GOLDSHIP

Frank Ross

BOOK CLUB ASSOCIATES LONDON

This edition published 1981 by
Book Club Associates
by arrangement with Macmillan London Ltd

Printed in Great Britain by
Richard Clay (The Chaucer Press) Ltd,
Bungay, Suffolk

The extract from Roy Campbell's translation
of Baudelaire's 'Man and the Sea'
is published by kind permission of the
Estate of Roy Campbell.

Many people have helped me in my attempt to make this book historically feasible and technically accurate:

Mr Arthur Smith of Isleworth; the editor of *Sea Breezes*, Craig J. M. Carter; the staff of the Records Section, Greenwich Maritime Museum; Arnold Kludas of the Stiftung Deutsches Schiffahrtsmuseum, Bremerhaven; special mention to Alfred Alexander of Swansea, whose remarkable memory and unflagging zeal still amazes me; E. W. Evans of Ruthin, Wales; Helmut Harksen, of Hamburg; Tony McGinnity, marine surveyor and architect, Brixham; Jan Needle, author, nautical buff and good friend; Don Spinks, who gave support when needed; my father, particularly, who sailed these waters in the days when the going was rough, and whose knowledge made *Goldship* possible; Teresa Sacco, of Macmillan, who kept me on course.

A long list that could be far longer, but incomplete without mention of my wife. Always my first reader. I dedicate this book to her.

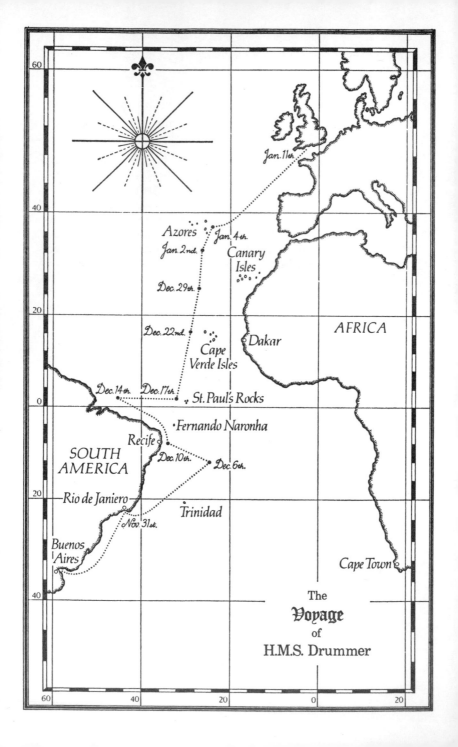

The
Voyage
of
H.M.S. Drummer

Free man, you'll always love the sea — for this,
That it's a mirror, where you see your soul
In its eternal waves that chafe and roll;
Nor is your soul less bitter an abyss ..

The two of you are shadowy, deep and wide.
Man! None has ever plummeted your floor —
Sea! None has ever known the wealth you store —
Both are so jealous of the things you hide!

Yet age on age is ended or begins,
While you without remorse or pity fight.
So much in death and carnage you delight,
Eternal wrestlers! Unrelenting twins!

from 'Man and the Sea'
by Baudelaire
translated by Roy Campbell

Part One

6 December 1918

The darkness held many shapes. Froze them, dissolved them. Eyes refusing to accept their sudden uselessness fought for something on which to bind themselves; a figure framed in the bolted doorway, a table with edges to be avoided, columns of iron, shelves of steel. Shadows in the mind.

He walked like a crab, head twisted to one side, waiting for the inevitable blow, the way blind men walk, an arm's length substituting for sight. Four strides took an age, and he found a corner, stretched his arms and shuffled, circumnavigating his prison. By slowly moving in a circle, arms wide like a hobbled dervish, he judged the room empty, apart from a bucket and a mattress. For its size it was over-furnished. A place where time had lost its meaning. Light made time. The time of the moon, the time of the sun, the time of the lamp's lighting: without light, time was fixed only by the need to sleep and the movement of the bowels – erratic chronometers in any man.

A slap and a shudder counted the reverberating seconds. One, TWO, three, FOUR. Up, DOWN, up, DOWN. And nothing counted the hours. Palms pressed against the steel bulkhead, Frank Judd marked the beat and speed of the ship's engine in braille. He listened to its rhythm like a man praying in a holy place, feet splayed, fingertips humming with energy; the body electric, collecting strength as sure as a Leyden Jar. He was part of the vessel, fused to it. The feeling pleased him. It could be night. Crossing his arms about him, he yawned. For some reason they hadn't shackled him, and for small things be thankful. There were degrees of freedom one learned to appreciate.

The storeroom was dry and smelled like an empty tea chest, an odd, fresh smell that had not felt the damp of sea. He sniffed it like a drug, lay back on the palliasse, eyes open, and tried to dream. It had always been a good way of coping, dreaming. But, as he grew older, more and more they failed to come. Old men had their dreams, they said, but he was coming on old and losing his. Once he had been able to use them between watches when, sodden and aching, without the energy or inclination to tug off his boots, he had lain in countless unventilated fo'c'sles, fogged with body heat and the smoke from a paint-drum-and-piping bogey stove, able to command the oblivion of his choice, according to his mood. Women, of course, but not always, and less and less as the years strode by. Women, lascivious or otherwise, never lived up to dreams and even a dream needed a touch of reality to garnish the fantasy. No, sometimes he had dreamed of strange things, like frosted fields with icicles of corn and huge shire-horses blowing steam, stamping them down with the sound of breaking glass. Another man's memories, they had to be. Someone in a strange port clutching familiarly at his arm and he turned to find a face he didn't recognise until, waking, it faced him again in his shaving mirror. And, the most persistent of all, a child bouncing on his shoulders, clutching his ears, his hair, feet drumming against his chest as a bonfire burned and they paraded around it, a man and a quarter high. That was the only one he had no control over, although he understood it well enough. A moment of untarnished happiness now was the nearest to pain. Yet there was no real pain. Frank Judd at fifty had never slept a nightmare in his life. Nightmares were reserved for days and readily coped with. Sleep was a different matter. The only solitude a sailor had. A private garden, jealously tended.

He blinked into the dark and thrust his hands between his knees, his body bent as it was born. One, TWO, the ship rose, three, FOUR, fell. His eyes had no need to close; the velvet blackness was total.

I am . . .

One, TWO . . .

Frank Judd . . .

Three, FOUR . . .

A shudder ran through the ship as it met a bad wave. The seventh wave. The time could be kept by the seventh wave, the big bad one, or so they said. But how many seventh waves in an hour? And who the hell cared? The sudden chill had gone and he began to sweat. His fist chafed and he felt the damp stickiness of blood, licked its salt.

It had been stupid by anyone's reckoning, let alone his own. But still, it had given him satisfaction, and wasn't a man entitled to a little of that in his lifetime? McGowan had been asking for it for over a year, maybe even from the time he first set foot aboard the ship. There was something about the coxswain that lit men's fuses. Once Judd had been slapped across the face by the second mate of an old barquentine, *The Nancy Down.* Slapped, as a woman might slap. He had hit that man too, not because it was a mark of the second mate's weakness – he was built like an orang-outang, only without the charm – but because it was demeaning, a sign of contempt for another's manhood. Judd had been just nineteen at the time. The second mate had gone down hard, his face barely finding time to register shock before it opened, melon-ripe, on the deck. Judd had felt no remorse then, nor had he felt it an hour – or was it three? – ago.

McGowan had set him up for it like a 'bucko' mate who had spent too long on a leash and felt his malice running to seed. If Judd had been five foot three he would have figured small in the coxswain's life, but being a foot taller he constituted a challenge no one of his rank, particularly a Scotsman, could ignore. It was as primitive as that. Darwin might have taken half a lifetime to divine it, but to a sailor on deep waters it had always been the natural order. Big men were felled by tougher men, tough men were put down by faster ones, old men beaten by younger. McGowan was younger, but he wasn't faster, and it had been his bad luck to have chosen the wrong day. After that there was little more to be said, except that as a defence before a court martial it would cut about as much ice as a heretic calling the Devil as character witness before the Inquisition. And then what? Three years? Ten? Fifteen? McGowan might die, he had been told. The coxswain had gone through life with a skull thin as an eggshell, and it had been Judd's misfortune to discover the fact. A child could have laid him out. How, in God's name, he had lived all his years with a handicap like that would forever be a mystery to Frank Judd. Maybe he had been lucky for a while.

'You on watch, Judd, or taking the air?'

'On watch.'

' "Coxswain." On watch, "coxswain"!'

' "Coxswain". On watch, "coxswain".'

A ship's coxswain, being the leading rating in direct charge of the lower decks and answerable to the senior officer, had a foot in both camps and, not surprisingly, was an object of little love to those he represented.

'Then whaddya doing strolling the decks, here?' McGowan had managed, with little effort, to turn his role of lower deck spy into something even worse, by sheer force of character.

'Going to the heads, "Coxswain".' Judd had been suffering

stomach cramps all day and most of the previous night and was not in the best of humour. His gut felt as if a live rat was running up and down it gnawing for an exit.

'Sly fag, eh? Quick tickler? Heard you're a bit of a hard man, Judd. Bit of a troublemaker? That right?'

'I don't account for what you hear, son. Now, if you'd just let me about my business, I'd be grateful.'

'*I* decide your business, *son*!' McGowan was stocky, a short, compressed stockiness as if raised too long in a cradle too small. His shoulders had continued growing sometime after the rest of him and had eaten up his neck to the point where the two were welded as one.

'My business is in King's Regulations. And, of this moment, King's Regulations are desiring me to make for the Heads and I'd be pleased if you didn't stand in the way. It could be a mite embarrassing for both of us, if you get my meaning.'

'A bag of shit, Judd!' McGowan cackled. 'Am I right?'

Judd had tried to brush past and the coxswain had grabbed his arm.

'I gave no order, Judd!'

The rest was inevitable. Both of them knew where it was leading. He had shaken the arm off, but still McGowan had barred his way. And then it had become tiring, and Judd's stomach more demanding. He tried once more, saw the coxswain's fist swing and blocked it with an arm. Without thinking, Judd had hit him, the blow beginning waist high, gathering its momentum from his body spin; an old trick that came with countless fights in the cramp of a fo'c'sle, the press of a bar or even, when the occasion demanded it, locked around a yardarm. It was a gesture, no more. But it had turned out to be an expensive one. If McGowan didn't pull through then the charge would be murder, and clemency was a late starter with a bad leg in any naval court he could even imagine.

Why McGowan? There had been twenty, thirty, he had had more reason to batten down in his time and in every case – bar a few – he had bitten on the bullet. For five years Frank Judd had contained the power in his fists, a power that had blighted his life so often. Had McGowan gone down for all the rest?

The ache in his wrist told him what kind of fool he was. Cradling it across his chest he felt the fingers swelling to the size of blood sausages.

'Sod you!' he said to the uncaring bulkhead. 'Sod you, one and all. Ay. Men.'

And slept in his garden.

The edge of the world was as sharp as a razor blade. After two days of desultory mist and cloud, the sun, poised on the rim of the horizon, blinked a single watery eye like an old man woken from sleep, uncertain of what was expected of him. A few white-caps foamed and fell in the southerly breeze that had come with dawn. Those apart, nothing broke the thousand or so square miles of ocean that His Majesty's Ship *Drummer* and her captain Jack Muir were sole heirs to.

In all his years at sea nothing had changed Muir's feelings about this kind of morning at this kind of hour. A moment of peace. While it lasted it was as if a benediction had been cast over the fears of the night past and the uncertainties of the coming day. A wedge of hope driven between the two: a moment of respite and reflection.

There were other, less philosophical, reasons to greet the day with at least a certain amount of pleasure. Armgard, the ship's cook, had, for once, woken without the usual poisonous spleen that invariably transmitted itself throughout *Drummer* in the form of waterlogged porridge, oily coffee and rubbery flapjacks. The coffee had been tolerably warm and the oats almost stuck to the spoon. Armguard had either rediscovered a long-lost pride in his culinary expertise or the law of averages had asserted itself.

The sun gained strength by the minute, visibly rising. They were leaving the Trades behind, moving into the uncertain Doldrums where storm and squall might spring from nowhere in a torrent of rain. Either that, or they might steam under a leaden, oppressive sky, sweltering in a sauna of hot air trapped between sea and cloud. The Doldrums were as fickle as a rich man's daughter.

25 deg w, 11 deg s. Muir took up his binoculars. A thin sheet of what looked like white cloud had begun to blur the horizon to the north. Sea mist. The heat of the night would soon seem no more than a prelude to the furnace. Behind him, in the wheelhouse, the quartermaster on the wooden grating stared over the wheel as if hypnotised.

'Steady as she goes!' called Muir.

'Steady as she goes, sir!' The voice was hollow as a shell.

The half hour of peace had passed. Another day. He knew what the quartermaster must be feeling. For a year Lieutenant-Commander Jack Muir had performed the same morning ritual and for a year the outcome had been the same. 'The war to end all bores,' Prettie, the gunnery officer, had once punned in a moment of uncontrollable frustration. Muir had given 'Guns' a sharp reminder of what war was all about, but even the reminder came by rote and didn't convince anyone, least of all himself. It was an empty, fabricated, reprimand and everyone in the wardroom had known it. Since December, 1917, the armed merchantman *Drummer* had been almost constantly at sea – and had seen little else.

True, it had been a bad war, so far. But who was to say what was good and bad? There was scant glory in death for those who died, no matter how stirring their eulogy. A million men had foundered in the mud pits of Flanders, ships blown to fragments in the Dardanelles, and yet here, in the middle of nowhere, a handful of men denied participation in similar carnage had seen it not as a blessing but a personal affront, as if being blackballed from a mass execution they had a God-given right to attend. It said a great deal for the motivating power of boredom.

Annoyed with himself, Muir wrapped the cloak of captaincy around him. There were seventy men aboard *Drummer*, every one of them in his care. There was nothing they could reproach themselves for. Or did he mean *him*self? The promise had gone out of the day and he was left with a nagging feeling of betrayal.

If it was a question of fault, then the next question was where it lay – with some nameless, bemedalled bureaucrat at the Admiralty who had seen fit to send them on this pointless patrol and then forgotten about them. *Drummer* had been Muir's first command. He had come to her with the enthusiasm of a boy scout and the hard experience of a shellback. Somewhere in between lay the real Muir. Lost at sea, maybe. His thoughts wandered to the misty sepia-tinted portraits he kept on his desk. An old man and his wife, he formal and bewhiskered above a starched collar, she Victorian-stern, crinolined and bonnetted, both staring from their frames like captured ostriches. His guardians. The word itself, suggesting as it did protection from mortal sin and moral turpitude, might have been coined for them alone. Life to them was a restless battlefield on which good and evil struggled for supremacy like Greek wrestlers on a stone jar.

Children, of course, were particularly vulnerable, unable as they were to resist temptation in its many guises: music halls, penny bazaars, picture postcards, gluttony, girls, comics, impure thoughts, idleness and disrespect. If he had managed to escape only three-quarters of them he might not have finished up as captain of the only fighting ship to miss the war, but a minor saint, or, give or take a transgression or two, the Archbishop of

York. Instead he had 'run away' to sea, as they insisted on calling it. And the sea ranked high in his guardians' list of avoidable vices, sailors by their very calling embodying most of the evils a body could be prey to.

'It's his father's blood coming out', he had once heard the old man say, the words reeking of condemnation. And he had lain fearful nights wondering how and where it was draining. Jack Muir had only a hazy recollection of his father – a naval officer, bearded and with a skin like leather. He had laughed a lot, he remembered that, at things most other people didn't find funny. And died when the boy was six, regretting nothing of a life that could have filled five men's with incident.

Two years later his widow, unable to support her son (or was there another reason?) had put him in care. And the old couple who had 'chosen' him had given him their affection as best they could. Then they too had died, within months of each other. At sixteen Muir had joined the Merchant Marine, using the small sum they had left him to pay the £35 of his apprentice's indentures.

It was a far cry from his dream of naval midshipman, but at least it was the sea. Where it had all begun. His father's blood.

The voice at his shoulder brought an abrupt end to his reverie. It was Barrow, his first lieutenant.

'Fine day, sir.' The observation was couched as a greeting.

'You know the worst thing in the world you can do on a bridge, Number One?' asked Muir.

'A number of things come to mind, sir.' Barrow gave an affable grin. 'Then again, perhaps they shouldn't.'

'Let the wind blow through your ears,' Muir answered his own question. 'I learned that from the mate of a Blackball packet, and just to make sure I remembered the lesson, he gave me an ear the size of a melon for thinking of some tootsie back ashore. Thought I'd never forget it. But I did, for a minute just then.' He pulled a face: 'Too old for tootsies now,' and brought together his palms in a characteristic 'clop' that signified the end of the topic. 'Flood, fire, famine? Sermon over, back to business. I'll take the bad news short and sharp, the good you can elaborate on in minute detail.' He smiled. 'So what is it to be?'

Barrow shook his head. 'Not a lot. The rudder trouble has been fixed by Garrett. Some kind of sleeving had worn, the intricacies of which are beyond me, even after listening to half an hour of sleeving lore. Anyway the upshot is he has improvised a new one which he reckons is better than the original. I don't doubt him. To be frank, I wouldn't dare.'

'Wise man. I tried it once. Thought I was playing Devil's Advocate and finished up battered with the history of the reciprocating engine from 1860. If I had a photographic memory I could have built one by the time he had finished.'

Barrow went on: 'A hell of a stink from the aft storeroom. Mould got to a crate of lemons. They're floating way back and heaven help any fish that find them. Armgard is still claiming he could have made a purée out of them. That apart, little else.'

Muir grunted. Barrow was a good eighteen years younger than he. A career officer with a gaggle of brass-hats in the service and a family estate in Wiltshire where he could ride to hounds and fish without the inconvenience of leaving his grounds. A posting to a requisitioned merchant ship must have dampened Barrow's spirits considerably, and Muir was certain that that was the reason for his posting in the first place. It sometimes worked out that relatives in high places guarded their gilded perches jealously and saw to it that a few judiciously placed obstacles fell in the way of those – be they *kinder* or not – who fancied it was a straight race from college to a cap peak of scrambled egg.

But war should have honed Barrow into an exceptional officer, given him ammunition that, when it was over, would cut a swathe through wardroom pink gins and battles played with champagne corks by 'social sailors' who had spent their lives running messages for gouty admirals. War hadn't. So far, Guy Barrow's war had been Jack Muir's. An endless anonymous travail. Latitudes, longitudes. Point A to point B and back again. Until a numbness set in that Muir had fought against night and day, like a parish priest who feels his flock slipping away from him into apathy and disbelief.

One good thing had come of it. He was tuned to nuances as if they were his own nerve-endings.

'*Little* else?'

Barrow oscillated his jaw. He was a handsome man in the uniquely patrician English mould. Long faced, perfectly proportioned, his features bore no permanent stamp whatsoever, but were a screen on which emotions were allowed to flicker as he chose. A space in the world had been awaiting him before he was born and he fitted into it as snugly as a foot into a hand-made shoe. Yet there was a strength there, beneath the reserve, that was not Muir's strength, but something altogether different. It was the strength of caste. Of rich and powerful ancestors who, down generations, had offered their lives in the service of their country, never seriously considering any other alternative. Barrow held the baton they handed on. It was formidable. Only *Drummer*'s bad luck might make him drop it.

'Short and sharp, sir,' said Barrow. 'Judd.'

Muir pinched the bridge of his nose. It had to be Judd. 'Destroy my breakfast,' he said resignedly.

'A lot of Jack Strop stuff,' went on Barrow. 'They don't like Judd being locked below. A case of more concern for the culprit than the victim. A storm in a teacup. There's a certain amount of restlessness.' He glanced over his shoulder to the quartermaster in the wheelhouse. Muir drew him out of earshot into the starboard wing of the bridge.

'I've been waiting for some such growl to start, Number One. It was bound to happen and we both know why : on a treadmill there's nothing else to do but think. An occupation that must be refreshingly new to some of them. I reckon I could put my finger on the ones involved.' He shook his head. 'To some extent I sympathise – but not if they're out looking for trouble. I'll give them enough of that to take their minds off anything! Fighting talk.' He looked at Barrow wryly. 'The irony is that Judd's seen more "action" in five minutes than we've seen in a year.' A throat-clearing cough erased the sudden flippancy. 'But Frank Judd as martyr is a lost, lost cause. And the first man to raise his voice in that direction will be sharing the lock-up with him.' He cocked an eyebrow. 'You think I'm being unreasonable?'

'I don't think reasonableness is the issue,' said Barrow eventually. 'Judd struck his superior and the rest is for a court to decide. At the moment he is an apprehended criminal like any other.'

'Exactly. And the man he struck is now fighting for his life. Judd could face a lot worse than he imagines. He has a contagious disease of the fists, I've seen it and know it.'

Barrow's eyes flickered momentarily and adjusted themselves to the distance. There was something odd in Muir's tone. Or was he imagining it?

'I know the coxswain leaned hard,' went on Muir. 'Maybe very hard. It makes no difference. When Judd lashed out he opened the scuttles of this ship and that I will not be having. The crew are dissatisfied, so am I, so are you, but it's not going to degenerate into a free-for-all. I want drills tightened up, calling the watch below. Boats, hoses, guns, checked and re-checked. And, if in some way you can communicate my feelings to any troublemakers below, it will be in their own interests to think again.' There was a long pause. 'I knew Judd twenty years ago,' Muir said suddenly. 'He was mate on a Blackball packet.' He turned to Barrow and there were the beginnings of a smile.

'The thick ear?' asked Barrow.

'Very thick,' said Muir. He tugged at a lobe. 'He was one of the toughest seamen I have ever chanced upon. He had to be. He was also a good one. As it happened, not a perfect combination. Some rise, some fall. Judd fell, I don't know how, though I can guess. I don't like sitting in judgement.' He rolled a finger. 'In the ship I was on with Judd they fitted brass caps to the yard ends in the unlikely event there was nothing for the crew to do. A job with no beginning, no end. But a purpose. Polishing them kept the mind from grappling with the bloody idiotic fact that you were a thousand miles from anywhere, eating food condemned by the Navy and snapped up by the shipowners; sleeping in a fo'c'sle stinking of sweat and galley-fat lamps; and spending a major part of one's best years making love to a bucking sail eighty feet above deck in weather that God himself disowned. There was,' he added pointedly, 'little time to reflect.' He was at the pinch end of a generation catapulted into a frantic world that was moving so fast no one's feet touched the ground. Maybe Barrow understood it. Sail was the horse; steam the lorry, the tank. Muir had been caught straddled between the two like a latecomer on a departing boat. One-footed he stepped out of a disappearing age with different values, or, at least, ragged old ones.

'I think,' Barrow was saying, 'the only question now is how long it can last.'

Six days ago, whilst refuelling from a collier off Rio, they had heard rumours that the war was drawing to an end. The German High Command had lost control. One story, at least, seemed to ring true. The battle-cruiser *Prinzregent*, anchored in the Lower Elbe, had been ordered to sail, but her crew had put out her fires. They were sentenced to penal servitude for terms ranging from one to fifteen years in an effort to bring the mutiny to heel. It hadn't worked. An uprising in Wilhelmshaven had blossomed – or degenerated – into full-scale revolution, and the commanders of the North Sea Fleet had been deposed. The Red Flag flew at the masts of the ships in the Imperial Dockyard and German sailors greeted each other with a clenched fist raised. In practical terms it meant little. The main body of the

Fleet had been tucked away in Kiel since the Battle of Jutland and had never ventured out. Socialism was running riot in a fleet that was moribund, like maggots on a carcase. It could mean everything, it might mean nothing. Spithead, the Nore – the British Navy had had its own pimples in the past and it hadn't shaken the order of things.

Muir had taken the talk with a large dose of salt-water. He had heard nothing officially.

The whitecaps had begun to lap under *Drummer*'s bow. He took up the binoculars and the world became small.

'Once again the *Emden* seems to have avoided us,' he said ironically. The binoculars banged against his chest. She was a strange old tub, *Drummer*, formerly the SS *Eden Starr*. Commissioned for service in the 10th Cruiser Squadron in the North Atlantic as the blockade had been stepped up against Germany, even her gross weight of 2500 tons had been no match for the northern seas that shook her like a wet dog in the storms. The squadron – more properly a fleet, for there were more ships in it than Nelson had ever commanded – had found that even its 20,000 tonners had a rough time of it. *Drummer* had been put to pasture. Her crew was as patched as the ship herself. The seamen were RNR ratings, the stokers the original Merchant Service firemen. Others were holding temporary commissions. The Royal Fleet Reserve, Royal Naval Reserve, Mercantile Marine, and a backbone of career naval officers; *Drummer* had them all. A spotty dog, but no one could blame her for that.

Barrow had turned aside and was in conversation with a crumpled figure wearing the wings and lightning of a wireless telegraphist third class. Horace Feeley bore his thirteen stone like a handicapped Zeus, carrying his messages with the resignation of a packhorse.

Barrow glanced at the paper. 'We have contact,' he said to Muir. '*Challenger*.'

Challenger, a light cruiser, had, for a while, been their only occasional company in the South Atlantic, but had eventually lost touch – or had been ordered to adhere to the rigid silence that *Drummer* had been subjected to from the first day of her putting to sea. Her W.T., infinitely more powerful than *Drummer*'s and transmitting coded messages as she moved north, had been the only source of real news since they had set sail.

'We are told to stand by for something important,' said Barrow, handing Muir the slip.

'Signal Officer Haden offers his compliments and reports that the message will be due shortly,' panted Feeley. 'The signals are very weak.' Feeley's back, despite its muscle, was bent in a question mark, as if perpetually avoiding a low door. His face, untouched by the sun, had an anaemic gloss. Muir had grown to like Feeley, whom, he knew, worked like a Trojan in the tiny sweat-shop of a wireless cabin, trying to pick up and untangle anything that might lead them to an enemy.

'Tell the signal officer to see me as soon as the message is received,' said Muir.

But it was Feeley who returned. 'The signal officer is still trying to hear more, and asks you excuse him a moment, sir.'

He held out the neatly folded message in a hand clenched so tight there was little doubt he knew every word it contained despite the fact it was intended for the captain's eyes only.

Muir read it. Re-folding the paper he said, 'Thank the signal officer and tell him to keep listening.'

Feeley saluted and nodded his way from the bridge as if offended by the prolonged exposure to daylight.

'Well, Number One,' said Muir lightly, 'we've run our course. Wherever the war was, it now isn't. Armistice. The Germans seem to have called it a day. We have orders to return home.'

Barrow slapped the rail with a dubious palm and held it out. They shook hands. It seemed the thing to do. 'So it's damn well over!'

'Armistice,' said Muir. 'Not quite the end yet.' It seemed the thing to say.

'As near as dammit, sir.'

'As near as.' Muir looked out over the sea. It hadn't heard the news. The whitecaps were still bunching in shoals as if driven by armies of tiny silver fish. 'Yes, as near as,' he repeated. 'It seems the breeze is freshening. Too hot for a storm.' Flipping off his cap, he ran a finger around its rim. 'Well, we must make a provisional course, Number One.'

Barrow gripped the rail. 'A long way from home,' he said, with a forced cheerfulness.

It was over. And had never really begun.

Able Seaman Morris Wylie, temporarily excused from serving King and Country, belched expansively and shook the small cork-stoppered bottle with the abrupt vigour of a man who had scorched his hand on a hot stove. The contents had thickened to the consistency of ox-blood. Satisfied, he poured a carefully gauged amount into his cupped palm.

'Jaysus help us!' came a muffled Irish voice from the hammock nearest to Wylie. 'As if the stink in here ain't bad enough!'

Unperturbed, Wylie slowly began to rub the foul-smelling liquid into his scalp with the rapt concentration of a phrenologist divining his own future.

The mess deck on *Drummer* was divided into four separate sections, each sleeping twelve men, the watches rotating between them in four-hour shifts. The unfortunate whose fate it had been to occupy the hammock next to Wylie's tossed like a harpooned seal and, thrusting a sweat-soaked face from beneath his sheet, glared down at his neighbour.

'In the name of mercy, knock it off, willya! The pong of the stuff is liftin' me off me back!' Paddy Hackett looked for support from the other occupants of the mess.

Penn Coker, stripped to the waist, lay back in his hammock, one leg trailing over its side, eyes hooded like a waiting lizard. His torso was the colour of stained pine, wedges of muscle interleaving like rough lumps of sculptor's clay still waiting to be smoothed into credibility. Coker allowed his head to loll to one side and looked at Wylie from beneath the thick eyelids. He seemed unconcerned. One word from Coker, a grunt even, and Wylie would have taken his business elsewhere. But Coker had lived with stink of one sort or another most of his days and one more wasn't going to make any difference. The whole damn world stank of something and that was the truth of it. The grey amber scraped from the guts of a whale smelled worse than a three-day-old corpse and yet they made perfume from it, high class tarts spraying themselves with the end product of a stomach complaint. His head rolled back and he slid his glance down along the valley of his chest to the flat plain of his midriff, supreme in his contempt for the human race.

Wylie, his toilet finished, rubbed his vivid hands on a rag and dropped it on the table. His hair was a brilliant red, with lesser pink patches on the balding crown. With his gaunt, gangling frame the nickname had come by that strangely fluent process of word association endemic in men who lived in elbow-jostling enforced intimacy. Wylie had become 'Tilley'. Tilley as from Vesta Tilley. Vesta as from the box of matches. The logic of it was undeniable. Standing there, his fifty-eight-year-old stick-like body topped by a burning bush, Morris Wylie couldn't have been anything else but Tilley.

The pained face of Hackett still drooped over the edge of his hammock. 'Baines? Can't you smell it? What you got for a nose?'

'Go burn a candle, Hackett,' said Stagg Baines without bothering to look up from the dry-stone balanced on his knee across which he was drawing the blade of his clasp knife. 'That pit of yours could do with some fumigation!'

The sweeping tolerance shown by most of the men towards Tilley's seemingly anti-social trichology stemmed less from charity than from the discovery that the seaman's perpetual companion, lice, impervious to sulphur, paraffin and burning tar, had capitulated in the face of the fumes from Tilley's bottle. Hackett opened his mouth twice, thought better of it and, with a mild oath, disappeared back under his sheet.

'Where you say you got that poison from, Tilley?' drawled Baines.

'Liverpool. A herbal emporium specialising in treatment of the follicles.'

'Again?'

'Hair. Dr Belton's Elixir. The composition is a closely guarded secret handed down through generations. The original Belton was of Chinese extraction, I believe, hence the mandarin on the label.' Tilley gave a small tug at a lock of hair as if to vouch for the mixture's efficacy. A small clump of it came away in his hand. 'Without it,' he went on, 'I am prostrate with itching. A hereditary illness, possibly as old as the mixture itself. All it needs is one application a week.' He stared doubtfully at the tuft.

'Any good for curing crabs?' said Baines.

'It all depends on the ailment the crabs are suffering from,' replied Tilley. There was a snort of laughter from the buried Hackett.

'Pretty clever with words, ain'tcha, professor?' Baines threw the knife lightly in the air and it turned once, to bury its point through Tilley's rag, pinning it to the table.

His pudding-like face, unhealthy and malevolent, broke into a grin. Swinging a boot under the table top he dislodged the knife with a titter and went back to honing it. Tilley busied himself with his ditty-box, not wishing to be drawn. The best way to deal with Baines was to ignore him. There was a long silence, broken only by Hackett's sniffing.

'Hey, Coker, you asleep?' asked Baines suddenly. There was no answer. The big man lay unmoving. 'Whaddya reckon to Juddy?' persisted Baines, as if his brain had been tortuously trying to find something to occupy it and had at last triumphed. He rasped the knife edge along his thumb.

'Judd? What am I supposed to reckon, Baines?' The head fell sideways once more and the eyes flickered.

Baines squinted along the knife edge as if sighting a rifle, aiming it provocatively at Coker for the space of a second and then clipping it, still open, to the lanyard at his waist, began to pare his nails with it. 'What I'm getting at, Coker, is that life on this lash-up ain't getting no better. You've seen the grub we're supposed to eat! Well I reckon afore long we're going to be prayin' for a slice of ratmeat the way things are going. I saw them ditching barrels of stuff overboard half an hour ago. Stank worser than Tilley's brainbox! Christ it's sodding Christmas soon — we could all do with a bit of fun! Sticking away Judd is just the start is what I reckon. Know what I hear?'

Coker's face might have been looking out over Easter Island.

'I hear the Old Man *asked* to stay in this God-forsaken steam bath! I hear too it suits him fine paddling around safe in his own private pond playing Admiral Fuckall along with Jimmy the One as Little Lord Whatsit!'

'You hear a lot, Baines,' said Coker, scrubbing a hand across his chest. 'Say a lot. What you looking for, mister, that we should meet a couple of battle-cruisers so you can show what a hero you are?' The voice made the rasp of Baines's knife sound like the rustle of silk.

'What I'm saying,' said Baines weakly, 'is that we should have been home and dry by now if the Old Man had wanted us to be.'

Listening to the conversation — if it could be called that — Tilley idly wondered whether, if it came to it, a knife such as the one Baines was playing with could ever manage to penetrate the massive muscle-shield of Coker's chest. A debatable issue.

'So we're not,' said Coker finally. 'What's it matter to you? You begun to fancy Judd?'

Stagg Baines's hand clenched over the handle of the knife. Oh, Christ, thought Tilley, here it comes. But Baines's unflinching cowardice won the day, camouflaging his anger beneath an all-purpose snort of derision.

Coker knew how far he had pushed him and had known the result. His teeth seemed to split across his face in a grimace of pain. He was grinning, but with no trace of humour. If a shark could grin, thought Tilley, this is how it would look. The mouth bared for a moment then snapped shut. With a rumble that might have been a substitute for laughter, Coker looked at his feet. His cross was to share the world with spouters and shit-heads.

The door burst open with a crash that had Hackett snapping upright, the blanket under which he had been incubating still draped over his head. Tilley whirled round to see Baines clasp his hand where the knife had suddenly dug into his fingertip and drawn blood.

'You stupid bastard!' said Baines to the intruder. The wound was no more than a pinprick, but he stared at it in alarm.

The figure in the doorway showed no remorse. Feeley had been running and stood like a burst bean-bag with the effort. He held out a silencing hand as he tried to work out how to breathe and speak at the same time. 'Finito!' he finally gasped, jowls trembling with excitement. 'Home. Over.' Finding a butt of air: 'Germans have given in! We're going home!' He gave a little nod of self-satisfaction and bounced off, having gained sufficient fuel for his next call.

Baines sucked his finger as Hackett disentangled himself from his blanket and swung down from his hammock, wiping the sweat from his face with the trailing edge of a sheet. If nothing else, all thought of sleep had evaporated.

'Tilley, I'm going up there! If it makes Feeley run it has to be something!'

They left together. Baines closed his knife and spat a gob of watery blood. Walking over to Tilley's trunk he lifted its lid with a toecap. The ditty-box lay on top of a pair of seaboots. The ditty-box – made to treasure and hold the most intimate secrets a sailor had – was inscribed with the name of its owner, which was, as a traditional point of honour, its only security. It was never locked. Baines opened it. The bottle was pushed under a score of postcards. Flicking them aside he picked it up. Tilley was getting a cocky bastard and it was time he was taught a lesson.

The cold, flat eyes needed no lateral movement to take in Baines's action. Penn Coker watched in silence, reserving judgement ...

The South East Trades had blown themselves ragged, puffing like a punctured bellows, and even the cherubims were gasping for breath. The Doldrums hung heavy about *Drummer*, the sea oily. The horizon had bunched into low, grey clouds, menacing as dust from the hooves of an approaching army. It was midday and hot.

Chief Engineer Tom Garrett had been working for five hours in the bowels of *Drummer*, unaware that night had become day. The care that had been lavished on the ship in her money-earning days had stood her in good stead, but it was foolish to ignore the strain the past year of almost ceaseless steaming had placed on her. Placed on them all. Despite the efforts of the teams of rust-chippers, the brown mould seemed to grow like fungus overnight and there were plates that were seeping water. The engine itself was working steadily enough, but Garrett could sense it was on borrowed time. *Drummer* needed a rest.

He washed in the small bowl in the corner of his cabin but, as always, it was no good. The water slid over his oil-impregnated skin without touching it. He scrubbed again and, towelling himself dry, studied the split and spaded fingernails. Spurs of black drove deep into the quick, ineradicable as a miner's coal-dust tattoo. He sat at his table. Spread against the sheet of white paper his fingers looked like freshly turned worms. He held the pen crookedly, cramp clawing them, and steadied the paper with his elbow.

'My Dearest', he wrote. Above it, in parentheses, he added 'My Beloved'. That could be sorted out later, this was only the first draft.

'Today we have heard we are coming home.' The thought suddenly crossed his mind that the rumour that had swept around the lower decks was just that and no more. That didn't matter either.

'It should not take too long if the ship keeps her end up. It has seemed like an age since last we saw each other. It *is* an age, I suppose. Sam must have forgotten what I look like. Tell him I still have my moustache and beard for him to pull, though sometimes the heat makes me think of shaving it right off. I'm not sure you would approve though, dearest. One other bit of news concerning my looks; I'm afraid I am short of a couple of teeth, lost after an accident a few days ago. I was hit – accidentally – by a spanner that flew out of one of my men's hands. I felt practically nothing at the time and he was very contrite. It twinges now and then, but, as they say, worse things happen at sea! The only thing I'll have to do is cut down on the smiles, though that will be difficult when at last we reach England and I see you and the boy again. I won't bore you with ship news, I reckon you'll hear enough of that when we are perched round the fire together. My dearest, I really do miss you more than I can say. It has been so long that ...'

That what? That I will ... that I can ...?

'That I sometimes feel our life together was all a dream.'

The words stared back at him.

When it came down to it, words were clumsy things in which

to try and wrap the heart. I love ... I believe ... I feel. A manifest of emotions piled one on top of the other, each one burying the last under a welter of adjectives and clauses and phrases, meaning nothing. She wouldn't be impressed by this. Who could be? Words belonged to everyone and there were some things that were soiled by such sharing. Hong Kong shopkeepers wrote love letters for illiterate sailors; clerks did the same thing in Liverpool. Only the name changed.

Tom Garrett threw the pen on the table. A shower of ink spattered across the letter, bleeding the words together, proof – if proof was needed – of their impermanence. He ran a hand roughly through his hair.

Tom Garrett had been married for four years before he sailed in *Drummer*. The war was an accident that temporarily robbed him of a personal Garden of Eden. Merely an interlude, he had thought. There were overriding forces that even a war couldn't compete with. Her name was Maggie. Maggie Gibbon. A girl of twenty-four, sixteen years younger than he, Maggie had come into his life like Fate's tap on the shoulder and afterwards nothing could ever be the same. He had married her and then waited for his luck to fade. A boy – Sam – had been the first cementing of the bond. And still Maggie had not changed. Each morning Tom Garrett had woken expecting his bliss to end. But life had chosen to take him on a pleasant path, and she had grown closer to him and more beautiful. Two years, and the marriage had survived three voyages lasting in all ten months. The boy had clung to him, Maggie's palms had made an unfailing crucible for his brow, her thighs a furnace for his desire, and her presence a reason for living. Then *Drummer* had been commissioned and he too had taken a temporary commission in the Royal Naval Reserve. A perfect solution. Again, he had been lucky.

But a long year at sea had made a mockery of good fortune.

Garrett had written fifteen letters to his wife, each of them, he knew, more awful than the last. None of them had been able to quieten his mind. Now he was certain beyond doubt that Maggie was unfaithful. He had managed to receive two letters from her, maybe all she had written, and they were as echoingly insubstantial as his to her. She loved him, she thought of him night and day, she was waiting, would wait for ever. Words. Maggie was a spirited girl, always had been. The kind never meant to be left alone. He didn't condemn her, but simply couldn't live without her.

Taking the ink-stained letter he slipped it beneath the rubber band that held all the others, none of which he had sent.

Biting the cramp from his fingers, he went on deck.

The forrard 4.7 inch gun on its strengthened steel base gleamed beneath its oil like a gigantic sporting trophy. A fact on which one no longer complimented the man Tom Garrett was now approaching. Lieutenant Arnold Prettie, Gunnery Officer of *Drummer* needed no reminding that his charges were as well nigh pristine as the day they were cast. Target practice had meant lobbing shells at the occasional dolphin or, when the dolphins had not obliged, shooting into a meaningless void.

Prettie was standing on the fore deck with Charlie Pickett, head down, hands behind his back like a schoolteacher listening to a pupil's recitation. With his deceptively studied movements, slow country drawl and shock of white hair, Prettie had an inborn implacability that invited confidences as a matter of course. There was a deep streak of sanity running through him, which, when tapped, yielded a country common sense capable of quietening a storm. Life was kept in its place and he refused to be elbowed by it. He was, Garrett had discovered, just thirty-two, though age seemed to have been unable, or reluctant, properly to put its finger on him. Prettie had, for the moment, one ambition in life: to kill. More specifically, to kill those who threatened, sought to dominate, or generally showed no respect for, the Shropshire village of Much Wenlock in which he had been born and raised. Much Wenlock figured large in Prettie's view of the Empire he was sworn to defend. There were four aunts and uncles there, two grandparents, one great-grandparent, three sisters, a mother and father, a wife, twenty-five chickens, a pig, and a house that had been built in the year that Cook had begun his third voyage in the Pacific and America had declared independence. Prettie had known no other life than that of the Navy – from a raw cadet in the old wooden-walled training ship *Britannia* anchored in the River Dart, to a highly specialised and infinitely complex gunnery course at Whale Island – but had never considered himself other than a country boy temporarily on leave. Now he squared himself between his village and the oncoming hordes with a solid determination.

'Tom?' he looked up as Garrett joined them. 'Charlie here is filling me in. You've heard?'

'It's true then?'

'Seems it,' said Pickett. 'The Old Man is going to copper-bottom it with an announcement any minute. I'm going up to the bridge.'

'I've been in kip,' said Prettie. They watched as Pickett walked towards the bridge, broad shoulders over a tight waist. 'Bounce of a boxer, that little bugger,' he said. He nodded at the disappearing figure. 'Do all right, that one.'

'Looks like the real thing then, this time.' Garrett kept his voice light. He wanted to talk with Prettie, the things on his mind were growing too large for one man to handle. He wanted to talk about his letters, his wife, the sudden end to isolation that was crowding him with decisions that had to be made. Each nautical mile was dragging him closer to the abyss.

'My feeling is that it's all been a bit of a sod,' said Prettie. It was rarely that he swore in conversation, such occasions being reserved for jollying the gun crews, and then he had been known to reach unequalled heights of profane eloquence.

'Surely you're glad it's all over?' said Garrett. The direction of the conversation was shredding like an unwhipped rope-end.

'It's not that. 'Course I'll want to get back, as much as the next man. New life for me, Tom. Hope this will be my last trip. Wife and I have been building up a bit of a smallholding over the years and it's not doing too bad. A man's got to make the break sometime and I don't think there'll be much problem about getting out of the service now it's all over. But just a crack at them, Tom, would have made it all worth while. As it is I feel I've been living under false pretences.' Arnold Prettie had decided at least five times before that he would leave the Navy and devote himself to the land. His 'smallholding', as it pleased him to think of it, was thirty acres of land and a squire's house (dilapidated) that had belonged to distant ancestral landed gentry (minor). Nothing much had been done with it, but, he kept telling himself, one day ... one day ...

Garrett nodded. Prettie was eight years younger than he and yet, like Charlie Pickett, seemed to have decided what life was going to give him for the rest of his days. He had no room for doubt, the kind of doubt that was gnawing at Garrett's very existence. 'I'm pleased for you, Arnold,' he said. 'Like to do the same kind of thing myself.'

'Then do it, Tom. No reason why you shouldn't.'

'Not so easy. What I mean is, these things have to be, well, arranged. Worked at. Me, I'm not much of an arranger.'

'You know what's wrong with you, Tom? Same as what's wrong with all of us. We've had too long to think. Fatal. Like being in a sanatorium, all you can fill your mind with is how ill you are. Look, anybody who can keep this old lady moving like you've done can make a fortune ashore. It's what they're going to be looking for, from now on. Men who understand machines. That's where the future really lies for you.'

'Maybe you're right. To tell the truth, I don't know exactly what's happening back home. Letters have been slow arriving and . . .' his voice trailed away. It didn't seem the time or the place.

'I know what you mean. It's been a long time, Tom, a hell of a long time. And sometimes we forget it's been *their* war too. The women. That's what sticks in the teeth. Nobody's to blame, but, as far as *Drummer*'s guns are concerned, I might as well have been blanching leeks for the war effort.'

Garrett fumbled in a pocket and held out an open wallet. Prettie gave a low whistle. The picture showed a young woman, three-quarters to the camera, looking over her shoulder, ringlets falling across a lace shawl. Her eyes were dark, her lips full, a smile playing at their corners. Garrett took it back, feeling foolish.

'If ever there was a reason for a war to end, you have it there, Tom,' said Prettie. 'My old lady must be built like a carthorse by now, digging up the spuds.'

'She sounds a good 'un,' said Garrett, regretting even more his moment of stupidity.

'Most of them are,' said Prettie. 'Only we don't give them credit for it.'

Muir gave out the news of the Armistice fully aware he was saying nothing that wasn't already known. The man able to extend indefinitely the manner in which news – particularly confidential news – travelled the length of a ship, would have in his grasp a telegraphic system Mr Edison could only weep to behold.

Drummer, Muir announced, would be altering course for a home port. But that didn't mean anyone could put his feet up. They were, still, technically at war and a German torpedo still exploded on impact, no matter how many white flags were flying in the Baltic.

'So what, in God's name, is an armistice then, if it means on the one hand we can still be sunk and on the other we're going home and the next they're flying the white flag?' said a perplexed Hackett. He was sitting on the mess table as Tilley knotted a bright green cloth bandana around his forehead.

'The fact you're talking as a man with three hands doesn't

help to create a one-armed brigand,' protested Tilley. Hackett had kept an old sail-hook as a horse-shoe charm and it was now protruding from his sleeve like a crab's claw. 'But, to answer your question,' went on Tilley, 'armistice is a truce right enough, which means hostilities are at an end – but only while the powers that be think it over. Horse trading. If one side or the other doesn't like the deal that's struck then it's a few hundred thousand more dead to see how it balances out.' He stood back. 'Remarkable. To the manner born.'

Hackett stood up doubtfully. His trousers were bunched five inches above the ankle and tied with cord over long white socks. A brilliant red sash split across his shoulder, ending in an extravagant tassel at the waist. Hackett had been Tilley's first recruit, stoker Melfort the second, Shadwell the carpenter third. Then others had begun to come forward until he was forced to turn a good dozen down.

Tilley's proposed concert – sod's opera in the lingua franca of the Royal Navy – had been received with a certain badly concealed amazement when he had first put it to Muir and Barrow. But Tilley's reasoning was simple: if you celebrate the end of a year, then surely you celebrate the end of a war. Muir had agreed to an extra-large tot of rum all round and a relaxing of all but the essential watches for an hour. Barrow, recovering from the initial shock, had quickly entered into the spirit of the thing and had come up with a collapsible opera hat for one of the performers with a nonchalance that suggested no man went to sea unless so equipped. At the present count there were fifteen artistes threatening their best for eight o'clock that evening. Their debut was less than two hours away.

Tilley had been hard at it all day and, to his surprise, found his project taking immediate root, sweeping away the flood of cynicism that had had a stranglehold on the ship for so long. He had long sensed the lack of purpose that was robbing *Drummer* of her life. A lot of it had to do with Baines and his kind, and, on another level, with Coker and Judd. A dissatisfied sailor was about as common as a virginal nun and the months they had been through were bound to increase the normal level of discontent. Even so, there was nothing in Tilley's lexicon that accepted the idea of an unhappy ship. Ships were happy, only *men* were not. Tilley was almost sixty years old and had been at sea so long the land was no more than a lighthouse in his life. The way of a ship was the way of the world, and it was a small, small world that one grew to know like a termite knows his tunnel. *Drummer* was a good ship, but things were threatening to go sour and, for some reason that he couldn't explain, Tilley had felt obliged to do something about it. It was the kind of thing the likes of which he had never done before. So why now? Perhaps the lotion was burning into his old, addled brain?

He laughed. Hackett was outrageously splendid, ready to be propelled on stage.

Penn Coker padded like a cat into the mess, tearing off his shirt. His eyes took in Hackett as he bent to tug off his boots. Strangely, Tilley had never been afraid of Coker, though believing him to be one of the most potentially dangerous men he had ever met. Coker's clenched violence defied imagination. Like Judd's. Both had come from the square riggers – as had Tilley – but Judd was older than Coker, and had managed to preserve a certain blush of humanity. They could have been born of sisters: Judd who exploded across the world collecting trouble like a volcano's lava gathering shale; Coker the glacier, moving slow and chill, grinding everything beneath heels of ice. Different men, but, to Tilley, more than that. They belonged to a different race – one he had lived alongside most of his life and still didn't understand.

'Coker?'

'Piss off, Tilley,' said Coker abruptly. Baines stood picking his teeth by the door.

'I need a feat of strength,' persisted Tilley. 'I'm looking for a strong-man act. A challenge, to get the others going.'

Coker slumped in his hammock and closed his eyes. Baines flicked away the sliver of wood that had been exploring his cavities and gave a grin. Strolling forward he tugged the tassel at Hackett's waist and nudged Tilley in the ribs. 'Leave it,' he said. 'Leave it to me.' A yellow tongue wetted his lips as he looked at the reclining figure of Coker. Stagg Baines appeared to have thought of something incredibly funny.

'Begging your pardon, sir.'

'Baines?'

'A minute of your valuable time, no more.'

'I'm ... I'm busy.'

'Terribly important, sir.' Baines greased his vowels as if speaking in a language he despised and sidled up to Midshipman Beattie Dandridge. His hand held him loosely by the elbow.

'Let go of me, Baines!' Dandridge's voice was in danger of

becoming shrill. The hand slid up his arm to squeeze the muscle at his shoulder. Dandridge tore himself away and stepped back with a suddenness that caused him to stagger off-balance. Breathing heavily he supported himself against the bulwark. 'I warn you, Baines . . .'

'Awww.' Baines grinned and held his hands wide in a gesture of innocence. 'There's no need to be like that. We know each other, don't we?'

Beattie Dandridge was eighteen, a midshipman who, according to naval discipline, was to be treated with the respect accorded to an officer. But at eighteen, on a ship full of hard-bitten seamen, it wasn't easy. For Dandridge, events had made it impossible.

'Look, lad,' Baines was at his side again, ingratiating as a dockside pimp. 'I want to do a little business, see? No need for a song and dance.'

'I want no more of this!'

'Ah, now, no harm done? Nice while it lasted? And now a little help, eh? No need for a scene.' His hand brushed Dandridge's cheek. 'For your *friends*, Betty.'

'Don't call me th —'

Baines cut him short. 'I want a key, son!' His voice had lost its banter. 'For half an hour. A bit of fun for Mister Coker.' He grinned. 'I want Juddy out. You've got them keys.'

Dandridge looked at him with amazement. 'You're mad! Do you realise what you are saying?'

'I'm saying I want the key, *Betty*. You're a lovely boy, but if I don't get it fast, then next time your fucking virginity ain't all you're going to lose.'

'Jesus, Beattie, it can't be *that* bad!' Charlie Pickett said, knowing it could be.

Dandridge was leaning back against the cabin door as if expecting it to be battered down behind him, swaying with the relief of a man finding temporary sanctuary and blocking the tears with effort. 'I'm sorry.' His voice trembled. 'Charlie, I'm in trouble!' The words came in choked-off gobbets of sound, as if he was about to suffocate on each syllable. 'I'm being blackmailed, Charlie!'

There were a few thousand places Charlie Pickett would have found more congenial at this precise moment. The wrong end of a confessional didn't appeal to him one iota. 'Just give me the bare bones of it, Beattie,' he said quickly. 'The background I don't want to know.'

Dandridge nodded, sweeping back a stray lock of blond hair that had tumbled over his forehead. He looked, thought Pickett, as lost as a shanghaied choirboy.

'They want me to let Judd out,' said Dandridge. He bit his lip. 'For Tilley's concert.'

Pickett stared at him. It wasn't as bad as he had feared, it was worse, far worse.

'Baines, some others, they ...' Dandridge wiped a thin film of sweat from his upper lip. He was breathing unevenly and incapable of keeping still. Pickett cut him off again. 'Not the details, Beattie! If you've made some mistake that they are using over you, then that's between you and them! Can you tell the Old Man?'

'No!' Dandridge jerked still at the thought of it.

'Why Judd? Why do they want Judd?'

'A joke, I think. To see the concert, I don't know ...'

'Some joke,' said Pickett.

'Baines is mad, Charlie!'

'I don't think any of us are totally all there,' said Pickett.

'You don't understand ...'

'I do.' Pickett stood up. 'Well, if you really can't tell the Old Man about it and Baines has it in his power to make things uncomfortable for you ...' he began.

'More than "uncomfortable" Charlie,' said Dandridge, and for a dreadful moment Pickett thought he was going to slip in the cause for Baines's hold over him.

'So what if *I* muscle in? I suppose I could have a word with Baines.'

'No!' Dandridge shouted it. 'I wouldn't want that, Charlie.'

'Then there's only one thing left – give them the key.'

'What?'

'Baines wants the keys, so you "lose" them. That way a broken snap-lock on a lanyard is at fault. Baines "finds" them and does what he wants to do. There's no way he's going to let Judd drop him in the cart, so whatever he has in mind isn't going to mean him dancing a hornpipe up there. Maybe he just wants to boast Judd saw the concert and he was the man who did it. Maybe he's, as you say, going off his rocker. One thing, once it's over Baines will have nothing on you, Beattie. If he says one word, all you have to say is that you'll tell the Old Man about Baines's doings and no matter how bad it might be for you it'll be twenty times worse for him. I'll vouch for the fact that you came to me in despair at having lost the key and we both went on a search for it, if anything comes out. I doubt that it will.'

Dandridge blinked. 'I hadn't expected you, Charlie ...'

No, thought Pickett, neither had I, but there was no going back now.

'If things go wrong ...'

'Things *have* gone wrong,' said Pickett. 'Just try and see they don't get any worse.' He looked at his watch. 'You'd better be on your way.'

'Charlie, I just want to say that ...'

'Don't kid yourself it's not a bloody mess,' said Pickett quickly. 'But a bloody mess isn't the end of the world.'

'Yes,' said Dandridge.

When he had gone Charlie Pickett stood a long time staring at the door. 'It's not the end of the world.' Philosopher Pickett putting his head into the lion's mouth on the doubtful premise that the wider the jaws the more time there was to avoid decapitation.

It had been one week ago that Beattie Dandridge's private hell had begun. Tilley had told Pickett everything. He too had heard it second hand, but there was no doubting its veracity. Dandridge was too pretty, too bloody innocent. Maybe something more, who could tell? Even so, Pickett had liked the odd messmate, who had come to *Drummer* with a bag full of books in his dunnage and a head full of Conrad, Zola and a weird Irishman named Joyce. Pickett had read all of them, never before having considered reading as anything other than an educational exercise, necessary but tedious. Dandridge had done his best to explain some of the more obscure references, and what the authors did with words made Pickett's 'journal' look as if it was written by a three-year-old. On the other hand the Irishman wrote a bit that way himself. Beattie explained that too, or at least tried.

It was a new world; not one that really mattered much to anyone, but one that seemed to be able to put down for ever what most people felt for a fleeting second and then forgot. In return Pickett had told Dandridge of ships and the sea. A strange friendship but it seemed to work. Dandridge had come to the sea like a pilgrim to Mecca, prepared to make any sacrifice in order to gain strength by it. It wasn't unusual. The sea, like the moon, drew thousands in its wake as if its very emptiness was offering a source of inspiration. As far as Charlie Pickett was concerned it offered callouses, gyp, hunger and bedbugs, but he'd never been able to explain the 'lure' of that to Dandridge. Even to himself. They had come on different roads and as it happened they liked each other. But now ...

One week ago Midshipman Beattie Dandridge had been asked to settle a dispute in the section of the crew's mess occupied by Baines and the others. Tilley, Coker and Hackett hadn't been there, otherwise the story might have been different. The row centred on the ventilation of the compartment, some wanting more, some less. It had been stifling and they had asked Dandridge to take off his jacket and shirt to appreciate just how bad it was. Half of them were already shirtless. The details of what happened next were irrelevant. But Dandridge, unaware of what was going on, had tried to adjudicate and made a fool of himself. The rest only he and the others could truly know. What seemed certain was that he had suddenly found himself in a cabin of half-naked men, vying for his attention. They had crowded him, arguing noisily, laughing, jostling. Beattie had probably made the mistake of trying to laugh it off, going along with their horseplay out of sheer embarrassment at his ridiculous situation, not knowing the mood was changing by the minute. Whatever he had done, it had been interpreted as acquiescence. The rest wasn't difficult to imagine. Clawing sweaty hands, snorts of breath, his body no longer his own. Baines had chosen his companions as well as he had chosen his sacrifice. Dandridge had been stripped and firmly splayed face down over a table, naked.

And they had used him, for the moment the masters.

Dandridge had said nothing afterwards, riddled perhaps with shame. Or was he? An uncharitable thought, but Pickett couldn't help it. Beattie had never had any sexual experience in his life before.

He leaned back in his chair with a groan. The advice he had just given might rank as the most stupid thing he had ever done. To be associated with any of it could wreck his career as surely as it could wreck Dandridge's if anything went wrong. He had thrown a lifeline that might become a noose.

The stage was on the forrard well deck. A series of planks laid over salt-cod crates nailed and lashed to keep them stable. Two uprights supported a canvas backdrop, behind which the 'artistes' awaited their moment. The 'orchestra', as Tilley resolutely referred to the squeeze-box, ukelele, tin whistle and drum, had seats on one side of the stage, partly obscured by a board on which someone had written *Tiley's Tivvoli*. The entertainers had begun to arrive, coyly taking cover behind the canvas that was rippling like an impatient sail.

From the bridge Muir could make out a procession of weirdly

garbed figures fussing like a chorus line behind the backdrop as the audience squatted on deck clutching their tots of rum. A few good natured jeers could be heard.

'I feel as if I'm peering into a ladies' dressing room,' said Barrow.

'Better you were,' said Muir. With a smile he went back to his cabin, leaving Barrow to peep.

Hackett strutted on stage and forgot his lines. He stood like a ventriloquist's dummy without a knee to sit on.

'I am a pirate, brave and bold,' hissed Tilley loudly from behind the canvas. 'Improvise!'

'Can't,' managed Hackett, over his shoulder. 'Just have to do what I can!'

Any answer he might have received was drowned by laughter. Puzzled, he regarded his audience.

'Somebody wind him up,' yelled a voice.

'Shut your gob, Whittle, you scranbag!'

Sounds of despair backstage.

Hackett coughed into his hook, wetted his lips and, throwing out his chest, began to sing:

> Lone is the house now, and lonely the moorland,
> The children are scattered, the old folk are gone.

The squeeze-box limped behind him.

> Why should I live like a ghost in the shadow?
> Tis time I was moving, tis time I passed on.

The Irish tenor John McCormack was being slowly crucified. Hackett flung out an arm with dramatic emphasis and the hook, detaching itself, scythed over the heads of the audience and fell into the sea. Baffled, he regarded his empty sleeve.

'Move on, move on!' came the roar. Red-faced he left the stage. Stoker Melfort followed with reluctance. *He* was supposed to be the comedian. But his jokes (known by heart by most of the crew) went down well, a chorus of voices bellowing every punch line with glee. Percy Armgard juggled eggs until, totally enwrapped in the backcloth, he was forced to slither off, leaving the trampled remains of a giant omelette. Shadwell the carpenter danced with a rag doll tied to his feet, its arms slung around his shoulders, ending in something that left little to the imagination and had nothing to do with dancing. Barker, a rating, did gymnastics that left him limping.

It was, if nothing else, an engaging hour.

Tilley came on stage. 'Now, for the final, breathtaking act . . .'

Baines, squatting at the rear of the audience, stood up, jerking his head silently. On either side the men moved with him. They met Dandridge in the compartment that led down to the storeroom.

'That's a good lad,' said Baines. 'Knew you'd turn up.'

Dandridge dropped the key and began to climb the ladder to the deck. Baines pulled him back. 'And what you think that means, sunny Jim?'

'You want a key. There it is,' said Dandridge. 'Now leave me be.'

Baines shook his head slowly. A cracked grin displayed a chaos of twisted teeth that seemed to fill his mouth entirely, as if he was chewing marble chippings. 'Pick it up, Dandridge!'

Dandridge whirled on him. 'You got what you wanted, damn you! Why can't you leave it at that?'

Baines's hand shot forward and grasped Dandridge's wrist, wrenching his arm behind him with a force that bent him to the deck. 'Now pick it up!'

Dandridge's shoulder was screaming for release. He scrabbled for the key with his free hand and held it up. Baines took it and let him go.

There was no point in resistance, not any more. He had lost everything. Dandridge stood unsteadily. Blackmail, striking an officer – Baines could be in worse trouble than Judd if only the captain knew. But for the captain to know would destroy both of them. As it was, the shame was simply eating him away, piece by piece. Dandridge knew he was weak, but there was something more to it than that. Something was happening to him that he couldn't understand. He should have felt loathing and disgust at what had happened to him and, initially, he had. But lying on his bunk on the evening of that terrible day he had been unable to prevent a sick, trembling excitement from sweeping over him. And what was left of his manhood mocked him with a throbbing firmness he couldn't control. He knew then that he had not been scarred but branded, and the scum of his baptism would cling to him for ever. He was lost.

Baines inspected him as they stood outside the door. 'Open it.'

As it swung back Baines reached in and flicked the switch. The light hit Judd a hammer blow across his eyes, turning his head spastically away from it. He squinted up between a lattice-work of fingers. 'Bloody hell on earth, wassis?' His voice was thick with sleep. He sat up batting his eyelids furiously. 'Sod me!' He made out the light switch that his groping had missed. 'A party, Juddy,' said Baines. 'Ain't that right, Mr Dandridge, sir?'

Tilley waved his arms for quiet. A rumbling 'shuuushhh' went around the deck. 'So you've heard the rules. Any of you sober enough to stand is welcome to take part. Mr Winslow is waiting.' Tilley nodded to the wings and two men walked on carrying a plank. 'Right, Tiny, it's all yours.'

'Tiny' Winslow was standing stage centre, sixteen stone of badly packed fat. Smiling, he puffed out his stomach and, like a sumo wrestler who had seen better days, sat on the plank held between the two men. With effort they lifted him and balanced the corners of the plank on the thick pads of canvas draped over their shoulders. He dangled, a grotesque Humpty Dumpty.

'One man,' said Tilley. 'A trial of stamina and strength. All he has to do is support the total weight of Tiny for ten seconds unaided. Surgeon Bellamy has vast experience of treating ruptures, he tells me, and everyone will receive the best of attention. Now, who's to start?'

Two challengers. The first sank slowly to the stage as if caught inadvertently beneath a descending steel press. The other, eyes bulging as he took the weight, panicked as he realised that his rum-induced confidence was about to reduce him to pressed ham. He slunk offstage to the accompaniment of hoots and jeers.

Tilley looked over at Penn Coker, who was lounging to one side of the stage tying a turk's head in a rope. He needed Coker to participate, show that he was in some part like other men. People like Judd, Baines, half a dozen others he could name, were in varying degrees rough, foul-mouthed, coarse, violent, savage. Coker was something else. His precise, uncoiling contempt had begun to obsess Tilley. It seemed everybody aboard *Drummer* had their own nervous tic and this was his. One vaguely human act. Why should it concern him so? Tilley coughed away the dryness in his throat. 'Mr Coker? The finale is in your hands.' He would have felt more at ease trying to house-train an anaconda.

The crowd responded immediately, stamping and shouting. Coker shook his head. But he was beaten, Tilley knew he was beaten. For the first time in his life—and by his own pride.

Still shaking his head Coker stood up and looked at Tilley. The applause stopped as he ambled towards the stage, smacking the turk's head into his open hand. It began to occur to Tilley that Coker might well have an unscheduled and impromptu act of his own — like tearing him limb from limb. But, to his relief, the big man tossed away the rope and positioned himself under the board, hands flattened, legs ready for the strain. He breathed deeply once and took it.

'Uuuuuuuup,' murmured the audience. Coker's stomach contracted and the men either side moved away. Tiny Winslow was suspended above Coker's head and the veins at his temples pulsed.

'One ... two ... three ... four ... five ...' counted Tilley. The board shook and Winslow gave a 'whoop', but it held. At the count of fifteen the men moved in at a sign from Tilley and Coker picked up his rope and walked offstage, nostrils flaring. The yelling and cheering drowned Tilley's words.

'... and seen the impossible,' he ended. There was a sudden burst of laughter. Walking on stage was a figure draped from head to foot in a sheet, two eyeholes slashed below a string that bunched it around the forehead, arab-style. Without a word a hand was flicked beneath the sheet and the men with the board moved back on stage. Winslow looked at Tilley. But Tilley had lost control.

The board was raised and, shrugging, Winslow sat suspended once more.

The count reached twenty-two before the fat man crashed to the deck. The white-robed figure patted him on the head and, with a curtsy, made a quick exit.

Tilley, nonplussed, could only stare after him. The audience was beside itself, mugs, hats and anything else hands could be laid on, thrown on the stage in an eruption of delight.

Penn Coker shook his head slowly, his lips bitten down into the beginnings of a smile. 'Judd,' he said to himself. 'Bloody Judd, as I live and breathe.'

Tilley rang down the curtain. Something had gone terribly wrong.

Barrow jabbed a finger at the quartermaster at the wheel. 'Keep her steady. Offord, come with me.'

Navigating Officer Offord had never heard Barrow speak with such brusqueness before.

'Now, man! Jump to it!'

'Sir!'

'Get someone to inform the captain ... no. I want the master at arms and three men immediately.' He stared from the bridge down at the deck, craning after the figure he had seen walk from the stage. 'Down to the storeroom fast as you can. I'll be there.' He raced from the bridge and took a wide circle across the deck and down to the companionway that led below.

He was there less than a minute before the sheet began to billow at the top of the steps.

'Judd! Stay where you are!' Beattie Dandridge, following, gave a cry and sank his head against the metal. Above him Barrow caught a glimpse of retreating legs.

Judd snatched the cloak over his head. 'What in bloody hell is going on?' His fists bunched in anger.

'Just hold it there, Judd. Dandridge, what are you doing here?'

Judd began to move forward.

'Don't move, Judd!' Offord and the master at arms hung from the ladder levelling pistols.

'You find the other one?' said Barrow.

'Saw nobody else, sir,' said Offord. He stepped down, his pistol pointing at Judd's stomach.

Dandridge stared at him wild-eyed.

'Look, I'll give you no trouble,' said Judd to Barrow. 'If you'll just ...' he had walked a pace closer. Offord's pistol split his cheek as the barrel tore down.

'Christ!' Judd doubled over, the blood running to his shoulder.

'Take him below,' said Barrow to the master at arms. 'And get him patched up.' Offord was a bloody fool, there had been no need for violence. Judd was bundled down to his cell, and he turned to the navigating officer. 'I suggest you might be serving me better above,' he said acidly. 'The question of who authorised you to carry that pistol is a matter I'll deal with later.'

'Judd,' began Offord, 'you could see what he was likely to do, I merely ...'

'Above, Offord!' Barrow turned to Dandridge. 'I saw some of what was going on down there, on the well deck. How are you involved in this? What are you doing here?'

'I don't know! It's nothing serious! If you just let it be, then ...'

'Dandridge!'

'I don't know anything! You leave me alone!'

'What? What's the matter with you, boy?' Barrow stepped

towards him and Dandridge shrank back. 'Have you been under duress?'

'Nothing! All right, do what you like!'

Barrow slapped him across the face and held him by the shoulders. The shocked boy stared at him hopelessly.

'I'm not threatening anything, Dandridge, I'm asking. What can you tell me?' The master at arms clattered past them.

'I've left a guard, sir.'

'Good.' Barrow waited until he and the rest of his men had gone. 'Dandridge, this is damn serious!'

'It's not the end of the world, sir.' Dandridge began to giggle hysterically.

Muir walked the cabin as Barrow ran through the sequence of events. How he had spotted the robed figure slipping away from the stage and had become suspicious, the height of the man alone suggesting Judd. Dandridge's unexplained presence; Offord's idiotic overreaction.

'I hold myself responsible,' said Barrow. 'Offord should never have had a pistol.'

'Nonsense!' Muir opened a small tooled-leather box and took out a cigar. 'Offord can answer for his own actions! Bloody fool!' He sighed. 'What do you make of the Dandridge thing?'

'Well, Dandridge was in charge of overseeing Judd's mealtimes, general security. He had the keys. They could have been lost, taken from him ...'

'Not by Judd. There's more to it than that. Somebody is trying to swing a point.'

'I think the boy was under duress. He's on the verge of cracking up.'

'One broken head in the sick bay, a rating in confinement, an officer wielding a pistol like Dick Turpin – the whole damn ship is cracking up!'

Muir's anger was total.

7 December

The sun, scudding through a mackerel sky, had finally sunk like a guttering ember in the sea. The moon rose, showering stars on the water, and a thin, hissing phosphorescence curdled at *Drummer*'s bow and stern. Her engines beat softly, apologetically, as the wind blew cat's paws across the ocean.

Some were maybe not as elegant as others, thought Charlie

Pickett, standing at the lee rail, but an ugly ship had never been created. Two thousand net tons of steel plate, copper piping, pumps, bilges, ballast, all squeezed around coal-fired boilers blasting steam into the racing pistons of the engine, that lay buried like a shackled locomotive in her bowels. In her holds a mountain of coal. On land *Drummer* would have been some disreputable factory, gracing a grimy street with the droppings from her smoke-stack and the rumblings of her stomach. At sea she was, if not exactly a queen, a rare old lady still, with a bearing and a pedigree handed down by the centuries. Every ship that sailed deep waters was born of a line that began with the first Phoenicians creeping their galleys past the 'Pillars' into the river they called 'The Ocean' and on to Cadiz and the Baltic. Beattie Dandridge's words. Pickett ran a finger around his collar. Three o'clock in the morning, the last hour of the 'graveyard watch' and sticky hot. Prettie had sworn by a storm but it hadn't come. At least not the weather kind.

Slim and ascetic over a tight, compact body, Pickett's physical neatness was only marred by shoulders that shot his shirt cuffs a good inch and a half above his wrists. It was hereditary. His father, who had risen to become engineer-lieutenant, had been something of a boxer in his day and had brought up his son as if nurturing a future sparring partner. His spasmodic homecomings were occasions for ferocious testing. Pickett had learned to dodge his father's well-meaning fists in between his mother's equally well-intentioned attempts to teach him Latin. To her consternation, father and son went about hammering each other with glee until she was on the verge of despair. And the day came when Pickett junior began to pull his punches, caught blows by intention. It wasn't until later, much later, after his father had died, that he realised that that was what love was all about. His mother had never understood and had still tried to find some excuse for his father's strange displays of affection. But how could a woman, even a mother, make sense of it? It was a man's world, rough and tumble. Charlie Pickett had never learned Latin.

A man's world. So where did Beattie Dandridge fit into it? He was sleeping fitfully after blurting out what had happened with Judd and Baines. It all added up to the bloody mess Pickett had dreaded. The business with Baines and company wasn't big news on any ship; moths found their lamp. But Dandridge didn't seem to be the type. 'The type'. What *was* the type? Pickett shook his head. One thing you learned – what went on in people's minds was a sight more complicated than what moved 2000 tons of ship.

His lean face peered over the rail. The thick warmth still clung to the ship, despite the breeze. The horizon, under a gibbous moon, had blown clear. He worked his way along it.

Three twigs.

He looked automatically up at the bridge. Turned back. They were still there. He could see the faint outline of white sail. Began to run.

'See her, sir?' he was calling before he had even reached the end of the stairway leading from the boat deck. Barrow was in the wheelhouse.

'Out to starboard, sir!'

'Do you have to come charging up here like an elephant, Pickett?'

'Couldn't sleep, sir.'

Barrow suddenly remembered that Pickett shared quarters with Dandridge. 'I see. So what have *you* seen?' They walked out to the bridge, Barrow holding his binoculars. Chief Petty Officer Muswell saluted them from the port wing.

'Any sign of life, Chief?'

'No, sir.'

Still holding his glasses at his waist, Barrow peered naked-eyed along the horizon.

'The lee, sir. Starboard quarter,' said Pickett. 'Difficult to make out from here.' He craned over the wing. 'There they are!' To Muswell: 'No chance of spotting her from this angle, Chief.' It took Muswell off the hook.

Barrow was training his glasses. 'I see her. Square-rigged. No lights. She could be in trouble.' Handing the glasses to Pickett, he blew into the speaking tube. 'Sparks? There's a ship on the starboard quarter showing no lights. Try and establish contact. Good man.' To Hardcastle: 'Have course made to intercept her. Watch on deck at full alert. I'm going to have a word with the captain. Pickett, stay here. And don't lose her, or I'll have your guts for garters.' He smiled. 'See what thanks you get?'

For two hours they had been closing on the sailing ship. She was making a course away from *Drummer* and moving as fast as the breeze would allow. But the breeze was strengthening and she was making good use of it. Muir watched from the bridge, having been dragged from a deep sleep. 'Nothing on the W.T?'

'Not a twitter,' said Barrow. 'The chances are she hasn't seen us.'

'Or heard us,' said Muir. 'And if she is in trouble it isn't affecting her progress. Keep after her, Number One, and give me a shout when we're closer.'

Barrow had the bit between his teeth, thought Pickett. One learned something every day. After the incident with Judd which had robbed him of shut-eye, Barrow couldn't have slept for the best part of a day, but the rising sails seemed to wash away any sign of fatigue. An hour passed and dawn began to blush. The binoculars had red-rimmed Pickett's eyes and his arms were leaden.

'Chief, get the yeoman up here sharp. If they're deaf they may not be blind. We'll try the signal lamps.' Barrow looked across at Pickett. 'Give it a rest.'

Pickett's brow wrinkled. 'The light's getting better,' he said. 'There's a flag ... wait ... got it ... she's a Frenchie. Definite!'

'And can you tell me her name and how many men on deck?' said Barrow with a grin. He took up his own binoculars. The flag was a dark smudge.

'There!' Pickett seemed about to reach out and touch it.

'I'll take your word for it, Pickett,' said Barrow.

Pickett re-focused the glasses.

A Frenchie.

But a memory stealing up from somewhere told him differently.

From spanker to jib the sails proclaimed a chance breeze that, after three days' calm, was not unwelcome. The full-rigged ship *Charlemagne*, flying French colours and, according to its manifest, carrying wood and general cargo, had been making nine knots under a full press of canvas when a hand perched high in the main top-gallant shrouds saw what those on deck could not see: a smear of smoke moving steadily across the horizon on the port bow. The news brought the mate and chief officer scrambling up the ratlines for confirmation. Within minutes the deck was a maelstrom of bodies as the violent change of course cracked her sails and the braces were stretched to breaking point as they hauled the yards to gain new power. *Charlemagne* had swung almost on her beam ends and wasn't liking it.

Standing at her midship wheel, the captain fixed his eyes, unblinking, on the seaman who had shinned high into the main royal, 120 feet above the deck. Everything depended on the next few minutes and the figure swaying there.

The activity of a moment before had given way to one of uncertain expectancy. Then the trapeze artist waved a hand. A bellow.

'Aaah!' The captain shook his head to one side and turned away in disgust. It was as he had guessed – they had been seen. The biggest disadvantage of all – albeit their only one – the soaring masts of *Charlemagne* stood like a semaphore above the sea's edge, visible long before the watch on deck could make out the squat shape of a steamship. And though he had kept men aloft as often as possible, the job of look-out on a pitching ship was fraught with problems. Another bellow: the stranger was altering course. Which could mean one of a dozen things; one learned to anticipate the worst.

'Well, Monsieur Vilhon?'

The chief officer wiped grease from his hands: 'A tramp steamer. But she has turned hard and is making for us, there is no doubt.' His accent was that of the Southern Cevennes, thick and raw, bouncing the final syllables. By contrast the captain spoke a different language – northern French, polished and Parisian smooth.

'You are doing well, *Monsieur* Vilhon.'

The chief officer gave a doubtful shrug. 'And you, Captain, are, I suspect, mocking me.'

'Not at all. It will do.'

'Need it?'

'I think so.'

The chief officer was three inches under six foot tall but alongside him the captain seemed minute, his uniform hanging loosely, dipping at an angle from a permanently drooped left shoulder. His face, equally lopsided, was cocked like an inquisitive bird's. Quick, dark eyes peered from caverns fringed by black fly-away eyebrows. The captain of *Charlemagne* hunched himself like a maître d'hôtel preparing to receive an unwelcome guest.

'They have been trying to communicate by wireless telegraph, but we have remained silent, as you ordered, sir. That and our lack of lights seem to have worried them.'

They watched the sailor as he scurried down the spider's web of ratlines to the deck.

'Well they have seen us, despite that,' said the captain, 'so we must make our plans.'

'You think . . .'

'Why should a tramp steamer change course? Every delay would have to be explained to her owners and no merchantman on these seas goes courting trouble. Have the ship's lights flicker and tell the wireless officer to give the impression he is having trouble with his equipment. Then signal that we are prepared to heave to if it is strictly necessary. She could be merely inquisitive, or starved of news.' He gave a short, decisive, hiss of breath. 'We will see.'

Charlemagne, under full power, could make fourteen knots, more than many an old steamship could hope to equal. But it took just one knot more to beat them down, and the sea held many knots. 'It might merely be tiresome,' added the captain. He jerked his shoulder, flexing the arm. 'Tell the men we are to be on our best behaviour. We are an impatient ship, already long overdue and any delay is a bad one. That will be made known. But maybe it will not be enough. We will go through the motions.'

'You feel we should . . .'

'I feel nothing. She is an interruption, no more. We will wait.' He regarded the approaching lights. Strange that the British thought of themselves as lions when they were, in fact, something far worse – terriers. Single-minded and wearing to a degree. He had endured their snapping before and shaken them off. It could be done again. His arm hung limply from his shoulder, having tested the pain. 'Bring her round,' he said to the helmsman. 'Lose the wind.'

Charlemagne's sails were punched flat as the mate communicated the order.

Now everything belonged to the fates. As the English would say, it was damnable. Damnable luck.

'Every man's death diminisheth me'. A noble thought. The unpalatable truth was that another's misfortune was a lightning conductor drawing the blow to a neighbour and eliciting only a sense of delivery from those it passed over, as if pain had an allotted allowance on earth which it couldn't exceed. The whistle of the sword was followed by a gasp of gratitude as it struck someone else. All the rest came later. Reflections in tranquillity. Death diminished no one, apart from the dead. The survivors of the lottery grew only more jealous of life. And blind with relief.

Jack Muir had ten depositions from his crew, each one of whom, from various positions, witnessed the blow that had put McGowan on the brink of death. None bore any relationship to the others. There was no doubt some had 'seen' what they had claimed to have seen – certain key events testified to that. But the rest was a mélange of imagination, half truths, fancy and romance. With a smattering of partisan lies. A ragbag from which reality had to be ferretted for.

McGowan had kicked Judd. Judd had hit McGowan. McGowan had hit his head on the rail. McGowan had slipped. Fainted. Judd had fallen accidentally across him. McGowan had had a heart attack. As yet there was no suggestion that McGowan had voluntarily smashed his brains out on the deck in a fit of pique, though no doubt to sponsor the idea would have met with a nod. Version after version. At least three from men who could see through bulkheads.

Muir shuffled the papers to one side. His report was half finished and he was unhappy with it. Sleep on it. But there was no way he could do that. Sleep wouldn't come. For a moment the sighting of the sailing ship had shaken off his sloth. Even at this late stage a prize ship wasn't too late to change their fortunes. But if, as it seemed, it was an ally, then once again they had been robbed.

Damn and blast Judd and McGowan! Damn and blast the whole business! He tore what he had written in half. All his life he had been criticised (or praised) for being 'blunt'. A 'bluntness' that had taken him from seaman to second mate and a princely £5 a month. Bluntness that had doubled that in a storm off the Cape Verde Islands when the role of chief officer had come to him on the spot, courtesy of the former chief officer found on his bunk too drunk to know one end of a ship from the other. Four years later Muir was the youngest executive officer in the history of the Baring Line. And then came the liners. And 'bluntness' became a hump on the back to be shaken off. Cocktails and canapés. He had learned. And won a wife. For months he had delighted in the evening soirées, if only for her company, and they had married a year later. It hadn't taken long for Muir to realise he was little more than a railway navvy in the eyes of her well-to-do parents.

Bluntness.

Say what you think, when the name of the game was think before you say.

His commission had brushed him with respectability. The cuff chains of a R.N.R. lieutenant had become straight bands and he was accepted. Muir, R.N. Command of *Drummer* had elevated him to the status of a minor managing director. He picked up the pen, wondering how bankruptcy would be received by his wife's parents.

Half an hour later he had finished his report, and was as satisfied as he would ever be. They could take it or leave it. A hundred Battles of the Nile that almost were, were fought on paper by lieutenant-commanders fighting for their careers and he'd be damned if he was going to join them. The Dandridge affair might complicate things, but it wouldn't alter his feelings. McGowan was a bully and a braggart: Judd a man unable to accept the realities of life aboard ship. Between them they constituted a small fester on the surface of life, no more.

'We have a signal, sir,' said Barrow. 'Their wireless is faulty, but Haden has ungarbled it. Her name is *Charlemagne*, bound from Montevideo to any port in France she can make.'

'Carrying?'

'Wood. They've been hit by a storm and her generator is giving trouble. She's prepared to heave to, but points out she needs the wind.'

'Does she need help?'

'I think not. No indication of that, sir.'

'Tell her the war is over.'

'The yeoman has signalled; it was the last message we sent. So far no reaction to that.'

'Well, I suppose we'd best let her go. I know how the captain must feel ...'

'Sir!' Pickett stood at the head of the steps leading from the boat deck into the wheelhouse.

Barrow raised a hand. 'Later, there's a good chap.'

'Sorry, sir, but it's about the ship.' Pickett caught Muir's eye.

'What is it, Pickett?'

'Well, sir, there's something strange about her.' He paused, as if debating with himself. 'I think I recognise her.'

Barrow arched an eyebrow. 'And when have you been on a French windjammer, Pickett?'

'That's it, sir ... the odd thing about it. I don't think she *is* French. Or wasn't ... I mean ...'

'You saw her flag, lad,' said Muir shortly.

'Sir. It's not the flag ... it's the *look* of her. My brother was on board a ship exactly like her, that is from the way she sits in the water, her trim, the rake of her jib-boom ...' Pickett's enthusiasm was waning, but not his conviction. 'I went aboard her a lot when she was in Pompey. I was only about fourteen at the time.'

'Pickett,' said Barrow, not unkindly, 'I'm sure your life-story is fascinating at the appropriate moment. Not now.'

The midshipman flushed. 'I collected them, sir.'

'Collected?' Muir was mellowing.

'Just the tall ships, sir. The ones that came into Pompey. I drew them – in profile – in a book. A hobby, like train spotting. The one I'm talking about I spent hours aboard.'

'And what was her name?'

'*Glencoe*,' said Charlie Pickett. 'Fifteen hundred tons, built on the Clyde. There were three of the line: *Glencoe, Argyll*, and I can't remember the name of the other. I'm not saying this is *Glencoe*, it might be any one of them, but ...' he looked defensively at Barrow. 'It's like not being sure you've seen someone you used to know, except for his way of walking.'

'The cut of his jib,' said Muir.

'Yes, sir. A manner. Some things stick in your mind, but you can't put a finger on it. I'm not totally sure, but I thought it was a point ... a point worth making.'

Pickett had begun to wonder whether he'd had a brainstorm.

'Ships get sold,' said Barrow. 'Maybe it *is* one of the line you're talking about, under new owners.' He was trying to be kind.

'Yes, sir,' said Charlie Pickett.

'Never mind,' nodded Muir, 'whatever she is, keep your eyes open lad, and you'll please me mightily.'

With a salute, Pickett left.

Muir had taken up the binoculars. '*McAllister*,' he said.

'Sir?'

'The ship Pickett couldn't remember. The third of the line. She was taken out of service years ago and used as a target ship. I've heard of *Argyll* and *McAllister*, not *Glencoe*.'

'He's a keen young fellow, Pickett,' said Barrow.

'When he was fourteen he was probably a damn sight keener. At that age they see things sharper than they'll ever see them. The world's still a fascinating place and they swallow lumps of information whole. They're not yet knocking corners off, they're building them. Do you know the exact button arrangement on the uniform of the Coldstream Guards, Number One?'

'Sir?'

'No, neither do I. But any schoolboy in England could tell you. It's all in the cigarette cards. The ship Pickett went on at fourteen wouldn't be forgotten lightly, is the point I'm trying to make.'

'We've told her to proceed,' said Barrow.

'Have a look in the L.C.L.,' said Muir. Lloyd's Confidential List of Ships was issued to all commanders of patrol ships and listed size, owners, and planned routes of all commercial shipping.

Barrow brought it from the chart-room and read: '*Charlemagne*. French. 1500 tons, square-rigged. Owners: Lefèbre Shipping. Trading with South America. Built 1893, Nazaire.'

'Try *Glencoe*,' said Muir.

Eventually Barrow found her. 'She's called *Pass of Glencoe*, but it sounds like the one Pickett described. Built on the Clyde 1888, 1571 tons. Sold to American Vance Line 1913.' He looked up. 'Similar, agreed. But different ships.'

'I wonder,' mused Muir. 'Assume for the moment she is *Pass of Glencoe*, or was. What if the Germans had taken her, rigged her out as *Charlemagne*, a ship they know exists and trades with South America – a very similar ship in all probability, as you say. Under a French flag they could run supplies back to Germany without being stopped. It's been done before.'

'They'd have to be convincing,' said Barrow. 'If they were boarded . . .'

'Yes. If they were boarded . . .' Muir came to a decision. 'I'd like to find out more about her, Number One! It's unfortunate we've given her clearance, but we'll have to live with that. Get the yeoman to use the lamp and tell her we would like to go aboard. A *social* call. Then we'll see how she jumps. At the very least we might get a few glasses of vino.'

The two ships were less than a thousand yards apart. *Charlemagne*'s captain had ordered men to the rails to wave at the steamer – which had proved to be a British armed merchantman with guns fore and aft, flying the white ensign.

A small buffet had been prepared using the last bottles of burgundy. The British responded to civility like no other nation on earth and it would provide a distraction. The wind would have to wait. There was a tap at the door and the chief officer nodded apologetically for his intrusion.

'The ship has signalled she has no further need to detain us, sir.'

The dark eyes flashed and the captain allowed himself the luxury of a smile. 'Then wish her well, and bon voyage.' He tapped a bottle. 'And afterwards join me.' The door closed silently.

Tidying the files he had arranged on his desk, he returned them to the safe and slipped the key into his pocket. 'The war is over. Armistice.' Why had they resorted to such nonsense? To force his hand? Not that it mattered. Now, as ever, luck was on his side. He walked awkwardly to the small washbasin.

Clutched his shoulder.

But the pain wasn't localised there any more. It swept throughout his body and sweat began to ooze from him, draining him of movement. He reached for the door of the small wooden cabinet above the basin. Stopped. No! Forcing himself to turn, he stumbled stiff-legged as far away from it and what it contained as the cabin would allow, clutching his stomach with both hands as if holding a writhing animal. Unable to stand, he collapsed into a chair, the pain robbing him of breath. But he knew now he wouldn't be able to reach the cabinet until it had stopped. And it would stop. *Would* stop. Everything could be defeated if a man was prepared to meet it. The secret was to know the nature of one's enemy, most of all the enemy within. A sudden movement pressed him back in the chair. *Charlemagne* had taken the breeze once more. The captain slapped his palms against the arms of the chair and, hooking his body forward, willed her on, moving her with his pain.

'Two points to starboard,' ordered Muir.

'Two points to starboard, sir,' repeated the quartermaster.

The windjammer was still moving away from them. Barrow came on the bridge. 'No joy, sir. Haden can't get a peep out of *Charlemagne*.'

'Fair enough, Number One. It was worth another try. Tell Hackett to give us as much steam as he can without putting too much strain on the engine. Yeoman!'

Yeoman Hollis snapped to attention.

'Signal her to heave to. We wish to come aboard.'

The yeoman scribbled down the words and moved to the signal lamp on the bridge wing.

'No, use the searchlight,' said Muir. The secondary searchlight, fitted with shutters, was mainly used in murky weather conditions, but its powerful beam would guarantee the message being seen.

'You think she might be running contraband cargo, sir?'

Muir shrugged. 'You know, Number One, I think if we came upon the *Queen Elizabeth* right now we'd try and convince ourselves it was a German cruiser.' *Queen Elizabeth* was the flagship of Admiral Sir David Beatty, C-in-C of the Grand Fleet. Slapping his pockets, Muir extracted his pipe and sucked on it until a faint gurgling sound came from its bowl like a faulty tap. There was every chance, he was thinking, that he might be about to make a complete fool of himself. Stopping a neutral was one thing, but to board an ally was another, particularly after second thoughts. Of course, done with tact it could have been a friendly visit and nothing more. But that moment had gone. Now it would only serve to annoy the French captain who, having lost way once already, might easily refuse to be trifled with again. And then what happened? If Muir ordered her to stop and she simply sailed on, or merely pretended she hadn't seen his signal? A shot across the bows? Muir had been told to make a course for home, but there had been nothing in those orders about carrying on with his duties. If hostilities had – no matter how temporarily – ceased against Germany, what was the situation regarding suspicious vessels? He bit the stem of his pipe. Doing the right thing at the wrong time was an occupational hazard.

They were closing fast on *Charlemagne* but there had been no response to the yeoman's signal.

'Keep her on the quarter,' he said. His mind was made up. 'Hoses on deck and stretcher parties at their posts. Tell the surgeon to be at the ready and all gun crews in place. Get Prettie up here, the gun-laying will be from the bridge. But for God's sake don't have people running everywhere like ants, Number One. Slowly does it.'

Barrow glanced up at the International Code flags Muir had ordered hoisted. M.N. Stop instantly. 'They must have seen them by now, sir!'

'If they want to,' rumbled Muir.

'I respectfully urge you, Captain! Not a moment can be lost!' The chief officer of *Charlemagne* had gone well beyond himself and he knew it. His tone fell. 'Forgive me, but ...' he waved a hand to nowhere and it dropped to his side.

'It is unfortunate they have changed their minds, but please do not presume to "urge" me.' The captain raised himself from behind his desk. The pain had gone but it had left him weak. His voice was uncomfortably reassuring, as if he were talking to a rude child. 'We are in danger of only one thing – falling under a spell. It must not be allowed to change how we think and act. Think like a peasant who has nothing to offer the robber who stops him. Nothing to give, nothing to lose. Don't toy with the gold ring on a finger, it will be taken from you. *Charlemagne* has nothing to hide. You understand me?'

The chief officer nodded. It was half an answer. Even a penniless peasant still had his life to lose.

'Good. Now signal the Britisher that we still welcome them aboard.'

'As you wish, sir.'

'But ... one has to be circumspect.' The officer caught the new note in the captain's voice. 'I think,' he went on smoothly, 'they may have seen the ring already.'

'I believe they have, sir!' The chief officer's tone was urgent. 'Nothing else can account for their persistence. They are suspicious.'

'The English are suspicious by nature. Intrigue is their national sport.'

Straker's prey had up till now been ill-equipped merchant-men, not armed patrol ships, which this must be. He looked at the lights approaching them. There was too much to lose and, in the end, it was better to lose his ship than let it be taken. To sink and drown. The final act of defiance and, in a way, an act of victory, though they would never know it. Everything had been changed because of their cargo, and the decision had been made for him.

'We take the initiative,' said von Bauer. He levered himself from his chair. The weakness had passed. 'The French language is for cafés, not for war,' he said in German.

'We fight?'

'We fight. They will send a boarding party. Sink it. Then all fire we have is to be on the stern. Cripple her, sink her. We have the element of surprise. It has won many battles.'

He waited until the chief officer had gone and regarded his outstretched hands. They were steady. 'The element of surprise'. A wasp sting. The bite of an adder. But wasps could be brushed aside, adders trodden on. It was a matter of who moved first. There was something else that set the coming encounter apart from all the others, and the thought of it was uppermost in his mind. This time there must be no survivors.

Pray God it could be done legitimately, in the heat of battle.

The boarding party was easing the boat in its davits.

'I want you to go with them, Number One,' said Muir. 'All guns out of sight, it's an "informal" visit. Get the victualling officer to put together a few things – fresh bread, some grog, anything he can lay his hands on. But tell him to go easy, it's not Christmas yet. And take the Chief with you, and Pickett here. Tell them we're prepared, if necessary, to escort them to the Channel. And keep your eyes open.'

Pickett was still studying the windjammer. 'There are two

pig pens forrard,' he said. 'See them clearly now. They weren't there before.' It was common sailing ship practice to carry livestock to provide fresh meat. Aboard some of the deep-water clippers the smell of porkers, and the ducks and chickens roaming the decks, gave a lively, if incongruous, barnyard effect. 'There's also what could be a life-raft locker on the poop deck. The rest looks just the same, as I remember it.'

'Let's be having you, Pickett,' said Barrow with a grin at Muir. 'I'm not laying any bets until I see for myself!'

Muir watched from the bridge as Barrow and Pickett supervised the loading of the boat. *Drummer* had moved ahead of the windjammer, which had begun to fall off the wind immediately after signalling they were waiting to be boarded, and was now directly in line. By lowering the boarding boat on the lee side and ordering the tall ship to move forward to meet it, little effort would be required of the boarding party – they simply drew away from *Drummer* and waited until *Charlemagne* came alongside. *Drummer* would then steam in an arc to come abaft and the pattern would be repeated to pick up Barrow and his crew on their return. Muir had practised it fifty times, but never with a sailing ship in mind – and the sea was beginning to swell.

Drummer slowed to two knots. Winches rattling, the boat slid from the davits and touched water, and the massive central hook and rear lizard were disengaged. The boat's helm over, the bowman let go of the forward lizard and held her off with a boathook. For a moment it refused to move away. A sickly thud and the transom knee smashed against *Drummer*'s hull. The chief petty officer let out a stream of curses.

'Bear off!' shouted Barrow.

The bowman bore off the bows and laid in his boathook as the stroke oarsman sprang the whaler ahead and the fenders were laid in, crutches and oars shipped. They waited.

'Oars!' yelled Barrow.

Grasping the looms, the boat's crew brought the oars athwartships, blades horizontal. The stroke was taken and they began to move away.

There were six of them in all: Barrow and five oarsmen, Pickett, Chief Petty Officer Muswell, Petty Officer Lorimer and two able seamen – Purvis and Baines.

'Pull away there!' shouted Muswell, heaving on his oar. 'Time for a bit of boatsmanship! We're bloody standing still! Tighten your arses, this isn't a fucking punt!'

His enthusiasm found little echo from Baines. Fumbling with

55

the crutch he held the oar between his knees. 'No good, Chief, it's me hand.' He raised it gingerly as if any sudden movement might topple the fingers. 'I cut meself. See it. Hardly move the sodding thing.' His tongue clicked in exasperation at having been robbed of a chance to participate in Muswell's 'boatsmanship'.

'Baines!' Lorimer's voice thundered from behind him. Baines turned to see the boathook in mid-air, travelling towards him sideways on. Instinctively he flung up both hands and caught it before it struck his face, the force throwing him backwards along the bottom boards.

'Miraculous recovery, Baines,' said the C.P.O dryly, with a nod to Lorimer. 'Now get on with it. Next time I'll personally chop your fucking fingers off if they get in the way!'

Baines slammed the oar into the crutch, head averted, chewing on his rage in silence.

'Keep her steady,' said Barrow. He looked back. 'She's coming up. When she's abeam move in – but *slowly*! It's a sailing ship we're dealing with and she'll be rolling and her speed not constant. Don't let her stick to us or we could go under. And watch the sea. If it picks up we can get thrown aboard her deck. Lorimer, when I shout, make sure those guns are out of sight. Right, here we go . . .'

Watching and waiting at the tiller, Barrow recalled a point-to-point held across the fields of *Brownlows*, the family home. In the distant mist the horses moved effortlessly, manes and tails flying, silent and light as if defying gravity. And then, as they approached, the ground began to shake and the illusion was gone with the wet slap of the rider's thighs, the creaking of leather, as the flashing iron hooves chewed up great gobbets of earth in a passage of sheer brute force. 'Santiago's Horses' – the Spanish children's name for thunder.

'Auxiliary!' shouted Muswell. 'She's got a hidden auxiliary!' They could see the curdling foam of her stern.

Charlemagne had swung out of line and was increasing speed.

'Oh Christ! What did I tell you?' moaned Baines. 'Do something, somebody!' He stood up. 'She's a bloody raider!' Muswell's boot caught him between the shoulder blades with a mighty kick that bent him like a jack-knife. He retched over the lazy oar.

'Shut it, you bastard! Pull!' Muswell was shouting at the top of his voice.

'All of you, *pull*!' said Barrow. He grabbed a spare oar and dipped it into the water indian-style. *Charlemagne* was putting them directly between herself and *Drummer* and there was no question of her being boarded.

'Move this bloody boat, you useless set of sods!' Lorimer addressed Purvis and Baines but, in the heat of the moment, added, '*All* of you! Bend your backs!'

'Don't look, just keep *pulling*!' grunted Barrow.

'They're running up a ...' Petty Officer Lorimer suddenly slid an arm awkwardly over Pickett's shoulder and the midshipman felt a soft pudding slide down his chest. The severed arm dropped across his knee like an eel as the P.O. collapsed over him, pumping blood in a fountain.

'Pickett! Hold him!' Barrow tried to move back. But there was nothing much for Pickett to hold. The limp body had been cut into slices.

'He's dead, sir.' Pickett was drenched in Lorimer's blood. None of them seemed to have heard the shots that had killed him. But now they could hear nothing else – a vicious hail of machine-gun fire was all around them.

'Get down!' ordered Muswell.

'No! Keep pulling!' Barrow jerked a hand at the chief petty officer. 'We have to keep moving, man!'

Muswell looked at him in astonishment and tried to say something but words seemed to fail him.

'Do as I say!'

Still Muswell stared, his face contorted as if about to reply with a stream of oaths.

'Muswell?' Pickett turned, wiping the blood from his face. But Muswell was long past obeying orders or even hearing them. The past seven seconds had been fully devoted to the bullets that had peppered his back. For the last time he tried to express himself and then, to Barrow's horror, he stood up and pitched overboard.

'Christ! Christ! Christ!' Baines had thrown himself into the bottom of the boat, clutching the boards and spitting out a frothing soup of blood and salt water in great belches. Purvis scrambled away from the remains of the petty officer that had slid from Pickett's lap down to his feet, still jerking in a parody of life, eyes open and glazed with oil.

Barrow hit Purvis across the face with a force that made his knuckles crack. Reaching down he grabbed Baines by the hair and hauled him bodily back on the thwart. 'Pickett! Guns! Get the guns!'

He let fire with the rifle that was thrown to him and realised the stupidity of it.

Charlemagne's first shell hit *Drummer* at some point behind the bridge and he could see debris falling into the sea. Simultaneously the flag of the Imperial German Navy broke at the windjammer's masthead. The boat was making no way.

'Baines, Purvis – grab a gun!' ordered Barrow. Any gesture was better than simply sitting there waiting to be picked off.

Crouched below the gunwales they began to fire, and even Baines seemed to gain strength by it.

'Fuggin' fuggers, fuggin' fuggers,' he chanted hoarsely.

Purvis had seemed to master his hysteria by considering himself already dead and therefore there was little point in making too much fuss. Taking careful aim, he loosed off one considered shot after another like a man in a dream. After each volley he crinkled his nose along the sights, blinked rapidly, and pronounced with deep reflection: 'As a doornail!'

'Fuggin' fuggers!'

'As a doornail!'

'Fuggers!'

'Doornail!'

Directly alongside Purvis, Pickett could see the A.B. had bitten clean through his lower lip and it hung like a piece of undigested raw meat at the edge of his mouth. Purvis seemed oblivious of it, his exposed teeth and gums ripped in an insane smile. Pickett looked back at Barrow.

'Stay with it, lad!'

'Sir!'

'It'll be all right!' *Drummer* was still turning and still not a shot had been fired from her. 'It can't be long. Hang on! Any minute!'

The boy nodded, the congealed blood cracking his face like sunburn.

Barrow turned his eyes away, aware of the paucity of his epitaph.

It was as if all the events that had passed *Drummer* and her crew by over the last year had, unknown to them, been squeezed into a secret cache that now had suddenly sprung its lock. The windjammer's 'pig pens' had collapsed, guns swinging and firing as their sides hit the deck; a rattle of Maxims and the boarding boat had stained the sea rose-pink. Muir had seen someone fall and, following the machine-guns, heard a dull unequivocal thud and *Drummer* had lurched. Prettie had been the first to realise what was happening. Standing on the bridge, he had not waited to see what would happen after the first rounds hit the boat, but ordered his guns aimed and ready to fire. Only then did he realise his speaking tubes had been cut. Like a man possessed he had raced down to the forrard gun and, falling headlong over the body of his gun-layer, cursed him with a violence he would later regret.

'Get this bugger out of my way!' The body was dragged unceremoniously across the deck as he began to lay the gun.

'Up! Up! Wait for the swing. Coming! Now!'

As *Charlemagne* dipped in unison with *Drummer* Prettie's shell took away half her mainmast. It fell in a tearing roar, slicing down to smash the rails into matchwood, and slid overboard in a tangle of blocks and ropes that refused to give, hanging like fallen knitting down her side.

'Lower,' he said. 'Put the bitch under!' He looked for confirmation from the bridge. It seemed to be on fire.

Muir's problem was straightforward. He could either fight it out broadside on, or move off and use his long-range guns to pound the windjammer. Moving off would mean temporarily abandoning Barrow. One thing was certain: this couldn't go on.

A rush of air swept from behind him, stinking of sulphur. A shell had passed through the wireless office, sweeping out equipment and men. Signal Officer Haden had disappeared, as had Wireless Telegraphist Horace Feeley and two others. Stretcher parties wandered at a loss among the fragments. Something that could have been an ear hung from a piece of ripped steel.

Offord, temporarily rehabilitated during the emergency, was in the wheelhouse, having taken over from the quartermaster who had been hit by blast and sat hunched, making strange purring noises to himself, refusing any aid. *Drummer*'s guns were beginning to shake her.

'Ten points to starboard,' said Muir. He walked out on to the bridge. The windjammer hadn't faltered. He saw a faint splash at her side and whirled to Offord. 'Evasive action! Swing her!' The ship lurched and Offord saw the thin ripple pass a cable's length in front of *Drummer*.

'Mother of God!' Hackett's arms were still shaking long after the Vicker's Maxim had stopped and another belt was being clipped to it. 'Did you see that?'

Coker pushed him aside and began to fire the gun as if watering a lawn.

'A torpedo! It was an' all!' Hackett watched the now-harmless wake disappear into the distance.

Coker shook the 250-round fabric belt from its box, helping the feed, and thrust Hackett towards the chain.

'As close as you like,' said Hackett.

'Mad bastards,' said Coker. 'They haven't got a cat in hell's!'

Hackett pointed to Coker's chest. A thin pencil-mark had creased it. Coker pushed his hand away and began to fire again. Neither of them noticed that Hackett had suddenly lost two fingers.

'Out you come, lad!'

'I'm not bloody moving from here, and that's a fact.' Frank Judd squatted with his back to the bulkhead and fixed the master at arms with a look of withering derision. 'What's the matter? Barrow want to exercise his hounds, so send for Frank Judd?' He spat on the floor. 'Tell Jimmy the One that I'd love to come and perform cartwheels for him, but must politely decline, being otherwise engaged. To put it another way, tell him to shove a thumb up his arse.' He fingered the wound on his cheek. 'What's going on anyway?'

Keble, *Drummer*'s master at arms, was a craggy-faced man of fifty, whose natural posture – one it seemed that had been with him from birth – was that of rigid attention. He stiffened even more than usual. 'Save the old stroppiness, Judd! Doesn't make any difference to me, so only wasting your breath!' Keble had never been known to speak other than in corporalese and had yet to discover a sentence that couldn't be barked. Life was a series of exclamation marks of varying emphasis. 'Captain's orders! Temporary basis, for your own safety! Matter of trust! Word of honour, Judd, that's what I need from you!'

Judd gave a grin. 'That's *dashed* civil of the Old Man, to be sure. He wants me to come aloft and shake hands with Offord?'

'Judd!' Keble was ostentatiously wearing an empty holster at his waist and had come alone. His own idea. Judd wouldn't be intimidated by a show of force so the gesture of a personal armistice might avoid a clash that, from Keble's side, could only be answered by a bullet. Not that the master at arms had any qualms about incapacitating Judd, or anyone else who overstepped the mark and threatened the internal security of the ship. But he believed fiercely in his position of ship's policeman and had not got this, the most independent and responsible of jobs, by cracking skulls open at random. He was also still smarting at Offord's flat-footed 'handling' of a situation he could have controlled with the minimum of fuss. 'Don't make it difficult, Judd! You can hear the rumpus up top! All hands needed! Stay here and you might well be cooked alive!'

Judd grew serious. 'Submarine?' Still squatting, he looked at Keble with genuine interest. 'I've been hearing the row. Don't tell me the Old Man has actually met a bloody German at last?'

'Decoy raider dolled up as a windjammer!' said Keble. 'The Number One and half a dozen others caught in an open boat between the two of us, poor devils!' There was the sound of an explosion followed by the grating of metal against metal.

'Well, so I might as well see what the bugger looks like.' Judd tugged himself to his feet. A sudden thought: 'What happens if she sinks us? Takes survivors? Reckon they won't be interested in me and my little "difference" with the coxswain? What you think?'

Keble led the way to the steps. 'Technical point! War ended! Armistice!'

'Jesus wept,' said Judd, 'even the fucking Germans aren't on my side.' There was a rattle along the hull and they both drew themselves away from it as if from a wind-whipped fire. A series of blisters stitched themselves at head height along the hull.

Keble bent over the hatch and helped Judd through it, straightening immediately as if having been caught committing some misdemeanour. The shellfire was echoing around them like a man hammering in a sewer pipe.

'One thing,' said Judd. 'Just one thing. Is this the way they always surrender?'

Three fires had swept *Charlemagne*, one of them disabling her diesel, two others eating at her sails. Muir had seen a score of men fall from the rigging like droplets of candle-fat, hitting the sea with a hiss that seemed audible. One torpedo had narrowly missed *Drummer*, another had exploded on hitting the water, throwing the windjammer on her side. *Drummer*'s decks were a spaghetti of hoses over which men were being carried to the sick bay. Men carrying shells from below — the forrard lifting derrick had been shot away — lurched like wet-nurses clutching fat black babies. Garrett had reported from the engine room that a pipe leading to one of the boilers had been split by an unexploding shell that had passed clean through the engine room and otherwise exited harmlessly. One of his men had rushed the spurting, scalding pipe and wrestled a canvas across it.

'Daftest thing I've ever seen,' said Garrett over the speaking tube. 'Mad bugger did it, though, and it gave us a chance to move in and shut it down. His name's Webster, sir. I've had him taken to the sick bay, red as a prawn, but pleased as a dog with two tails. Do they *make* medals for engineers?'

'Webster.'

Muir would remember the name. In the space of the past few minutes he had seen Websters swarming all over his ship. Two Websters had slid on their stomachs into part of the blazing deck-housing and brought out three men, horribly burned, but alive. Another Webster, sitting cross-legged like a duck-shooter in the hide of the bow had steadily been decimating the Maxim gunners aboard *Charlemagne* who had fired at Barrow's boat, his tripod-mounted Lewis gun being punched back into position as it regularly bounced across part of Tilley's stage which had been dragged forward to serve as a platform. He seemed oblivious of the fact that twenty five per cent of the air around him was solid lead.

Muir tried to take stock. *Drummer* had suffered badly from the initial blow, but failing some unimaginable tour de force *Charlemagne* had up her sleeve, the outcome was now inevitable. He had ordered the yeoman to signal the windjammer that her situation was hopeless and surrender would not be dishonourable. The message had been met with a fusillade that Prettie and his gun crews had answered threefold. The fires on *Charlemagne* were covering her with smoke. It was insane, thought Muir. The German captain was slaughtering his crew. For what? The war was over, done – even if it wasn't there were limits beyond which bravery became senseless carnage. The fool of a German was drawing Muir himself into the butchery. Another few minutes and there was no doubt that *Charlemagne* – or whatever her true name was – would go under, dragging down with her like flies most of her crew, caught in the web of twisted rigging.

'We'll turn away,' said Muir. 'Hard a-starboard.'

'Aye, aye, sir.' Offord was streaked with dirt and the bottom of his jacket was ragged from the blast that had taken away the wireless room. He disappeared into the wheelhouse.

As *Drummer* began to turn, Muir saw Prettie at the forrard gun hold up his hands in despair. But Guns had had his moment and done well by it. Enough was enough. Whatever his counterpart aboard *Charlemagne* might feel, Muir had no intention of being the most successful of two floating coffins. He would bring *Drummer* round, stand off and, if the German hadn't come to his senses, shell her from a distance.

If they went on firing at Barrow he would shell her anyway. He tried to put the thought to the back of his mind.

Captain Count Nikolas von Bauer was neither a fool nor a murderer. In a long career he had, when the time demanded, killed men with no regret, no satisfaction. In war the terms had no intrinsic meaning. A foolish man was one who died. A man who found pleasure in killing was a fool. And fools inevitably catapulted themselves into a disaster of their own making.

After the debacle of Jutland he had decided the way *his* war would be fought. Feint, lunge, strike. But not killing for killing's sake. There was still room for chivalry. *Was*.

The events of the past few minutes had meant no quarter was left.

'Captain?' Mueller, his chief officer (it had been so long he still tended to think in merchant terms) was with the mate, Hasso Detweiler. Detweiler's moon face had been pummelled into shape by old winds, his nose bent like battered driftwood, no hair to talk of and a blue jaw permanently clamped, when not in use, like a bulldog's.

'They have us, sir,' said Mueller.

'We have no sail and the engine is finished,' added Detweiler. Blood was oozing from a cut on the back of his hand.

'Have the surgeon look at that,' said von Bauer.

'The surgeon is dead, sir.' Mueller caught the mate's eye. 'We are doing our best for the wounded, but conditions are . . .'

A yardarm drove into the deck like a falling pine. A scream. Detweiler began to move forward, but von Bauer put a restraining hand on his arm. 'We need to talk.'

The spar rolled back, hideously stained, across the two men who had been crushed beneath it.

'We must keep our heads,' said von Bauer. He seemed oblivious of the danger they were all in, staring above it all, as if he had momentarily lost his train of thought and was trying to regain it. Mueller recognised the mood and it filled him with foreboding. At the best of times a cold fish, von Bauer had begun, on occasions, to seem almost totally detached from events around him. It was unnatural and Mueller was hard put to explain it rationally. The strain of the past two years had begun to claim its due. And, there again, there was the possibility that had long been whispered below decks – and above it.

Detweiler walked away, not bothering to hide his disgust.

63

'Tell the mate to come back,' said von Bauer evenly. 'There are things to discuss.' So they would capitulate, that he had decided. For the moment. But only for the moment. A short-term surrender could be as strategic as battle itself, if one used it well.

Mueller found Detweiler staring at his clenched fists. 'Good God!' The mate shook off Mueller's hand.

'The captain wants ...' began Mueller.

'The captain *wants*!' said Detweiler bitterly. '*Wants*? The man is drunk! Anyone can see it! All this ...' he broke off and waved an arm hopelessly. 'Do you know how many men are dead?'

'He is not drunk,' said Mueller. 'Ill, but not what you think. Sick in some way ...'

'Pig sick!' Detweiler battered a hand on his thighs. 'Pig sick on drink! Why do you cover up for him? It's all the same now. The Britisher is just waiting to finish us off. It was madness to take her on!'

'You know why!' Mueller shouted. 'There was too much to lose, he had no choice!'

'Every choice,' said Detweiler. 'Every choice. It's we who have no choice.' He stepped over a puddle of blood and collided with a sailor running along the deck. 'Recke!'

'Yes.' Winded, the sailor blinked at him. His face was completely blackened, his clothes in tatters.

'What happened, Recke?'

The figure regarded them both for a moment, as if chancing on old acquaintances he couldn't quite recall. Then: 'What happened? Don't ask me, Mr Mate.' He gave a grotesque smile. 'It's over. The war is over, didn't you hear? The new one has just begun!'

'He's stunned,' said Mueller moving towards him.

Karl Recke drew away, holding up a palm smothered in soot. 'Sandel is dead,' he said. 'Dead.'

Mueller remembered Felix Sandel as a lumbering old sea dog who, over the past two years, had become a father figure to many of the younger hands on board *Charlemagne*.

'A nice end,' said Recke. 'His head was blown off as he tried to shout something to me.' He still held up his smeared hands. 'Now his war is over. You fight your own bloody war. I know who I fight!'

He stumbled away. Around his waist was knotted a white sheet.

Detweiler ignored Mueller's order to return to the captain. He had no argument with the first lieutenant and regretted having to disobey him, but for the moment there were a number of more pressing duties than chewing over some hopeless formula with a captain who, he was still convinced, was incapable of rational thought. In Detweiler's view, Mueller ought to assume command anyway and end it all.

'I can't do that, Hasso,' said Mueller. The two had been friends long before their time aboard *Charlemagne* and now the formalities of rank were vaguely absurd. 'I can't do it, and there's no reason I should do it. You know why the captain is pushing us to the limits, as well as I do. In his position I would do the same.'

'And what does that mean to those poor devils forced up the rigging to fry?' Hasso Detweiler almost spat the words on the deck. 'Remember, *I* was the one who had to send them up there!'

'As long as there's a chance . . .' began Mueller. The sentence died in a vacuum of doubt. There was no call for him to explain or justify. All he knew was that if von Bauer had ordered *him* into the rigging, even now, he would have gone. Was it blindness, stupidity, as Detweiler was claiming? Once he — they — had called it loyalty, and no one had questioned it.

Even so, there was something in what Detweiler was saying. For the past few months the captain had not been himself. There had been small errors, moments of indecision disguised as reflection, so fleeting that probably only he, Mueller, had noticed them. Once he had opened the captain's door, fancying he had heard permission to enter, and found von Bauer lolling helplessly in a chair, eyes glazed, saliva flecking the corners of his mouth. So, if he was drinking, who could blame him? The strain of the past two years had been enormous and coupled with that was the wound he had sustained at Jutland. Even so, it was out of character. Mueller worried about it a great deal, even more so when members of the crew began to notice that there was something odd at times about their captain.

After all they had been through together it was distressing to see the cracks appear. Mueller was not by nature a man who normally dwelt on such things. A career officer, he had been proud to serve under von Bauer, delighted in the strict formality that, at any moment, could be thrown aside with the relish of a buccaneer. They had gone from triumph to triumph, capping it all with perhaps the greatest triumph any ship of any navy had achieved since the days of Cortez. Von Bauer had seemed invincible and it had brushed them all with the same feeling. Now it had gone, thrown away ... given ... lost. And Hasso Detweiler was cursing his captain.

'I'll say you've gone to the sick bay,' said Mueller. 'Your arm.'

Detweiler shrugged as if the damage was too petty to dwell upon and bent to pick up a writhing hose. Mueller helped him grapple with it until they could play it on the smouldering holds.

'One shell in there, and von Bauer might sober up,' said Detweiler. They were standing directly over the ammunition of the ship's magazine. 'Kapper!' A huge seaman pounding a jammed Maxim turned at the sound of his name. 'Get down here! Take this damned thing, guns are no use now!'

Head averted from the heat, Kapper raced across and took the hose from them. It barely trembled in his hand. Bending close to the nozzle, he bathed his face in the fine spray. 'This is madness,' he howled.

'They've stopped,' said Detweiler, peering through the smoke that was enveloping the windjammer. 'They'll be taking our range. Any minute now. Christ, why doesn't somebody *do* something?' Dabbing the foul taste of Stockholm tar from his lips with the back of a hand he leaned over the rails. 'Where's the boat?' Then: 'Mueller, look at this!'

The lieutenant, coughing, joined him, and, as the smoke blew clear, saw it. The pulling boat was less than three hundred yards away. Around it floated three men, two motionless, one thrashing desperately in the water. Two officers and a rating were kneeling in the boat, and a series of rifle shots rang out.

Detweiler had found a light machine-gun and was balancing it on the rail. 'See them?' He pointed the barrel like a finger, snuggling the butt into his shoulder for support. 'We're not the only madmen on the sea!' Swinging the gun, he sighted carefully. 'I hate the bastards!'

'Leave them, Hasso, there is no point now.'

Detweiler ignored him.

'Hasso! That's an order!'

There was a rapid burst of fire and Detweiler struggled to stop the gun from jumping away.

Mueller drew his revolver and grasped Detweiler's shoulder.

'Look at them!' Detweiler squeezed the trigger again. 'Sharks! They're eating the poor swines alive!' The bullets ripped into the water around the boat. A tail flipped high. 'Bastards!' said Detweiler of every seaman's traditional enemy. The gunfire formed a perfect circle until he ran out of am-

66

munition. He let the gun topple over the side in disgust. 'I just hope the Britisher does the same for us,' he said.

Mueller, still clutching his pistol, was staring at a figure clinging to *Charlemagne*'s fore royal yard, barely visible through the smoke that lapped around it.

'Recke,' said Detweiler, following his eyes. 'It's Recke. What in hell is he doing?'

'I know what he's doing,' said Mueller quietly. 'Get him down, Hasso, before the captain sees him. Otherwise he's a dead man.'

'God!' Detweiler drew a breath as the white sheet broke at the yardarm. He began to run forrard, cursing. Ignoring his injury he swung himself into the ratlines and began to climb. Mueller could hear him calling Karl Recke's name.

'I think we're on our own, sir.'

'I believe you're right, Pickett,' said Barrow. They were still feeling the wash from *Drummer*'s sudden turn. 'I don't think it will be for much longer.'

Pickett didn't wish to dwell on the possible interpretation of the sentence. He assumed Barrow was being optimistic. The small boat, both buoyancy tanks punctured, was slowly filling with water and threatening to sink. They had been forced to put Lorimer's body overboard to join that of Muswell. In the process Purvis had fallen with it, and, weighed down by his heavy sea-boots, he had been unable to reach the gunwale. They had watched helplessly as he drifted away, threshing in the water and calling for help, and had tried to take the boat to him, but it was leaden, scarcely moving a yard. And then the sharks had come, first dealing with the two corpses and, as they began to dwindle, fighting among themselves, maddened by the smell of blood. The diversion had given Purvis, struggling to kick off his boots, five more minutes of life.

Baines, swinging an oar, had rained blow after blow at the black surging backs, moaning with fear as they rasped alongside, his throttled keening a descant to Purvis's sudden wild screams. In a burst of anger Barrow had, irrationally, begun to fire on *Charlemagne*. And the end had come with a returning rattle of machine-gun fire that had left one shark jerking spasmodically across the surface of the water and had put Purvis out of his agony. His body disappeared in a slick of foam.

Baines was still beating the sea, gagging now. 'Fugging cannibals,' he screamed.

'I reckon they were shooting at the sharks,' said Pickett. Both he and Barrow had run out of ammunition simultaneously and were now reduced to observers, or, more accurately, prey.

Barrow nodded dubiously. Pickett had reserves of charity that he didn't share. All he knew was that it had spared him having to shoot Purvis himself.

'Why don't the buggers come and help us, then?' said Baines, jabbing an oar towards *Drummer*. 'They're just fucking watching us, the swines!' He turned on Barrow. 'Get the bastards to come, can't you!'

'They'll come,' said Barrow. After the last few rounds from *Charlemagne*, she too was silent.

'What's going on, sir?' Pickett was shaking his head as he looked first at one ship then the other.

Barrow picked up a wooden bailer. 'I don't know. But whatever it is we're not going to be around to find out if we don't get this boat seaworthy.' His steady voice gave the lie to the desperation he was feeling. And he was regretting bitterly using the last of his ammunition so stupidly. If things got worse there could no longer be the anodyne of a bullet before they sank. His hands rose and fell, jettisoning the pathetically small scoops of water. 'Bale! Use your hands, anything.

Pickett slopped water over the side in his cap. Baines raised his head. In his mind he had already felt the yellow teeth snap.

'Bale!' repeated Barrow. 'Unless you want to join Purvis!'

Baines came to life. 'Bale,' he echoed woodenly. Then at tremendous speed began to cup the water like a man possessed, swilling it up from beneath his feet.

None of them saw the white flag break at the windjammer's bow. If they had its significance would have been purely academic. The enemy they faced now had never been known to make bargains.

Muir saw the flag.

Drummer was scarcely moving and Prettie, given breathing space, had prepared for the coup de grâce with the pains of a conductor building up to a finale. Twenty-two men were dead, as many injured and *Drummer* herself, despite everything Garrett could do, was beginning to wheeze. The wireless office was no more than a gap through the ship's superstructure; the funnel was a colander, threatening to crack at its base, and everywhere were shards of metal and wood, red hot and smouldering. Bellamy had taken over part of the engineer's quarters as an additional sick bay and prepared it as best he could. And the victualling officer had politely informed Muir that if 'victory' meant another thirty men aboard then, on present supplies, there was every possibility of them all starving to death – *Drummer*'s crew included.

Whichever way one looked at it, thought Muir, it was going to be a fairly hollow triumph. The war is over. He repeated the phrase for the fourth time and shook his head. So whose war was *this*? He blew the ash from his pipe and banged it against his heel as the men he had summoned trooped out on to the bridge.

'Is the cutter ready, Chief?'

Chief Petty Officer Hardcastle nodded.

'Good.' Muir moved across to where yeoman Hollis was standing in the shelter. 'Ask her her name – her real name.'

The reply came surprisingly swiftly. *Straker.*

'At least they are responding. Now tell her to put every man in her boats except for the captain and three of his officers.' They waited. 'You sure they have that?'

The lamp flashed once more. 'They don't seem to acknowledge, sir.'

'Tell them they have one minute. If they don't respond they will be sunk.'

The yeoman worked his lamp and an answer blinked through the smoke. Muir breathed a sigh of relief.

'They're telling us their ship is badly on fire, sir.' Hollis looked up from his message pad. 'The captain regrets not being able to comply, sir,' he said, as apologetically as a waiter informing Muir that a dish had been discontinued.

'*Really?*' Muir shook his head.

'He says that *Straker* is an ammunition ship and liable to explode at any moment. He urges you to move away in your own interests while they fight the fires.'

Hardcastle blew a despairing puff of breath.

'Tell the captain of *Straker*,' said Muir heavily, 'that she is a raider and has shown herself as such.'

The reply was blunt: 'A ship can be many things.'

'Codswallop!' said Hardcastle.

Muir bit on his pipe. What was *Straker*'s captain hoping to gain? Time? For what? There was the vague possibility that he was telling the truth – any ship with free licence to roam the Atlantic would be perfect for ferrying ammunition from base depots to German cruisers. Except that it would require the presence of a hidden supply base that had, somehow, miraculously survived the exhaustive search by the Royal Navy of every inch of the scattered South Atlantic islands. And it would require the presence too of German cruisers – which for the past two years had been well-nigh eliminated south of the equator. An ammunition ship flying the white flag and blazing merrily, plus a captain who was using the fact to call his own tune. Muir began to feel a grudging respect for his adversary and, even more, a growing puzzlement as to what was driving him on.

'Sir,' began Garrett, 'if that *is* an ammunition ...' The rest of his words were drowned by a tremendous explosion as the aft of *Straker* erupted in a sheet of yellow flame and smoke, spinning six-foot long timbers in the air like blazing cartwheels.

'Right, Chief, off you go,' snapped Muir. Then, to the yeoman: 'Tell them we are going to board her.'

'Volunteers?' ventured Hardcastle.

He wasn't being awkward, or even stupid, but Muir had to choke back a certain testiness. The whole thing had dragged on too long. However it was a fair question under the circumstances.

'No volunteers,' said Muir. 'I want the hardest men you can find. First pick up the Number One and the rest. If they are injured bring them back here as fast as you can. But if not, and they wish to go with you, carry on. There will be no repetition of what has happened, I assure you. The first sign of trouble and we'll hit her so hard she won't know what day it is. So – hard men, who'll brook no messing about. You can handle that?'

Hardcastle had spent three-quarters of his life handling 'hard men' as the captain put it. 'No problem with the men, sir, no problem at all ...'

'So?'

'It's the formalities, sir. I'm not used to ordering a captain around, even a German bugger, and I was wondering how I stand. The rank thing. If I give him an order is he bound to jump or what?' Hardcastle was in deadly earnest over the intricacies of protocol.

'Considering yourself acting coxswain, Chief, if it helps.'

'And in the event of any sort of resistance ... ?'

'I tell you exactly what you do,' interrupted Muir with a tight grin. 'You kick him in the arse, Chief. And if that fails you kick him again. With *my* say-so.'

They watched the cutter pull away.

'Get yourself ready, Guns,' said Muir. 'When I say, hit her with everything you've got.'

'That explosion was fireworks, sir,' said Prettie. 'A blast like

70

that should have blown the bottom out of her! It was as calculated as anything she's ever done.'

'I don't suppose it's an original thought,' said Garrett, 'but they did the dirty on us once and, well ...'

'It was bloody treacherous!' burst out Prettie, unable to contain himself any longer. 'Who's to say they won't try it again? Last time it was a French flag, then a German one. Now a white one. As far as those buggers are concerned I've suddenly gone very colour blind!'

Muir packed his pipe assiduously and when he was satisfied looked up at Prettie and Garrett. 'Right, so we blow her to kingdom come without more ado? What would that leave us with? I'll tell you, gentlemen: tacky consciences and little else. "Well, it was like this, she was flying a flag of surrender but we were a bit worried as to whether we could believe it so we decided to sink her while she wasn't firing at us." No, I don't like the sound of that either. I'd sooner be heading into Pompey leading that bugger out there by the nose. And if we have to sweat it out for a while then we sweat it out. So far they've played it straight – no matter what you may think. They have broken no international law. They struck their true colours before hostilities began. They can do one of two things, if they are planning any more tricks: they can use more torpedoes; or they can take the boarding party hostage – though I don't fancy their chances in that direction. The first sign of them doing either and we lose our very first ship. I for one don't want that to happen. I want to have a gander at her captain.' He nodded. 'So don't go colour blind; watch out for any moment of that flag. Then it's all yours, Guns. In the meantime they're sweating too, only a damn sight more than we are.'

Unwritten but rigid, the code of the Imperial German Navy made no room for surrender. Explosive charges laid along the keel left no doubt in a captain's mind what action was to be taken if his ship was in danger of being taken. Self destruction. The ship was to be scuttled.

Those very charges, stripped from the keel on von Bauer's orders, had exploded only minutes after he had informed the Britisher that *Straker* was an ammunition ship. Stacked in the rear hold, many of them had become damp but the fire had found enough to provide a convincing spectacle. Cushioned by the timbers on which they rested (*Straker*'s ostensible cargo as a merchant ship) the blast had been channelled harmlessly upwards, blowing out most of the real fire. A useful coincidence.

Even so, von Bauer had gone back to his cabin and finished the task of destroying the papers that had, earlier, earned a short-lived reprieve. He watched the last of them burn in the small stove.

Mindless, brute force had never been to his taste. When war degenerated into a toe-to-toe battle of sheer strength it reduced men to mechanics, little more than wind-blown drones at the mercy of a jammed gun or the roll of a ship. For the first time he had used a sabre and not a foil and it had failed. A wrong analogy. He had knocked over the chess board, no matter what extenuating circumstances could be argued.

He watched until the last fragment of paper had twisted into carbon, and crumpled it to ash with the blackened point of an ivory paper-knife. The American schooner *Nancy B. Johnson*, the French barque *Carcassonne*, the *Ivy Cutler*, a British tramp bound from Cardiff to Buenos Aires, *Garonne*, another Frenchman, and half a dozen others. Last of all *Voortrekker*. He burned them in strict order. Fewer lives had been lost among them all than had been destroyed in the last few hours. The foil not the sabre. Two hundred prisoners had been transferred from *Straker* to *Voortrekker* and, under the command of a third officer and skeleton crew, had made for Montevideo. Von Bauer had heard the last wireless message himself. The South African steamer was less than a hundred miles away and listing. Then came the squalls and loss of contact. But it was imperative that *Straker* moved from the area, which in all probability was being swept by English ships. There was nothing he could do. He had ordered them to keep to their course.

That night he had slept badly and had woken with a hollowness that had remained with him ever since.

'*Es besteht die Gefahr, dass wir verzaubert werden* – we are in danger of falling under a spell.' His own words came back to him, bubbling to the surface of his consciousness like barnacle-encrusted amphora, shapeless, unrecognisable. He had gone to the cabinet then as he had done less than half an hour ago – the only time he had ever turned to it when there was no pain. And the crisis was past. Did it matter how?

He bent over the stove until the past had disappeared.

Mueller didn't knock on the door for the singular reason that there was little left to knock. It lay blasted wide, swinging from one hinge like a drunkard from a lamp-post. 'Recke is with me, sir,' he said hesitantly, standing as if to block an unwanted guest.

'Let him face me.' Von Bauer had ordered Recke's arrest as soon as the white flag had broken at the yardarm. His eyes glittered as Mueller stood aside.

Recke was holding a pistol and the lieutenant's movement left it pointed uncompromisingly at von Bauer.

'This ship is no longer under your command,' said Recke, evenly. 'These men with me form part of the People's Marine Division of the Revolutionary Committee. Your officers are under arrest. For weeks this moment has been drawing close and now the slaughter has prompted us to act.'

'Don't be a fool,' said von Bauer. 'Your socialist nonsense has no place at sea.'

'There have been many meetings, Captain, and this is no idle, unpremeditated act. It is the concerted will of a majority.' Recke was twenty-five, thin blond hair wisping over a domed forehead. His face was pale, but unlike Detweiler's paleness alongside him it was not of the moment but one that would follow him to the grave. Only his eyes held any heat. Slight and with a sharp tongue, he had been endured as *Straker*'s fo'c'sle lawyer and resident iconoclast since the day he joined her. Every ship had one. They served as both a safety valve and a lightning conductor for the myriad petty nigglings that went on below deck. Recke wasn't unaware of the fact. What a man believed was rarely reflected in how others saw him. Once, on a ship sunk by a British destroyer, he had found himself in a boat full of half-drowned and wounded survivors. As one of the fittest, he had been ordered by an officer to prevent others still in the water scrambling aboard and sinking them all. Recke had refused, dragging as many as he could to safety. The boat seemed little the worse. But the officer had drawn his gun. Again Recke ignored him. The gun was sodden, but they had all heard the click of the hammer as it fell on a dead round.

Three days later the same officer, delirious after drinking sea-water, was one of the many half-dead whose presence was, as the weather got worse, genuinely threatening to drag them down. A vote had been taken among those still capable of thought as to whether the hopeless cases should be thrown overboard. Recke had refereed the secret ballot (handshakes, during which a hidden finger pressed into his palm indicated a yea) and lied as to its result. No one was abandoned. Twelve hours later they were picked up by a fishing boat. The officer had lived and recovered sufficiently to bring Recke before a court-martial accused of disobeying orders. Of course it was ridiculous. The officer was making a fool of himself admitting that he had been prepared to leave men to drown rather than take his chance along with them. A dozen of the boat's survivors came forward to testify on Recke's behalf. They were all asked the same question: had the accused disobeyed an order?

Recke was demoted to ordinary seaman with six months' loss of privileges and two months' loss of pay.

He bore no grudge. It only served to underline the truth that nothing would change the order of things but revolution, not revolt. And he had seen it work. In the spring of 1914 a strike of 1300 merchant sailors aboard the liner S.S. *Vaterland,* in Cuxhaven, had been declared illegal. The multi-millionaire overlords of the Hamburg-Amerika line had ordered the rebels to work, threatening reprisals for those who didn't heed them, promising benevolence towards those who did. The wedge didn't work. And neither did the seamen. Every day a ship lies idle it becomes a hole in the sea into which money is poured, and watching its money drain away had a sobering effect on the Hamburg-Amerika line. It capitulated totally, agreeing unconditionally to every one of the sailors' demands. An isolated action in itself, it was still the beginnings of something far wider. Recke had been at Cuxhaven on a light cruiser and had followed events on the S.S. *Vaterland* with interest. Two days after the sailors' unprecedented victory he had met some of the crew, and through them had come to know Karl Liebknecht and Rosa Luxemburg and the Communist movement that had split the Social Democrats apart. Recke and many others had begun to listen to the new voices. And when Liebknecht – a conscripted soldier – in an open but unlawful rally on May Day, 1916, had rocked Berlin and the rest of Germany with his cry: 'Down with the war! *Der Feind steht in eigenen land* – the real enemy is in your own country', Recke had been among the hundreds who cheered. Liebknecht, by then an M.P., had been arrestèd and sentenced to six years' hard labour. But for the old Germany the writing was on the wall. The Junkers had had their day: the von Bauers.

'You do not understand,' said Recke. He had planned to use a burst of rhetoric that had come to him as he tied the white sheet to the yardarm, but now it all seemed vaguely melodramatic and cheap. And even now it was not von Bauer whom he felt to be the enemy but the system he represented, and there were no words that would ever convince this captain that his command could justly be taken from him.

Words might serve to impress the instant praetorian guard Recke had gathered about him, but was that necessary? To what purpose? The revolution was inevitable. Words might smooth its path, but in the end action alone would decide its validity.

Mueller pushed forward. 'Sir, I am afraid ...' he spluttered.

Recke saved him any further embarrassment. 'The men around me are representatives of the crew. I am *not* acting alone, Captain. It has been decided — by democratic process — that, a pointless war being over, there is nothing further to be gained by bravado. We are all aware of why you are urging the ship and the men to their limits, but now it is of no consequence. We have been prepared to die in the past, but not now. You do not hold power of life or death over us any more. Not for a cause that has died, not even for your "cargo" ' — he picked at the word carefully, 'which I see as no more than the oil to grease the palms of those who exploit the working class. I will not go on. This is not a discussion, it is an ultimatum. I give it to you with respect, but not humility. If you choose not to recognise our authority you will be arrested.'

'I see.' Von Bauer's face twisted in contempt. 'Piracy. Common piracy, Recke. Don't attempt to clothe it in pomposity! You want my ship so desperately? Then take it. It is your nowhere-island, and you and the rest of your rabble will be shot when the tide comes in. It will, incidentally, be extremely interesting to see whether the British save a German court the bother of passing sentence.' He turned his back and began to shuffle the few remaining papers on his desk, ignoring the tableau behind him. He had noticed the first flicker of alarm among Recke's 'escort'. He murmured: 'You intend to surrender openly, I take it?'

'Of course. The British will understand.'

Von Bauer spun round. 'I wonder, Recke? How much do you know about the Royal Navy? About the British? They have a remarkable tradition when it comes to dealing with people who don't quite live up to their standards of behaviour. Do you realise something else — that we were sailing under colours that mean the British can do with us what they will? No, you don't. We are outsiders, Recke. Think of that, and what it might mean for you.'

'We are not going to listen to any more of this ...' growled one of the men at Recke's shoulder, plainly uneasy at the way the conversation was going.

'One more thing,' said von Bauer. It would be a pity not to hammer home the lie while he had the chance. 'Do you really think I do not know the position we are in? That I am not

75

aware of what is happening? You and your ... friends ... could have been dead a dozen times over if it was not for me. I had no "delegation" coming to me when we were surprised by the British cruiser a year ago and bluffed our way through; no "delegation" when we took on ships as heavily armed as *Voortrekker*. Why now? Do these men suddenly feel they know their own salvation? They do *not* know it! And you do not understand the implications of the flag we flew.' His voice fell. 'Take the ship. All you have is the strength to leave it. I am not interested in your absurd "revolution", nor your battle with the social order. I am only interested in keeping this ship, and the men who serve it, alive.' He braced a hand on his desk. 'You may or may not know that I intended to capitulate too? It would not have been done at the expense of dragging our self-respect through the mud. Ironic, Recke?'

'It makes no difference now,' said Recke. 'The die is cast.'

'It may not be, Recke. Tell these men to go away, I would like to talk to you alone. There is still a chance, and I am sure you would prefer that your "revolution" did not see its finest hour in a British internment camp.'

Recke shook his head in wonder. 'Captain, you are a resourceful man, that there can be no denying.' He turned to the guard. 'Make the rest of the ship secure. If there are those who are still misguided, arrest them. No killing. Return here in ten minutes. One of you position yourself at the end of the alleyway.'

'I would like Mueller and Detweiler to remain.' Von Bauer looked questioningly at Recke. 'You have my word no move will be made against you. If you wish for one of your more, how shall I say, *perceptive* colleagues to balance the numbers, I ...'

'No,' said Recke. 'It will not be necessary. The one I would have chosen is already dead. Felix Sandel. A fine man and a true friend. *Your* war killed him, Captain.'

'And would he have approved of *yours*?' Von Bauer passed lightly over the venom contained in his question. 'I am truly sorry you have lost a friend.'

'Don't be.' Recke was businesslike. 'No doubt I will lose many more.'

Acting Coxswain Jethro Hardcastle had taken Muir at his word. The cutter was double-banked with the biggest collection of rogues he could lay hands on, all armed to the teeth. Apart from McGowan in the sick bay, no other man aboard *Drummer* could have made the selection so fast and so confidently. Hardcastle knew them all: the Bully Boys, he called them, and they bothered him not a hoot. The wrong end of fifty, Hardcastle had been as tough as any of them in his time and as tough as most now, though he had long grown tired of the shoulder-squaring that had given McGowan a smashed skull for his pains. Once he had strolled the decks of deep-water clippers with a belaying pin stuck in his boot top and a knuckle duster in his cap. It seemed two lifetimes ago. But he had learned one thing from it all that still held good: the Bully Boys didn't like the idea of pain any more than the next man – on the whole they liked it less, and they didn't give him any trouble.

Hardcastle sat on the cutter's keel-box as they slipped away from *Drummer*, his eyes missing nothing, sharp as an alley-cat's. What he would never quite understand was that his Bully Boys knew the measure of Jethro Hardcastle like a prizefighter knows his reach: in any other place on earth it would be called respect.

'Point your oars,' he bellowed. The inner stroke oarsman at the stern and the two bowmen held the boat off, as the remaining nine unplugged the wooden poppets in the crutches and, taking their oars by the looms, held them over the washstrake in a movement as ceremonial as it was prudent. One wrong move and the lot of them would be treading water.

'Bear off! Fenders in! Oars down!' The blades hovered over the water. 'Give way together!' The bowmen hurled in the fenders and, raising their oars, kissed them together above their heads before swinging them down to meet the rhythm. 'Not bad for a bunch of bloody brigands,' snorted Hardcastle. 'Now puuulll! First bugger to catch a crab catches my fist.' They began to move like a thrashing centipede towards Barrow's stricken boat.

'Who put you up to it?' hissed Penn Coker as he bent forward.

'Dunno,' exhaled Frank Judd. They heaved back together. 'You tell me.'

Coker shrugged.

'What the bloody hell's this about anyway?' said Judd. 'They killing us off in relays?'

'Judd,' bawled Hardcastle, 'this may be an outing for you, it isn't for me. Save your breath!' He snapped a glance at the bowman whose eyes had begun to round to marbles as they drew nearer Barrow. 'Eyes in the boat.'

They were coming alongside. Barrow was standing calf-deep

in water the colour of rosé wine. Picket waited in the bow with a boathook.

'Fenders out,' said Hardcastle. He waited until they were less than twenty yards away. Only then did he take notice of the sharks that were still snapping at small chunks of waterlogged flesh. 'A couple of you get some guns on these vermin!'

Within seconds the sharks began to break away to a safe distance, waiting.

'Bows!' In perfect unison the bowmen's oars were tossed, blades kissed together and laid amidships. They reached for their boathooks. They were closing on Barrow's boat. 'Way enough!' shouted Hardcastle. The rest of the crew waited. 'Toss and boat your oars!' They bumped alongside and a dozen hands locked the two boats together.

'Bloody hell!' said Hardcastle. 'You all right, sir? Pickett, that you? Sir, I mean.' He could hardly recognise the midshipman, covered as he was with all manner of filth.

'In you go, Pickett, you too Baines,' called Barrow. He scrambled after them into the cutter. All of them were sodden from the waist down. Barrow shook Hardcastle by the hand. 'We're not quite as bad as we look,' he said, managing a grin. 'But, God, are we glad to see you!'

'You'll be wanting to get back, sir. My orders are to board the German. I'll get another boat sent out to meet us.'

'Is that strictly necessary?'

'Well, no sir. The captain did say that if you wished to come with us ... but I'd have thought that ...'

'I'll consult my "crew",' said Barrow. He called Pickett and Baines in the boat's bow: 'Do you want to go aboard her or make tracks back to *Drummer*?'

'Having got this far, sir ...' Pickett said. Baines nodded numbly.

'Right, we come with you, Hardcastle. Not the most prepossessing additions to your crew, I admit, but I do have an urge to see the gentleman who was responsible for this.' He nodded towards the windjammer. 'Are they expecting us?'

'They have been told we are boarding and I think the captain has warned them of what will happen if there's any more nonsense. He also said we should be firm, and I'd say he intended us to be a little less than nice if they play silly buggers again.'

'I don't feel particularly "nice", now you mention it, Hardcastle.' Barrow suddenly saw Frank Judd. 'Judd, I take it, is an accredited member of the party?'

'He is, sir. Parole, sir.'

'Good. Maybe this time we can put his natural exuberance to good use.'

'No question of that, sir.'

'What's her name? Her real name?' Barrow was still staring at the tall ship. As long as he kept talking he felt better. The heat had begun to steam his trousers in a clammy feverishness and there was a pit of bile where his stomach had once been.

He looked across to where Judd was mopping the blood from Pickett's face with a rag. Pickett tore off his shirt and the process continued. By all reasoning the boy should have been either gibbering or prostrate, or both. He was neither, though God knew what might happen later, when it had all sunk in.

'*Straker.*'

He realised Hardcastle had repeated the name a number of times.

'She says she's carrying ammunition, sir. It's all a bit cagey. Her captain reckons she might explode.' He sounded apologetic, as if somehow partly to blame.

'We saw an explosion,' said Charlie Pickett. Reasonably clean, he had worked his way aft through the straining oars to sit alongside Barrow. A red weal had begun to blossom across his chest. The acting coxswain touched it gently. 'That bad?'

Pickett looked sheepish. 'I fell on my own boathook as I got aboard,' he said. He pulled a face. 'Call it a war wound.'

'I see, sir.' It wasn't difficult for Hardcastle to change the subject. *Straker* loomed above them. He ordered the fenders over the side and oars shipped. The windjammer had dropped ladders and that at least was promising.

'Toss oars!' The blades swept up.

'Steady, steady. Get it right!'

The inner stroke stood in the stern sheets ready to fend off. They were alongside and holding their own.

'Arm,' said Barrow. 'Bayonets fixed aboard.'

Hardcastle grasped the ladder. 'Begging your pardon sir, but after me ...'

'Right behind you.' Out of the corner of his eye Barrow saw Frank Judd pick up his rifle.

Four empty glasses stood on the saloon table and the captain rose to greet them with a nod. Captain Count Nikolas von Bauer introduced himself.

'First Lieutenant Barrow of His Majesty's ship *Drummer*. Chief Petty Officer Hardcastle,' said Barrow.

'Acting Coxswain, sir,' said Hardcastle.

'To welcome you would be hypocrisy,' said von Bauer. 'But a little wine and then the formalities.'

Barrow stood in the doorway. 'A trifle inappropriate, Captain. Your ship is on fire,' he said dryly. 'As for "formalities", there *are* none. You have surrendered. Now if you would care to step outside and order your men into the boats . . .'

'Very well.' Von Bauer nodded at a chart on the saloon table. 'But I think this might interest you.'

Barrow took a step forward and felt Hardcastle pluck at his shoulder. 'He's playing for time, sir. I don't like it. Would you be talking about wine and maps if you were sitting on top of what this ship is supposed to be carrying?' Hardcastle shook his head. Without realising it, he was grasping Barrow's wrist. 'I don't like it.'

'Come on, Captain, and bring your map with you, we'll talk about it on deck.' Barrow disengaged an apologetic Hardcastle's hand from his wrist and nodded the captain out. They stood in the alleyway outside the saloon. Von Bauer had ignored the map and the fact hadn't escaped Hardcastle.

'It will not be necessary,' said the German.

'I bet it won't,' said the acting coxswain.

'Now, now, Hardcastle,' said Barrow, 'we mustn't be too hard.' It was said in a way that lacked all conviction. Hardcastle's comments on von Bauer's strange disregard for the danger he was in had been perceptive, but perhaps there was a simple explanation for it.

'Do you intend to be insulting, Lieutenant, or am I to assume you have been ordered to act in this manner?'

'I respect one thing, Captain,' said Barrow. 'Your rank. But I have little need to inform you that your ship is now a prize of *Drummer* and her commanding officer, Captain Muir. In the meantime I am assuming command of *Straker* and ask you to order your men to acknowledge this and act according to my orders.'

Von Bauer was tight-lipped.

'I trust you intend to comply? It will be unfortunate if you do not.'

'I think you are only partly aware of the situation,' said von Bauer eventually. '*Straker* is armed, of course, and was flying false colours. But she is not a raider. Our duty has been to provide ammunition for capital ships in the area, no more. The armament is purely defensive. We are an ammunition ship. An ammunition ship badly on fire. Need I say more?'

'An ammunition ship is vulnerable, Captain,' said Barrow.

'Highly vulnerable. And yet you fought?'

'Orders, Lieutenant. Simply orders.'

'If what you say is true then I must verify it.'

'You have seen the fires. There is no time.'

'Nevertheless.'

'I repeat: this ship is highly dangerous. We are risking men's lives every moment that they stay aboard. It is best we abandon her now. As her captain, I am prepared to stay aboard with volunteers and ensure we keep clear of your ship. Then you can signal other ships – I assume you have others in the vicinity – of the risk. You know our position and realise we can make little speed. God willing we may be able to save her.'

'For what?' Barrow tried to keep the annoyance from his voice.

'Because she is a *ship*, Lieutenant. Your prize, remember? Better a ship than nothing, even if the war has ended.'

The two men faced each other in silence.

It could still work, thought von Bauer. Something could be snatched from it. The meeting in the saloon had gone wrong, inexplicably wrong, but it wasn't the end. The auxiliary might be fixed, a jury rig hoisted until new sails were raised, and they still had guns and ammunition. The Britisher wouldn't shoot on men trying to save their ship, and *Straker* would refuse to be boarded again. The English were still gentlemen and to sink her in that state would amount to plain murder. He looked at his watch.

'What is the time, Captain?' asked Barrow suddenly.

'What?' Von Bauer had simply wanted to cover his deliberations. He hadn't noticed the time.

'It doesn't matter,' said Barrow. 'Now kindly show me the ammunition.'

Von Bauer felt the initiative slipping from him. 'Lieutenant ...'

'Have you a cigarette, Coxswain?' asked Barrow. Hardcastle had. A yellow, crumpled object was passed to the first lieutenant. 'A light?'

'Sorry, sir ...'

'Captain?'

'No, I ...'

'It will wait. Hardcastle, get Coker, Judd, a few others. And half a dozen of *Straker*'s crew.'

It took five minutes to muster them. When at last they arrived von Bauer's agitation had frozen his face into a death mask. He led the way below.

'Beyond this bulkhead is the ammunition.'

'Tell your men to open it,' said Barrow.

'Lieutenant, I consider that unwise. There are fires, and the draught will add to them.'

'I share your concern,' hummed Barrow. 'Even so, I think we will take a look.'

Von Bauer seemed not to have heard.

'Will *you* tell your men, Captain? Or shall I do so?'

'The danger,' began von Bauer. 'As captain of this ship . . .'

'No, sir. No longer.' He looked around. 'Does *anyone* have a light?' The cigarette hung uselessly from the corner of his mouth. Coker lit it. 'Good man.' Barrow drew deeply on the second cigarette of his life, squashing the match beneath a heel. 'Better. Now, Captain, I ask you again: will you have this door opened?'

Von Bauer was silent and none of the German crew moved.

Barrow shrugged, silently wrestling with the smoke that was pickling his lungs.

'Leave it to me, sir.' Hardcastle, who seemed to have taken an immediate and intense dislike to von Bauer, waved his revolver. 'Judd, Coker! Sort this out.'

The two men stepped forward, Judd taking one of the crew by the forearm and, seemingly with no effort at all, propelling him to the bulkhead door, Coker achieving the same effect by laying a hand between another's shoulders and hurtling him forward with a force that brought his nose against the steel. The rest of Hardcastle's party, at the order, detached their bayonets and gripped them like cutlasses in the confined space. Coker was holding the wriggling German sailor hard against the door, squashing him like a strawberry. The man groaned until Coker was vaguely satisfied. Judd was performing complicated manoeuvres with the other sailor's arm, hoisting him on tiptoe and beyond. Barrow gave a wry glance at von Bauer.

'I thought you an officer of some sophistication,' said *Straker*'s captain with distaste.

'After a time under your machine-guns, I begin to wonder about yours, Captain. Now cut the cackle, there's a good chap, otherwise I'll regard this as a hostile action. Judd and Coker here are little concerned about matters of sophistication and I do not want to prolong this nonsense.'

Von Bauer waved a hand. 'Open it.'

'Stand off!' yelled Hardcastle. Judd and Coker stepped back, their victims sliding to the deck like rag dolls. The securing clips were swung up. Barrow looked at his watch. They had been on *Straker* almost half-an-hour and every passing minute underpinned a wild hunch. The next few might justify it or blow them all to blazes. A gamble that offered no consolation prizes. He stamped out the cigarette. Von Bauer had not said a word about it, even now, when the door began to open. So concerned — yet how concerned? A man smoking a cigarette in an ammunition ship was a man seeking a gas leak with a naked match. A pariah. It was automatic and instinctive to react to it. No one had.

Hardcastle followed two of the Germans into the hold and the rest trooped behind. It was excruciatingly hot. A light was found and Barrow stepped among the crates. 'Prise a few of them open,' he said to von Bauer. The order was given in German and the tops sprung. The first held shells, as did the second. The third was full of engine spares for the auxiliary.

'There are a few other artefacts,' said von Bauer acidly. Barrow wondered where he had picked up the word. 'Marine artefacts. The rest is ammunition. Volatile.' He drew two fingers across his brow, but didn't seem to be perspiring. 'It is dangerously hot.'

'I want *all* the crates opened,' said Barrow.

'Unthinkable. It would take an hour!'

'Have them opened, Captain!'

Ten minutes later twelve of the crates had been opened. Half of them contained shells, the rest everyday hardware supplies of any ship on an extended voyage. Time was still the judge. And Barrow was still convinced that the German crew's attitude was incompatible with that of men sitting on a tinder box. If they were, an army of Judds and Cokers wouldn't have been able to restrain them.

'A question, sir?'

'Fire away, Hardcastle.'

The acting coxswain nodded around the hold. 'There must be acres of room on this ship, so why is everything stuck here like this. Makes no sense.'

Barrow looked at the German captain: 'I assume there is of course a simple answer?'

'It was necessary,' said von Bauer. No other explanation seemed forthcoming.

'That seems hardly ...' began Hardcastle brusquely. Frank Judd cut off any further interrogation.

' 'Ere!' Stalking between the toiling men, Judd had suddenly felt the deck give beneath his feet in a small area that had been cleared of crates. He banged a heel. 'This lot's a lash-up. I can feel it.'

Barrow didn't have to test it – looking at the timbers was enough. 'What happened here, Captain?'

'We were hit, Lieutenant, some time ago. The leak was patched as well as was possible, but it is faulty. The bottom hold is full of water. *Straker* swings badly because of it.'

'Prise a bit of it up, Judd,' ordered Barrow.

'Move one of those boards and this ship will sink,' said von Bauer bluntly. 'Here there is nothing between us and the sea.' His face was still dry, but his collar had a film of damp discolouring it. He looked ill.

'So you stick all your vital stores on top of it,' jumped in Hardcastle, 'bang in the place where you stand to lose the lot!'

'There is nothing to be gained, Lieutenant! Nothing!' Von Bauer swayed and Barrow held out a supporting arm. 'I am all right, Lieutenant. But I think we should leave now and put an end to the ship.'

'I am sorry, Captain. Maybe, if you would like to leave us, a little air would help.' He felt the sickness begin again, boring through his stomach. Perhaps von Bauer was right, it had gone on long enough.

'Will you bugger off, Judd!' Hardcastle's throat was as dry as a toad's back and he was beginning to wonder whether Jimmy the One wouldn't have been wiser to have packed it all in an hour ago. Muir hadn't said anything about this kind of nit-picking being necessary.

Judd, tugging at a plank, lurched and fell back as it split.

'Fools!' Von Bauer began to stride forward and was checked by Hardcastle. As Judd began to rise, one of the German sailors leapt at his back, fists flailing. Another grabbed an iron rod that had been spilled from a crate. Judd spun, carrying the German like a hump. Hardcastle swung a boot and the rod flew past Barrow's head as he dived across the hold, hitting the sailor double-fisted in the stomach. Coker had snatched the attacker from Judd's back and was stamping him to the deck. The four remaining German sailors tried to make for the door. Rifle bolts clicked. 'Easy!' yelled Barrow. Two of Hardcastle's men had levelled their rifles. On his knees, Hardcastle waved his pistol at von Bauer. 'Knock it off!'

The German captain stood impassive.

'Do as he says, Captain!' Barrow was holding back the rifle fire with a raised hand. The three Germans held up their arms.

'Now then, get back there,' said Hardcastle. Coker and Judd

stood back reluctantly as the men shuffled across to them. 'Tear up those planks,' said Hardcastle. 'Judd, Coker – encourage them.'

Barrow waved the rifles down. The sailor who had flung himself at Judd was unconscious, the other squirming from the blow that had buried itself in his stomach.

'One more incident like that, Captain, and my men will open fire,' said Barrow. His face was white with anger. 'Now stand with your back to the bulkhead and don't move until I say!'

The makeshift deck was torn open. Judd peered down through the gap that had been made. 'Well, we're not sinking yet.'

'Out of the way, there!' Hardcastle barged forward and began to lower himself into the hole until only his fingers could be seen, clutching the splintered wood. There was a faint splash.

'Be careful,' called Barrow.

'Give me a light!' shouted back Hardcastle. A lamp was passed down by Coker. There was a long silence. Then: 'A bayonet. Hand me a bayonet.' The bayonet was lowered and there came the sound of more wood being split.

'Lieutenant?'

'What is it, Hardcastle? Let me come down there and . . .'

'No, it's all right. I . . . Christ!'

Barrow swung his legs over the gap, but was pushed back from below by something pressing against his feet.

'Can you see it, sir? Tell me when you see it. I'm almost at full stretch, difficult . . . it's heavy . . . there!'

Barrow got to his feet. A dull yellow block of metal rose from the hold, thrust upwards in Hardcastle's trembling hands.

'See it? I can't hold . . . much . . .'

Coker and Judd took it from him and dropped it on the deck.

'We have it,' called Barrow. 'Get on up here, Coxswain.'

'There's more to come.'

'Get on up here!' Barrow looked at von Bauer, but the captain was staring at the object as if life was draining from him. Hardcastle pulled himself out of his tomb, his grizzled face pouring with sweat. 'You wouldn't believe it, sir! Crates of the stuff. The water's only a couple of feet deep and I can't reckon to a leak.'

Barrow traced a foot over the ingot of gold. 'I think, Captain von Bauer, you have been less than honest with me.'

Von Bauer turned away. There was nothing to be said.

Part Two

No words were needed to convey to Karl Recke the failure of von Bauer's final ploy – it was written across the captain's face as he walked behind the English lieutenant along the alleyway. Positioning himself squarely in the middle of it, Recke waited.

''Scuse me!' Hardcastle had gathered his party and was ushering the German crewmen along at bayonet point. The door to the hold had been re-sealed and two armed guards left with instructions to shoot anyone – British or German – who tried to enter. Now, pushing past Barrow and von Bauer, he reached Recke and gave an impatient growl: 'Out of the way there, laddie!'

'I speak English,' said Recke.

'Right then, you'll understand "hoppit!" Come on, sharpish, you're making the place untidy!'

'Captain!' Recke raised his voice to reach von Bauer. 'Tell these men who I represent!' He struggled as Hardcastle gripped his arm. 'The People's Marine Division of the Revolution has taken charge of this ship,' he shouted.

'Wrong,' countered Hardcastle, spinning him half-circle, '*we* have taken charge of it.' One of the boarding party pushed the point of a bayonet against Recke's back and began to march him down the alleyway.

'Who is that man?' Barrow nodded at the protesting figure.

'Recke. A seaman,' said von Bauer. His voice was expressionless.

'Is there anything in what he claims?'

'No. He is an opportunist criminal who, but for the events of the past hour, would have been shot. I trust you will punish him.'

'You are aware that the Imperial Fleet is in the hands of factions claiming to have taken command and demanding to negotiate surrender terms?'

'*You* tell me this, Lieutenant!' Von Bauer's eyes clouded with a sudden anger. 'It does not mean there is a grain of truth in it! If I informed you at second hand, maybe third, that your navy had been taken over by pirates and cut-throats would you lend it credence? Or would you prefer to rely on your own knowledge and judgement? I realise, of course, it would give you great pleasure to believe it, but would counsel otherwise.'

'It is a subject you will be free to discuss with my commanding officer,' said Barrow abruptly. There was clearly no point in dwelling on it. The captain obviously preferred his own interpretation. Maybe he had better information. 'But I assure you there *is* an armistice and until the picture becomes clearer, you should bear it in mind.' Barrow was studiously avoiding any reference to the gold. That would be Captain Muir's province.

They reached the deck and the warm wind dried the sweat on their faces. Most of the fires had been dampened and there were none that looked incapable of being contained. Still, the air was a foul-smelling pomander of nameless acrid burnings.

'Have the boats made ready, Coxswain,' said Barrow. 'You and some of your men stay aboard, with whatever of the German crew you may need – not too many, though. Keep a guard below. Signal Captain Muir we are preparing to join him and bring the prisoners off. We'll send you reinforcements from *Drummer*.'

Hardcastle raised his Bosun's Call, piped the short low, long high, short low of the Special Call, and boomed out: 'D'ya hear there?' He drew breath for an encore and gasped. Pickett was walking from the poop.

'He's got a woman with him!' said Judd. 'Couple of them!'

Barrow turned to von Bauer in a blaze of anger: 'What other damned secrets have you got I should know about?'

Von Bauer lost any semblance of poise. He was shocked. 'Lieutenant, I swear ...'

'Who are they?'

'They ... they were taken from a ship ... a sailor was sent to see to their safety when the shooting began and he ... on my word as an officer, I was told they were dead!'

There were not two women, but three. Pickett was walking slowly and carefully, supporting a young girl. Alongside them a middle-aged woman with raven hair walked alone, a sailor hovering at her shoulder. In front of them a short dumpy figure, older than the other two, clutched her shawl around her, her dress billowing in full sail. All three were streaked with dirt.

'I found these ladies below,' said Pickett. The young girl began to shake. Throwing off Pickett's hand, she wrapped herself around the dark-haired woman.

'Don't quite know what to make of it, sir, except they seem to be badly shaken up.'

'I am perfectly well,' said the old woman.

'I assure you once more, Lieutenant . . .'

'Please be quiet, Captain! Coxswain, get these ladies into a boat right away. Put a reliable man with them. Explanations can wait.'

'My name is Rose.' The dumpy figure planted herself in front of Barrow. 'You'll be English?'

'And you, ma'am, are Irish?'

'I am indeed.'

'We will talk about all this later, Rose,' said Barrow, 'for the moment the most important thing is to get you off this ship.'

'I agree. You wouldn't be after having a drop of brandy with you by any chance?'

'Have a gander in the captain's cabin, Pickett, I'm sure you'll come up with something.'

'This way, please, ladies,' said Hardcastle. But Frank Judd cannoned into him and, swooping between them, grasped the old woman by the wrist, holding it like a twig. Hardcastle, regaining his balance, lunged after the madman, but met Judd's shoulder and fell back against Barrow. Before anyone knew what was happening, Judd had gently opened the old woman's clenched fist and disentangled it from beneath the shawl.

'Sorry if I caught you, Chief,' said Judd.

'Think nothing of it, Judd.' Panting, Hardcastle stared as the hatpin the woman had been clutching like a stiletto fell to the deck. Barrow kicked it away.

'Leave it be. Get them out of here.' He waited until they had gone and picked up the vicious-looking pin, holding it out to von Bauer. 'Unless I'm very much mistaken, Captain, I believe this was intended for you.'

'My name is Kapper. You understand me?'

Frank Judd stared blankly at the German beside him in the boat. If his name had been Kaiser Wilhelm, the information at that precise moment would have elicited the same response. He along with twenty others, mostly Germans, were in one of *Straker*'s boats heading towards *Drummer*. And *Drummer*, whatever it might mean for the rest, held no promises for Judd.

'Kapper,' repeated the sailor.

'Shut it,' said Judd.

'Ah, you are a man who hates chatter.'

'For Christ's sake put a sock in it!'

'I too have no time for words. But sometimes if they are not idle . . .'

Judd considered hitting him, but the man who called himself

Kapper was built like a house, his face pockmarked as if he had spent a lifetime shot by desert sand. And Judd wasn't in the mood.

'You were down there? Saw it?' went on the German. 'Do you not think about it?'

Judd felt his mouth go dry. He didn't want to hear. There were more than enough problems to be going on with. But yes, he had seen it, unless they had all been caught up in the same dream. If Hardcastle was right in his estimate and all the other crates in the dummy hold were filled like the one he had opened, then they had been standing over a king's ransom. It meant trouble just as the women meant trouble. Barrow might not see it, Hardcastle not see it, not yet – but Frank Judd saw it, building up like the subterranean waves from a distant explosion. 'Row this bloody boat,' he said.

'It belongs to no one,' said Kapper, undaunted.

'In that case we'll all get one each to take home,' said Judd. 'Will you fucking shut up!'

Penn Coker, on the backboard of the boat, studied the German, having heard every word. One day he might have to take the big man on and, though he was running to fat about the gut and didn't sound too bright upstairs, in sheer weight he wouldn't be easy. Judd had lost the will even to try, but then nobody ever knew which way Judd would go and therefore he would have to be watched. No, Kapper, or whatever his name was, would be no danger, not at first. He would be an ally. Though, as yet, he didn't know it . . .

'Captain?' Prettie was leaning over the rail. 'Lieutenant Barrow is coming alongside.' The winches began to creak the boat aloft.

'Barrow!' Muir helped him over the gunwale as it hovered above the deck. 'What can I say?' He held him by the shoulders. 'God, it's good to see you!'

'Multiply that by ten, sir, and it's mutual.' Barrow looked back at the boat. 'I didn't get the vino. This is Captain Count von Bauer of *Straker*.' The German captain stood formally at his side. 'Captain Muir.' Barrow introduced them as if bringing together two hostile diplomats at an embassy cocktail party.

Von Bauer gave a nod. 'I am at your disposal, Captain Muir.' In his left hand he held a small black briefcase. 'My personal papers,' he said, following Muir's glance. 'I trust I will be able to retain them.'

'Of course.' Muir turned to Barrow with concern. 'Are you in one piece, Number One?'

'Body intact, mind slightly rearranged, I must admit, sir. A little grubby, somewhat damp. I think, however we need a few words ...'

'Yes. Of course.' Muir beckoned Dandridge. 'Captain von Bauer, I have arranged a small cabin for your accommodation. I think you will find it satisfactory. Later we will talk, but, in the meantime there are the injured and many other problems.'

'As you wish.' A curt bow. He followed Dandridge clutching the bag rigidly at his side.

'Has he been injured?'

'No, sir. An old wound, I think. He never mentioned it.'

'So what do you make of him?'

'More sides than a diamond and twice as sharp,' said Barrow without hesitation. 'He gave us something of a run-around. And Pickett tells me that half of *Straker* is equipped with bunks. She's a raider all right, built – or at least adapted – specifically for it. She's riddled with alleyways.'

'And what about you? Are you sure you are all right? What happened in the boat? Is anyone else ... no, you need a rest and a change of gear.'

'I don't think it will wait, sir.' Barrow went over what had happened on the boat.

'And where's Pickett now?'

Barrow held up his hands in supplication: 'He's with the ... women.'

'What?'

'What indeed, sir. Women. We – Pickett – found three of them aboard *Straker*. One Irish, two who I think are Americans – again according to Pickett, they haven't said a word to me. They should be coming aboard any moment. They are a bit shaken.'

'Shaken. Yes.' Muir was desperately trying to locate his pipe.

'The women aren't the end of the story.'

'Of course not. The best stories need a punch line.' Muir shook his head, 'I think I'm ready, Number One.'

Again Barrow turned to the boat. Two men were marshalling a tarpaulin-wrapped package over its side. It was laid at Muir's feet like an offering and Barrow scuffed the wrapping from it. 'It's what a tradesman might call a "sample". There seems to be a hold full of it.'

Muir dropped to his haunches. For no reason that made sense to him, he tapped it. Lifted it by a corner. Laid a palm flat against it. 'Gold.'

'An ingot.'

For the past quarter of an hour Muir had seen litter after litter of half dead carried past him and now, despite himself, the ghastliness of it all was eclipsed. Almost guiltily he looked up at Barrow. 'I begin to understand a little more about the fighting spirit of our Captain von Bauer.'

'It explains a lot.'

'Have this taken to my cabin,' Muir said, waving across the two A.B.s who had hauled it from the boat. 'Try not to lose it,' he added.

Straker had been fitted with twenty lifeboats, of which ten remained seaworthy. The injured were the first to be hoisted aboard *Drummer* and taken to the makeshift sick bay which Bellamy had created by requisitioning part of the engineers' quarters amidships. Stretcher parties moved in a constant procession of pain.

The surgeon had decided at the outset that those who could walk, stagger or shuffle would be classified as nominally fit. Lacerations and abrasions, broken wrists, second degree burns, impressed Bellamy not at all, and they were treated perfunctorily. As for the rest, he would fight to keep them alive, though most of them wouldn't be thanking him for it.

'Wood splinters.' The surgeon nodded at a figure being carried past, hunched on a stretcher. He had left the sick bay to try and find out just how many more he would be expected to cope with and was standing alongside Muir on the forrard well deck, his cadaverous face scarcely healthier than some of his intended patients. Muir had often wondered what it must be like to blink up from a sick bed after regaining consciousness and be confronted by Bellamy. The relief at discovering eventually that he was a doctor and not an undertaker must have spurred many on to thankful health.

'More than half of them so far,' said the surgeon dolefully. 'Peppered with them. The blast drives the splinters through anything, bone, liver, muscle. It's like trying to get out a fish hook from a gullet. The more you try, the more damage it can cause. Festering ... blood poisoning. Amputation where possible.' His prognosis died away in a sigh. 'I'll do what I can, but we're hard pushed to handle our own injured. All of them need proper hospital attention.' He paused, weighing his words. 'Half of them will be dead long before we reach England.'

Muir watched as two bearers lowered their stretcher and bent over a convulsing, screaming man who had clawed at his eyes until the charcoal strips of skin came away beneath his fingernails. His arms were pinned to his sides and lashed. He began to sob.

'The nearest port is Recife,' said Muir. 'I don't know what medical facilities they might have.'

'*Whatever* they are like, they would make ours look primitive,' said Bellamy.

Recife lay on the Brazilian coast, seven hundred miles to the west. They could reach it in under a week – four days if things went well. But what would happen when they arrived? The story of the gold aboard *Straker* would spread like wildfire and Muir had no faith whatsoever in the Brazilian government's idly watching it slip through their fingers. There would be red tape, quasi-legal blocking moves dragging on for months. Either that or *Straker* would mysteriously sink in harbour, where, of course, the mud would be too deep to lift her or her cargo. That is until *Drummer* and her crew had been sent packing, and then it would rise quicker than a bubble.

'The Cape Verde Islands are two thousand miles north,' said Muir. 'Perhaps twelve days. I'd feel happier there.'

'I'm sorry, sir, I realise the problems, but these men need attention of the kind I simply haven't the ability to give. I do not have the drugs nor the equipment to cope.'

'In that case, there can only be one decision,' said Muir. 'We head for Recife.'

Bellamy gave a nod. 'Now, if you'll excuse me, sir ...'

Muir watched him catch up with the stretcher carrying the pinioned sailor, shake his head and walk hurriedly on to the sick bay. Despite his graveside manner Bellamy was a good doctor, still able to regard a corpse as a personal failure, which it wasn't. The pressure on him would be intense and Muir made a mental note to second as many men as possible to the sick bay.

Recife.

Would the dying die anyway, their ordeal made worse by the blistering heat of the place? It was less than ten degrees south of the equator and probably riven with disease. By juggling with the checks and balances, Muir knew he could have made out a case for pushing on north.

It would have been the wrong case.

Straker's crew – those who were uninjured or merely 'damaged', as Bellamy referred to it – had been lined up above the Number Two hold beneath the bridge, where a million years ago Tilley had held his 'sod's opera'.

'There's Pickett,' said Barrow.

Charlie Pickett's boat had been drawn up aft. The young girl was being held between the midshipman and the dark-haired woman.

'The ladies, sir,' said Pickett as he approached Muir. 'I'm afraid I don't know their names, apart from Rose.'

The old woman crooked her head and strode forward as if examining a prospective escort for the evening. Apparently satisfied at what she saw, she gave a brief dip of her head.

'Captain Muir, ma'am.'

She proffered the back of her hand and he bent to it, gallantly.

'And your friends . . .'

'Are tired, Captain. Excuse them.'

'Of course, of course. Number One, get Dandridge, if he's sorted out von Bauer, to find them private quarters.'

Excusing himself, he took Pickett to one side. 'Good work, lad. Let's have a long talk soon.'

'Grateful, sir.'

Dandridge, having been winkled out by Barrow, stood as far as possible from the captain.

'I'll take care of them,' Rose was saying. She fluttered the others in front of her.

'I am indebted,' said Muir. 'Anything you require Dandridge will do his best to supply. Dandridge?'

'Aye, aye, sir.' Dandridge flushed and led them off.

'I confess I'm still finding all this a bit bizarre, Number One,' admitted Muir. 'But if you're up to talking there are a few things I'd like to go over.'

'Of course. What do they say about a whiff of grapeshot?'

'It's a shot of whisky I'm thinking of, Number One. Hell with the grape. Where's Pickett?'

But Pickett had gone.

'Bloody slaughterhouse. Shells everywhere. Jimmy the One pissing himself in panic. Never seen the likes of it. Sodding idiot Purvis chucked himself over the side, shit scared, round the twist. Way I saw it, the only thing left was to get the fug out of it, said as much. Pickett was blubbering, suppose might have expected it, so had to handle it meself. Mind you, I don't mind admitting, I was getting a bit worried.'

Baines was leaning against a winch and was in full flight, his face assiduously streaked with other men's blood. 'Sharks ten foot long. Killed two of them with a boathook. Stuck it in their eyes. Heard them scream, the buggers.'

'Scream?' Hackett's nose wrinkled as he tried to recall whether such a thing was possible.

Baines nodded sagely. 'They scream like sodding lobsters.' Setting the seal on his authority in the matter: 'How many sharks you killed, Hackett?'

Hackett, shifting his bandaged, three-fingered hand in its sling, had to admit shark-killing was something he had yet to experience. He had been sent over to Baines to tend his wounds but, as yet, the returning hero hadn't stopped recounting his adventures long enough to indicate what they might be.

'Take it easy, Baines,' said Tilley. He too was on sick bay duty, and had a personal interest in Baines's welfare. He tugged at the woollen cap he had taken to wearing. There was a chance that Baines was in a state of shock, or even mad. Madder.

'You telling me to take it easy? Like to have seen you out there, up to your arse in blood and guts!' Baines gave a cackle. 'Smelled worse than your bloody hair oil!' His voice fell, conspiratorially, but without pause. 'Seen the women have you? Not bad, eh? Not bad! The young bit! The black-haired piece? Hackett can have the old bag! And the other little beauties? Little gold beauties? Fugging ship is full of them! Falling over 'em! If I hadn't torn up the deck with me bare hands, nobody would've known it was there.'

'It was hidden?' inquired Tilley innocently.

' 'Course it was hidden! Silly sod!' Baines showered a spittle of rage over Tilley's idiot question.

'And you were falling over it?'

'Falling over it, right!' burbled Baines, failing to see the inconsistency.

'Where's it come from?' Hackett hadn't seen it either, and was hanging on every word.

'Pinched. Nobody's now. Bloody insurance company will have coughed up now it's just sitting there.' Another cackle. 'Coker's eyes fell out of his head! Thought he was going to dive over and swim home with his pockets full.' Baines wiped his mouth across his cuff. 'Christ, I could sink some coffee. No bleeding coffee on this ship for a bloke who found you a fortune?'

'The galley's boiling up,' said Hackett. 'Can you walk?'

Baines moved a leg experimentally. 'Bit of shrapnel.' He shrugged. 'It'll work its way out.' Catching Tilley's stare: 'What the fug you looking at?'

Tilley blinked. 'Just thinking.'

'All the bloody good some buggers are, "thinking",' snapped

Baines. He limped theatrically off to the galley supported by Hackett's good arm.

Tilley felt the trembling begin to subside. Anger always had the same effect on him. Sweeping over him like a fever that wouldn't break, immobilising him with fear of its terrible energy. It happened rarely, but on the few occasions when he had been unable to control it – many years ago now – he had seen himself as a stranger might; gripped by a diabolical madness that, later, sickened him to the core. An animal! Capable of gouging and tearing and ripping without thought; insensible to any injury inflicted on him, he had been dragged off the focus of his rage like a lunatic. For days afterwards he had been physically exhausted and mentally drained.

He took a breath. All that had been long ago, now he was old enough to know better. But it had shocked him to know the embers hadn't been completely extinguished. The trouble was he kept it all locked up, instead of doing what all the others did – rant and rave and curse, letting off in short bursts the accumulated aggravations of their unnatural life. But it wasn't in his character, he couldn't let it be, and that was that.

He smiled: Tilley the Tiger! Pulling the woollen cap down atop his ears he tried to ignore the burning needles drilling into his brain. Baines was a bastard. He was also a liar. Tilley had been breech loader on the forrard 4.7 inch gun, and on Prettie's orders had been conning the windjammer through binoculars when he had caught the open boat in the corner of the lens. He had seen Baines hiding below the gunwales and, almost able to smell the panic, had seen Barrow forcibly drag him back onto the thwart.

It would have been easy to have destroyed his braggart tale, and he had every reason for doing so. But no. Maybe later, in some other way. Revenge was only another form of self-destruction. Tilley began to make his way back to the sick bay. Some time Stagg Baines might find life not quite so accommodating and he, Tilley, reserved the right, when that day came, to be among the first to cheer.

The gold ingot sat on Muir's desk like a ridiculous paperweight bought in some Turkish bazaar. Von Bauer sat facing it, his hunched frame sunk in a low chair, bringing it a little below the level of his eyes, but he ignored it. Barrow was sitting to one side, having washed, shaved and changed his uniform. Muir, having pushed back his chair, was studying his outstretched toecaps. Already, in private, Barrow had outlined the basic sequence of events that had taken place on *Straker,* and both were agreed that they raised more questions than they answered — whether von Bauer would oblige by filling in the blanks remained to be seen. His composure, having suffered the rare indignity of being openly dismissed as a liar and further shaken by the discovery of the women, had reasserted itself. His uniform remained immaculate, and he sat at ease, one leg draped over another. All it needed, thought Muir, was a glass of port balanced in his hand.

'Captain,' began Muir, blinking over the ingot, 'I find myself as you have perhaps often found yourself ...' The words must be chosen carefully. To drive him into his shell at this stage would achieve nothing. 'The fight is over and every conflict has its victor and its loser.' Was it because the man was a foreigner that he found himself speaking in a Biblical pidgin-English? Muir changed tack. What was the point of beating about the bush now? 'I want some explanation, Captain. You are of course free to remain silent until placed in the hands of other authorities, but one thing I must explain is that, as far as this ship — and *Straker* — are concerned, I am the law and will decide its process as I think fit.'

Von Bauer gave a precise tug at his trouser and the crease fell along it like a blade. 'That is the law in my navy too, Captain.' He leaned back in the chair still retaining the air of formality, though there was something distinctly waspish in the way he had stated the obvious. Muir noticed the dark circles beneath his eyes.

'We have sick men from both sides, and many problems we must share, Captain von Bauer. None of which is going to be helped by a battle of words between us. Lieutenant Barrow has explained to me what took place on *Straker* and some of it disturbs me greatly. However I do not intend to dwell on my personal feelings at this stage.'

'I am in your hands, Captain.' This time there was no hint of sarcasm. 'I have nothing to hide from you. Nothing more. If your "personal" feelings are an immediate consequence of events following the boarding of my ship, then I offer no apology. When one has only duplicity left in one's armoury, one uses that. Now I am prepared to answer any questions you care to ask. Within reason.'

The rider was there. Ask me what you like and I merely reserve the right to decide whether you are asking the right question. Even so, Muir had the feeling that the man's attitude, his whole pose, was artificial. The Germanic brusqueness was

98

serving as a smoke-screen for a personality infinitely more complex.

'That, if I may say so, Captain, is damned civil of you.' Muir's expression was thoughtful and this time von Bauer missed the raillery, recognising only the idiosyncratic language of the British officer-class. 'I would like to begin with a few, perhaps obvious, questions. First, I take it the gold was taken from another ship?'

'It was.'

'English?'

'A ship bound for England. A legitimate spoil of war.'

'Carrying gold, with no escort? You are telling me that *Straker* alone simply took it from a ship she chanced upon?' Muir frowned disbelievingly.

'No, Captain, I am not saying that. There *was* an escort. The ship had become detached from it in a storm. There were two British sloops less than thirty miles away, but the weather was foul. We damaged her steering gear and, after a small affray, boarded her. A false position was telegraphed to the sloops and, as luck would have it, we saw neither of them.'

'The ship's name?'

'*Voortrekker.*'

'You sank her?'

'I did not. There were one hundred and fifty men aboard *Straker* who had been removed from previous vessels we had engaged. They were sunk – the ships – *after* I had seen to the safety of those on board. All the officers and crew of this particular ship were treated in the same manner. Obviously we could not go on supporting so many additional people indefinitely. After the gold bullion was transferred to *Straker* ...'

'In a storm?' interrupted Muir.

Von Bauer picked an imaginary piece of lint from his knee. 'In a storm. I lost seven men and, as it happened, a considerable amount of gold. May I continue?'

'Do.' What was the description Barrow had given of the German captain? 'Sharp as a diamond, with twice as many sides.'

'The steering gear was mended – it was a ridiculously small defect that could have been put right very quickly if her captain had acted promptly. I transferred our "passengers" to her and, under the command of certain officers and men from *Straker*, I ordered her to make for Montevideo. After that, Captain ... Well, there was nothing after that. Until now.'

'How much gold do you have aboard your ship?'

'It has not been assessed. A considerable amount.'

'And this ship, the one that was carrying it – presumably it arrived safely in Montevideo?'

Von Bauer shuffled in his seat. 'I have no reason to believe otherwise.'

Muir had caught something in the German's voice. It lacked the same, sure firmness. 'You mean you are not wholly sure?'

'I am not in the habit of killing people in cold blood, Captain. The ship surrendered and all aboard were treated according to both the law of the sea and that of basic humanity.'

'Can you tell me something more about the ship.'

'She was voyaging from South Africa to England. Perhaps your country too, Captain, is feeling some financial strain?'

Muir ignored the jibe. 'One other thing, for the moment, Captain. *Straker*. Was she once a British ship?'

Von Bauer mellowed immediately. 'Yes. Yes, she was. Now may I ask *you* something? Was that how you knew ... what made you change your mind?'

'In a way. The *Glencoe*?'

Von Bauer gave a small nod that might have been tinged with admiration. 'The *Glencoe*, indeed. You recognised her.'

'One of my crew.'

'Astute. There were many changes. Her original name was *Pass of Glencoe*, built on the Clyde and later sold to an American line, delivering cotton to my country when your blockade ships stopped her. A strange story.'

Barrow guessed von Bauer was as animated as he had ever been.

'The blockading ship put a prize crew on board her and they were sailing towards Lerwick when they, in turn, were stopped by a submarine and escorted to Germany, complete with the boarders who had hidden below. They were found, of course. After that she lay in dock. A year later I came across her. You may be surprised, Captain, that, as a young man I served on an English clipper. You are familiar with sail?'

'The hard way, Captain von Bauer.'

'Surely there is no easy way?'

Muir laughed. 'No, there isn't.'

For a moment Barrow thought the two were about to start exchanging shellback stories.

'Then we have a little in common, Captain,' said von Bauer without enthusiasm.

'Any points, Number One?'

'The women, sir. Maybe some explanation.'

A pink flush brushed von Bauer's cheeks. 'I have already ...'

'I think that may wait, Number One. That will be all, Captain, for the moment. If there is anything that has ... slipped your memory ... and you later wish to communicate, I am available. There will be no guard at your cabin, but I must ask you to remain in your quarters for the moment. A steward will be at your disposal.'

'Naturally,' said von Bauer.

Naturally a steward? Or naturally he would be confined to his cabin?

'I'll see the captain there, sir,' said Barrow.

'Then a rest, Number One.'

'As you say, sir.'

When they had gone, Jack Muir reached into his desk and drew out an object resembling a six-inch long sharp-ended sausage and sniffed it reflectively. The modern tins of expensive, blended, boudoir-smelling tobacco would never manage to wean him from the traditional rough-plug. When ashore the instantly recognisable aroma had raised more than a few eyebrows in the drawing rooms of his father-in-law's Admiralty-bound relatives, who regarded it as a passing reminder of the fo'c'sle rabble they preferred to forget. The dried, cured leaves, cut to size and laid on the deck after being moistened with rum, were rolled into shape with the full pressure of a bare foot and the compact mass covered in canvas, whipped with yarn and left to mature. Primitive, maybe, but the end result could not be bettered. Muir had been damned if he'd give it up. It was just unfortunate that the name of the finished plug was derived from that of the leaf from which it was made: *'prique'*. Muir unrolled the 'prick' and, after tapping a wad of folded cardboard into the bowl of his pipe, covered it with a frugal knife-paring of tobacco. The trick was to burn the weed slowly, since his supply of 'pricks' was reaching famine level. The first inhalation scorched his tongue, the second filled his cheeks with a rich satisfaction. He sat back in his chair.

There were many more questions he would have liked to put to the German. But there was time, and most of the answers he had received made sense. Von Bauer had stumbled on a crock of gold bound for the British Treasury and had taken an almost suicidal option to intercept her. The sheer flair of it was astonishing: the fact that it had succeeded, a crushing condemnation of whoever had organised the escort. Even so, Muir managed to feel sympathy for the captains of the two sloops, arriving back in port, shotguns intact, having lost their stagecoach.

Von Bauer had faltered only once: when questioned as to the fate of *Voortrekker*. Why? It intrigued him. But then, so did the man. Neat, precise, *proper*. On the surface only the monocle was missing. But the smack of the sea had a deeper imprint. Von Bauer was first and foremost a sailor – a fighting sailor – and nothing could disguise the fact. The sea seemed an unlikely place for a count to prosper, unless at heart he was an adventurer. And an adventurer at sea needed to be more than a stiff-backed, heel-clicking Junker. Muir blew an extravagant plume of blue smoke into the air. How different were they? And how much the same? It might turn out to be the most important question of all.

'*Surely there is no easy way?*'

West Tarn. Clutching his dunnage, he had struggled into eight-foot square quarters on her half deck. Quarters covered with the coal dust legacy of the cargo. Two scuttles and a skylight. Then into steam as apprentice in *Messenger*, painting the funnel, holystoning the deck and, within a year, quartermaster, capable of steering her. Exams in London at the Navigation School near the Sailor's Home in Dock Street, where he bedded down. Emerging as a young, qualified second mate, at £5 a month for five years in *The Sussex* as fourth officer. Then third officer: £6 a month. Second officer: £8 a month. First Mate and navigator: £10. At twenty-six a master's ticket. And the war. Acting lieutenant RNR in H.M.S. *Fortitude* – fully fledged lieutenant at ten shillings a day. Muir couldn't imagine von Bauer remembering the financial stepping-stones in quite the same way. His first fighting ship saw him as boarding officer and, in the last month of 1916, *Drummer* was his command. Lieutenant-Commander Jack Muir. It had been a hard slog, but von Bauer couldn't have got where he was much more easily. Differently, but no more easily, in the final reckoning. The sea was a great leveller and ate bad seamen alive.

Lieutenant-commander. A fine ring to it. But for Jack Muir it meant the most critical stage of his career. He had put in his qualified time for promotion to commander and – if it hadn't happened already without him knowing – the Admiralty was due to signal its List to the Fleet and shore bases. If his name wasn't on it he would be 'passed over', shunted into some bureaucratic backwater; a 'stone-frigate' training establishment or a fishery protection vessel. The big full stop. A week ago Muir had known what that verdict would be after the spectacularly uneventful voyage of *Drummer*. Now all that had changed.

Only the Admiralty didn't know it.

Karl Recke's co-operation with von Bauer had backfired with frightening implications. Having lost everything, the captain now owed him nothing. The tenuous union had ended. And though the war seemed over, Recke was uneasy. Von Bauer had regarded them as common mutineers, to be hanged. It needed to be established, and established quickly, that the uprising on *Straker* had been a political one. The gesture of defiance and loathing at the senseless killing had already been perverted by von Bauer into nothing more than gangsterism. And whose version would the English captain choose to believe? Was von Bauer now telling him that they had risen to claim the gold? He had, no doubt, been given a cabin and was chatting amiably with his counterpart.

His mind in turmoil, Recke saw everything sliding away, sordid and defiled. There could only be one way to rescue anything from the debacle. Quietly, under the cover of the general confusion, he had moved among as many of *Straker*'s men as possible. *His* men. His voice grew hoarse with urgency. They had to be given a fair hearing. At least he owed them that.

He sat down on the deck, legs crossed, arms wrapped across his chest to quieten the beating of his heart. After an age, a sailor sat down beside him, sliding back on his hands, focusing on the deck. Another. Two more. Misunderstanding, the British officers began to rail at their idleness. Still they sat. Twenty now.

'They dare not fire!' shouted Recke in German. A few more were convinced.

Arms waving like a choirmaster in a congregational chapel, a petty officer tried to get them to their feet. No response. 'Up, all of you!'

Fewer than half of them knew what he was saying, but it didn't need to be translated. Nobody moved.

'Up! Up!' screeched the P.O. Sailors with fixed bayonets began to move among the squatters, staring down at the bent heads and then at the P.O. A few nudges with the flat of a blade. The P.O., whose name was Crutchley, and who had never confidently ordered around more than two men at a time in his life — and then only after verbal guarantees from a superior ensured he couldn't be held responsible for anything — began to lose his temper. Aware that *his* temper was of no consequence whatsoever, he looked around for an officer, aggrieved at being left in the lurch.

Two of the German sailors were lifted forcibly to their feet, only to subside like wet sacks when they were released.

Karl Recke stood of his own volition and motioned the rest to stay where they were. Recke's English was far from perfect, but the issue was clear enough not to need any elaborate dressing. 'We wish to talk to your captain!' he said loudly.

'Sit down,' said Crutchley. 'No, stand up! The rest of you! Get up!' He had sent one of the watch off to fetch Muir or Barrow – anybody to take the weight off him.

'We have no argument with you,' said Recke, addressing the encircling bayonets. 'We are all seamen, don't you understand? An injustice has been done.'

The P.O. was blotched at the collar and had reached his agitation threshold by the time Muir arrived. He began barking orders wildly.

Muir waved him quiet and faced Recke. 'You claim to represent these men? You do not. You are prisoners! Now go about your business!'

'I cannot do that, sir. You are being misled. We are being ...'

'What's your name?'

'Recke. Karl Recke!'

'And what's your grievance, Recke? I assume you have one?'

'I do, Captain, and ...'

Muir gave a short chop of the hand. 'No! Simply answer my question! You have some grievance?'

'Yes. It is not of your making. Allow me to explain ...'

'Get these men on their feet, before any "explanations".'

'I do not give orders, Captain,' said Recke. 'These men chose to do what they are doing.'

Muir turned to Crutchley. 'Get the German captain down here fast. At the double.'

'We members of *Straker*'s crew, ordinary seamen, sit here for recognition, Captain,' Recke was saying. 'When you took our ship she was not under the command of von Bauer and he is not entitled to negotiate with you in any way. We ask to be accepted as the sole authority in command of *Straker* when you defeated her.'

Muir, aware of the audience that had been gathering, raked them with a single glance. 'To your posts!' They began reluctantly to dwindle away, leaving only the armed guard. The pale figure of Recke stood almost at attention above the bowed heads around him. There could, reasoned Muir, be no possible way the sailor might have known that the Imperial German Navy had risen in exactly the same manner – if the report was true – so was it mere coincidence? *Drummer*, and *Straker* for that matter, had been at sea for an age. When they got back home it would be to a changed world, against the pace of which they had marked time.

Von Bauer had been brought from his brief rest and was looking less than pleased. Muir, turning his back on Recke, spoke softly, but forcefully: 'I have explained my attitude towards continued resistance, Captain. I will not repeat it.' Each word was clipped. 'Tell them, in simple terms, once and for all, that I am not interested in their arguments with you and less so in their politics. Neither they, nor you, are in any kind of position to make demands. For some reason they strike me as frightened men, Captain, and maybe you alone know why that is. Just get them about things!' He glared at the captain. 'There will be no reprisals for any foolishness that may have occurred in the past, which I suppose this nonsense is all about. I need their muscle, not their minds, if we are to get back at all. It is their choice.'

Von Bauer stepped past him, his face a mask. He spoke for less than a minute in rapid sentences. One by one the men stood and were filtered down to their quarters by the guard. Recke pointed a finger at Muir, trembling with anger, choking on his words. He was dragged away before he could speak.

Muir took control of his surprise at the sudden turn of events quickly enough to order that Recke should not be confined. He was plainly broken. Then, to von Bauer: 'You did well, Captain. It seems at last the air has been cleared.'

'For you, Captain,' von Bauer said tersely.

Tilley's jaw hung slackly. The deck had been cleared and the last of the wounded taken to the sick bay. He had been unloading medical supplies taken from *Straker* when the German captain had spoken to the sailors sitting on the deck. Now he stood by the boat watching as Muir talked to him. Petty Officer Crutchley, who had been hovering hoping to discover whether he had done the right thing or not and armed to lay any blame in at least three other areas, was the only other remaining on the well deck. Tilley hardly noticed him. He was dumbstruck.

Von Bauer had returned to his cabin and Muir gave a cursory glance around the deck. 'No home to go to, Tilley?'

The P.O. stepped forward eagerly. 'No malingering, there, sailor,' he bustled. Tilley stared through him.

'Please go away, Crutchley,' said Muir in exasperation. The P.O. had the same effect on him as fingernails scraping along a blackboard.

Mortified, Crutchley melted away.

'Come over here, Tilley,' said Muir. 'Now, what's the matter with you, man? You've been looking at me as if I just murdered your grannie.'

'Was I, sir? Suppose I was, sir. Sorry, sir.' He tugged down his cap apologetically.

'So what's it all about? It's not like you to hang about when there's work to be done.' There was no other member of the crew that Muir would have talked to so familiarly; but then there was no other member of the crew quite like Tilley.

'Truth is, sir, I was a bit stunned.'

'I see that,' said Muir nodding at the woollen cap. 'Is it bandaged?'

'No sir. I mean, not that kind of stunned. The cap's for an affliction. Hope it's all right, sir . . .'

Muir was as aware as anyone of Tilley's singular problem. 'Then what *do* you mean? Come on, there's a good fellow, we've all got work to do.' Muir was about to turn away.

'Did you mean what you said,' burst out Tilley, 'about the Germans?'

Muir stopped. '*Mean?* Look Tilley, I think you *are* stunned. Have a word with one of the sick bay ratings and . . .'

'Do you *intend* to shoot them, sir?'

The captain's face passed through a variety of mild contortions before settling on one of blank incomprehension. 'Shoot? What in blazes are you burbling about, man? You heard what I said, dammit!' The look in Tilley's eyes began to ring a small warning bell.

'I didn't catch what you said to them, sir, I only came on deck when the German captain was talking. I know a little of the language, sir. Worked in Hamburg some time ago. But maybe it's rusty and I got it wrong . . .'

The bell was beginning to peal.

'I think I must have, sir.'

'Tell me what the captain said, Tilley. Assume you heard it right and tell me exactly what he said.' Muir was half-way towards guessing.

'Well, sir, he said the fact they were flying an allied flag put them outside the law. That was the first bit. Then he said that as they had risen against their captain — that's him, sir, not you — the British regarded them as criminals, mutineers I suppose he meant. Something like that. Anyway, putting them both together gave you a free hand to . . . to execute them on the spot unless they moved sharpish. There was another bit about him —

that's the German captain – pardoning them if they were loyal to him from now on.' Tilley paused. 'That was about the meat of it, sir.'

Muir rocked backwards and forwards on his heels. 'Mmm. That's what he said, was it? I'm glad you've been able to clear it up, Tilley.'

'Oh, I see ...'

'Yes, so do I.'

'If you'll excuse the suggestion, sir, I think he pulled a bit of a fast one.'

'Something our friend is adept at, I'm beginning to discover, Tilley. Thank you again. And I hope your head gets better.' Muir walked thoughtfully in the direction of the bridge.

Tilley heard a fist smack into a palm.

'I'll have three bunks made up as soon as I can. The water in the jug is drinkable. The ... er ... toilet facilities are through that door. They are used by the officers, but ...'

A dozen dreadful incidents suddenly loomed even as Beattie Dandridge uttered the words. He blushed. 'I'll make a notice to hang on the door,' he said hurriedly. 'Like they have in hotels.'

At a loss where to quarter the women, he had, in desperation, asked Barrow if they could use the wardroom. It was the only place aboard *Drummer* that would afford them any privacy.

'Are you hungry?'

The old woman, Rose, shook her head. 'Hannah? Elizabeth?' They were sitting together at the table, Hannah, the young girl's mother, still with a protective arm about her daughter. They looked like refugees waiting to be moved. Dandridge hadn't yet heard them utter a single word.

'Tell them I can ask the surgeon to attend the girl, if she is unwell. You speak their language, ma'am?'

Rose shook her head. 'They're not German, son. Americans. Just a bit tired and shook up.'

'I'm sorry ... I thought ... of course.'

'That's Hannah Lange and Elizabeth is her daughter. You're ...'

'Midshipman Dandridge.'

'I can't remember that mouthful.'

'Beattie.'

'That's better. Beattie.'

Hannah Lange looked across at Dandridge, seeming to notice his presence for the first time. 'A lock. Is there a lock?'

'A lock?'

'The door.' Her voice was barely audible, with the smallest trace of an American accent, and yet it managed to build a steel wall around her. Her eyes were even blacker than the shoulder length hair, drawn into a ragged bun, wisps curling at her temples. She had been – still was – a handsome woman. Dandridge began to blush again and made a pretence of examining the door minutely. 'Yes. A lock. I will find you the keys.' A hundred keys, a steel door, anything! Had Muir done this as a punishment? If so he had chosen it with diabolical care.

'You're doing fine, my boy,' said Rose. 'We aren't wanting for anything at the moment. Just to settle ourselves in.' There was something on her mind. 'I don't know whether it's possible . . . no, I won't be worrying you . . .'

'Please.' Dandridge almost shouted it. He was growing more and more uncomfortable. She must know, the woman with the dark hair. She had still not taken her eyes off him. Women could tell! Feeling naked, he tried to concentrate on the old woman's words.

'I was thinking of a medicament,' she said, holding a hand across her ample bosom. 'The condition.'

'You feel ill?' If she fainted there was no way he could pick her up.

'A little faintness now and then, is all.' Rose's face reflected a lifetime's martyrdom to the mysterious 'condition'. 'The old heart is willing, but at times things get too much for it. Faithful servant, so I shouldn't be going on complaining, just now and then . . .' the rich Irish brogue faded in contemplation and she looked down at her hand as if that alone was containing some imminent explosion. 'You wouldn't be having a drop of brandy, would you now?'

In his haste to get away from the searching eyes, Dandridge was prepared to conjure up a gallon of poteen with chasers of porter. Anything to leave the claustrophobic atmosphere bearing down on him.

'The merest drop. The smallest bottle. It eases the night's trepidation and brings the blessing of sleep. Gall in my mouth, but we cannot choose our own medicine can we now? Whisky will do, if no other. Irish, if you'd be having it.'

Dandridge nodded his exit.

Rose took a deep breath. 'It's no good, Hannah. You fair scared the boy away and him here to help us.' Waddling over she took the arm from around the girl. 'Leave her be, Hannah, Elizabeth is stronger than you give her credit for.'

The girl looked at her.

'Elizabeth, everything is going to be grand, I feel it in my bones. Look at the place we have here! A palace, no less! And we don't have to pay a penny piece for it! We're going back in style, waited on hand and foot. And here you both are looking glum as steerage passengers. Shame on you!'

Elizabeth Lange smiled.

'Now isn't that what we could all do a bit more with? Me, I've decided to sit back and enjoy myself.' Her boisterous good humour managed to disguise the sudden note of warning intended for Hannah alone. 'You too, my dear. For everyone's sake. We must forget the past.'

Elizabeth had begun to explore the saloon.

'I know, I know, Hannah,' whispered Rose. 'But no more.' Raising her voice, breezily. 'It smells of tobacco and boot polish. What this place is after having is a woman's touch.'

Hannah walked across to the water jug and, dampening the hem of her dress, dabbed it to her forehead. Inadvertently Rose caught Elizabeth's eye as they both turned their glance from the sheen of hair above the china bowl. And, in one brief, unprepared-for moment the young girl at the threshold of womanhood and the old lady deliberating at its exit were bound together as surely as sisters sharing a sworn-to intimacy. The vulnerability of their sex that one had learned from sixty-five years of life and the other within days was drawn together in a nakedness and exposure that no man could ever understand.

8 December

Drummer's chief engineer had spent two hours assessing the damage to the engine room and, for a while, it had managed to take his mind off many things. Now, aimlessly, he went on deck. He needed a word with the stokers. After that there was the reorganisation of his men to account for the loss in dead and injured. The stocks of coal were dwindling rapidly. He must see Webster in the sick bay. Must write a letter. More than anything, write a letter. A definitive one, this time. He would lay all the cards on the table, get it over and done with. He began to wonder how she would take it. Would she admit everything, openly, or would it gradually show itself over days, months? What if he knew the man? He stopped abruptly. *Men*, he had always thought of *men*, but one man! Taking everything and living each day with what was rightly his! The thought of

Maggie laughing, smiling, forgetting him, sent a spear through him. He couldn't go on like this: he was going mad! How could he condemn her, when he knew nothing? The hopelessness of it all hit him as it never had before; a mixture of exhaustion and defeat. Still it didn't stop his mind from plunging him down into despair.

'If it's one man, I'll kill him,' he said aloud. 'Yes, that's exactly what I'll do. Openly.'

'Problems, Chief?'

Garrett whirled violently, feeling the arm of the law already descending.

Muir stepped back, raising his hands in mock self-protection. 'You were a thousand miles away. Which is where we all ought to be.'

Garrett babbled his apologies, feeling foolish. How much had Muir heard? What had he said? He couldn't remember.

'So who is it you're about to take an axe to?' Muir grinned. 'When you've finished, lend it me, there's one or two I wouldn't mind bothering with it.'

'I ... yes ...' stumbled Garrett. But Muir didn't seem to notice his confusion. 'I was going to talk to the stokers, sir.'

'Before you do, a quick word. Be totally frank, bordering on the optimistic. I want to take *Straker* in tow. And I want to know if *Drummer* can stand it. Her engines, that is. It'll be a dead weight of around 2000 tons, steered by a skeleton crew. If the auxiliary can be repaired, well and good, but I'm not banking on that. You'll have heard about the gold on the windjammer – I intend to have a meeting of all officers about that soon – but between you and me, it would take days transferring it, and if a squall blows up we're in real trouble.' He paused. 'There is another reason. If possible I want to take *Straker* home as she is; gold, captain, crew, the lot. We owe it to ourselves to try.'

Garrett had recovered and, while taking in what Muir was saying, had been calculating stresses, engine power and fuel supplies. 'It would be a grand way to end our war, sir. One that not a man on board wouldn't appreciate. Barring the Germans, of course.'

'Yes, well they've had their moments of glory.' Muir clopped his hands. 'But can it be done? I'm not asking you to make a decision, that will be up to me. And if anything goes wrong it will be my error. I simply want a technical appraisal of probability, no more.'

'The engines aren't in bad shape,' said Garrett eventually,

his mind's eyes having moved through the engine room dial by dial. 'It'll slow things by a few knots, and I don't know how we stand for time. Coal is so-so, but if the worst comes to the worst we can always strip the windjammer and burn her wooden fittings. It'd mean gutting her insides, but it's a useful standby. The matter of handling *Drummer* is another thing. Power we have, at the moment. The main problem is keeping the hawser from whipping or breaking. To prevent that we need to keep a smooth, constant speed, and, in a bad sea . . .' he shrugged. 'I'd say, to your question, sir, it's possible. From my end, that is.'

'Good man! Have you ever been on a ship towing before?'

'Not towing a sailing ship, sir.'

'Neither have I. In which case it is going to be an interesting exercise for all of us, Chief.'

'I suppose it is, sir.'

'Keep me posted as to exactly how things are going below. And once we get under way, I'd like you on the bridge now and then, just to feel things from that end. Don't hesitate to speak out. A lot could depend on it.' He tapped Garrett on the shoulder. 'I believe I've kept you from weighty matters . . .'

Garrett managed a confused smile.

Drummer's mess deck, formerly depleted of men now in the sick bay, was packed to overflowing as the survivors of *Straker* were jammed into it. After what had happened on deck, Muir had thought it unwise to segregate the Germans; by mixing them with *Drummer*'s crew at least an eye could be kept on them. In theory.

Tilley, Baines, and Coker found themselves turn and turn about with three of *Straker*'s crew who, like the rest, were to share watches. Nothing as yet had been worked out in detail and the three hovered awkwardly in the small cabin like in-laws arriving unheralded, unsure of their welcome. Tilley pulled chests across for them to sit on. The one anchor on Tilley's jacket marked him as a 'killick' – two steps up from an ordinary seaman and charged with keeping order in the particular part of the mess that was his domain. Normally he was entitled to a private cubicle, but the architecture of *Drummer* had dictated otherwise, for which he was supremely thankful. He had little desire to give orders and the thought of separate quarters was not to his liking.

As 'killick' it was up to Tilley to show the first sign of charity – exactly where the second would come from was another matter. He introduced the men in the cabin. The Germans responded. 'Kapper, Recke, Fischer,' said Tilley, 'well, that shouldn't be too hard to remember.' He found it difficult to take his eyes off Kapper. He was, without doubt, the ugliest man he had ever seen. His body was huge, bigger even than Coker's but nothing could dominate the face that hung over it like a half-finished gargoyle. The eyes were pale and flat as a dab's, a lantern jaw jutting beneath a mouth designed to devour. Tilley judged it to be a good five inches wide, sensual and somehow disgusting.

'It's a fuggin' liberty,' said Baines, speaking with his new-found authority of master-strategist and war hero. 'These bastards tried to shoot my guts out not a day ago, and now I'm expected to kip down with 'em! Fuggin' liberty!'

'I speak English,' said the ugly giant.

Baines visibly blanched. 'Yes, well ... I mean ... how would you like it?' He sank into his hammock, mumbling.

Karl Recke said: 'We appreciate your problems, but we have no say ...'

'I think it'll sort itself out,' said Tilley. 'We're all in the same boat.'

Hackett laughed. Penn Coker looked up from the turk's head and, straddling his sea chest, leaned back on the bulwark. 'That stuff back there – where'd you get it?' He was talking to Kapper.

'It was taken,' said the German, warily.

'What about the women?' came Baines's voice hidden deep in the hammock. 'They "taken" too?' He cackled wildly.

Kapper said something rapidly in German.

'Let's have it, then, Tilley. What's he rabbiting on about? Least they can do is speak the King's English.'

'He was saying, from what I could catch – and I translate it loosely – that you have too much mouth and no balls,' said Tilley smoothly. He corrected himself: 'He *may* have meant you have balls at the moment but are in danger of losing them in the near future. It is a difficult language in the vernacular.'

'I want no trouble ... bin through enough ... if he's threatening, then Captain Muir ought to ...' whined Baines.

'SHUT it!' Coker lashed out at the interruption. 'One more word and I'll save him the job, Baines, are you hearing?'

'Listen to me, please,' Recke looked around the company. 'We are not here to cause dissent. Our fight must go on, but not with you. We *need* you all. Our lives are in danger. *Straker's* crew are being treated as mutineers by your captain and there is no telling what he might do. He has already threatened what may happen. *Straker* was taken over by us, but in the name of sanity – the name of the revolution.'

'You took over the whole works?' Hackett looked as if he had just been introduced to Genghis Khan.

'That's what he means,' said Tilley. He felt he should say more, explain his conversation with the Old Man, but was uncertain. The captain would want to work it out in his own way and he didn't fancy putting himself forward as the filling in the sandwich when the two captains collided as he reckoned they eventually must. Even so, the thought of Recke turning the mess deck into Hyde Park Corner wasn't appealing either.

Kapper clenched a fist and held it in front of him, elegant as a knobkerrie. 'Recke is right. You understand me? We are all together.'

'The German Fleet has surrendered,' said Recke, somewhat disconcerted at Kapper's lightning conversion to a cause he had so far ignored. 'You have all heard by now that the sailors in the Baltic are in control of the ships and the admirals are obeying *their* orders. So it was with *Straker*. We were fighting for you, too! What are you going back to? Nothing. How many dead on *Drummer*? How many dead on *Straker*? And yet there is no war. *Was no war when they died!* Just two captains deciding their fate between them – for a few more rings on their arms! We fly different flags, but are people first and last. At sea, on land. Seamen, workers – people!' Breathing heavily he sat down abruptly on a trunk.

Tilley cleared his throat. 'Quite. Very interesting, I'm sure, Mr Recke. But at the moment, before we think of, er, over-throwing the British Empire, I think the matter of sorting out accommodation ...'

'No, he's right!' Hackett burst out, his brow wrinkled as if whatever lay behind it was capable of penetrating thought. 'After all, what kind of a life is this, anyway? Did I ask for it? He may be just a German but what he's saying makes sense to me.' Then, with an impish grin: 'Just imagine an admiral fetching your coffee a-mornings. That's the life for me!' He beamed at the thought. Hackett had joined the Navy at fifteen and was now thirty-eight. The only revolutions he would ever be familiar with were the ones that turned the propeller shaft.

Coker lifted himself to his feet. 'There's too much wind in this hole. Too much *voice*!' He jerked his head at Kapper. 'You and me, mister, need a breath of air.'

They leaned against opposite walls of the alleyway and conducted their business in murmurs, neither of them capable of descending to a whisper. Penn Coker banged in the nail: 'You'd like to lay your hands on that stuff.'

The German sailor's lower lip slid forward, moistening. 'Ask yourself the question. You have the answer.'

Coker closed his eyes. 'Or are you just full of shit?' The provocation was deliberate. Throw these bastards a ball and it could come back before it reached them.

'*Ich habe gebrochen ...*', Kapper smoothed his palms together as if rubbing off paint.

'Shit to me, mister. Talk English, or talk nothing. If you're waving flags and all that slop I've been hearing back there, then go and dream. We've got a couple of minutes. If you want to use it dancing, I say piss off.'

Kapper weighed a fist.

'Put it away, you might need it,' said Coker. 'We can take *Drummer* and *Straker*. You've seen them, they're wide open. How many men could you get?'

'You move quick. Those who followed Recke. Some others. I begin to like you, *mister*.'

'Use the men who followed Recke, they sound scared enough. Play on it. I can raise ten men. It only needs twenty to take this ship if we know what we are about. Check them out and make sure they don't say a word, big man, otherwise the only people shot on this derelict are you and me. Savvy?'

'Savvy?'

'Understand?'

'We have big ideas, but one mistake ...' Kapper rippled his lips. 'We will need guns. A layout of the ship. And we cannot talk to all the men with us together. It will be necessary they know what they do at the moment it happens.' He wagged a thumb. 'A list. Their names will be written on a list – that way there is no turning back.' He sliced a hand across his throat holding an imaginary piece of paper.

Coker punched him gently on the chest. He had found his man. 'Give it twenty-four hours and we talk again.'

'O.K., *mister*.'

Coker walked back to the mess without looking back.

Kapper swilled saliva in his mouth and swallowed it. The sailor was the first link forged, and the strongest. The rest could be hammered into shape, and were dispensable. Not this one. He bit the hard skin on the edge of a forefinger. Never again would he set foot in Germany.

Friedrich Kapper had good reason for his satisfaction.

Two weeks before putting to sea he had been on leave in Berlin, visiting his wife. 'Trade' had been doing nicely and she barely interrupted it to welcome him, spending her nights with a succession of greasy shopkeepers who promenaded from bar to café, club to hotel room. It didn't worry him, as long as she kept herself clean. He could have her any time and anyway there were others who didn't need to *perform*. Not like the cows.

Rape? Fools! It was the way any woman secretly liked it, and all they regretted later was that they hadn't been wined and dined before! The girl had withdrawn her charge as soon as she realised her stupidity, like all the others. He had gone back to her. Again and again. Who would believe her? She had been good – better than all the simpering nonsense the whores played at. The last time was better than them all. His hands began to sweat, feeling the blond hair running through them.

Bared breasts, nipples firm (wasn't that proof?), unlocked thighs, a muffled scream, forcing ... until he drained into her with a roar. Two weeks later she had killed herself. Which left only his wife – the cow – but she had long forgotten the rules of the game.

'Looove me ...' Pirouetting in front of him, full of beer and another man's sperm, squeezing herself, touching him, gripping.

'Loove me ...'

The stain had spread across his trousers to the accompaniment of her wild laughter.

'Too long at sea! Little boys come like that! Tie a knot in it, sailor *boy*, can't you *looove* me?'

He had hit her once and she had died with a startled flap of a hand. The body was buried a borrowed cart journey away in thick woods, dug with a coal scuttle and lighted by a candle in the dead of night.

An hour later he had stamped her grave flat and scattered leaves. Gone back to sea.

Friedrich Kapper was now about to disappear from the face of the earth that contained her. And there would be other women to take their punishment for what she had done to him, even more than she had taken hers.

Everything was in his grasp now. A step away.

Everything.

Including Hannah Lange.

'Please make yourselves as comfortable as you can.' Muir helped fuss with the seats. The three women settled themselves and he moved his chair from behind his desk to join the circle. 'That will be all, Dandridge. No. Coffee. Four coffees? Ladies?'

'Grand, Captain.' Rose gave a tug at Beattie Dandridge's sleeve as he moved past her to the door. 'With a little medicament, perhaps?'

'Well, here we are, ladies,' began Muir briskly. 'Forgive me for not having spoken at length before, but, well, there have been a few things ...' The grating of cables across the fore deck. Muir had been studying the weather since dawn. It could go either way and the tow would have to be shackled up within the hour.

'And now, if you feel so disposed, there are a few things you can enlighten me about, at the same time as we get to know each other.' He looked at Rose and she smiled, displaying a perfect set of brown teeth.

'I think it might be best if I started the tale, Captain.'

'Whatever you wish.' There seemed to be little forthcoming from the others.

'First, my name is Rose. That'll do as far as I am concerned. Nobody needs be bothered about an old woman.' She stated it with a firmness that suggested, bothered or not, it would take hot irons to squeeze any more from her on the subject. 'Hannah Lange and Elizabeth, her daughter. Hannah is American. Doesn't sound it, I know, a name like that, but husbands give a woman half her name in this world and, as to the other half, well, "Hannah" was once "Anne".' She broke off. 'You don't mind me telling the captain all this, Hannah?'

'I suppose he should know ...' the wisps of hair fluttered against her cheek. Suddenly she seemed to awaken. 'It had been bad,' she said. 'Very bad. Our little business collapsed. A shop selling flowers. In Hamburg. It seemed people didn't want flowers any more, even for graves. Only pawnbrokers made money. We used the little we had saved to sail to a new life. As far away as possible.'

Muir realised she wasn't talking to him or to Rose, or even to her daughter. Hannah Lange was talking to herself, as if the process of gathering events in some order might explain what had gone wrong, exactly where the fault had occurred. She picked over the past like a woman retracing her path in search of a lost wedding ring.

'Oskar had an uncle who lived in Montevideo and owned a factory making steel ... or iron, I don't know what it was he said. He wrote that South America would soon need more and more railroads and there would be the need for steel. I think it was steel. He was a very rich man who had left Germany as a youngster, vowing he would make his fortune. Oskar wrote to him saying we were going there and that he would do anything, anything at all, in his factory, as long as he could be given a chance. We sailed two weeks later, still not having had a reply, but Oskar knew it would be all right. He was more confident than I have ever seen him before. Happy. It made me happy too.' Her voice fell. 'He was a simple man.' Then, with a defiant flash that resurrected her untended beauty: 'Good men are always simple men.'

They were interrupted by coffee. Dandridge discreetly sniffed them and handed Rose's to her first. When he had gone it seemed as if no one was going to take up the threads.

'You mean your . . . ah, Oskar . . .' said Muir, not quite certain what he was prompting.

'I was a secretary,' said Hannah. 'My family lived in Hamburg.'

'But let's be having what happened *then*!' said Rose with emphasis. 'Railroads! Factories! Ha!' She sipped the coffee and began to cough.

'Is it too strong?'

'No, no,' Rose reassured Muir. She wiped her eyes. 'Bejiminey, your young man can make a good coffee, that there's no denying.' She held the mug admiringly, her eyes still watering.

'There was no factory,' said Hannah flatly. 'No steel. No one waiting for us. We spent a week visiting every place Oskar's uncle might have owned, thinking he might have fallen sick, or been called away on business. All our letters had been sent to the post office, because it was easier that way, we had been told, so we had no address. No one had heard of him. Then one day Oskar saw him going into a bar. It was as sudden as that. On a big, wide street. Oskar said his clothes were covered in dust and he looked like . . . like a tramp. He called after him, but he ran away. We never saw him again.'

'Imagine it,' said Rose as if Muir might miss the implication of their plight, 'stuck in a foreign country, with hardly any money and no friends. What would you think of a man who lied like that one lied! Pie in the sky!'

'I'm sorry,' said Muir. Hannah Lange was not a weak woman, but she seemed to have been stretched to her limit, almost beyond, and was fighting not to show it.

'Oskar got a job,' said Hannah, as if driven to see the story through to its bitter end, no matter what the cost. 'Mending shoes. He wasn't very good, but he did his best. Elizabeth was ill and I couldn't go out to work. She has asthma. We didn't realise it until later, but the air was terrible for her. We saved hard. I have a mother in America. She returned there after my father died. We decided to go to her. It seemed our only hope. She said she would help us in any way she could, though Oskar didn't want charity. For Elizabeth's sake I persuaded him to go.'

'They boarded an American ship bound for New York, carrying cargo and a few passengers – including me,' said Rose.

'And *Straker* stopped her,' said Muir.

'She did that, Captain,' said Rose, 'stopped us, took everyone on board and then sank her – bang, just like that!'

'I still don't quite understand.'

'Ah, but there were hundreds of prisoners aboard the German ship, Captain. All kinds. Then they captured a big ship and decided to put us all on it and send us off. It was the way they did things.'

'So I gather,' said Muir. 'But you didn't go?'

'No.' Rose drained the last of her coffee.

'It *is* difficult to understand,' said Hannah. For the first time she looked directly at Muir. 'Oskar was a man who loved his country. He left it because of what he saw as his own failure. But when war broke out he kept saying he should go back and fight. I managed to persuade him that it would be foolish. Then, on board *Straker*, he changed. He felt a coward. He said that: a coward. Here are my countrymen, thousands of miles from their homes, fighting, and I am running away. This time I couldn't change his mind.'

'He asked von Bauer if he could serve on *Straker*,' said Rose. She shook her head. 'He was obsessed. I spoke to him straight: "What," I said "do you mean by leaving a wife and daughter, just like that?" And he said something about borrowing some money which meant Hannah could travel to New York, and after the war was over he would take her back to Germany and they would start again. "What does the German captain need with a cobbler?" I said. I laid it on thick. "What does a flower seller know about ships? Fighting?" It was no good. I don't think he was thinking straight, poor dear.'

'He stayed?' Muir could imagine von Bauer's reaction to the request.

'He did that,' said Rose. She looked wistfully at the empty coffee mug. 'When the time came for us all to be loaded on to the steamship, Oskar told us he was staying. Without his knowledge, Hannah here hid herself away, along with Elizabeth. It wasn't difficult, nobody was counting. And there were a few other women so our absence didn't stick out like a sore thumb. Hannah stayed, so what could I do? They found us two days later, rather we presented ourselves to them — the steamboat was too far away to turn back by then.'

'Oskar flew into a rage,' said Hannah. 'He didn't realise that, on his own, he would have been lost.'

Hannah Lange clasped her hands between her knees, forming a deep 'V' in her grimy skirt. 'He was not a good sailor, Captain. He tried, but the men were ... they were different. He shared their quarters and I hardly saw him, but I knew it was difficult for him.'

Muir didn't need to be told the tensions that were set up. A man playing at sailor with an attractive wife below deck, not to mention an equally attractive daughter, was just about as unstable a cargo as could be imagined.

'He worked in the food ... the kitchens ...'

'The galley.'

'Yes, that.' Her voice had lost even the vaguest of inflections.

'Hannah, rest yourself,' said the old woman.

Muir had the feeling that all of it was leading into a very dark alleyway the woman felt compelled to walk down. Her attitude had changed. Her hands were clenched, fingernails cutting into her palms, and even the old woman showed signs of agitation. 'Well, I sincerely hope that now all of you can put it behind ...' but things were out of his control.

'He died, Captain,' said Hannah.

'Hannah ...' Rose looked at the captain. 'One night he disappeared. Nobody knew what happened.'

Muir looked for some reaction from the young girl but, despite a feverish flush on her cheeks, she seemed composed and almost uninterested.

Hannah stood up as if there was nothing worth adding to the terrible finality of her sentence.

'I'm sorry,' repeated Muir. Dandridge was standing in the alleyway as Muir opened the cabin door.

'Show the ladies to their quarters.'

Hannah didn't look back and the girl followed, her head bowed like a penitent.

'A word in your ear, Captain.' Rose held back as they left.

'It is a very difficult situation, Rose. Perhaps only you can really help them.'

'You have heard a long story, but still only half of it. There were other things, terrible things.'

'Do you wish to tell me?'

'Not now. There has been enough.'

'Were they the reason for your hatpin, Rose?' ventured Muir.

'A moment's foolishness, Captain. No more. The captain couldn't be blamed, but ... just foolishness.'

'Then I'll ask no more questions, Rose. Save one. We have heard a lot. But nothing about you. How did you come to be aboard the American ship alone?'

'I've said – I'm an old woman. And old women are entitled to their secrets.'

'They are. But I admit to being intrigued.'

'I am flattered, Captain. And I'll let you into one little secret. Old or not – I have no intention of finishing my days on your ship. So be on your mettle, eh? I want to be buried among the green of home and not in this terrible wetness.'

'I'll do my very best, Rose,' assured Muir. 'I think we'll be all right.'

'Sure we will. Right enough.' She stood in the doorway. 'I know my way back.' Correcting a slight mis-step she sailed down the alleyway.

Muir could have sworn he smelled brandy.

The steel rope was laid out on the poop deck attached to a coir hawser made of coconut husk, light and floatable. Lashed to its end was an empty oil drum, serving as a buoy. The cable itself was connected to a capstan which, in the event of undue strain, could let it out immediately.

Slowly it was lowered over the stern, Barrow, fresh from a few hours sleep, supervising. A boat secured the drum to its side and began to make for *Straker*. Once shackled to the sailing ship, a manilla rope would be tied to the main cable to retrieve it if it came loose, and, hopefully, to control it if it snapped. That, above all else, was the thought that would be occupying every man on deck for a long time to come.

The wire lifeline consisted of six strands twisted left-handed around a jute core. Each strand, in turn, was made up of thirty smaller ones with a similar, smaller heart of jute that, like the parent core, would act as a cushion as the hawser stretched, and would squeeze out the lubricating linseed oil in which it had been soaked. If it parted at any point the dynamic power built up would crack it like a whip, capable of slicing through iron and steel with the ease of wire through cheese. There was very little on *Drummer*'s decks that could withstand such a blow and if it broke from her poop and struck *Straker*, the result might be final.

Barrow watched the boat as it neared the windjammer and Hardcastle's men began to haul the coir hawser on deck. He turned to *Drummer*'s wheelhouse. It was going to take some extraordinary seamanship.

Muir, standing alongside Offord on Monkey Island above the wheelhouse, grunted as *Straker* took the hawser. Offord had been doing his damnedest to redeem himself, but even so he was still a reminder of something that wouldn't go away. Offord, Judd, Dandridge – he had to sort them out sometime, gold or no gold. According to Bellamy, McGowan was out of danger and, compared with those around him, in the pink. Unfortunately amnesia wasn't one of the side-effects. He would have to get down to it. The thought soured him.

Offord leaned over the compass. 'Steady,' he said, into the speaking tube attached to the front of it. 'Steady,' came the voice of the quartermaster at the wheel below.

'Stop engines!'

'Stop engines, sir.' Alongside the quartermaster the telegraph was moved, relaying the order visually to Garrett in the engine room. A bell would ring four times, pausing between the first two and last two peals.

The engines throttled, *Drummer* waited.

A lamp blinked from the windjammer's bow.

Offord turned to Muir.

'Slow ahead,' said the captain.

'Slow ahead, sir.' *Drummer* made steerage way. Three knots. The hawser, oil drum cut from it, snaked across the water.

'I think we have her, sir!'

'If we don't, Lieutenant, then we have mighty problems.' Muir was watching Barrow on the poop. The Number One raised two upturned thumbs. Now, wait. Wait! They could do nothing else. The only question remaining was whether *Straker*'s weakened bow, with the hawser shackled to its anchor chain, would be ripped off.

Three minutes later, Muir began to relax. They were moving, both of them. 'Try half ahead.'

'Half ahead!' Offord barked into the speaking tube.

The hawser began to lift like a gigantic washing line. 'Keep it dipped,' said Muir.

A shudder ran the length of *Drummer* as she accepted her burden. 'Slacken off. Five knots.'

'Five knots, sir.'

The 'half ahead' had been a little rash but it was better to find out now if the tow could take more strain than wait for a storm to tell them. Muir took out his pipe. 'Well, we survived. I'll leave it to you for the moment, Lieutenant. Keep your eyes peeled and at the first sign of trouble, sing out. And keep her steady.'

'As a rock, sir.'

'Steadier.'

The British captain had given him access to von Bauer's cabin and, stretching the privilege, Mueller had taken Detweiler with him. The captain seemed pleased to see them. His old self. 'They are towing *Straker*,' he said. 'I didn't think they would care to sink her. Now the conqueror is making a ball and chain of his spoils. What condition is the ship in?'

'I have heard that the English captain is prepared to hand over the men who defied you to an English court martial,' said Mueller, avoiding the question.

'You have heard that? It could well be.'

'He has no jurisdiction!' said Detweiler angrily. 'How can it concern the English?'

'If — as you seem to believe — the English have defeated our country, Detweiler, then they have whatever jurisdiction they choose.'

'They are confused men, sir,' said Detweiler. 'Neither the lieutenant nor I support what they did, but now the situation has changed. They were good sailors for you, and,' his face hardened, 'they are Germans. They need a voice to speak for them.'

'Surely they have one? Recke.'

Detweiler was in no mood for banter. 'Talk to the English captain! Tell him!'

'Tell him what?'

'That it *wasn't* mutiny,' said Detweiler flatly. 'That it had nothing to do with the gold. They were misguided, misled, but all they wanted was an end to the slaughter.'

Von Bauer looked disparagingly at Detweiler: 'You sound in sympathy with their cause.'

'No! You know it is not that!'

Mueller was calm. 'We came to see you, sir, because we believe elements of the crew — maybe both crews — are volatile. There is an undercurrent. The gold may prove too powerful a temptation. If the men who went along with Recke believe they have no hope – face trial and almost certain execution – they may see no alternative but to . . .'

'Mutiny again? Is that what you are saying, Mueller? I think it is.'

'They form a large body of men, sir. In their eyes they would be merely freeing themselves from captivity by an enemy,' said Mueller.

'Only this time,' added Detweiler, 'they would be branded as criminals if they followed those who tried to take the gold. They are being blown backwards and forwards, sir! If they could be reassured it might prevent a bloodbath.'

Von Bauer tapped the table thoughtfully. Then: 'Very well. I will talk with the English captain. On condition that the men who mutinied – I call it that still – swear to place themselves unequivocally under my command. And Karl Recke stands trial in a German court for fomenting an uprising.'

Detweiler looked uneasily at Mueller and seemed about to speak, but Mueller gave a faint shake of the head. 'We will talk to them, sir,' he said. Saluted. 'Thank you, sir.'

Detweiler added his salute. At the end of the alleyway he broke the silence. 'Do you think they'll accept the idea of Recke as whipping-boy?'

'I don't know, Hasso. But there was no point in trying to get better terms. The captain wants to come out of this with something. He wants his power restored and he wants retribution. This way he gets both.'

'He doesn't believe the war is over, Viktor. *Won't* believe it.'

'I have a feeling he has no intention of *letting* it end,' said Mueller heavily. Suddenly: 'Do you think we are right about all this, Hasso?'

'There's *something* going on,' said Detweiler. 'I know those men and just by looking at their faces I know there's trouble blowing up.'

'Recke was as misguided as any of them,' said Mueller.

'I don't like it either, but he knew what he was doing when he took over the ship and knew the penalties if it went wrong. Anyway, it's up to the men to decide, not us. And how do we go about telling them the situation?'

'Tomorrow at noon, I will get Recke out of the way while you talk to the men below deck. They must make their decision immediately. If they agree, come back to the cabin and jointly we will detain Recke and inform him what has happened. After that it's up to Captain von Bauer.'

'Tomorrow, then,' said Detweiler. Neither of them had any enthusiasm for the coming day.

The cabin was small, but made large by their absence. Von Bauer sat on his bunk and drew his fingers beneath his eyes, teasing the sacs. He had sown the fear of a trial in the minds of Recke's men and now he would be their saviour – and again their captain. They would have every reason for unswerving loyalty in the days to come. Every reason for following him when the time came.

And when it did the English captain would have good reason to believe the war had not ended.

Frank Judd's reaction to Penn Coker's suggestion had been laughter.

Coker had somehow managed to slip down to the holds where, along with the victualling officer and four others, Judd was re-stacking supplies. Steering him away to a quiet corner, Coker had put the proposition as coolly as though offering him a part-nership in a street-corner greengrocery. Already a number of others were going along and most of the German crew didn't have any choice. The implication was there: what choice did Frank Judd have? Coker was talking about mutiny; not even provoked mutiny, but a calculated take-over. In any classified list of crime at sea not much came higher.

Judd had once worked aboard a clipper, *The Connie* out of Nantucket, under a captain and second mate who had spent the run vying as to who could be the bigger bastard. Half a dozen seamen, the rest 'Paddy Westers' with fake discharge papers: the dregs, on the run from the law or the waterfront loan sharks. A Spaniard who had argued with the second mate disappeared from a yardarm at night: another had lost his life as the result of a blow from the captain's brass knuckles. Two had committed suicide. On starvation rations, driven like dogs, the crew had tried to make representations to the skipper.

Erickson, a Norwegian, had been kicked before he could finish his sentence, falling poleaxed with a ruptured spleen. That night the crew had mutinied and the second mate was met by ten men. The mixture of loathing and fear had found its outlet in uncontrollable savagery. He was dissected by knife blades. But the captain had been ready for them. As they burst open his cabin door a shotgun had maimed half a dozen of them. The rest of the crew had fallen into line.

'They hanged the buggers,' Judd had told the tale to Coker. 'The rest of us were lucky.' Coker had shrugged. 'So stink your life away in gaol. Think about it.' Judd had. On one hand certain disaster. On the other ... The alternatives were bleak: the frying pan or the fire.

Gaol. And, if he was lucky, they would let an old man out for the last few years of 'freedom' in the nearest flophouse.

A sailor – his generation of sailor – saw life ashore as a second-hand existence, but with that same arrogance of spirit came a realisation that too much was being left behind, nothing stored for the future. Each callous was a tree's ring-knot marking the days until the tree fell. At the end, whitewashed by the sea, it left no legacy, told no stories that meant anything at all. And out of it, for some, grew a dumb treadmill mentality and, for others, a last-minute rag-picking at anything that might be salvaged.

A few – a very few – were strong enough to think it through and make provision for the time when a ship wouldn't want them and the land owed them nothing. Judd had thought it through but only when it was too late. The little he had saved was pathetically inadequate.

And then three, almost four, years ago everything had changed. One letter suggesting a meeting. It had been sent to an old boarding house where he sometimes used to room and used as his postal address, where he had found it by chance. A letter from his son. They met. The boy, twenty, was big-muscled and handsome, dressed in the uniform of the Sussex Regiment and ready to go off to war. The first time they had talked for ten years and it was a journey of discovery for both of them. Judd had married at thirty and the boy had been born one year later. Five years after that his wife had left him and gone off with an undertaker. Judd didn't blame her for going, he hadn't been able to give her much of a life – but she had taken the boy and he hadn't been given the opportunity to see him.

Judd had been at sea when the boy married and never received the invitation or knew of it until he was sent photographs of a small, bright-eyed girl named Gwen, now running their pub at Greenwich while her husband fought the good fight. He was going off to Belgium and the letter had arrived just in time. They had talked late into the night, growing closer than Judd had dared hope. And the boy had said: 'After it's over, dad, you're coming to stay with us. For good.' Judd had found it difficult to say anything, something was tugging at his throat. 'Why?' he had managed, eventually.

'Because you're my dad and never had the chance to be. Better late than never.'

It was as simple and unbelievable as that. They wrote regularly afterwards, Gwen gently admonishing him for 'messing about at sea' at an age when he should be doing something useful. She wanted him to settle down.

A month before *Drummer* had sailed, Judd had gone to see her, and it was then that he realised the future was going to be all right. But an hour before he had left to join his ship they learned that the boy had been badly injured and was being brought home. For three months and more at sea Judd had heard nothing. Then the agony came to an end in a letter transferred among the mail from a sloop that had put into Port Alegre. The injury had left one leg a little shorter than the other but, 'apart from walking a bit like you do, dad' he was fine. And out of the war, thank God.

One blow had put paid to all that. One punch.

Now did he join Coker, or did he wait for the final winding up of a life that had lost its last chance?

Judd saw only one chink of light, one possible redemption.

He made his choice.

9 *December*

The small bird lay on the deck, wings outstretched, trembling with exhaustion. Hannah Lange had almost trodden on it as she left the galley with a mug of warm lemon juice for her daughter. It was long past midnight, exactly how long past she wasn't sure. There were no stars and the moon was flickering through gaps in the low, swirling cloud, casting erratic blobs of light that seemed to originate from below the sea itself, like diver's lamps. She had been watching the sky, reminded of an opera – the only one she had ever seen – that Oskar had taken her to in Hamburg. One scene had had the whole of the backstage whirling with storm clouds, frightening and magnificent and unforgettable. She tried to summon the emotions she had felt then, but nothing came.

And the little bird had fallen like a stone at her feet. There were noises above her head. The ventilator was covered with birds, as they tried to find their balance on its smoothness. Three more tumbled, dead. The first one's wings still fluttered helplessly. She splashed a little of the warm lemon on the deck in front of it, but it seemed blind. Gently picking it up, she walked towards the wardroom, wondering where it had come from; what desperate urge had made its journey so necessary. Oskar and Elizabeth and herself had fared little better. America, Germany, South America and the promise of America again. Long, storm-tossed journeys, always full of hope, until, like the little bird, everything had crashed to the deck for them too and there was no longer the will to carry on.

She shuddered. None had fallen further than she, and *that* memory would never go away. Oskar had been a man, but now she had to forgive him for that. If he had been alive she could never have touched him again, not even he, whom she loved. Shaking the thought from her mind she crooned to the little bird. Stopped.

The man walking towards her had been caught by the moon's searchlight for a brief second. The mug fell from her hand. 'No!'

The huge, twisted face found her. Peered. Friedrich Kapper's face split into a grin, as she shrank away. 'Lovely Hannah? Is that you? Ah, it is!' He threw his arms wide in greeting. Slowly they came together and he laid his hands on her head like a priest calming doubt. 'No word for me? Remember how you talked, little woman? And now ... Nothing?'

Her body was shaking fitfully. 'No!'

'No? We have an understanding.' Kapper's voice came as near to a lilt as a wood-saw could come to a symphony. 'Soon, little woman, soon, eh?' He reached down and squeezed her breast, feeling for the nipple.

Tearing herself away she crouched against the bulkhead. With a guttural laugh he left her.

... the three women were together in their cabin. He stood in the doorway and ordered the old woman out. The door closed and only then did Hannah realise what he wanted.

'Please. My girl is sleeping. She is ill. No good for you.'

He drew back the sheet on the bunk and ran a finger from Elizabeth's throat to her navel until she shook in her sleep.

'No good! You speak English? Look!' She tore the dress from her own breasts and held them to him. 'She knows nothing a man would want. I can satisfy you. Not her!'

He turned on her and beat her quietly and methodically, lacerating her stomach with his fingernails until she squirmed, naked, across the cabin floor to escape him. She had never thought it could be so bad. Half-delirious she chanted obscenities like an exorcism, turning him from her daughter. For

127

ten minutes, or hours, she debased herself according to his needs, until he gurgled in release and she was forced to swallow his filth, knowing he was spent.

'One word and the girl is dead' was all he said as he left.

She knew, if necessary, she would do it again.

Now all that was left was for her to protect her daughter from the creatures that waited for her in the jungle.

One had to be strong. For her sake, strong.

Her hand had become sticky. The crushed bird oozed its lifeblood between the knuckles of her clenched fist.

She screamed.

Charlie Pickett had been lying on his bunk for three hours and had slept all of twenty minutes. Under the mattress was a letter that Frank Judd had given him, sealed, and bearing no name or address. 'Open it if I'm dead before we get home,' Judd had said. 'Or when I ask you to, if I live.'

It wasn't the kind of thing one slept on easily.

'The Old Man has said he wants to see me,' said Dandridge, 'but you know what just happened? I spoke to Judd. He said . . .'

'What did he say?'

'He said he had no recollection of my being anywhere near him the night of Tilley's concert. That is, *before* it. He swears the first he saw of me was when I came running after him down to the storeroom.'

'That's Judd,' said Pickett. 'And the end of the problem. Baines is out on a limb.'

'But why did he say that? He *must* remember!'

'He remembers what he chooses, Beattie. And thank your lucky stars he's on your side.'

Dandridge was walking the tiny cabin – no bigger than a locker room – that had been allotted them as Bellamy's need for space grew and he had taken over their quarters. 'I suppose he must be. And Baines . . .'

'Baines is shit,' said Pickett. He tried to change the subject, hoping they wouldn't get back to it. 'How are the women?'

'Women?'

'I don't envy you that job,' Pickett stretched back, bending his cramped toes. 'In a way.'

'It doesn't exactly come up to what you've been through, Charlie, not by a long shot.'

'To me it does. Who are they? You know? Must do.'

'Don't know much. The young girl doesn't say anything and

her mother is ... I spend most of my time topping the old lady up on brandy.'

'She's not a bad looker. And I don't mean the old woman.'

'I think she's frightened. Nice, though. A nice girl, I would say.'

'It's a bloody rum life,' said Pickett. 'Have you ever thought about it, Beattie? Sure you must have. I mean, whoever said we had any business out here anyway?' Stretching more, he crooked his hands behind his head. 'What I mean is: here we are in the middle of nowhere and all kinds of things are going on. If we weren't here none of it would have happened. That sounds daft, but it's what I'm trying to say, somehow. It's all artificial. A pile of gold slap bang in the middle of the ocean, causing all kinds of trouble, and nobody apart from us knows a damn thing about it. When it's all over what will it add up to? It doesn't add up to a scratch, really. Leastways, in five years it won't. Reckon it will?'

'Charlie, you're done in. Tired. It's not like you to have doubts. But yes, it adds up to a lot. For you more than me. If the Old Man takes it all back it'll be the marzipan on the end of the war that everyone needs. Not just us.'

'I don't get you.'

'Everybody is sick of the war, has been for years. You're sick of it, Charlie, that's why you're talking like you're talking. But even if we've won, there's going to be a let-down. What are people going to think? For four years we've been fighting and killing, triumphing over a couple of sunken ships, a few thousand men moved forward a quarter of a mile into another trench. So what do we look back on? As far as I'm concerned it leaves me with the feeling of having blundered into a madhouse where the doctors are killing the patients. That apart, it means returning to the way things were. And sweeping under the carpet men like the ones who died on your boat. A million dead, and then back to business. They'll build monuments, Charlie, and swear it'll never happen again. Not just us, the Germans too. You're right in a way, nobody will *really* remember, but they'll all pretend to. No one will remember this war like they should. They couldn't live with what they've done.'

Pickett tugged his head forward. 'You think the war was wrong?'

Dandridge paced rapidly. 'It's not what I expected, Charlie. All this killing. That must sound stupid. What else is war? I'd thought we'd missed all that, and I was glad. I haven't got the stomach for it. A little bit of metal passes through a man and he's gone – gone forever. He doesn't know why, the man who shot him doesn't know why. It's senseless and I can't come to terms with it.'

'I don't think war's meant to make sense, Beattie,' said Pickett. 'It's what happens when sense flies out of the window. It's crazy to me too, you know.'

'But you've got an anger, Charlie, deep down it's a fight and in a way that makes *some* kind of sense to you. I wish I could feel the same way. My mother was killed by a Gotha's bomb that fell on Chatham and, ever since, I've been trying to find an anger that would make me cheer when we slam a shell into a ship like *Straker*. I can't. Perhaps I'm just a coward, covering up behind words.'

'If you were, you wouldn't have said that.'

'We're swatting each other like flies,' said Dandridge doggedly.

'They swat, we swat,' said Pickett.

'Yes, I know you're right.'

'I started all this. Only difference is I just spout it, you think about it. But we're on the same course, coming from different directions. It's bloody crazy. We're in our prime, Beattie, aren't we? And yet I haven't touched a girl for a year. Haven't seen more than a dozen. Some prime!' He gave a grin, and blinked through tired eyes. 'So long that I could fall for the old woman, true I could. Now come on, let's get some kip. At least I can drea –'

The scream seemed to burn through the bulkhead.

'Christ, what was that?' Pickett leapt from his bunk, but Dandridge was already at the door, running barefooted out on deck.

'There she is!' Hannah Lange began to run away from them. 'Call her back, Beattie! She'll listen to you!'

But Beattie Dandridge didn't hear. He was running like the devil, leaving Pickett behind.

Hannah had reached the ventilator in the well deck and was scrambling across the hatch cover towards the port rail. There was no doubting her intentions. 'Christ,' muttered Pickett.

The men manning the hawser on the poop watched in amazement as the young midshipman skirted the hatch cover and threw himself at her as she grasped the rail, pinning her arms to her sides, as, shaking her head wildly, she fought to break away. He swung his head with a groan as her knee caught him between the legs, but was still holding her when Pickett reached them. The men on the poop began to clatter down the ladders.

'Charlie,' wheezed Dandridge. 'She's hysterical . . .'

Pickett hit her across the cheek, a single, stunning blow with the flat of his hand. Someone spun him away.

'What are you about!' Arnold Prettie was the first to reach them and his voice shook with outrage at what he had seen. Hannah Lange stood limply and Dandridge released her to slump down on the hatch cover clutching himself, tears of pain welling in his eyes.

'By Jesus!' said Prettie. He bunched his fists. Two men had taken hold of Pickett. 'You —'

Pickett shook his head. 'In your place I'd be thinking the same, Guns, but it's not like that. She looked about to do herself . . .'

Prettie turned. 'Dandridge?' He looked down at the midshipman's bare feet, and back at Pickett.

Muir came trotting over, a greatcoat over his pyjamas. 'What in hell's name is going on now?'

'I don't know, sir,' said Prettie grimly, 'but there was a scream and the next thing I saw was the lady running away from these two.'

Hannah Lange was staring white-faced at some private vision of horror.

'Madam?' began Muir, then, aware of the extent of her distress, turned angrily. 'Get the rest of these gawpers away from here, Guns, the lady is upset enough as it is.' Bending towards her he tried to bring himself into her focus. 'Madam? What happened? Can you tell me?'

Hannah Lange looked vacantly at Beattie Dandridge. He hadn't raised his head and a thin trail of spittle hung in small globules like early-morning dew from the corner of his mouth to the deck. Pickett froze. There was something in her expression that was dangerous. A wild light was glowing behind her eyes. Whatever had led to her terror in the first place seemed now to be finding its outlet in the form of Dandridge. She was confused, anyone could see that . . . and one wrong word . . . a woman fleeing across the deck . . . a barefoot sailor clutching his balls . . . it only needed that confusion to mislead her and . . . He stepped forward. 'Sir, she's in no state to think clearly!'

'Be quiet Pickett! When I want your advice I'll ask for it!'

Hannah Lange wiped her hand on her skirt. 'It was . . . it was a bird,' she said. 'I ran, and . . .'

'Midshipman Dandridge stopped you? Was that it? You were frightened and ran? No one has molested you?'

'No.'

Pickett swallowed a sigh of relief.

Prettie looked uncomfortable. 'Sorry about that, lad, but, well, it looked ... didn't stop to think.'

'Then I think we'd all be well off back in our quarters,' said Muir.

'I'll see to the lady, sir, if someone could give Beattie a hand,' said Pickett. To Hannah Lange: 'Thank you. It must be ...' Her eyelids fluttered and he moved forward quickly, catching her as she fainted.

A knock at the door. Or was it? She couldn't awake to open it. Noises. Someone was in the room. Elizabeth was dimly aware of voices. Whispers.

'She'll sleep now,' A man's voice. Silence. Dreams. Her mother was in the room. A man. Men.

'*No good for you, take me!*' The voice was her mother's. A memory. She heard the rustle of clothes, a mumbling. Precise now, clear.

'*Look! Do you like that?*'

'*For you.*'

'*Give it to me, let me, let me ...*'

Voices. Elizabeth twisted on the bunk. 'Look.' Her nightdress was smoothed to her throat as a hand thrust it from her stomach. 'More!' She felt the hurt and wanted more. Someone was squatting on her belly, firing her – a man with no face. 'Again!' Her hips began to move. 'No,' she said. She was on the edge of a cliff, wanting to fall, but every step forward was taking her back. 'Pleeeaase!'

'My darling.' A hand touched her forehead, sweeping across it. She couldn't breathe. 'Elizabeth?'

Hannah crouched by her daughter, awakened from her stupor by her cries. Rose stood behind her.

'A nightmare,' said the old woman.

'All of it is a nightmare!' Hannah bit her knuckles.

'Sleep,' said Rose.

'How can I sleep?' wailed Hannah.

'You will.' Rose poured her a glass of brandy. 'Drink this.' She traced the smear of blood down Hannah's dress. 'What has happened?'

'Nothing.'

'You have been out on deck? Why?'

'Has somebody ...'

'Nobody. Nobody.' Hannah allowed herself to be led back to her bunk and Rose saw that she swallowed the brandy. For ten minutes she held Hannah's hand until she was asleep and then looked across at the girl. 'Elizabeth?' There was no response. Her breathing was heavy and laboured. Kneeling by the bunk Rose placed a finger against the girl's temple and the poison began to bleed through her, shaking her with the effort. Never again, she had once vowed: there was evil in hindering God's will. But a little boy had walked once more; an old man's arm, once locked, had moved; a sick baby had been made well. Who could understand it? She was an old, drunken woman and, despite what they had once said in the village, no saint.

She took her finger from Elizabeth's temple and felt the pulse at her wrist. It was calm, as she knew it would be.

10 December

Holding a clandestine meeting aboard a ship such as *Drummer* was as practicable as seeking privacy in the middle of a dance floor. There was little unoccupied space and, in addition, each man's day was broken into watches, beginning with Middle (midnight to 4 a.m.), Morning, Forenoon, Afternoon (all of four hours), First Dog and Last Dog (two hours) and First (8 p.m. to midnight). Every minute of the working day was accounted for and supervised. Watch below was used for snatching sleep, mending clothes, writing letters.

It was a formidable barrier that prevented any group of disaffected men from bolstering each other's grievances. Aware of this, Penn Coker had known they would have to take a chance. The recruitment of men could only be accomplished at an individual level, with the possibility that, at the last moment, they might back out. There could be no mass meetings. Even so, the organisation had to be perfect and for that it was essential the prime movers got together. He had managed to slip away from duty, as had Baines, and with luck their absence might go unnoticed – for a while. But every minute was vital. Along with Kapper and Recke they were hunched in the alleyway leading to the mess. It was three in the morning.

Kapper began. 'At least twenty-four men. I am certain.' The dim oil lamp Baines was holding threw the huge German's face into a Neanderthal relief of shades and highlights.

'I reckon on eight to ten,' said Coker. 'Cast iron.'

Kapper looked puzzled.

'Certain.'

'Ah. Good.' Kapper looked at Recke. 'Our men will be listening to you, Recke. Impress upon them that there is no going back.'

Recke looked about to speak, but merely shrugged.

'You have doubts?'

'I am to blame for the situation they are in,' he said gloomily. 'They followed me and now it seems for that they could be shot, at the very least imprisoned. I owe something to them.'

'Yes. In the eyes of both captains they have already mutinied. Whatever they do now makes no difference to them,' said Kapper. 'You talk about a "revolution", I shall give it to you. The gold is a symbol of what none of us – them – could ever hope for, because they have been kept in their place. The swines who mined it got nothing either. Hand it over to the boss, and make his fortune for him! If we take it, it is a blow to the very people you despise.'

Coker sensed Kapper was urging Recke to become totally committed. 'Revolution or whatever you want to call it, we're on our way,' he said. 'Any messing about and the whole thing goes off at half cock. It's too late for second thoughts.'

'Probably half his fugging relations are English, anyway,' said Baines obscurely. 'Look at the Royals – all bloody Germans. Battensomething . . .'

'I'll do what I can,' said Recke.

'Right. Then we move at the end of the morning watch,' said Coker. Kapper looked at him sharply. 'We *need* to move fast! As yet we have no guns, but that needn't matter. First we take the two 4.7s and disarm any of the crew on guard duty. You got the knives?'

Kapper nodded. Despite the original search of the German sailors on *Straker*, many of them had managed to retain their knives. They had been taken from them on *Drummer* and, in the mêlée, had been left in a heap on the deck. An enterprising German sailor had scooped up a dozen of them with an aim to selling them later. Now they would be put to better use.

'We cannot take the ship with knives alone,' said Kapper.

'I know!' Coker was impatient. 'We're not going to leap around the sodding deck stabbing everyone to death! What we need is another of Recke's sit-downs. Listen. Get them over the well deck forrard, same as before, and cause a lot of row. I want Muir and Barrow down there. Take them and we take the ship. One knife is all it needs.'

Kapper looked at him slyly. 'That is *half* right. We think the same. But you underestimate your captain, as we underestimated von Bauer. You think a knife at his throat will stop him calling on his crew to demolish us? No, I don't think that will happen. And we would be left with two dead men and no ship. He knows he would only be useful alive. The bluff would be in his hands, not ours.'

'He's right,' said Recke. For the past few minutes he had been wondering about Kapper. Nothing the man had said or done in the past two years had given an indication of anything but a simple low-grade intelligence. He was an ox, not easily shackled, maybe, but fundamentally incapable of responding to anything but the most basic urges. Felix Sandel had once said that Kapper was the only man he had ever met whose muscles gave orders to his brain. But now, on the verge of the most momentous and monstrous event in his life, it was if something had been stimulated that had been lying dormant until now. It made him even more chilling. Coker seemed to be keeping something in reserve, giving Kapper rein.

'So what do you have in mind, big man?' asked Coker.

'You play cards? The ace. You put it — the ace up the sleeve?'

He began to spell it out.

'Oh, hell and damnation,' murmured Barrow as he looked down from the bridge. He tipped his cap back in despair. From out of nowhere men had suddenly emerged and begun to sit down on the hatch covers.

A matinée performance.

The tow was going well and the long-threatened storm was still playing ducks and drakes. They had been making good way and he had begun to feel that perhaps it might still all work out well.

'Hold her steady,' he said to the helmsman.

Muir was at his desk with a calendar and countless scraps of scribbled-upon paper. Barrow held his hands wide: 'The carnival as before, sir. Some of the German crew are on deck. I suppose this time they are missing their schnapps. I think we're going to have to put a few of them in jankers before they see sense.'

'Is this that bugger von Bauer's doing?'

'I don't see how it can be, sir. But then, who knows? The guard are at a disadvantage — they obviously can't *shoot* them, but they get no response to threats. Only thing we can do is drag them below and keep them on hard rations until they stop playing up.'

Muir gave a hiss of breath. 'He's fighting me, Number One,

I feel it in my bones. Somehow all this is tied up with von Bauer, don't ask me how. I'm going there. He'd fed his men with something before they even set foot on *Drummer* and we're reaping it now. You know he lied through his teeth in front of me last time this happened? Well, no more! I'm going to root it out, by thunder I am!'

He walked down to the deck trying to contain his rage. Von Bauer had struck a pose from the very beginning. He, Muir, was the third-rate skipper of a tramp for whom an aristocrat on his sailing boat didn't choose to bow his head. Well, this time he'd learn who won the damn war! He stalked across to the well deck and for the second time faced the squatting men.

'Right! Get up! NOW!' he boomed. 'Barrow, where are you? Get the guard over here and when I say wade in ...' Someone brushed his side. 'Barrow, move ...'

But it wasn't Barrow. Penn Coker stood at his shoulder. 'Very still, Captain. Very still. I have a knife against your side.'

The words didn't register. Muir half turned and Coker grasped his arm. 'No, Captain.' The knife had been worked through Muir's jacket and was touching the flesh below his rib cage.

'Are you mad? What is this?'

A number of *Drummer*'s crew stood idly around, unaware of what was happening.

'We have the guns,' said Coker, looking quickly for confirmation. Both 4.7s were pointing inwards, the forrard one at the bridge.

'For what? Put that knife away and you'll be treated decently, sailor. If not, I warn you ...' he stepped to one side, no more than half a pace, hindered by Coker's grip. Barrow was standing below the bridge, two Germans on either side of him. 'Your last chance, sailor. Put it away. Very well, I suggest you use it, and use it rapidly, it'll be the last thing you do out of irons.' Muir jerked a head at the armed guard standing around the deck. 'Arrest these men and open fire if they resist!' he shouted. 'Do as I order!'

Suddenly aware, the guard lifted their rifles.

'Muir!' Kapper's voice was a howl. He was standing by the wardroom and pushing the three women in front of him. 'It is over! Tell those men to lower their guns and throw them on the deck. I have a bayonet at the girl's back.'

'Don't think he's bullshitting,' said Coker. 'If it was his mother he wouldn't hesitate.' He stuffed his knife into his belt. One up to Kapper. In the end they had compromised, using both plans – but the German's assessment of Muir had been sharp.

Muir began to walk towards Kapper and the women, and Coker grabbed him. 'Don't be a madman! If you want three dead women on your conscience keep walking. But one more step and I'll lay you out personally. For their sake!'

'You seriously think you can get away with this?' Muir stared at the women and then back at Coker.

'Just give your orders, Captain. Guns on the deck. We aren't going to wait.'

Not a shot had been fired. Prettie's guns had been taken under the sheer force of shock alone. The men on the poop faced an assortment of knives, and Baines was on the bridge. Garrett, in the engine room, had been slammed against a bulkhead, searched, and told to get on with his job. Charlie Pickett and Dandridge were tipped from their bunks and frogmarched on deck. Tilley, at the end of his watch, had been gratuitously kicked and hurled headlong into the scuppers by a man he had once played checkers with. There was only one man left aboard *Drummer* who was not aware of what had happened.

Karl Recke knocked on the cabin door and waited, holding his pistol at his side. It opened and von Bauer stood there dishevelled, dressed in a long red nightgown.

'Stand back, Captain,' said Recke. 'Back into the cabin. I am armed.'

Von Bauer was immediately awake.

'Sit down.'

'If you intend to kill me, Recke, then I would prefer it to occur while I was standing.' He appeared to have grasped exactly what had happened and displayed no confusion. 'The attitude of my body can be of little importance. Well?'

'I am not here to shoot you, Captain, merely to inform you that *Drummer* has been taken from the charge of the English captain and this time you will do as we say.'

'Incredible.' Von Bauer sat down. 'Unique. To mutiny against *two* captains, *two* navies. Whatever happens, Recke, you will cheat one or the other – they cannot hang you twice!'

'*Drummer* will stay taken,' said Recke doggedly.

'In the name of the "revolution"?'

'In the name of the men.'

'Ah. A subtle difference. And the gold? Assuming you manage to avoid the British Navy – unlikely, but assuming you do – I suppose it will be donated to the poor and the fatherless,

the sick and the dispossessed? Is that what will happen, Recke?'
There was no attempt to lighten the sarcasm.

Recke flushed angrily. 'I am not interested in the gold, Captain! It will not drive me to kill men for its sake, as it drove you!'

It was von Bauer's turn to feel the barb. 'And your colleagues feel the same?'

'They are entitled to their own thoughts. I have mine. They coincide on one point: I will not have the men who followed me put on trial for what was a political act that is no concern of the English. The captain of *Drummer* has been pig-headed and it is he who has led to this.'

'Why are you telling me all this, Recke?' Von Bauer's face was pale.

'Because, Captain, I want you to know that the uprising on *Straker* had nothing to do with the gold she was carrying. Do you believe me now?'

'Now less than ever.'

'Can you not see that other motives *can* exist? That you have no divine right, Captain? All your life you have believed that the von Bauers of this world are the only ones capable of judgement. Anyone who goes against that judgement, by his very opposition, is marked as being corrupt, misguided and ... yes ... *ungrateful.* You can not understand why and how men, of their own free will, had the right to take power from you. It is long overdue. These men and men like them have been kept "in their place" for so long that they began to believe in their own subservience, like dogs grateful for a bone and thankful for a collar if that is the means toward obtaining one. Their livelihood could be taken from them and they would be thrown on a human scrap-heap.' Recke lowered his voice. 'I am not a fanatic, Captain. I simply want you to acknowledge the situation. If you will do that, then there still may be something to be gained from all this.'

Von Bauer turned in his chair so that Recke was unable to see his face. 'There is an order to things, Recke, as you will discover when you try to run this ship. Who is captain now? There *has* to be one. You do not have ...' he tried to rise. Collapsed in the chair, his head falling back to display a face running with sweat. His tongue slid from his mouth.

'Captain?' Recke cupped von Bauer's head in both hands. 'Is it your heart? Can you speak?'

Van Bauer was trembling violently. 'My case ...'

'This?' Recke pulled across the small briefcase from beside the bunk, and opened it.

Von Bauer fumbled awkwardly, and took out a small sachet of powder. 'Mix it ... put it ...' he tried to hold a small bottle in his other hand.

Recke unscrewed it. Alcohol. He tipped the powder into it and shook it.

'Now ...' Von Bauer hugged his arms to his sides to ease the trembling and managed to pour the contents into a syringe. Drawing back the sleeves of his nightgown, he plunged the needle into his forearm, and lay back.

'For God's sake, what is it?'

'A ... pain ... killing ... it is passing ... will pass.' Some of the liquid had stained his nightgown.

'Your injury?' Everyone had heard of the captain's wound at Jutland – the reason for his laboured walk.

Von Bauer massaged the back of his neck. 'A fragment chipped from the bone, here. Now it is crumbling, crushing the nerve. At times it is painful. Eventually it will mean paralysis.' He sat up, his eyes unclouded. 'It has gone.'

Recke took the syringe and placed it back in the case. On reflection, he took it out again. 'It needs to be cleaned?'

'Leave it, I know the way.'

'What is it?'

'A powder. A ...' Von Bauer seemed reluctant to elaborate.

Recke knew it could only be opium. It explained everything about the captain's secret 'drinking'.

'How often, Captain? The pain?'

'Rarely.'

He was lying. 'We will perhaps talk some other time, Captain.'

But von Bauer checked his departure with a raised hand. 'Recke, is the ship taken by Germans only? Our own people?'

'No, there are English too.'

'Then it might not be too late.' Von Bauer's voice had found its strength.

'They will not take orders from you, Captain,' said Recke, exasperated by the man's intractibility. 'You have no control. You said you could take the lieutenant hostage and it failed. I could have delivered *you* to *them*, but instead went along with you. I was a fool!'

'Things went wrong, Recke. Tell me, the men who have taken the ship, are they the men who followed you on *Straker*?'

'There is a core of villains. The men who, as you put it,

"followed me" have no alternative but to join them, if they value their freedom.'

'You have been misled, Recke. The English captain had no intention of arraigning your men.'

'What?'

'Fear was the only way I could hope to wean them away from you. In law the English captain cannot do anything and the English follow the law as the gosling follows the goose. If "your" men had stood behind *me* there would have been an uprising on *Drummer*, but a very different one to yours. Ironically, you have shown it *could* have succeeded. It would have been in the name of the Imperial Germany Navy – not in the name of greed.'

Karl Recke fumbled for a reply. 'You have thrown a net over us all,' he managed, eventually. 'If we had known . . . then . . .'

'Then you would not be in the hands of criminals – surely you must agree this time they *are* criminals?' said von Bauer. 'Your "revolution" has led you into deep water, Recke. And still I am the only one who can save you all from drowning. You will come to realise that.'

'Is this the lot?' shouted Penn Coker, standing, legs braced, on the foredeck with a Lee Enfield tucked under his arm. The armoury in the chartroom had yielded twenty weapons, none less than ten years old, but all capable of serving their purpose. Baines, similarly equipped, stood outside the wheelhouse smoking a cigar.

Every member of *Drummer*'s crew who had not been among Coker or Kapper's 'selection' had been lined up on deck beneath the open arms of the derrick. Only the sick had been left in peace.

'The tables are turned well, eh?' said a jubilant Kapper.

Coker had the look of a man who distrusted good fortune. 'Fuck the tables,' he said. 'Let's get this finished properly and then we might think about how we spend Christmas.'

Kapper shrugged and faced the men, speaking loudly in German. There was an undercurrent of mumbling and five of them got to their feet.

'You get the general idea,' said Coker to the rest. 'You can be either with us or against us. Now's the time to make your choice. It doesn't matter a bugger to me – it might to you.'

Four men stood up.

'That the lot?' He looked pointedly at Frank Judd, sitting with his back against the winch. 'A test of strength, Judd?'

'Well, I've been thinking, Coker. And maybe a little bit of sun, a little bit of fun and some cash is better than I got at the moment.' He pulled himself to his feet and stretched himself.

Muir, Barrow, Offord and the rest of the officers had been lined up in front of the wardroom. Barrow shook his head. 'This isn't Judd's pitch, Captain,' he said. 'He's being driven into it.' Raising his voice: 'Judd, don't be a fool!'

'Shut that bastard up,' spat Coker. Barrow was thrown to the deck by two of the Germans. 'Next one to speak out of turn gets this,' added Coker, raising his rifle. 'Right, the rest of you, get moving. I want Garrett kept on board along with the rest on the list.'

'And *you*!' said Kapper, pointing to where Pickett and Dandridge were standing. Baines leaned forward from the bridge, gave a grin and disappeared with a chortle.

'I need a steward,' said Kapper.

Pickett tugged at Dandridge's sleeve, and stepped forward. 'I make better coffee than you,' he whispered.

Coker had complete control, rattling off orders as if he had spent a lifetime doing nothing else.

'Officer material,' muttered Barrow sardonically, brushing himself down.

Those who hadn't chosen to join Coker were prodded towards the waiting boats. 'Now, then,' Coker jerked a thumb at the yeoman and led him to the rail. 'Get it right and dead right.'

Yeoman Hollis's hand shook as he held the lamp. He looked at the piece of paper Coker was holding in front of him, read it through quickly and began to signal. It was a long message, but he repeated it, imagining what Hardcastle would be feeling on the receiving end.

'Finished?'

'Yes.' Respectfully: 'Sir.'

When the reply came he dictated it directly, dispensing with the signal pad. 'We understand and must accept.'

Coker nodded. 'Hardcastle's no fool. Now you get back with the rest.' As Hollis scampered off, he strode forrard. Baines had come down from the bridge. 'Get these men out of here right away, there'll be no trouble *Straker*'s end.' Facing Muir: 'You little lot go last. Now let me just put you clear, Muir. There'll be no guard on *Straker*, because we don't need one. You'll do exactly as we order otherwise the buggers we're keeping here — Bellamy, Prettie, Garrett, the rest, will be put over the side. And I don't mean in a boat. Two: there's nowhere you can go in that tub, even if the tow breaks, but if you get any fancy ideas, forget them now. You'll be given enough food and water for a week. One week. If you behave yourselves you'll get some more next week. I don't have to explain that without water you'll last four days. And if you starve to death, that'll be *your* fault, Muir.'

'May I ask where you hope to land?'

'No. You listen from here on in.' A thought struck him and he called across to Kapper. 'Where's Recke and that mad bloody captain? Get them down here and stick him on a boat – he's the last one I need on this lash-up!'

Kapper waved a hand.

'Everything clear?'

'It couldn't be clearer,' said Barrow.

'There is one thing,' said Muir. 'What is to happen to the ladies?'

It was obviously a question Coker hadn't catered for. Confused, he walked back to Kapper and the two began to talk animatedly – the beginnings of an argument.

'I suspect,' said Barrow, 'that this might well be a stormy partnership.'

'We can only hope so,' said Muir. The women were beginning to worry him. 'Is Bellamy around?'

'In the sick bay. He's staying aboard *Drummer* from what Coker implied.'

'Then get him. Quickly, while they're talking.' Prettie slid away before he had finished.

'This is a joint deal,' Kapper waved a finger in Coker's face.

'Women on a ship are bad luck and bad sense,' said Coker. 'Trouble.'

'No trouble. I will see they are no trouble.'

'Shit to that! Half these bastards will be slicing each other apart to get at them before the day's out. No.'

Kapper drew himself to his full height: 'I want them to stay.'

'Coker!' Muir was now certain as to what was going on. He called again.

Coker stared at him as if contemplating murder – whose was uncertain. Muir searched for some vague rapport. Bellamy had been found and knew exactly what was wanted of him; all it needed was Coker to read between the lines.

'Get in those bloody boats!'

'Coker, it's about the women. Something you should hear.'

'There's nothing you ...' Coker broke off. Muir's eyes hadn't flickered. 'C'mon over here.'

Bellamy's angular frame accompanied Muir across to the two men. 'Tell them,' said Muir. He readjusted his cap.

Bellamy twirled a hand. When he spoke, his tone was detached, befitting someone reciting facts over which he had no control. 'Yesterday I reported to Captain Muir that, in my opinion, the young girl, Elizabeth Lange, has pulmonary tuberculosis, transmittable by breath and sputum – spittle. I further advocated that she should be isolated. There is every chance that the two other women are infected too, though I have had no chance to confirm this. However, I cannot see, living in such proximity, that it is possible for them to escape it. It remains, medically, conjecture . . .'

'What is he saying?' Kapper was at a loss to follow the surgeon's mannered style.

'They've got something,' said Coker succinctly. 'He's saying they've got some bloody disease. What did I tell you : trouble.'

'I think you understand when I say that, needing isolation, they will not be isolated for long on this ship,' said Muir pointedly.

Kapper shrugged : 'A little sickness . . .'

Bellamy looked at him as if examining the contents of a specimen jar. 'It begins with a wasting away. You have seen how thin the girl is. You . . .' he stressed the word '*you* cannot eat. Breathing becomes difficult. You may not have heard her breathing. Part of her lung is not working. She will lose first the will to live and then the ability to live. There will be no air reaching her lungs. It is most distressing, and I will do my best to give her drugs that will help her.'

Kapper had been listening intently. Like so many big men who shrugged off the hardest of physical punishment, the thought of an unseen decay eating away from the inside was anathema. He wiped his mouth with the back of his hand.

'In that case, Kapper,' said Coker, 'if you still want them aboard then they're in your bloody cabin! And put that to Recke's vote! Do you realise what would happen if whatever she's got went through this ship?'

'Aaach!' Kapper shrugged again. Uneasily.

Bellamy drove in the nail : 'Whatever has happened on this ship is incidental at the moment. I am here first and foremost to keep men alive. Do you understand that? You would be extremely foolish not to allow me to examine every member of the crew. It needs only one man who has come into close contact with one of these women and there is no real treatment I can give once it has taken hold.'

'Do what you want!' Kapper's voice was hoarse. With a curse he turned and walked away.

Coker regarded Bellamy and Muir, his eyes moving between them. When he eventually spoke the words seemed to be coming directly from his throat, by-passing his lips. 'Get the women on the boat. You're a lying bastard, Bellamy.'

He waved them away.

Even when the last boats emptied their passengers onto *Straker*, Hardcastle still didn't seem to have grasped completely what was happening or what had happened. Barrow gave him a brief resumé.

'And they're leaving us, no guard or anything?' said Hardcastle. Ten of the mutineers had been aboard and, with unrestrained delight, had vandalised the main guns and taken back to *Drummer* the rifles from the armoury.

'They don't have to have a guard,' answered the first lieutenant.

Hardcastle thought about it for a moment: 'No, I suppose they don't. They seem to have put a bit of thought into it, then?'

'They've put a lot of thought, I would say. Apart from what happens if we meet a British ship.'

'You think we might?'

'No,' admitted Barrow. 'They'll be looking for somewhere to land, and that means turning back to South America. We don't have any ships in those waters.'

Muir had said little since coming aboard *Straker*, except to convene a meeting of the senior officers at midday. Barrow could imagine what the Old Man was feeling: for one glorious moment everything had been tight in his palm. Without doubt he would have been a popular hero on his return to England – bloody combat, hazardous voyage, the capture of one of Germany's top fighting captains and, above all, the gold. By the time *War Illustrated* and the newspapers had finished with it, they'd be singing about him on the music halls. Now – nothing. And, perhaps, the only man who could fully share the irony was the very captain he had defeated.

'Reckon we'd better be going in,' said Hardcastle. 'Nigh on time.' The acting coxswain's experience of handling *Straker* was the reason for his presence; Muir didn't want to rely on German knowledge alone.

'How do you feel about it now?' asked Barrow. 'The saloon, I mean?'

'Oh, that, sir? Strange, I dunno. But, soon as you opened the door, looking at the table and the rest, it gave me the creeps. He was up to something. Never felt like it before. Like the Last Supper. Sorry, sir, did you think I acted a bit daft?'

'Not at all. From the way von Bauer took it I'd say he was up to something. Still, this time it's the Old Man in there – so grit your teeth and on you go.'

Muir and von Bauer were already waiting, seated at opposite ends of the saloon's polished Brazilian rosewood table like joint chairmen about to announce the winding up of their company. The room was sumptuously furnished in Second Empire style : a plush velvet sofa, two half tables of darkened pear wood with mother of pearl inlay, revolving bookcases, oil paintings. In the centre of the table stood a splendid crystal water jug and glasses. Muir waved the two men to their seats. Mueller and Detweiler filed in behind and, for a moment, the six of them sat in silence. It was a fascinating situation, Barrow was thinking, as he waited for one of the captains to make a move. Who exactly *could* claim to be *Straker*'s commanding officer now? Muir had to be very quick on his feet if he was to keep the little edge he had. His opening words left no doubt that he was well aware of the fact.

'First of all, gentlemen, before we settle down to discuss the predicament and what may be salvaged from it, I would like to deal with something that can only fester if not brought out into the open and sorted out now.' He looked directly at von Bauer and the German stared back, unblinking. Hardcastle began to gnaw his bottom lip, concentrating on von Bauer's fogged reflection in the table top.

'Every ship needs a captain,' said Muir crisply. 'But there is a saying that no ship can have two. At this moment there must be discipline if *Straker* is not to become a ragged, dispirited collection of disorganised men. If that were to happen we would be finally lost. I'm sure all of you would agree with the plain common sense of that.'

Nobody disagreed.

'By dint of battle I took command of *Straker* and her crew. Command of *Drummer* has been – I believe temporarily – taken from me by an act of mutiny. I am still her captain. And, consequently, I am still in command of this ship which, in spite of everything that has taken place, is still a prize of His Majesty's Navy.' He sat back in his seat. 'Comments?'

'It is an interesting argument, Captain,' said von Bauer after an age.

'A fact, Captain. The circumstances are extreme, the facts simple and clear.' He reached for the jug and splashed water into a glass. 'Of course, I depend on your co-operation and advice. All of you. It is imperative we work in harmony.'

Von Bauer had still not shown any clear reaction and Mueller, as if prompting him, slid the water jug down the table.

'To what end, Captain?' the German captain asked suddenly, frowning.

'What?'

'To work in harmony for what end? As I have said, your argument is interesting, but more immediately interesting is the fact that you consider we have any say in what happens to us. That intrigues me. To be commander of a ship that has no independence is something of a phantom role. A man blindfolded and bound and placed back to front on a horse can hardly be in a position to think of himself as a jockey? Please go on.'

Neat and witty. But that was all. Barrow knew that the moment had passed and the German was already accepting the fait accompli. He could see from their expressions that Mueller and Detweiler knew it too. They looked relieved. Even so, their captain had again acted too rapidly for Barrow's peace of mind, as if impatient to dismiss a scenario that he had already worked out an hour before.

Muir sipped his water. 'In reply, Captain, all I can say is that, no matter how hopeless things seem, we must do *something*. *Straker* must be made properly seaworthy, whatever sails can be mended or replaced worked on below deck. The auxiliary seen to. Guns examined. It may not be as bad as we assume.'

'And then?' said Mueller. 'Then?' He shook his head.

'Then we see,' said Muir bluntly. 'You have had *two* defeats, Lieutenant – and I mean that in no derogatory way. But you are all weary. I have had one, call it "defeat", and am a little weary too – not as much as you.' Despite the calm in his voice, there was an obvious undercurrent of excitement that was brushing aside all the impossibilities. He was, thought Barrow, bloody well enjoying himself!

'Why not!' Hardcastle slammed a palm on the table and water jumped from Muir's glass, trickling like quicksilver across the polish. 'What have we got to lose? For one, I'd sooner put up a show than sit here twiddling our pinkies waiting until . . . until . . .' he fell silent, the final word hanging like a sword. 'Sorry, sir.'

Von Bauer stood up and walked the width of the saloon. 'They will make for the coast. With the wealth they have here on *Straker* they know it is possible to bribe enough people to spirit them away. Before that happens they will have to kill us all, of that there is no question. There can be no witnesses.' He turned from the panelled wall. 'You are a man who likes challenge, Captain. I have, on occasion, found it stimulating too. But – in principle – I accept what you say.' He took in Mueller and Detweiler. They nodded.

'Thank you,' said Muir, making no attempt to hide his relief. 'Now we have twice the strength.'

The sparring was over. For the moment.

At the saloon door Barrow turned to see Muir and von Bauer in deep conversation. The German captain, dwarfed alongside his counterpart, was enumerating points one by one on the fingers of his left hand, like a lawyer running through his scoring points before entering court.

'Well, the Old Man laid down the law all right,' said Hardcastle. 'Even got me thinking we might have a chance, bugger his socks!'

'I wonder,' said Barrow.

'Eh?'

'Nothing. I was thinking about von Bauer.'

'Don't think he'll be any more trouble,' said Hardcastle.

Barrow inclined his head: 'I hope you're right. But I'd take insurance against it.'

Evening fell, slab-banked clouds dark as the inside of a coffin lid lowering over the two ships. Neither of them was showing more than the bare minimum of lights and, to Tilley, crouched on the foredeck with a slush-bucket of linseed oil, it seemed as if the bobbing shape of *Drummer* was pulling away, disappearing into the gloom. A trick of the light. The steel hawser, tight on the anchor chain, left no doubt of that. He sloshed linseed over it. The jib boom had been smashed away by a shell, leaving only the stump of the bowsprit sticking forward like a finger amputated at the first joint. Bobstays and backstays trailed from the still-intact dolphin striker that dipped towards the rake of the bow. *Straker*'s hull was steel, but that alone didn't offer many guarantees. A few bad waves – when were they going to come? – could pile on enough tension to tear the plates apart like a sardine can being opened. Everyone worried about the hawser snapping – if the damn thing *didn't* snap in a blow then *Straker* could be torn in half.

Tilley was left with a mental picture of himself clutching the steel rope and being towed like shark bait in *Drummer*'s wake. One needed a sense of humour.

'I don't know who's the worse off.' Beattie Dandridge had

finished his nursemaiding for the night, but, unable to sleep had needed to talk. 'What do you think is going on out there ... Tilley?' It was the first time he had ever used Morris Wylie's nickname, though Charlie Pickett and everybody else did. Dandridge wasn't even sure what it meant, but now anything else would hardly have opened a conversation. It was a gesture. Tilley knew exactly what it was.

'They'll be all right,' he said. 'They wouldn't have kept them on if they didn't need them and if they need them then they're not going to knock them about.'

'I suppose you're right. I was thinking about Charlie. Charlie Pickett.'

'Mr Pickett, I gather, is going to be where the grub is, and I don't reckon that fact will pass him by.'

'No, I don't think that's why ...' Dandridge began.

'He's not a bad lad,' said Tilley.

There was a long, awkward silence. They watched the rolling ship in the enveloping darkness.

'Funny,' said Tilley. 'See now – all you can make out clearly are the derricks and the funnel.'

'Funny?'

'Wrong word. What I'm getting at is ... look again ... what's it like?'

Dandridge studied the swinging boom, just making out the topping lift and guy pendants. 'An insect? I don't know.'

'A gallows,' said Tilley. 'You know why they're called "derricks"? After a Tyburn hangman. Two hanging trees, fore and aft. What could be more appropriate? Plan was to take them down, but the Old Man said no. Reckon he's a bit of a raider himself.' He gave a little laugh. 'Funny.'

'Yes. I see.' Dandridge looked for somewhere to sit, and, finding nothing, crouched on his haunches. Tilley was squatting, one leg bent neatly under another like a gipsy fiddler.

'Tilley, you're an educated man,' Dandridge shook his head at the response. 'You *are*. It makes no difference where the education came from – but you've seen a lot of things, a lot of people – more than I'll ever see.' He was doing it again : foisting his problems on to others. After he had spoken to Charlie Pickett he had vowed he would never do it again. He would come to terms with it himself. But he couldn't. It was too much to be, alone, both the accused and the inquisition.

Tilley guessed what was on the young boy's mind. He had told Charlie Pickett of the disgusting ordeal in the mess, hoping he would be better equipped, as a youngster too, to talk with

Dandridge when the inevitable storm broke. He also knew that the most difficult thing in the world was to convince a man his 'illness' was imaginary, whether in the mind or body.

'Tilley ...' said Dandridge. 'You must know, people talk ...' He would have it out. Now.

'Well, sir ...'

'Beattie.'

'As you say ... Beattie ...' went on Tilley, swilling the linseed in the bucket, 'I've seen a lot of things. Nothing much like what's been going on for the past few days, but, yes, I know the men, the life. Don't know any other, come to think about it. Maybe that's what you mean by "education". I've managed to read a bit too, here and there. A scrappy kind o' learning, no better than any sailor's.' He sniffed and spat out the taste of oil.

'Go on. Please.'

'Ramblings. Let's just say that one thing I've learned is that if you can depend on anything it's that the world is waiting round a corner to hit you on the head.' He laughed. 'Most times it hits you with a big, fat balloon, but, like a pimple in the mouth, it feels large as a house and twice as heavy. It all depends on what you're expecting – sometimes on what you feel you deserve.' He tapped his temple. 'We're all a bit cracked, one way or the other.' He looked at Dandridge. 'Things happen, son,' he said softly. 'Good and bad. If they didn't we wouldn't know we were alive. And how bad is bad? Who knows? Never as bad as it seems.' He tugged off his woollen hat.

Dandridge recoiled, stubbing a hand behind to stop himself tumbling backwards. Tilley's head was virtually hairless, his scalp burned or scalded in black and ochre patches, some weeping a thin fluid.

'You see, Beattie, we all have our problems; even the old 'uns who have been through it all are as vulnerable as the rest.'

'God! What ... what happened?'

'Baines,' said Tilley evenly. 'It could only have been Baines. He changed my ointment, put something in it – cooking soda, an acid from the sick bay – it doesn't matter. He went to a lot of trouble.'

Dandridge stood up, clenching his fists. 'Why? Why?'

'Because that is what happens,' said Tilley. 'It'll pass, be forgotten. But only if *I* forget it. Baines already has. Gone on to greater things.'

'If you had spoken to the captain, told him ...'

'Nooo! Where would that have led? You see, Beattie, that would be Baines's strength. I can rob him of it only by despising and forgetting him. It sounds like weakness – it certainly isn't forgiveness. Do the same. Shake your head and wonder, but don't ever despair. When you do that, the likes of you and me have lost and *they* have won. D'you see what I mean?'

Dandridge looked down at Tilley stirring his slosh-bucket, his cap covering his pain. 'I do see. I think I do.' Impulsively he bent and grasped Tilley's free hand. Shook it. Too full for anything more, he walked away.

Tilley stared into the dark. Christ, the air had made it itch! Smearing a dab of linseed on to his finger he teased it under his cap. If it worked for hawsers . . .

'Oh, dear.' He sighed, shifting himself into a different uncomfortable position. How many times had he heard it himself? Seamen, like country folk and quack doctors, made up their makeshift philosophy on the basis of homilies and home-spun sermons. A herbal for the mind, using anything that came to hand.

Crazy Tilley, giving his advice on the world and its ways. A world which, he was convinced more than ever, was venal and mad.

11 December

A ship without sails; a bird without wings. Muir, having completed his first full inspection of *Straker*, stood on the poop deck looking forward over a scene of furtive industry. Stripped to their waists, bodies glistening with sweat, the watch moved among a riot of huge wooden lift-blocks, tackles, chain slings, jack-pins, sheaves and pulleys. Spars that could be salvaged from the destruction had been lashed to the deck, along with spares brought from below. The splintered mainmast had been cut from the ship's side. Of the major sails left, the mizzen and fore clew garnetts hung in scorched but possibly stitchable tatters. as did those above them. The topsails had been furled, and *Straker* was making no headway of her own and taking the sea badly. She was down at the head which meant, probably, a leak somewhere, though as yet no one had been able to find it. Muir's guess was that water had gone down the hawse pipe and was, invisibly, seeping among the wood ostensibly carried as cargo in the forrard hold. That would have to be looked at too. The wireless transmitter was beyond salvaging. All the activity on deck was being carried out in a way that would arouse no suspicion if seen from *Drummer*. Running repairs, no more.

He gave a snort of self-disparagement. It was unlikely that anyone *could* believe they were trying to make *Straker* whole again, considering the state she was in. Had he been fooling himself? Between the desire and the performance were a hundred obstacles, each one in itself requiring skill, time and sheer physical effort to master. On full rations, with a contented crew, it would have been fanciful enough. Now food was inadequate and the men – though not showing it – must be aware of the odds against them. Half of them had lost a war, the other half had lost their ship. But then, thought Muir, all of them stood to lose a lot more – their lives. He couldn't think of any better justification for attempting the impossible.

Von Bauer had been the first to voice what ultimately it must lead to and, in that, he had been the hard-headed realist. Muir still found it unthinkable – yet it had to be thought. He had gone over the permutations endlessly, first trying to think as Penn Coker, then as Baines, finally as Judd. The German captain was convinced that, when the time came, those on board *Straker* would be killed in the classic way that a murderer disposes of his witnesses. They would be shot, starved to death or put into boats ('we gave them a chance'). Only it would not be murder, but slaughter. Could Coker, Judd and the rest cold-bloodedly kill fifty men and three women? Muir didn't believe that any man, no matter how diabolically driven by greed, could compound his crime by such proportions. It had nothing to do with any innate belief in the limits of barbarity – he knew those limits were as elastic as belief itself. It just didn't make sense. Coker, Baines, Judd, all of them, had spent most of their lives, fourteen and more hours a day if need be, coaxing, cursing, beating, the ships they had sailed. Rough, violent survivors some of them might be, but ten men sprawled along a yardarm, shoulder to shoulder, needed other qualities too, which few gave them credit for. A casual arm outstretched to prevent a man toppling; a job shared when another was too ill to do more than retch, terrified the mate's eye might find him. A rough and ready comradeship that, the next moment, could erupt in a fist fight without quarter. It didn't breed the kind of men von Bauer was talking about – unless there was a wild card. Friedrich Kapper. Muir knew nothing about him. Who *had* started it all : Kapper or Coker? He settled for Kapper. Maybe von Bauer was right.

Straker swung leewards and he stabbed out a leg to keep his balance. The jigsaw of tackle laid out on the decks, deliberately slipshod to mislead any boarders from *Drummer*, had been allotted its place with care. If and when the time came – and Muir no longer thought of 'if' – everything must go smoothly. The auxiliary and the guns were another matter. Even so, it was coming together. What had been a vague, ill-defined scrap of an idea seemed to take shape of its own volition, outrageous, improbable – inevitable.

Straker trembled in her disgrace as she was shaken into line. Muir began to feel at home. All it needed was for the wings to grow again.

'There is a saying: "People live for the morrow, because the day after tomorrow is doubtful".' Viktor Mueller slapped a hand across the barrel of the gun standing forlorn among the remains of its 'pig pen' camouflage and shook his head. The breech block had been removed, rendering it useless. He looked at Barrow: 'How do you see our tomorrows?'

The two officers, in their shirtsleeves, had come on deck after inspecting the sabotaged four-cylinder diesel. A brief look at the main guns was all that was needed to complete the picture: it was bleak.

'If I was a gambling man,' said Barrow, after a moment's thought, 'I might invest my money elsewhere, say in tapioca or zulu shields, but then, if you don't gamble you can't win.'

'And you think we can *win*?' Mueller slapped the barrel once more. 'No armament, no power, no food to talk of. For a moment your captain was convincing, but words can only fire men's enthusiasm, they cannot fire these guns.'

'Not so very long ago I would have agreed with you, Mueller. It looks hopeless. But not now. You see, having spent an hour in a far more hopeless situation, suddenly fate took a hand. Isn't that the way the story writers put it: "suddenly fate took a hand"? Anyway, it did. What would you have put the chances of survival as in that damned boat?'

Mueller rubbed the stubble on his chin awkwardly, avoiding Barrow's eyes.

'Come to that, Mueller,' went on the lieutenant, easing the other's discomfort. 'If it hadn't been for a timely white flag, how long would *Straker* have remained afloat? Two minutes? Three?'

'Up till now she has always been a lucky ship,' said Mueller. 'Some of it may still be left.' He shrugged and attempted a smile. 'To blazes with tomorrow, and the day after – have you eaten?'

The question awakened a reply in Barrow's stomach.

'If you have to think about it, then you haven't,' said Mueller. 'Neither have I, not for a day. Let's "feast" ourselves.' They walked back towards the galley.

Armgard had not, to his infinite relief, been detained on board *Drummer*. Barrow couldn't help wondering whether Kapper had heard something of his culinary reputation. He was stripped to the waist, stirring a huge tureen that held a green liquid of indeterminate odour, but reminiscent of *Zebra* hob polish. 'Aaah,' sniffed Barrow. 'Clam chowder? No, no ... bouillabaisse à la Marseille ... ?'

'Pea soup,' growled Armgard querulously, 'with stockfish.' He ground his teeth in rhythm with the revolving spoon. 'It's all we got apart from salt pork and rice, and I'm not touching that yet.' Exactly why he wasn't touching it was best not inquired into, decided Barrow, soon they might have to eat it. He and Mueller took a bowl of soup each, struggled out of the cramped, steaming galley into relatively fresh air, and made their way towards the cabin they were sharing (at Muir's suggestion). They drank it in silence, balancing the bowls on their knees to avoid clearing the mass of diagrams off the table – Mueller's and Detweiler's breakdown of how the sails might be jury-rigged or repaired, along with a few charts the vandals from *Drummer* had overlooked.

The soup was nauseating. Mueller gave up the struggle and placed it on the floor with a shudder. 'Maybe later,' he said, 'I am not so hungry now.' He watched with admiration as Barrow finished it. 'You *like* it?'

'I have been trained to eat under Armgard,' said Barrow, grinning. 'It was much better than usual. Simply foul.'

Mueller laughed and stood up.

'Before you get involved out there,' Barrow went on, 'I wonder if we could have a few words? Nothing that'll keep us long?'

Mueller looked at him inquiringly.

'And do you think we can – at least here – call each other something a bit less formal? It's Guy Barrow.'

'Viktor. Viktor Mueller. An unfortunate name under the circumstances.'

'Good. Well, at least we aren't talking at arm's length, Viktor.' In the few hours since Barrow had made a point of getting to know Mueller, the more he saw, the more he liked. The first lieutenant of *Straker* (or 'chief officer' in his raider's role) was as open as his commanding officer was devious. The plain, almost blank, face did no justice to his alertness of mind.

Mueller, reckoned Barrow, had learned the hard way to become an astute listener.

'None of this is anything more than my own curiosity, but something Captain von Bauer said about the ship that was heading for Montevideo . . .'

Mueller stiffened defensively.

'Is there a mystery, or am I imagining it?'

'What Captain von Bauer said, I cannot add to. I am sorry.'

'Well, he didn't say very much at all, Viktor, that's really the point. A little about the storm, how you eventually lost contact, and all that. And, as *Straker*'s log books are missing, it is . . . no doubt it will all become clear.'

Mueller made no move to leave. He seemed to be engrossed in his thoughts.

'She sank, didn't she, Viktor?'

Mueller pulled back a chair and sat down, his hands resting across the charts. 'You have spoken to others?'

'Not yet. I hope it won't be necessary. Which is why I asked you.'

'We did *not* sink her,' said Mueller emphatically. 'You have my word.'

'But something happened? Something of which the memory alone can upset both you and your captain?'

Mueller drew a hand across his eyes and bowed himself across the table, staring at an upside-down fragment of the North Atlantic. 'Recke knows, I am sure. Others guessed. None of them can really know the reasoning. There was nothing we could do. If there had been, do you think Captain von Bauer would . . .'

'She sank?'

'Yes. She was ninety miles away when the storm-squall, no more, struck her. *Straker* rode easily on its edge. There was a wireless message, that was all. Then nothing.' He spoke precisely. 'My cousin was among the crew handling her – only a handful of men, not enough. No one knew that some of the ship's plates had buckled under the waterline during the action.'

'There were no survivors?'

Mueller looked up, his eyes still. He rolled the edge of the chart, curling it between finger and thumb. 'In the end he was right. There would have been no hope of finding anyone alive. A terrible – that is, *difficult* – decision. He had to make it. Risk all our lives, or . . .'

'You didn't alter course to search for survivors?' Barrow suddenly realised what had so obviously disturbed the German captain when Muir had questioned him.

'I have said – it would have been useless.'

'You agreed. At the time?'

'No. But I was wrong. Which is why he is captain and I am not. One must think of the wider issue.'

'You mean *you* would have thought the risk worth taking?' Barrow was determined to have every inch of it.

'I have told you!'

'But if that ship reached Montevideo, the fact that *Straker* was on the high seas with a fortune in gold would soon have become known ...'

'You are suggesting that Captain von Bauer *wanted* her to sink! No!' Mueller flattened the Cape Verde Islands with a fist. 'You do not know him!' He smoothed the chart and rose heavily. 'Our war would have seen scarcely a man killed if not for that.'

'But how did Recke and the rest see it?'

Mueller shrugged wearily. 'As they wanted to see it.'

'I'll get you something eatable,' said Barrow.

Mueller shook his head. 'You believe what I have said?'

'Yes,' said Barrow. 'The dead can't be resurrected.' He had no stomach to say more.

Hackett swore. For the past fifteen minutes he had been crawling over slime-covered wood in the hold, searching for the source of the leak that Muir was convinced was making *Straker* unstable. It was wet enough, no doubting that, but where was the water coming from? More than likely, reckoned Hackett, the wood itself was jammed against the damaged hull somewhere below the waterline, holding it in place but slowly absorbing what was able to ooze through the fracture. The worst that could happen was for the hold to become flooded, and even then the wood was buoyant enough to compensate in part. *Straker* would become more sluggish, that was all, and what the hell did that matter, they weren't going anywhere special he knew of. He swore again, louder this time. No matter how much care he took, his bandaged hand seemed to be making painful contact with just about everything. First he had cracked it against the flashlight tucked into his belt, now, forgetting, he had tried to lever himself on to the ladder that led up from the hold. The two missing fingers shot an excruciating pain up to his armpit. He felt them move, knowing they were no longer there. Bellamy had managed to find enough torn skin left to wrap over the stumps and had sewn them up as neat as mittens. Later, Hackett had unwrapped the bandages and smeared hot Stockholm tar over the joints, almost passing out in the process. Re-bandaged, there wasn't a germ small enough to infect them and, apart from the throbbing, he had felt little. Until the last blows had reminded him.

Struggling up the ladder he reached the deck and the covers were hastily slammed across the hatch and sealed. If there was one thing every seaman hated it was a hatch that was open. One roll, one breaking wave, and the weight of water entering it would take the biggest ship to the bottom. Hackett was glad to be out of it.

Tilley handed him a rag to wipe his face. 'Take it easy, Paddy. I'll carry on.' He looked at the oil-smeared bandage wrapped around Hackett's fist. 'What the hell you doing messing about down there?'

'I'm fine,' said Hackett. 'It's like toothache, except it gives you hammer when the tooth isn't there.'

Hackett had a private conviction that, no matter what anyone said, his fingers would grow again. It was only natural, after all. Even more, he was determined not to be some kind of cripple. 'There's water in there,' he said, 'but it's been there a hell of a long time. Tadpole water. Not what we're bothering about. That's coming from somewhere else.' Tucking his hand inside his shirt, he swallowed a mouthful of mucus. 'I'll be keeping these buggers out of harm's way.'

Tilley went back to the fishing lines he had trailed from the lower yardarms in search of Bonito.

One didn't argue with captains, unless particularly desirous of a week chipping rust, but Hackett personally didn't rate the Old Man's theory of the sea coming in at the head as amounting to much. The hawse pipe, through which the anchor chain passed into the forepeak, was normally cemented over at sea, but the tow line connecting it to *Drummer* had meant it remained open. Lowering himself through the hatch, Hackett realised what Muir was getting at. His feet met water after five steps down the ladder. Two more and he was up to his knees. Unwilling to chance another blow to his hand, he left the flashlight in his belt and flailed out with a leg. Two feet away he felt the coiled anchor chain rising like an island and swung on to it, holding the flashlight before it went under. The smell was strong enough to make him squint. He shone the light.

The yellow face stared at him between parted legs over a bloated body that was moving towards him in a vice.

'Oh Jesus Mercy! Fucking ...' Hackett's wrapped fingers hooked the ladder, feeling no pain. The flashlamp held in his other hand threw the sign of the cross over the scum, as slowly the outstretched feet of the corpse bumped against the bulwark and began to move back again in a mockery of life.

Hackett, teeth clenched, stepped down a rung and stopped the movement with a boot against its head. The throat had been slashed so violently that everything above it bobbed independently. An upraised knife cut the water like a shark's fin, in a hand shrivelled by salt.

He fumbled for, and found, a sodden wallet and transferred it to his mouth as he snatched at the knife blade and prised it from the dead fingers. An inquiring fish poked its head from a distended nostril.

'What's the problem, Hackett?' Muir gave a quarter of his attention to the question. But Hackett had bulldozed insistently through Barrow with his request and stood, reeking, in front of the captain.

'I found a man floating dead in the forepeak, sir. It's full of water.'

'Ah, *is* it, now? Down the hawse pipe? Thought as much. We'll have it pumped out.'

'He was dead, sir.'

'What?'

'His wallet, sir.' He handed over the dripping leather and placed the knife on Muir's desk. 'He killed himself, sir. A quick job.' Hackett looked down at his sodden, burst boots. Water trickled from the bandage around his hand.

'A nasty business.'

'A suicide can damn a ship, sir,' said Hackett impulsively. 'He died without a blessing of any sort.'

'So did quite a few others, Hackett. But I appreciate what you are saying. How is your hand bothering you?'

'Hardly at all, sir.'

'Other things are?'

'A restless spirit, sir, with an unforgiven sin as its only comfort. The man took his life, for what reason we'll never know, and he's damned sir, damned forever.' It was the longest speech Hackett had ever made outside the confines of a public house.

'We have different faiths, Hackett,' said Muir, 'but, in the end, perhaps not so very different.'

'A proper Committal to the Deep service would be in order, sir.'

'I'm afraid, Hackett, a formal ceremony right now is, well, it could pose problems.' Muir didn't want anyone from *Straker* asking any questions. 'Seal off the forepeak with my authority. The leak is there and you are in charge of stopping it. Refer any questions to me. Can you move him?'

'To where, sir?'

'Over the side,' said Muir. 'Your blessing alone will have to do, Hackett. I'm sorry.'

Hackett saluted. It didn't hide the look in his eyes. Stepping smartly back he closed the cabin door with difficulty.

Muir tugged it square on its broken hinge and sat at von Bauer's desk. A dead body in the forepeak interested him as much as a seagull alighting on a mast. Until Hackett had spoken. His words were a needed reminder that it was *men* who were his prime concern, not machinery or sails, or strategy. No one was expendable. Those killed in war shared a communal sympathy when it was over — a tombstone in common and a collective memory enshrined in some tattered flag on a wardroom wall. But they still left widows and sons and daughters. 'Glory', 'sacrifice' was no comfort to them.

He reached for the wallet. *'Over the side.'* War turned men into rubbish, dumped and shovelled unceremoniously out of sight and out of mind.

There was a single photograph. The young woman was kneeling, an arm curled around an Alsatian dog's neck. Beside her a child, blurred by the turning of a head. The stain of the sea had not managed to obliterate their moment of happiness.

Hannah Lange and her daughter smiled at him.

Part Three

The old man's mutton-chop whiskers were all that could be seen: two white tufts on either side of the black barrel. Kapper squinted along the backsight and steadied over a spot that must be in the middle of the forehead. He was too close. Tipping his chair back on two legs he planted his heels against the edge of the desk and slid it away from him. It had the opposite effect from the one he had imagined. Now the old man was completely obliterated. Kapper grinned; it would be like shooting a pigeon with a six-inch gun. He squeezed the trigger and the hammer clicked on the empty chamber.

'Pistol, self-loading, Webley & Scott, 0.455 Mark 1' it had read inside the box he had found after smashing open Muir's locked desk drawer. A fancy name for a piece of equipment that seemed to have been made for a double-jointed dwarf. The square-angled butt fitted awkwardly into Kapper's hand and he fumbled with it before hurling it across the desk in disgust, splintering the glass frame holding the photograph of Muir's guardian. There was a brief knock at the cabin door.

'Yes?'

Bellamy opened it. 'You wish to see me?'

'Come in, and shut that.' Kapper crossed the cabin and turned the key in the lock. 'Where have you been, mister? I sent for you an hour ago!'

'I received your message in the past ten minutes. I was removing a man's leg at the time and, rather than leave it half off and half on, I indulged myself, at the risk of inconveniencing you.' Bellamy's eyes roamed imperturbably around the cabin. He had the air of a traveller whose connection was being jeopardised by some half-witted ticket collector.

Kapper frowned and rapped a knuckle against the surgeon's shoulder. 'You speak slow, mister, so I get what you're saying. And speak *English*!'

Bellamy inspected his fingernails. They were riven with dried blood. The loutish German's attempts to intimidate him were laughable. After what he had been through over the last few days the surgeon had developed an immunity to pain and suffering. Seeing so much of it had cauterised his nerve endings and the thought of being personally struck or shot was a matter of complete indifference to him, apart from the fact that it might give him an excuse to lie down and sleep. 'What do you want? There are sick men who need me, some of them your own countrymen. I can't waste time here.'

Kapper seemed impressed by Bellamy's abruptness. It smacked of efficiency and professionalism. He took off his shirt and stood, hands akimbo, in front of the surgeon. 'You inspect me. Inspect me good. The others can wait. Without me it doesn't matter whether they are ill or not, they will be finished.'

Bellamy managed to recall Muir's gambit on the foredeck and his own venture into amateur dramatics. It appeared to have sown richer seeds than they might have guessed. But then the thought of sickness always did.

'Take off your trousers and lie on the bunk,' he said.

After a moment's pause Kapper stripped to his underpants and lay down, stabbing his knife into the side of the bunk within easy reach.

'Turn over.'

Kapper turned.

Placing the fore and middle finger of his left hand on Kapper's upper back, Bellamy rapped them with the corresponding fingers of his right hand, sounding out the chest for fluid. The response was hollow – and perfectly normal . . . Tap. Tap. Moving over the lungs, he stopped. Tap. Harder: tap, tap. His fingers drummed over the right lower lobe. Kapper twisted his head and stared up, anxiously. Bellamy ignored him. 'Turn over.' He pressed an ear to the German's chest, stood back and was silent. Kapper began to rise, but he eased him back, casually. 'You *feel* sick? Ill in any way?'

'I feel good. Don't *ask* me, *doctor*, tell me! You find something, then you tell me!'

'How "good" do you feel?'

Kapper jerked his huge shoulders. 'Sometimes a little . . . no . . . nothing. I feel nothing.'

He was lying, Bellamy knew it. Kapper was a frightened man. Why?

'Keep anything from me, mister, and you're in trouble, big trouble!'

'Raise your arms and breathe deeply.' Bellamy tapped Kapper's chest.

161

The abscess was under the German's left armpit: a *gumma*.
Dead tissue on an overgrown scar. He passed over it as if having
seen nothing and moved his hand down to feel a knee joint.
Kapper winced as his fingers squeezed it. The surgeon turned
away, motioning him to dress. 'Are you tired? At times very
tired?'

Kapper pulled on his trousers. 'Tired? I sleep five hours a
day since taking over and that is enough.'

'On occasion, *very* tired, just for a few minutes?'

Kapper sniffed. 'No more than anyone gets tired,' he said,
defensively.

'I see.' Bellamy nodded.

'So? You have found something? You try to fool me into
thinking you haven't!'

That was all he wanted – for Kapper to be the first to suggest
there *was* some lurking disease. That way the German would
believe everything that followed; after all, it had had to be
dragged from the surgeon!

'You have fluid in your right lung,' said Bellamy. 'It's bad and
there's a lot of it. Speaking "English" that means, without
treatment, you will drown.'

'Drown!' Kapper, dressed, was no longer unmanned. He
towered over Bellamy, his face black. 'You tell me I "drown"?
What kind of doctor are you? I swallow nothing . . . noth . . .'

'From inside,' lied Bellamy smoothly. 'Water goes into your
chest. Your *own* water – fluid from your body. Like the girl
aboard *Straker*. I have told you before!'

'Then get rid of it, mister!'

The 'mister' was a borrowing from Coker, thought Bellamy;
how much were they influencing each other? 'It will need a
poison. Arsenic.' He spoke it slowly, 'Ar – sen – ic,' so there
appeared no attempt to gloss over it. 'I have very little. In small
doses it will help make you well, but it can be dangerous and it
is your decision . . .'

'Get it!'

Bellamy had already worked out the dosage. Enough to show
some initial improvement in the debility that was now incurable
and then, slowly, its medicinal properties would be nullified as
the quantity and strength was increased.

'You get me some of that, and we start right away,' said
Kapper, pulling the knife from the bunk.

'I will have to mix it first, and one must be careful,' said the
surgeon.

'Well, what are you waiting for?'

The man's sweat followed Bellamy out on to the boat deck and for a moment he let the wind waft it away. How odd: in the course of fabricating an illness, he had found a genuine one. Friedrich Kapper had tertiary syphilis – the third and final stage of a disease that could have lain dormant for years. The outward physical signs – the abscess and inflamed knee joints – were not yet pronounced, which characterised it as *general paresis*. Kapper was teetering on the edge of chronic mental derangement as his personality deteriorated into delusion and, eventually, total insanity. The collapse could be rapid, and the only mercy Kapper might expect was that by the time his body began to decay he would be beyond comprehending what was happening to him. The arsenic could – ironically – help him for a while. But not in the doses Bellamy had in mind.

The surgeon took a deep breath. In the midst of fighting death he had become its partner in crime.

Penn Coker tugged off his sea-boots and massaged his feet. He had been on the bridge for four hours, three of them at the wheel, and he felt like a wrung rag. 'Half the buggers we've got crewing this lash-up couldn't take a paddle steamer down the Mersey,' he snorted. 'Horse Marines! Two of them took turns at the wheel and the bloody ship was running wild! Your bunch still think the wind blows us along. If we hope to make it *anywhere* we've got to knock some sense into this fish's tit. Judd's up there now, so we might stand a chance of surviving, but there's a storm about, has been for too long and when it hits, if they're all still walking around in a dream counting the bottles of booze they'll be able to buy ashore, then we've got about as much chance as a fucking pig in an abattoir. Another thing, the course ...' Cramp locked his toes and he massaged them rapidly, cursing.

Kapper, still shirtless after Bellamy's 'medical', was back at Muir's desk. He hadn't bothered to acknowledge Coker's entrance, absorbed as he was in running his fingers across his chest. He breathed in. Exhaled. Coughed.

Coker stared at his back, cracking the joints of his toes. 'You got something wrong?'

'The doctor says yes.'

'Bellamy!'

'Water.' Kapper banged two fingers across his lung as he fancied the surgeon had done.

'Balls! You're fit as an ox,' snarled Coker. 'Bellamy's trying

163

to give you the shits, that's all. He's another bastard who needs sorting out!'

'I can tell. He wasn't lying. If I hadn't made him, he wouldn't have told me. I feel it, Coker. Something inside, all over. Sometimes I don't feel so good.'

Coker groaned. This was all he needed; Kapper wetting himself into a panic because of Bellamy's bullshit. 'My feet are more painful than anything you've got, Kapper! Now, for Christ's sake snap out of it. I tell you, there's nothing wrong with you and, better than that, I'll get Bellamy to tell you the same, damn his eyes!'

Kapper stood and, still breathing awkwardly as a consequence of his concentration on it, kicked the chair on which he had been sitting across the cabin. 'I want we put ashore, mister! This is taking too long!' His face was red. 'They're just waiting back there – von Bauer and the rest of the swines. I'll show them! Once and for all! What are they to us? A dead weight. Get rid of them and we go twice, three times, as fast! We bring the gold aboard and then . . .'

'And then *what*?' Coker flexed each toe, one by one.

'What?' Kapper's sudden rage was shaking him. His jaw jutted and a fleck of foam formed at the corner of his mouth. He swung an arm wildly. 'Get rid of them! Give the sharks a meal! It will have to come, so why not now? I will do it myself!'

'If we make for an offshore island,' said Coker, 'we could dump *Straker*, leave behind some food, and later tell anyone who's interested where they are. By which time we'll be miles away. Kill them and every navy, every country in the bloody world, won't rest till they've found us, gold or no gold. O.K., half the governments in South America are crooked and the other half waiting for the chance to be, but mass murder and they won't help us, Kapper. We'll be lepers. Think about it. And while you're thinking, make a few guesses at the course we're on, because as far as I can see we've to make up our minds fast.'

Kapper's eyes had narrowed to slits. 'No! We need to get rid of them.'

'Why? So you can prop yourself up in some fucking hospital bed eating grapes because Bellamy has rattled some bones over you? That's what it's all about, Kapper, isn't it? He's really got to you!' Coker stood up and stamped his feet vigorously. 'Think! Like you thought a couple of days ago, and stop being such a bloody big wench!' His toes bounced him up and down.

Kapper wiped the spittle from his mouth. As suddenly as it

had begun, the frenzy had blown itself out. 'Wench?' he mumbled, 'I do not know "wench".'

'It means you're not stupid, Kapper.' Coker brought his own imminent anger to heel.

'We will wait, a little while,' said Kapper finally. He sounded exhausted.

'Bellamy!' roared Coker. Thundering between the hanging cots of the sick bay, he brushed aside anyone in his path, injured or orderly. The surgeon was probing at a windpipe, searching for a sliver of metal that had buried itself there, and was moving inexorably down into the trachea. He gave a 'tut' of annoyance that had nothing to do with Coker's arrival and took up a scalpel. 'Tilley? Give me that rubber tube.' He shook his hand abstractedly without looking up. 'The kidney dish. In the dish. And a clean scalpel.'

Coker handed it to him. 'I want to talk to you, Bellamy.'

The surgeon bent over the etherised patient and slit the sailor's throat expertly, forcing the tube into the open wound and down to the lung. He blew into it intermittently, and dug out the splinter with a pair of forceps. 'Needle.'

Tilley, racing back from the far end of the sick bay, where a delirious German officer had fallen from his cot, handed Bellamy the threaded needle with a passing look of astonishment at Coker.

'Right.' The surgeon stitched, knotted. The sailor began to breathe. 'Tough chap,' said Bellamy, to himself. 'And *now*, Mr Coker?' He eased the muscles in the small of his back.

'Come out here.' Coker looked impossibly seasick.

'It's a very fine day,' said Bellamy, as they walked out on deck, 'I had no idea.'

'What have you been telling Kapper, mister?'

'Nothing that he wanted to hear.'

'Don't be smart with me, I'm not some thick-headed Boche!'

'Then tell your friend Kapper that it is your decision I no longer treat him. If that's the way you want it, I happily comply.'

'I know your game and went along with it to get those bloody women off the ship and out of my hair. Now the fun's over — you tell Kapper he's O.K. Fit as a fucking stoker! And make it sound good!'

'Kapper is sick, did you know that?'

'I know *you*, Bellamy!'

'You see more of him than I do — thankfully. Rages? Inexplicable tempers? Strange decisions? The outward signs. You are right, of course, his chest is sound, but I thought it best for him to believe in the lesser of two evils. If you insist I will tell him he is incurable and will deteriorate into gibbering lunacy and death. I don't think it will improve his attitude.'

'You're lying!'

'Not this time. His mind is collapsing like a rotten fruit. Observe him for yourself and, if you are still doubtful, you may borrow my medical books and look it up in all its technical detail. It is quite explicit, even for a layman. A strange disease, syphilis. It can take many forms. In some cases there is a terrible degeneration of the body, followed by madness. In others the madness comes first. It can attack the heart, the muscles, the skin, the brain, sometimes all at once. In Kapper's case it has chosen to eat away his reason first. One word of advice: don't let him see the pages I mark. It might upset him somewhat. Normally, of course, he would be my responsibility; now, I fancy, he is yours.'

Coker swallowed, began a sentence, checked himself and rethought it. 'Just watch yourself, mister. Watch you don't fall over yourself!'

'Absolutely, Coker. I watch myself continually, with evergrowing amazement.'

He hardly noticed that he was suddenly alone.

Coker's hands were filthy. Had he handed him the scalpel blade-first? He tried to remember, staring at the limitless sea.

12 December

The way the galley was moving it would have made scrambled eggs of its own accord. But there were no eggs. Pickett was boiling sausages that had been preserved in salt. The simplest movements, that legs could cope with, reduced a pan's contents to a heavy swell, slopping over its sides like sea through the scuppers. He oscillated a wrist helplessly, reassessing all his thoughts of the maligned Percy Armgard. This was the front line. Stubbing a thumb into the water, he shook his head. It wouldn't take the skin off any sausage, never mind these.

Kapper had called for his meal four minutes ago with a tenor to his voice that suggested his 'steward' should be advanced in mind-reading. The German cook – Hoffman – thin as a lath, as if the preparation of countless ghastly meals had turned him forever against food, had thrown up his hands in despair as Pickett stole the ring on which the inevitable pea soup was bubbling, and bustled out in a huff.

Sitting on the galley stool the young midshipman shrugged. Even Kapper couldn't make water boil, whatever personal head of steam he might generate. And he'd been doing enough of that over the past few hours. The whole of *Drummer* was dominated by his ranting and raving and, barring Coker and Judd, no one was free of his intimidation. It was something more than simply stamping his authority – Kapper prowled the ship restlessly, as if in the grip of nervous energy he couldn't control.

'Jesus!' Pickett leapt at the pan as the water bubbled, frothed and swamped the stove in a hiss of vapour. Grabbing the handle he gave a howl of pain, stuffing his burned hand beneath his shirt. The pan skittered across the stove and clattered to the floor. He kicked it away from his feet.

'God damn! What happens here?' Kapper stared around the galley.

Pickett held up his blistered hand in answer.

Knocking it aside, Kapper clutched Pickett's shirt front and dragged him across the galley. 'You learn, mister steward!' Swinging him off-balance, he kicked his feet away and Pickett pitched into the spreading pool of water. Kapper's boot bunched him double as he tried to rise. Shuddering for breath he hurled the pan at the German as the foot drew back for more. Fending it off with a rumble of contempt, Kapper positioned himself with care as Pickett curled himself into a ball, wrapping his arms around his head.

Nothing came.

He blinked an eye, peering under a protective armpit. A huge pair of boots were inches away from him. But they weren't Kapper's.

'Trouble?' The voice of Frank Judd.

Kapper spoke in German.

'Don't know the lingo, son. Come again?'

'This little swine!'

'Aah!' Judd had insinuated himself between Kapper and the sprawled Pickett. He looked down at the midshipman. 'Get up and take it, Pickett, you son of a bitch! Show some guts or have them kicked out of you!' He winked at Kapper.

Pickett struggled to his feet holding his ribs and leaned against the bulkhead, eyes wet, but not with tears. 'He touches me again, Judd – or you try anything – and if I die in the attempt, I'll blind you!' He bunched his fists, hooking the thumbs outward like talons. He groaned as the pain bent him double.

Kapper moved to push Judd aside. 'So a fighter? Good. I break every finger and . . .'

'Later.' Judd wasn't to be moved. 'I take *my* turn now, Kapper.'

'I start this, mister!' Again Kapper tried to push him away.

'Listen, I *owe* this little bastard one, Kapper. He got me stuck below facing the rest of my time in gaol. Now's as good a time as any to sort him out. I came down for some coffee, but I'll settle for this. Take the bridge for a couple of minutes and I'll tell you about it.' His voice changed. 'There's something wrong with our course.'

Kapper looked at him doubtfully.

With an abrupt backward swing of his arm, Judd caught Pickett full across the face. The midshipman, unprepared, buckled.

Kapper grinned, as if reassured. 'Five minutes, mister.' He wet his lips and, with a throaty laugh, left him to it.

'Get up, Pickett,' said Judd.

The midshipman shook his head.

'Get up and listen to me.' Judd hauled him to his feet and propped him on the stool.

'You're as mad as he is . . .' struggled Pickett through split lips.

'That was nothing to what Kapper would have done to you, lad. You shouldn't have faced him.'

Pickett bowed forward on the stool, hugging himself. 'Bastards!'

'By the time I leave here, Pickett, you won't be able to walk. Your ribs will be broken and whatever else you can think of. See Bellamy and tell him you are to be quartered there. Make sure Kapper steers well clear of you. But, by Christ, you're going to be bad.'

Pickett raised his head. 'What . . . talking about?' he licked his bloated lips.

'Do as I say. I'll send in two men to take you to Bellamy. They'll be carrying the next best thing to a corpse. Don't walk. Be carried.'

'Carried?'

'*Listen*, you silly young bugger, get some of that blood . . .' he drew a finger across the midshipman's mouth. 'Spread it around. Warpaint, all right?' He held out his shirtsleeve. 'Some on here. Suck at it and spit.'

Pickett spat and Judd smeared it across his sleeve, dabbing the rest across Pickett's forehead. 'Lie down!'

He didn't find it difficult to slide back to the floor.

'Now stay there.' Judd punched his still-swollen fist against the bulkhead. Again, until the knuckles turned purple and he examined them critically.

The galley door slammed.

Some time later two sailors rolled him on to a stretcher and delivered him to the sick bay. Bellamy seemed to know exactly what had happened.

Neither of them could be one hundred per cent sure, but the area of doubt was so small as to be almost negligible. 'I can't imagine anyone else carrying a photograph of the woman and the girl,' said Barrow, 'so we must assume that the body in the forepeak is that of Otto Lange. Suicide. It fits with what might have happened.' He handed the photograph back to Muir. 'Otto was being hazed and couldn't stand it any longer. He must have been in a state, poor devil.'

Muir shook his head at the thought. 'All that sea out there and yet he chose to hide himself away and cut his throat. Strange. He must have realised his body would be found eventually.'

'Well, whatever impression one might have of him, he wasn't so weak after all.'

'Eh?' Muir slid the wallet into a drawer and covered it with papers.

'Nerve. It must have taken nerve to do what he did,' explained Barrow.

'Nerve?' Muir looked doubtful. Then: 'Yes, I suppose it might have. I wasn't quite looking at it like that, Number One. Suicide doesn't normally rate very highly in my list of a man's strengths. I was always taught to think of it as a crime.'

'Against who, sir?'

'God.'

'I see.' Barrow had no intention of being drawn into a theological debate. It had happened only once before and had ended with Muir as unshakeable as ever behind an unscaleable wall of scriptural dogma. The captain's religious beliefs were not such that they coloured his every action, but when they did occasionally surface they were uncompromisingly puritanical and worth avoiding. Barrow moved quickly on to the story Mueller had told him about von Bauer and the circumstances surrounding the loss of the original bullion ship, wondering what judgement would be heaped on the German's head. Muir passed none.

'Whatever the truth is, only von Bauer can know, and it's a pound to a pinch of salt he isn't going to tell anyone. I just hope he sleeps well at nights. I doubt it. Now, about the body: nothing can be served by telling the women about this, so I propose to draw a veil over Hackett's discovery. The corpse will be ... put to rest. I don't have to tell you how distasteful I find the whole business, but a funeral service and the *manner* of death might have alarming effects on his wife and daughter. The shock, you understand.' Muir was trying to talk it through in a way that might make it palatable and was not entirely succeeding.

'She would have to identify the body. That alone ... well, Hannah Lange has suffered enough, I would say.'

'Exactly.' Muir seemed relieved. 'Make sure Hackett doesn't breathe a word. God, we sound like conspirators! But I think it's all for the best.' He dug ash out of his pipe bowl, sifted through it and reluctantly threw it into the stove, tugging out the remaining roll from his top pocket. 'What's happening below?'

'The auxiliary is in a bad way,' said Barrow. 'I don't know whether anything can be done with it. Maybe Garrett might have been able to perform one of his miracles, but I doubt if anyone else would know where to begin.'

'And the guns?' Muir lit the cut plug.

'Minus breech blocks, so there's nothing more to be said in that direction. The sails are coming together nicely.'

It was small comfort. But if Muir was depressed, he didn't show it. 'Get the men down among the gold and have them go through all the crates with care. There was a lot of engineering stuff mixed among them. Breech blocks wear and it's unlikely von Bauer wouldn't have covered that eventuality. I'll question him about it, but we might as well start looking now.' He smiled ruefully. 'An answer from our German friend isn't always the correct one.' He concentrated on building up the combustion in his pipe and, when it was glowing to his satisfaction, looked up at Barrow. 'As for the auxiliary, you've just given me a thought, Number One. It worked once, it might work twice. No harm trying. It'll make demands on Bellamy's powers of perception, but he has plenty of that. Yes, why not! Let's run it up the flagpole and see what happens!'

Barrow waited patiently for the captain to disclose his plan.

'Signal a message to *Drummer*. Routine stuff. The hawser is holding, steering under control – and ask when the next food is coming aboard. Add a rider asking Bellamy how Garrett is progressing. Whether the symptoms are better or worse. The reason we are asking is that if there are any more isolation cases we will have to be prepared in advance.'

There was a long silence as both men tossed it around, prodded it for faults and came to their conclusions. Barrow held out both palms, weighing the idea. His hands found a common level. He grinned. 'If it works then, you must understand, von Bauer moves a notch down from being, in my opinion, the most wily, devious, Machiavellian captain aboard this ship.'

Muir accepted the admonishment solemnly, nodding at the verdict. Then, unable to contain himself any longer, slapped his thigh and burst out laughing. 'So if I'm Machiavelli, what will that make Bellamy?'

'Cardinal Richelieu, without the naïveté,' said Barrow without a second thought.

She was moving badly, shaking her head like a tethered animal. The ignominy of what was happening to his beloved *Straker* had threatened to plunge von Bauer into a bottomless despair. Since rejoining her he had not set foot outside his cabin save for the meeting with Muir. He didn't want to see her like this and had begun to hope she might founder and sink and be out of her misery. His misery. For wasn't he alone responsible? There was nothing left to be salvaged from his war, nothing. A broken, humiliated ship; men who had turned not only against their captain, but against the trust of the sea itself, and the rest, crippled either in body or spirit, finding his name wormwood on their tongue. Those who had not died.

A mistake. He had made one mistake – as the British captain had made his. Or was it merely a challenge, the greatest he had ever had to face? There was still one thing in his favour : time. And time could turn everything on its head once more, as it had already twice before.

Von Bauer had managed to smuggle his sachets of powdered opium back to *Straker*, stuffing them in his hat lining. The hypodermic and small bottle of alcohol had been hidden in his waistband. The alcohol wasn't so important, water could be used. But there were only fifteen sachets left and six unbroken needles. He had used one of them a quarter of an hour ago. The pain in his neck had been no more than a dull ache, a workaday handicap he normally wouldn't think twice about, but this time there was a different pain to kill: a despondency more malignant than anything the body could devise. Unless it went he knew he was destroyed. And he had injected himself, clearly aware of what he was doing and why. The justification was showing signs of birth. His sole purpose now was to rectify his mistake, and that would mean, first . . .

He reached for a sheet of paper and began to write, point by point. The Englishman was no more in control of his own destiny than any of them. Less, because he was fighting the wrong enemy. So let him fight them – give him everything and, in his moment of triumph, take it away. Von Bauer looked at the future and rearranged it with a few strokes of his pen. Now the details would have to be worked out . . .

'Captain?' Muir stood in the doorway. 'I knocked, but you didn't hear me.'

Von Bauer turned the paper over.

'I am sorry.' He stood up.

'We haven't seen much of each other, Captain,' went on Muir, accepting the seat the German captain drew towards him. 'Forgive me.'

'You have problems, Captain.'

'I won't beat about the bush. What I mean is . . .'

'You do not intend to prevaricate,' von Bauer finished his sentence for him. 'I am familiar with the saying, Captain.'

'Prevaricate. Your English is excellent. So . . . What chance is there of spare breech blocks being in the hold?'

'If they have not been removed there are five replacements.' He looked at the paper on his table. 'I have been making a list of such things, which may be of some help.'

'The men who came aboard were cursory saboteurs,' said Muir, 'and my guess is that they had been told not to go any-where near the gold.'

'In which case they are still there, along with engine parts. After so long I had almost forgotten.'

And yet could recall them sufficiently to know the exact number and write a list from memory, thought Muir. 'The auxiliary is in a mess. There are enough parts to overhaul it?'

'I am no engineer, Captain. But possibly.'

With extraordinary familiarity he took Muir by the elbow. 'May we go to the saloon?'

Muir allowed himself to be led from the cabin. Von Bauer's sudden strange co-operativeness was intriguing, but that was only part of it. The German captain was a man who seemed to change like the wind, and, like the wind, was worth studying for future storms.

They stood in the saloon and von Bauer positioned Muir with his back against a panelled wall, situating himself directly opposite. 'My own design, Captain. A refinement, sophistication, call it what you will – a frippery, it seemed, at the time of my first enthusiasm. I lean back, Captain Muir, as you see, and behind me is a barometer. Behind that is a small switch. Before I touch it I will explain. The idea came to me when the hydraulic lifts were being fitted in *Straker* to bring her ammunition from the hold. A wild idea, but I talked with experts and, well, you will see ...'

On his final word he reached behind him, pushed the barometer aside and pressed a switch. The entire centre of the saloon, table, chairs, sank rapidly into the hold without so much as a ripple in the water jug.

Speechless, Muir looked down.

'If your officers had accepted my hospitality, then that is where they would have finished, Captain. Your lieutenant was either uncommonly lucky or strangely perceptive. As you can see, there is no way of getting out.' He touched the switch again and the floor rose and was locked in place.

'A bag of tricks,' said Muir. On his inspection of *Straker* he had discovered her to be a maze of compartments, trap-doors and tunnels riddling her like an ant's nest. And what he had found must be only half of it. 'Incredible.'

'I did not believe it possible myself. A Swede devised the mechanism. A very clever man.'

Rapping a foot over the invisible join in the floor, Muir could only agree. 'This could be useful.'

'It adds to your list of "armaments". How, I am not as yet sure,' said von Bauer.

'Come, Captain, you know as well as I how this particular rabbit can be taken from the hat?'

'I am sorry, you leave me ... rabbits ... I do not understand.'

Oh yes, you damn well do, thought Muir.

Elizabeth Lange studied herself section by section in the tiny mirror propped on the cocktail cabinet. By walking to the far end of the cabin they had been given she could view first the area from throat to bosom, then, moving away, waist to knee and, finally, knee to the hem of her dress. She dipped slowly, as if curtseying, and a fleeting picture of herself ran across the small glass. Rose stepped forward and with a nimble rearrangement of pins ruched the material across the shoulder.

'A tuck here, tuck there, less at the waist, bit of fancy work around the hem – and we can use some of the material from the old one to finish the sleeves off. I think it'll do. Now take it off and we'll see if my old fingers are what they once were. I'll be wanting more of those pins on the table.'

Rose had decided Elizabeth was in need of a new dress and had spent the day tramping *Straker* looking for odds and ends that might serve to spirit one together. There was no shortage of needles and yarn, essentials in every sailor's 'hussif', and she had found a pair of what might pass for tailor's shears in the sail locker. The material itself had been the greatest problem, but eventually a man named Tilley had shown her to a pile of spare and unused nightgowns in red flannel that would serve the purpose nicely. She had had little trouble after that discovering buttons and everything else that was needed. The thought of all those big, brawny men bent over a running stitch had made her giggle. And, as for the men, they had taken to her as a mother, her formidable spirit gently shaming some, inspiring others. *Straker* had no figurehead, but in a very short space of time Rose had become its living embodiment. A talisman. Her words to Muir about having no intention of dying at sea had soon been passed around the ship (a shrewd piece of morale-boosting propaganda by the Captain) and had impressed themselves deeply on men who, by their nature and environment, were never slow to find portents of good or evil.

'We need some lace,' said Rose. 'I've seen some somewhere, can't think where. Yes, I can. Over a kind of trunk it was, in a cabin. Perfect! Now will you look at it, Hannah!'

Hannah Lange had remained silent throughout the fitting. Elizabeth slipped on the stained and torn dress she had been obliged to wear every day since they had been taken from the American schooner.

'Cinderella, poor lass. Never mind, give me a little time and she'll be a picture. What do you think, Hannah?'

Hannah Lange was non-committal. She had no desire to hurt Rose's feelings and Elizabeth seemed pleased at having something new to wear – no matter how improvised – but in her heart Hannah wished for nothing more than that her daughter be dowdy, unattractive and, if such a thing was possible, repulsive. That way she might be safe. Rose didn't seem to understand that they were still women amongst men, that Elizabeth was a young attractive girl, whose sex and youth alone placed her in danger. To flaunt her was inviting ... she felt invisible hands run over her body and turned away. 'A walk, Rose. Some air.'

She would tell her. Explain that men — such men as these — needed no temptation and that even she, an old woman, was not beyond their lust. Animals! All men were, after Oskar.

'We'll find that lace while we're about it,' said Rose. 'You can be cutting out that paper pattern, Lisbeth, and neat I want it.' She took Hannah's arm and the two women went on deck, Rose linking arms as if taking a constitutional along Brighton pier.

Picking up the shears, Elizabeth began to follow the traced lines. She had made up her mind. Why be captive? It was ridiculous! Day after day in a cabin, and for how much longer? Why? Because Hannah saw her still as a young child, to be cosseted and smothered. No one could change what had happened, the death of her father, the rape. She said the word out loud: 'Rape.' It had been meant for her and she had lain in a fever hearing it all, unable to distinguish dream from reality. But it had been no dream. She had to forget it, lock it away, or end it. No tears. Tomorrow she would ask Captain Muir if she could help with the cooking or the sick, anything! And Hannah must do the same. The shell was growing around her mother until now she was almost a stranger. Elizabeth began to sing an old school song. It was good to sing, they had told her at the clinic: breathe and sing. She stopped.

'Who is that?'

'Me. Midshipman Dandridge,' came the voice from the other side of the cabin door.

She opened it. Dandridge was inexpertly balancing three bowls of soup and was incapable of movement. She took two of them from him with a smile. Most of the contents of the third had disappeared down his sleeve.

She placed the bowls on the table, took the other from him and mopped his sleeve.

'I'll get some others,' stammered Dandridge. 'And some bread and ...'

'It can wait a while,' said the girl. 'Can you be excused your duties just a moment?'

He coloured.

'Here, sit down.'

He sat opposite her.

'I talk to no one my own age,' she said. 'I'm twenty, you must be ...'

'Eighteen,' said Dandridge.

'There! So we can talk?'

175

'The other ladies are ...'

'They've gone for a walk and won't be back just yet.' She held up the red flannel. 'Do you like it?'

'It's a nightshirt.'

'Wrong. It's Rose's latest creation. She's making me a dress. Don't you think I need one?' She picked at the skimpy frock she was wearing.

'It's nice,' said Dandridge. 'The new one. I mean, I'm sure it will be.'

'Men know nothing about dresses. You're just being polite. I expect it looks terrible.'

'No, really. It *will* be very nice.'

'Well, Mr Dandridge, I'll invite you to the first showing and we'll see what you have to say then.'

'I'm no judge, miss, you're right.'

'Is it *Mr* Dandridge, or do sailors have other names like ordinary people? My name is ...'

'Elizabeth.'

'*Beattie*! There, I've remembered it now!' She smiled. 'You've been very good to us, Beattie. We are grateful, though sometimes mother may not seem it.' Suddenly: 'Tell me about yourself.'

They talked for a quarter of an hour, about anything and everything that came into their heads. At the end of it Dandridge had seen a swathe cut through his problems, sharing his thoughts more openly than he would have thought possible. The girl seemed to absorb without question everything he said, nodding her interest as she snipped, adding her comments, until the dialogue flowed between them without pause: two streams of water sparkling from different sources, but eventually joining. The nervous drumbeat in his stomach had gone.

'I must get back,' he said reluctantly.

'Of course. Maybe we can talk again.'

'I'd like that.' He looked at the soup. 'It's cold. I'll have it heated up.'

'No, I'm sure ...'

'Really, I'll enjoy doing it.' He stood at the cabin door. 'I've ... it's been very nice talking ...'

'Yes.' She handed him the soup bowls.

'Perhaps tomorrow.'

'Lisbeth.'

'Lisbeth.'

'One very important thing, Beattie, and be honest with me or I won't sleep tonight for thinking of it,' she said.

He coughed. Cold soup splashed on his boot.

'Tell me – how did you knock the door holding three soup bowls in your hands?'

Dandridge stared at her. 'Oh. With my head.' He nodded forward. 'Bump, bump. How else?'

She began to laugh. It was the most incredibly beatuiful sound Beattie Dandridge had ever heard. 'I really must go,' he said with a smile.

Leaning forward she kissed him on the forehead. 'Bump, bump,' she said.

Bellamy was annoyed. He had willingly gone along with Muir's bit of nonsense in order to protect the women and had even managed to raise the ante – Kapper was decidedly unnerved. But now things were being taken too far. He didn't know what made it so important for Garrett to be on *Straker*, but, whatever the reason, it was out of proportion to what might be lost by stretching Kapper's credulity to the limit.

In short, to pull the same trick again might set the German thinking and, in his present condition, if he realised he had been made a fool of there was no telling what might happen. Pickett had been the first to taste the strength of his madness. The surgeon stalked along the deck to Garrett's cabin like an offended ostrich. The chief engineer was poring over a mass of calculations.

'Look here, Garrett,' said Bellamy, shortly, 'this is not my doing and I don't quite understand it, but Captain Muir has been inquiring after your health – to the puzzlement of Coker and Kapper. At the moment they are none the wiser, but reading between the lines I'd say Muir wants you in *Straker* for some reason and he's playing on the T.B. the girl is supposed to have.'

'T.B? What the hell are you talking about?' Garrett was untypically brusque, the result of a tremendous ache in his jaw and the depressing conclusions that his calculations were beginning to indicate. *Drummer*, no matter how he fined it down, would not have enough fuel to take them back to England even if they were to set course immediately. So if the mutineers abandoned the ship and went off with the gold, those who were left would have to put into a South American port. And it might take weeks to find sufficient clean-burning coal. Back home, Maggie would be justified in believing him dead. It was a new permutation, and one that had kept him sleepless at night. To lose her by default was something he hadn't reckoned with.

'The Old Man flashed a message,' Bellamy was saying, 'part of which added up to the fact that he wants you to feign T.B. so you can be "isolated" on *Straker*. If that isn't what he wants then I've no idea what he's playing at. Anyway, I'm afraid we're going to have to go along with it.'

'What do I have to do?'

Bellamy ignored the question. 'Open your mouth.' He gently prised back the upper lip. 'God, man, how long has it been in this state?'

'The ones that were knocked out ...' mumbled Garrett.

'The gum's poisoned,' said Bellamy. 'You've been jabbing at it. Why didn't you come to me with this?' He bristled.

'Just toothache,' said Garrett with a shrug, 'didn't seem worth it.' He had seen some of the injured brought aboard and the thought of complaining about toothache seemed in distinctly poor taste.

'You need it lancing,' said Bellamy, sharply. 'And, as it happens, the fact that you do might convince Coker you really have got T.B.' He was doubtful. To link poisoned gums with the first stages of pulmonary tuberculosis was a medical feat as viable as divining the weather from the entrails of a chicken. Still, it was all they had.

'If you just take the swelling away, it should be all right,' said Garrett.

'I'll have a look at. But before I do, listen carefully to what I'm going to say.' He briefly sketched out the symptoms of the illness the chief engineer had 'contracted'.

'You mean I sham it?' said Garrett. He wasn't sure he could have got it right.

'Precisely.'

'They'll never be taken in by it. It's bloody daft, Bellamy!'

'Kapper will. Coker? We'll have to wait and see who pulls the most weight.'

'Do we really have to go along with it? I've got work to do here, and anyway ...' Garrett pushed his calculations aside. 'Oh, I don't know! I've never heard anything so barmy in all my life!'

'Barmy or not, we'll have to try it.' Bellamy wiped the fatigue from his face. 'Let's say it's just what the captain ordered.'

There were some people you could never understand, thought Rose, no matter how hard you tried. She drew her shawl around her shoulders. Hannah Lange had gone back to the cabin, leaving her on the half deck still not having found the lace she was looking for. Lace had not been on Hannah's mind. Twice she had tried to tell Rose something and twice she had stopped in confusion. Rose sensed what it was all about and had been determined to ignore it. Hannah disapproved of her efforts to rehabilitate Elizabeth – she wanted her daughter left alone, camouflaged from harm and dependent on one person alone: Hannah Lange. That way she could control her life, steer her where it was safe to go, teach her how to hide away in anticipation of the worst. It was a life lived in a state of barely controlled terror, waiting for an ogre around every corner. She had no idea just what harm she was causing. But then, thought Rose, Hannah didn't know her daughter at all.

Straker heeled and, caught off-balance, Rose dance-stepped sideways across the deck. Tiny Winslow, permanently stable due to a complex interrelation between body height, girth and gravitational weight, checked her chassé with an open arm.

'It's a dream I'm in,' said the old woman archly, locking her fingers around two thirds of his waist. They promenaded unsteadily to the fo'c'sle.

'Young lady, it has been a pleasure and a privilege,' said Winslow, readjusting the leather belt that, as ever, had detached itself from his trouser top and bowing a tweedledum bow. Stoker Melfort and Tilley caught the scene in passing. A burst of applause.

'Ah, Mr Tilley,' said Rose, recognising her benefactor of the red flannel nightgown. 'I have yet another favour to ask of you. Lace. Now where can I be after getting some lace?'

Tilley squinted in thought.

'I saw some, where I can't remember. On a box of sorts in a cabin.'

It jogged Tilley's memory. 'Ah yes. For you, Rose, I think we can manage it.' Tilley remembered the French lace covering the sea chests.

Stoker Melfort introduced himself. He had not actually seen the old lady, buried as he had been in the depths of *Drummer,* but he had heard of her. 'My pleasure, ma'am. *Vous parlez Anglais très bon.*'

'Rose is Irish, you wet ha'porth,' said Winslow.

'Oh. But used to the social graces despite that,' recovered Melfort. It didn't sound right, somehow, but Rose seemed to appreciate the sentiment behind it.

'Lead on, Mr Tilley and ...' she tugged on a breath. The ship was turning, turning. 'Mr Tilley?' Her voice was small.

Straker spun to the beat of her heart, drowning Tilley's reply. She blew out her cheeks as Winslow and Melfort supported her. 'Oh, dear.' It had passed. Why were they looking at her like that?

'Rose?' said Tilley. The old woman's face was grey.

'I'm all right.'

Melfort held her wrist, counting the pulse. He glanced at Tilley and gave a slight shake of his head.

'Come on, Rose, easy does it,' said Tilley. 'Back to your cabin and a lie-down. I'll bring you the lace, don't worry about that. Don't worry about anything.'

13 December

One might have guessed it. For three days they had been hoping for rain to replenish *Straker*'s drinking water and now, when it did come, the timing couldn't have been worse. Muir looked along the ship's length. Buckets, tarpaulins, mugs and pans were placed everywhere: it looked like an Arab market. Men were racing around the decks laying out anything that came to hand that was capable of catching the precious liquid. Others had come up from watch below and, stripping off their clothes, began to wash away the accumulated grime of the past months. Gnarled and knobbly nymphs capered over the hatches. Muir let them get on with it, almost envious, as rain dripped from his cap peak in a constant waterfall. He suppressed a grin. All it needed now was for Rose to come up on deck!

'Steady,' he said to the quartermaster at the wheel. 'Keep her from swinging.' Leaning over the starboard poop rail he looked at a point mid-way between *Straker* and *Drummer* and at a small dinghy heaving in the swell. Garrett was alone, trying desperately to keep the bow facing the windjammer and away from the hawser. The sea was beginning to pile, driving the dinghy dangerously close to the cable, and whatever qualities Garrett undoubtedly had when it came to engines, coping single-handed with a boat in a deceptive sea was another matter.

Bellamy had pulled off the impossible. Less than ten minutes ago *Drummer* had signalled them to prepare to receive the chief engineer. Whether they had chosen the moment out of spite or simply in haste to get rid of the 'contagious' Garrett, Muir didn't know. What he did know was that Garrett was in considerable peril. If the dinghy touched the hawser it would be sawn in pieces and if *Straker* didn't meet him at precisely the correct angle it would be run down or simply float away for ever. *Drummer* had refused to stop for the operation and the pick-up was having to be done while moving – literally scooping Garrett up the windjammer's side.

Buried beneath an oilskin two sizes too big for him, von Bauer climbed the ladder to the poop and stood alongside Muir, peering from beneath the voluminous hood like a penitent monk. 'So they aren't prepared to starve us to death just yet,' he said, conning the dinghy.

'They're not supplies,' said Muir. 'My chief engineer.'

The German captain didn't question why Muir's chief engineer should be bobbing around the ocean like a cork – or, perhaps more aptly, like a nut between the jaws of a nutcracker.

'You intend to take him aboard while moving?'

'No option, Captain.'

'I see. In that case ...' von Bauer touched the wheel. 'With your permission, Captain?'

'Of course.' Von Bauer didn't look strong enough to hold the huge wooden wheel but, edging the quartermaster off the grating, he took the helm and, jamming his heels against the projecting iron bolts on either side of him, began to move *Straker* crab-wise towards the dinghy. Muir looked at him sharply. Garrett was less than thirty feet from the hawser.

'We have to come almost dead astern of *Drummer*,' said von Bauer in answer to the glare. 'If we stay on this course the dinghy will be left yards on the port lee. And there's no turning round. One chance, Captain.'

The problem didn't have to be explained: how to get round it had been uppermost in Muir's mind ever since Garrett had begun to drift towards the hawser. The windjammer had moved badly out of line in the swell and was being towed at an angle to *Drummer* instead of directly behind her. In seaman's terms, *Drummer* was fine on the starboard bow – which meant that *Straker* had to overcome the momentum of the tow and move as rapidly as possible dead astern without dragging the wire across the dinghy. Muir reckoned that to do so would leave Garrett less than twenty feet from the hawser during the final stages of the approach.

'Can she be coaxed fine enough?'

Von Bauer nodded. 'Under sail, yes. Even now, I think.' He grimaced as the wheel wrenched his arm. 'Her bottom is foul, dragging her.'

'And there's water in the forepeak,' said Muir.

'I feel it. Her head is lazy. Even so, a good ship.' He was

wrestling with the wheel but there was nothing Muir could do. One man only could steer a ship in an exercise like this, feeling its strengths and weaknesses, checking, releasing, channelling the tremendous power where he ordered.

The hawser was straightening, but Garrett was so close it seemed he might be able to reach out and touch it. Aware of what was happening the men, who had only moments before been frolicking like schoolgirls, grew silent. All eyes were on the little boat. And then back to von Bauer.

'Every man to the ropes,' yelled Muir. 'Barrow?'

'Sir!' Barrow's voice came back.

'Men up at the peak. Start there and move her length, port side only.' A succession of ropes and ladders had been trailed over *Straker*'s sides and if Garrett missed one there were ten others. If he missed them all . . .

'Now!' called von Bauer. The dinghy passed out of danger from the hawser, but was still too far away from the tall ship. He bore down on the wheel and there was the singing of stretched wire as the hawser leapt from the water. 'Now!' repeated von Bauer. The cable sagged and splashed, but it had served to bring *Straker* violently to port. The men, some still half-naked, began to scramble down the trailing ropes and ladders until their feet brushed the wavetops. There was silence, then a voice shouted triumphantly: 'Got him!'

'Quickly, quickly!' urged von Bauer. He had brushed back the oilskin hood and the rain, mingling with perspiration, blinded him. Muir drew a hand across the German's brow.

'Scran!' came another voice.

Muir gripped the rail and looked down at the dinghy. Garrett had been grabbed from it and was at the top of the rope ladder and somehow a purchase had been made on his boat. A winch began to hum, as it was lifted up.

'Well, a bonus, Captain,' said Muir. 'We have some food too.'

'The man is safe?'

'Yes.'

Von Bauer beckoned the quartermaster back to the helm. 'Then she is still a good ship.' The effort had left him shaking.

'Let me see you to your cabin, Captain,' said Muir.

'No. Thank you, Captain, but I am capable.'

'Very capable, Captain von Bauer. Mr Garrett would be the first to vouch for that.'

'She is my ship,' said the German. 'We still understand each other, despite everything. Now if you will excuse me . . .' He stepped slowly down the ladder, to the well deck.

Muir heard a ragged cheer begin somewhere amidships. Louder, as von Bauer passed on his way to his cabin.

He didn't begrudge it.

'Dried peas, some flour, two casks of fortified lime juice, fifteen pounds of salt pork and a couple of bags of rice.' Barrow glanced up from the meagre list. 'If everyone eats just sufficient to keep body and soul together it will – might – last three days with what little we have aboard. On a starvation diet it could last a week. The rain helped a little, but the fresh water tank has forty tons in it. It's designed to hold three hundred.'

Muir threw his cap on the desk. 'Well, they did say they were going to keep us in line, but judging by this I'd say there's another purpose.' He ran a hand through his hair. 'From that list there doesn't seem much doubt about the real name of Kapper's game, does there? Which makes what I'm going to put to you doubly important, Number One. Take a pew.' He dragged forward a chair. 'Don't mind me standing, I think better that way. So, one more week and, as you say, we won't have the strength to look after ourselves. I've never seen anyone starve to death, but heard tales of those who have and can think of a few better ways of ending my days. The brain goes weak and sluggish and after that you go downhill so fast you don't even know what's happening to you. Which means we must act and act quickly, while we're all *compos mentis* and have the strength to act. That, as far as it goes, would seem fairly logical.'

Barrow didn't interrupt, despite the first gnawing doubts. It was all very well to talk of 'acting' but was it 'logical' to act if acting was suicidal?

'Did the men find anything for the guns?'

'What?' Barrow shook himself. 'I'm sorry sir, I was drifting ...'

'Don't apologise. The effect of what you went through on that boat is going to be around for a little while, Number One. I was talking about the guns.'

'It had gone out of my head. I do beg your pardon, sir, how bloody stupid of me. Damn fool! I was too preoccupied with the wretched food ...'

'Butter before guns,' smiled Muir.

'There *are* breech blocks and they hadn't touched the ammunition, presumably thinking that if we had nothing to fire it it wasn't worth bothering about. The blocks were piled haphazardly among the ones containing gold. It was rather like opening Christmas parcels and pushing aside the goodies in search of a pair of socks. Every time the men discovered gold they groaned with disappointment!'

'Marvellous.' Muir 'clopped' his hands mightily. 'And Garrett?'

Barrow frowned. 'Garrett doesn't say much, but his face seems to be getting worse. Bellamy gave him some tablets and I'm keeping my fingers crossed they'll clear it up. I don't know. He needs rest.'

'I had a word with him and couldn't get a lot out of him either. Apparently there was hell to pay on *Drummer*. Coker saw right through it and had an up-and-downer with the German but in the end washed his hands of it all and left him to it. Garrett seems to think they can't make up their mind what to do – at least come to any agreement, and this is more on Coker's mind than anything else. He also says that Bellamy has discovered Kapper has syphilis.'

'What?'

'Yes, I felt the same. It's advanced and he's far from rational. It puts everyone on *Drummer* in a great deal of danger – including Coker. Not that I'm too worried about that one. But the rest, yes. It was Garrett's information that finally made up my mind. And now, with the good news about the guns, it's Garrett who holds the key. I want the auxiliary working. After that he can have all the rest he needs.'

'He's pushing himself,' said Barrow. 'I don't think he'll let you down.'

'There's something on his mind, has been for some time, even before all this started. He's married, isn't he?'

'Yes. You think it's that? Trouble at home?'

'It usually is. Poor bugger. You're not wed, Barrow, you don't know what a trip like this can do to a marriage. I'll have a word with him as soon as possible, though I don't know if it'll do much good. Right, having been helped by von Bauer's squirrel-like memory, and hoping Garrett can fix the auxiliary, we can get down to the next item on the agenda. I want you to hand-pick the most reliable men – keep the German crew out of it for the moment – for a job that requires one major ability: that of keeping their mouths shut. They'll be working at night and under a great deal of difficulty, so the stronger they are the better. Tell them if they breathe a word to anyone else they are throwing their lives away – and everybody else's. Come on very strong over that, Number One. It's no exaggeration. There will be a curfew on *Straker* and no one who isn't authorised will be allowed on deck after midnight. The explanation for it will come soon enough, so I'm not going to attempt to make one now. Mueller and Detweiler will be put in charge of ensuring it is adhered to – but they too will be below decks.'

'Mysterious, sir.' Barrow raised an eyebrow.

'So let's go over it.'

Fifteen minutes later Muir finished speaking, sat down and scratched his chest. 'Well?'

'You intend to tell von Bauer all this?'

'Not yet, no.'

'And how soon before we start?'

'The first stage immediately. Tonight. The second within a day. I don't need to stress that it needs only one man to blab and that's the end of it. It's going to require extraordinary self-control.'

'They are extraordinary men,' said Barrow. 'They won't talk.'

For the past two days Muir had pored over the slender chance of its working until sheer fatigue had riddled his mind with doubt. He felt inordinately tired and realised he hadn't eaten anything but soup for a day. Smoothing out a deck plan he had made of *Straker* with von Bauer's help, he forced his eyes to focus.

There could be no turning back now.

14 December

The rain had passed as quickly as it came, sliding away to the east locked in a ridge of black cloud. Steam began to rise along the length of *Drummer*'s sodden deck as the sun burned across it.

Kapper, Coker and Baines were standing around the azimuth compass on Monkey Island. Kapper had taken off his shirt and, realising the folly of it, knotted its arms around his neck, protecting his back. Baines sizzled in his own sweat, occasionally scratching himself. Only Coker seemed unperturbed.

The two ships were curving west, following the Brazilian coastline. The Equator lay less than a hundred miles due south.

One foot in the Atlantic, the other in the forests of the Matto Grosso, Kapper looked down at the map he had spread at his feet like a colossus. Tracing the toe of his boot across it: 'Along here there are towns.'

It had been Coker who had called the meeting – for the simple reason that they were off course. Or, more precisely, without one. For most of the four days since they had taken control of

Drummer, Kapper had been on the bridge. The first argument had occurred after they had overshot the island of Fernando de Norohna, 350 miles north east of Recife and the place where they had agreed the sick should be put ashore along with the rest. Coker was certain that, for whatever wild reason, Kapper had wilfully avoided landing there. Now they were running into nowhere.

'Here,' said Kapper eventually, still looking down at the map. 'We can land here.'

'Camocim,' read Coker. 'You know it?'

'It looks a good place,' said Kapper.

'*Looks* good?' said Coker. 'I've never heard of the place, but I know this coastline. Most of it is solid rock and the "ports" would have trouble with a coracle, for Christ's sake!'

'Nobody will find us here,' insisted Kapper. Since taking over the gold he had become obsessed with the thought that the murder of his wife would be the only thing to take it from him. There was a vast German community in South America and perhaps even now his name and description had been circulated. He had to be very, very careful ...

Coker detected the first signs of one of Kapper's rages. The German had been solely responsible for plotting their course and now, confronted with the fact that he had made a complete mess of it, was likely to find comfort in going berserk. The illness that Bellamy had diagnosed might not be far off the mark after all. Kapper seemed to be deteriorating rapidly. He had been adamant that Garrett should be put back on *Straker*, despite Coker's arguments, and now he spent the best part of the day waiting to be prescribed his drug by the surgeon, proclaiming improvement with each dose. There were more Germans than English aboard *Drummer* and he hadn't been slow making that fact known to Coker. They weren't going to listen to an Englishman.

Coker said: 'We cut our losses, head south — but first drop everyone off we don't want.' He looked down at the chart. 'St Paul's Rocks, here.' He jabbed a finger. 'This coast is as wild as a hurricane and offers nothing. Have you ever thought, Kapper, what happens when we get ashore?'

'So what happens?' Kapper was derisive.

'We lug it ashore and start living it up in some one-horse town where the peons would as soon slit your throat as offer you a glass of water? Once word gets round we are carrying this lot they'll be riding in from every point of the compass swinging their bolas.'

Baines looked uneasy. 'We can get to some place and sell it. Don't be so bloody off-putting, we don't need it.'

'There is no *place*,' said Coker. 'You expect a millionaire to be picking his teeth in a straw hut waiting for us? Don't be a fucking idiot!'

'You're being awkward, mister,' insisted Kapper. He stubbed a toecap against the chart.

'We leave them at St Paul's Rocks then head south, as far south as possible,' said Coker grimly. 'Salvador or Rio. We anchor way offshore and take a boat in. Then we start talking. Rio is big enough to disappear in and find the right kind of money we need. At the moment this stuff is ballast. We want someone who can turn it into cash. That will take a few days, in the meantime Muir and the rest will be O.K. When we do the deal we let someone know they are stuck out there. Two or three days, no more. By the time they are picked up – we tell some vague story – we can have bought a boat and be miles away. Peru doesn't care a damn about a war that's happening four thousand miles away.'

'I like the sound of that,' Baines said eagerly. 'That's bloody good. Everything taken care of.'

Coker met Kapper's red-rimmed stare, playing out the cord of his own anger.

Kapper shrugged. 'Perhaps. If we do, you have forgotten one important fact. People talk, Mr Coker. Talk. So we go and buy a boat. All the rest. But no. First we get rid of *Straker*. We take the gold and go alone.'

Baines's face fell. He looked for some reaction from Coker. 'You mean we do like he said?' He didn't believe that was what Kapper meant at all.

'No! They are plotting! They are tricking us!' Kapper was shouting, his fists pounding the binnacle.

'Garrett,' said Coker.

Kapper banged his clenched fist against his hips. 'That was your doing, mister! You Englishmen!' He was sweating profusely. 'The gold is taken on to *Drummer* and the hawser cut, that is my decision. They make their own way!'

'Which is murder, *mister*,' said Coker quietly.

'Murder? It's ... it's ...' Baines spluttered. 'Let them starve to death? I want no part of that! They'll have the whole bloody Fleet looking for us!'

'So, go with them!' Kapper spat on his palm and rubbed the back of his neck.

'And if the men won't go with you?' Coker, back to the sun, seemed unaffected by it.

'The swine will do as they are told!' said Kapper. His eyes held thunderstorms. 'We get the gold on this ship!' Snatching his shirt to his shoulders he stumped into the wheelhouse.

'Christ!' said Baines. 'He's crackers. The sun's got him!'

Coker wasn't listening. Kapper was becoming a liability and would have to be seen to. With every sentence he uttered the German was drawing that time nearer.

He ordered the change of course.

Frank Judd was in the stokehold, streaked with coal dust, a shovel in his hand. *Drummer's* performance had been getting steadily worse, and at times she had almost lost way entirely. The reason was obvious: the stokers were not *Drummer's* regulars but made up of a cross-section of British and German mutineers, most of whom resented being put to work in the traditional hell-hole of a steam ship. The gold had changed them from sailors to gentlemen of leisure.

Judd had heard their protestations and watched them work. Then, taking up a shovel, had steadily fed the fire for ten minutes.

'Right, I don't want to have to show you again!' He threw the shovel across to one of the stokers. It had taken the man, along with two others, twenty minutes to move the equivalent amount of coal. 'Steam drops off once more and next time I bring Coker and Kapper down here with me. And we won't be shovelling!'

Clapping the dust from his chest he left them.

Baines was running around the quarter deck like a chicken with its head cut off. Spotting Judd he grabbed him by the sleeve. 'Where you been,' he whined. 'I been looking all over. Come here, in here ...'

He pushed open the galley door. 'Piss off,' he said to Hoffman, pushing him out on the deck.

He looked furtively at Judd. 'Listen ... get an earful of ... you won't ...'

'Go easy. You might fall into the pea soup,' said Judd, regarding the agitated Baines. Judd shared everyone else's opinion of Stagg Baines. It was probably the only thing the crew of *Drummer* would share, apart from the gold.

'Kapper,' said Baines. 'He's stark raving mad! Half his cogs are missing! I've been up top listening to him. He wants to chuck the injured overboard, cut *Straker* adrift and sod off, leaving them!'

Judd scooped a wedge of coal dust from between his fingers. 'We'll all get topped!'

'So what you going to do, Baines?'

'Eh? Me? Well, I've thought it out, see. Stick Kapper over the side, for a start. Give him half the chance and he'll do us all in, I tell you he's round the bend. So we drop him over, then we start to do things proper. He's already fucked up the course. What do you say?'

'I hope we're not supposed to eat this,' said Judd, dipping a spoon into the soup.

'Sodding hell! That *all* you got to say?' Baines's lip curled. 'You're bloody shit-scared, that's it! Kapper puts the wind up you! Eech! You make me sick!' He yanked at the galley door and flung it back in disgust.

Karl Recke made no pretence of not having heard every word. He stepped back allowing passage for Baines.

'Talk,' said Baines in a diluted mixture of anger and shock. 'Just a bit of talk. Judd started it, not me.'

Recke walked past him into the galley and closed the door without a word.

'Recke.'

'Judd. I think it is time *we* talked.'

'Less talk and more shovelling and maybe we'd be getting someplace.' Judd grinned. Recke wasn't a bad sort. 'Talk away, comrade.'

Recke was circumspect, choosing his words with care, but Judd knew where he was leading.

Trouble. Again trouble.

Only this time it might be terminal.

15 December

Tilley had been right. A cliché maybe – but things *weren't* ever as bad as at first they seemed. Beattie Dandridge had begun to find life tolerable once more, the sickness and shame that had dogged him slowly being overlaid with the first veneer of strength. A thin, delicate crust, but the beginning. As Tilley might have added: time heals all wounds. Only in Dandridge's case time was only part of it, a small part. The real healer was Elizabeth Lange. Without knowing it she had given him back all that he had lost. His thoughts were crowded with every word she had said, every gesture she had made and there was no room for anything else. He was absorbed, but no longer in himself. Psychologically speaking, Beattie Dandridge had found an emotional safety-valve preventing an inner collapse and breakdown — which was another way of saying something he had, as yet, been fearful to admit.

He had fallen in love.

Standing outside the cabin door he felt the thin sheets of paper grow impossibly heavy in his hand. What if she laughed? He stuffed the poems he had written into his shirt and stared at the door. No. If she laughed, he would laugh too. 'Damn it all!' he said aloud. She owed him nothing more. They would laugh together. He pulled them out, smoothing the creases and knocked.

Elizabeth opened it and he automatically looked over her shoulder, though only a few minutes before he had seen Rose and Hannah on deck.

'Beattie!' She followed his glance. 'They're not here.' Smiled.

'Oh, then I, er . . .'

'And I don't need a chaperone, I assure you.' She gave a curtsy. 'You enter as my guest.'

He stepped over the threshold and into her warmth, forgetting completely the elaborate reasons he had fabricated for visiting the cabin. Seeing her had erased all rational thought. He sat facing her, feeling stupid. Since the first time they had sat together like this they had only managed to meet briefly, and usually with one or both of the women present. 'I hoped we might talk again, like this,' he said.

'So did I,' said Elizabeth. She had come to the conclusion that, so far, it was a most unsatisfactory way to conduct a love affair. She fell deliberately silent, drawing him out of himself. Beattie was the second boy in her life that she had felt anything other than friendship for. The first had been at the German clinic when she was barely sixteen, and the memory was still with her. Her mother had taken her away because of him. At the time it had seemed cruel, heartless — even spiteful, and she had hated her mother for months afterwards. And then he died of tuberculosis and Elizabeth realised that Hannah had been trying to cushion the blow that she had guessed must fall. A litmus of love. The hatred had drained with the tears, but left something else — a realisation that she had been robbed of the chance to show her strength, to decide for herself. The young boy had died with only an ageing uncle at his bedside, she later learned. Love had been taken away from him when he most needed it. Hannah would never see that. And now there was Beattie. It mustn't be the same.

Perhaps she should feel what Hannah felt, but she had tried and couldn't. The sickening disgust of her mother's ordeal at the hands of the German sailor had seemed to become part of yet another distant memory. The small two-roomed apartment in Montevideo where they had lived, and the hushed night sounds of lovemaking through booming paper-thin walls. How different was it? Would she ever be given the chance to find out?

'I've brought some scribblings,' said Dandridge. 'Do you like poetry?'

'Yes. You wrote it?'

'It's not very good ...'

'But first I have something to show you.' Her voice was low. She plucked a bundle of material off the bunk. Holding it to her she glided across the cabin in mock splendour.

'Your dress. It's finished?'

'Yes. If you laugh when you see it on I won't listen to your poems. Turn around.'

Dandridge twisted the chair away and braced his arms across its back. A secretive rustle.

'Wait.' A muffled word.

He turned. Had she said 'now', or 'oh'? He had heard it as 'now'. Elizabeth's head was obscured by the dress that had stuck over it. She was wearing no petticoat, no stockings ... nothing. He tried to turn away. Couldn't. She was the first naked woman he had ever seen.

'There! Ah!' Elizabeth forced the neck-opening over her face and let the dress fall, brushing it smooth against her hips, down over her legs. 'You can turn around now.' She looked up.

'Beautiful,' said Beattie Dandridge hoarsely.

She knew, staring at him silently.

'I ... I thought ...'

'You like it, Beattie?' Her voice was a whisper. 'Like what you ... see?'

'Lisbeth ... I ... didn't ...'

'Come and sit beside me, Beattie.' She sat on the bunk, her face pale.

He held her around the waist and she began to tremble. 'Beattie, hold me, hold me tighter.'

'Elizabeth, please,' he tried to draw away, but she drew his head towards her and the kiss she gave him bore no relation to the peck of their first meeting.

'Beattie ... Please ...'

'No! Oh, God.' He drew breath. 'We can't, I ...'

His belt was undone and she moved her hand under it as he began to moan. 'Don't think, Beattie ... don't think ...' Her breasts were suddenly bare as she lifted the dress and threw it away. Pressing him against them she forced a nipple towards his mouth.

Hannah Lange had taken her daughter's words to heart and Barrow had been more than delighted at her request to be of some practical help on *Straker*. In a short space of time they had drawn up an area where she could work, helping in the galley and with the sick. Rose had gone with her and, though she looked worn after her 'turn', as she put it, of the day before, had nonetheless insisted on going in search of Garrett, whose mouth was the colour and consistency of a bruised pumpkin. All that Hannah felt was a weariness that ate through her with every movement of the ship, and sleep didn't make it go away. But at least she had made a gesture. Elizabeth would be pleased and she needed to please her. To win her back.

She put the key to the lock of the cabin door and frowned. It was open. She had told Elizabeth to use it, always use it when alone. 'Rose?'

Her daughter was naked. Across her sprawled a figure, twitching, its hands entwined in her hair.

Hannah toppled forward clutching at the table for balance. Still they hadn't heard her. Stumbling over a pair of trousers she fumbled for Rose's scissors.

Down.

Down.

The twin finger hooks stood upright of their own accord as she drew back.

Dandridge's hands fell from the girl's hair, his nails biting into her breasts as his back curled. Spitting blood into her face, he spent his love on her stomach.

And began to die.

With one last spasmodic jerk he slid across Elizabeth and fell face downwards to the floor with a force that smashed his teeth. The blood ran from the wound beneath his shirt – high, just missing the bone-shield of the scapula that might have saved him – and down between his buttocks.

Hannah, her eyes closed, stood as if in a trance, swaying gently to some catatonic rhythm. Her daughter's orgasm had been transformed into a hysterical, asthmatic convulsion. Gobbling for air, eyes bulging, she shook herself across the bunk, her head thrashing the pillow.

Which is how Rose found them.

They had followed the old woman without quite knowing why. Whatever it was – and it seemed to revolve around the young girl being taken ill – Rose was so shaken by it as to be incapable of expressing herself. Her huge bosom trembled as she half ran, half walked in front of them, urging them on, tears streaming down her face. Muir and Barrow broke into a trot, fearing the worst.

The captain was the first to enter the cabin and he stopped as if he had walked into an invisible wall. Barrow looked over his shoulder. Hannah Lange was singing softly in her daughter's ear, oblivious of their presence. Barrow knelt and raised the edge of the red flannel dress that Rose had draped over the boy. 'It's ... Dandridge, sir.'

Placing himself to shield the girl from any view of the body, Muir pulled the flannel back to expose the source of the wound. The scissors were still protruding from the midshipman's back. There was no point in feeling his pulse. Covering him, they both stood and for a moment it seemed as if neither of them could move. Muir swallowed. 'Can she walk?' he asked Rose.

'Walk, sir?'

'They must leave here,' said Muir. 'Now. Take her. Number One, help them. In your cabin.'

Elizabeth, wrapped in a blanket, was breathing a stuttered apology for breath, poisoned by the stale air in her lungs.

'Hannah!' Rose caressed the woman's forehead. 'Come with me. Both of you, away from here. Hannah?'

To Muir's relief she managed to get them to their feet.

'I'll be with you presently,' said Muir to Barrow. He closed the cabin door.

'Dandridge.' He had been looking down at the body, shrouded in the flannel dress, for some minutes, and at the end of it it was all he could say. He gave the corpse a name and that gave it respect. And the memory of poor, damned Dandridge needed that now as much as when he had been alive. Kneeling once more, he drew the flannel back and turned the boy's face towards him. The mouth was ragged where he had fallen, his eyes open wide as if looking for an explanation. Muir closed them with a thumb.

'Lord, in Thy infinite wisdom,' he improvised, 'accept this soul into Thy house. Bless him with mercy and forgiveness, for we are all sinners. Regard this, Thy child, as a sheep who has strayed and ...' he paused, '... been led into a wayward world he did not fully understand. Forgive those too who took his life, the confused, the frightened.' He stood up. 'Forgive all of us.'

Picking up a sheaf of papers that had scattered across the floor, he riffled through them. Poems.

He took the key from the table, stepped outside and locked the door. Beattie Dandridge hadn't locked the door. The fact exonerated him from premeditation. But it had condemned him all the same.

To death.

Twenty-four hours and *Straker* must make her move. The thought was no longer vying with the memory of Dandridge's body huddled beneath the bloodied flannel. The dead must now bury their dead. Jack Muir could concern himself only with the living.

Hannah Lange had seemed unaware or unconcerned at what she had done. Her daughter was in a deep sleep on Barrow's bunk and she herself had slumped, head on her chest, asleep in a chair alongside it, eyelids flickering. Rose had cleaned the girl up and was standing alongside Barrow as Muir entered the cabin. He had brought with him the last half bottle of brandy from the back of von Bauer's hospitality cabinet (the rest had been looted by Kapper's men or requisitioned by Dandridge for the old woman). He found three glasses and poured Rose a measure. She took it and her hand shook.

'A drop, Number One?'

'I think it might be in order, sir.'

'So do I.' They sipped their drinks in silence. Muir looked across at Hannah and the girl. 'Will they wake if we talk?'

Rose shook her head. 'The girl sleeps for hours after an attack of asthma and Hannah ... I don't think Hannah ever wants to wake up.'

Muir splashed more brandy into her glass. 'Why, Rose? Why did she *kill* him?' He shook his head. 'Anger, hate, panic, fear — yes I can understand what she must have felt, but to *kill*?'

'I know.' Rose was haggard. Barrow pulled his chair close to her and held her wrist lightly. She gave him a wan smile: 'What will you do to her?'

He caught Muir's eye and the captain nodded.

'First, Rose,' began Barrow, 'we must know exactly what happened. The picture paints itself in some ways, but not in others. As Captain Muir said, whatever was going on, to kill the boy seems out of proportion. But we are only saying that from *our* point of view. Perhaps circumstances were different. Did you hear Elizabeth scream?'

'I got there when it ... it had happened,' said Rose. 'If only I had got there sooner, none of it would have happened.' Muir watched the glass, calculating the remaining contents of the bottle and feeling desperately sorry for the old woman.

'But you didn't hear a scream, Rose? While you were approaching the door ... on the deck ... any time at all?'

'No scream,' said Rose firmly.

'No shouts?'

'I heard nothing, Mr Barrow.'

'And had Elizabeth mentioned Midshipman Dandridge to you at all?'

'She liked him and told me so. He seemed a good boy – immature in a way, but kind enough. When she had the chance she liked to talk with him. Company, you see. Our company must have been a bit ... well, I got on with her, but I'm old. For Hannah it was different ... difficult.'

'Hannah didn't mind them talking?'

'She would never have let them be alone together.'

'Because she didn't trust Dandridge?'

Rose swallowed the contents of her glass and Muir moved forward with a prompt refill. 'Hannah doesn't trust any man born under the sun, Mr Barrow.'

'Rose, I know this is very painful for you, but I must ask you – do you believe Beattie Dandridge raped Elizabeth Lange?'

The old woman looked at him in surprise: 'Oh, no. I never entertained the thought.'

'You didn't?'

'Hannah is a good woman but she has seen too much tragedy and pain. Before all this – before your ship saw us – a man came to our cabin and told me the captain wanted to see me. It took me a long time to find him and when I did he couldn't recall having sent for me. He was still a little angry at us being aboard, but spoke for a while about this and that. When I got back to the cabin she was – she was as I found her with the boy just now. Staring into space, not speaking. Her dress was badly torn and she was bruised. It was obvious what had happened, but she refused to go and tell the captain and made me swear that I wouldn't either. She said the girl would suffer. Only afterwards did I discover to what extent it had gone on. Elizabeth told me.'

'Her daughter? She was there?' Muir looked aghast.

'Hannah was raped while the girl was in a deep sleep, but

somehow she seemed to have heard it all in her fever. The man was an animal. The most terrible thing was that Hannah allowed it to happen, encouraged it.'

Muir leaned forward. 'Are you sure you've got this right, Rose? If the girl was delirious surely she could have imagined ...'

'Hannah offered herself,' said Rose, 'in place of her daughter. I know that, Captain. Believe me.'

Barrow broke the silence that settled over them: 'Who was it, Rose?'

'The man called Kapper. Now understand her fear.'

'And it was presumably Kapper who was sent down to see if you were safe when we started shelling,' said Muir, 'which is why von Bauer thought you were dead.'

'We never saw Kapper. It would have been convenient to leave us there to die if a British ship was about to take us and someone might get to hear what had happened. It hadn't occurred to me that the captain didn't know what was going on.'

'After what happened, Rose,' went on Barrow, 'how did they react? Hannah and Elizabeth?'

'Hannah was frightened, not for herself, but for her daughter. Kapper might return. In the end protection came even before love. But Elizabeth had found something she needed in the young boy and felt everything was being held back by her mother. I think it was like that. She is a very strange young girl at times. What happened to her mother had a funny kind of effect on her. I think of her as girl – she is a young woman, twenty years old.'

'What?' Muir couldn't help himself. 'Twenty?'

'Twenty, almost twenty-one, Captain. She had been repressed for so long ...'

'I thought, well it seemed ... Barrow?'

'I would have said sixteen, perhaps.'

'The poor boy, it will look bad for him,' said Rose as if Dandridge was still alive. 'Elizabeth will believe she was responsible for his death, but to say that will hurt Hannah even more and I don't think she will do that. Not now. Who else have they got now, but each other?'

'And she will say it was rape – to protect her mother?' asked Barrow.

'It depends on what will happen to Hannah. What *will* happen?'

Muir drew a deep breath. 'Rose, I'm going to need your help once more, only this time more than ever. Everyone is right and everyone is wrong. Hannah, Elizabeth, Dandridge have been caught up in a terrible tragedy. Whatever the truth behind it makes no difference now – it is up to us to retrieve what we can from it. Hannah did what she did because she believed her daughter was being attacked, and having suffered herself, well ... no one can condemn her. As for Beattie Dandridge and Elizabeth ...' He coughed. 'They were doing ... what ... er ... young people are sometimes rashly led to do. To pursue the matter further would be pointless. Tell Hannah and her daughter that no one will speak of it any more. And Rose? Help them. They need you.'

The old woman put down her glass. 'The boy must be laid out, Captain. Have you the key?'

'I can't let you distress yourself any more,' said Muir.

'The key, Captain. I want to do it. And alone.'

Muir handed her the key and Barrow opened the cabin door for her. 'Do you want me to come with you, Rose?'

'Alone, Mr Barrow, thank you. I have seen a lot of death in my time.' She looked at Muir. 'Captain, the brandy was very welcome, but I say what I have to say with a head never so clear. Perhaps you will not understand me, I don't know. Just let me say that some of we Irish feel things other people can't – or don't want to – feel. There is something bad on this ship, and whatever it is began when Hannah Lange's husband disappeared. I *feel* it. I feel him watching over his wife and daughter, trying to reach for them. All this is not Hannah's doing alone, Captain – someone was guiding her hand. A presence. This ship doesn't need any more sailors, it needs a man of God. To purge it!'

'Well?' said Muir.

'They say the hair rises on the back of your neck,' said Barrow. 'I never believed it. Until they just did.'

'Has somebody blabbed?'

'No, she just feels what she says she feels. Extraordinary woman. I saw her with Garrett, just briefly. She was stroking his jaw and I could *see* the swelling going down.'

'I can't even begin to *think* about that,' said Muir. 'The first thing is that we can't let the boy's memory be trailed in the mud. After listening to Rose I'm convinced rape never entered into it. He was foolish, but that was all. Which is why I intend to break every law in the book.' It was becoming a habit, he reflected. 'Beattie Dandridge has been killed in the course of ...' he checked the unfortunate phrase '... he died honourably and that is how he will be remembered. He was trying to help locate the leak and was crushed by moving ballast. It's the best I can think of and will have to do, but we're all getting used enough to death by now and it won't be questioned. The funeral will be first thing tomorrow. Now, what do you make of the sudden change of course?'

'It's less surprising than where we were going,' said Barrow. 'We're heading directly for Sao Pedro e Sao Paulo – St Paul's Rocks. Presumably they'll dump us there. That really isn't the most pressing news, sir.'

'Tell me.'

'As I was bringing the women here I was told *Drummer* has signalled. It's bad news, I'm afraid. They want Garrett returned.'

'They've got wind of something,' said Muir. 'I wondered how long we could keep pushing them. Sod and damnation, we need him desperately!'

'I've been thinking about that, sir. There is a possible way out, if I might venture . . .'

'Venture away, Number One. Anything.'

'Tomorrow we have a funeral service for poor old Beattie Dandridge. *Drummer* will have to be told. Now one thing any captain would turn from is fabricating a funeral at sea – it invites all manner of trouble, and I think as far as that is concerned I'd be as superstitious as the next man. *Drummer* would know there was no trick being played.'

'Trick? Why "trick"? I may have cut a few corners, but messing about with a man's death . . .'

'Exactly. No "messing about" at all, sir. Dandridge is accorded the proper rites, the service properly conducted, *Drummer* told everything. I will signal them myself and what I say will be seen by no one aboard *Straker* and everyone aboard *Drummer*.'

'And what,' said Muir warily, 'is it you plan to signal, Number One?'

'I will signal that Garrett cannot go back to *Drummer* for a reason they can see with their own eyes. Garrett has died of his illness. We are burying him.'

16 December

Death had burrowed through *Straker* like a wasp through a peach, infecting it from inside, leaving the sheen on the skin

198

but slowly fermenting corruption. From the spars where hooked hands had frozen in rigor mortis and been cracked open by the weight of a falling body, to the deck, where headless men had momentarily walked, and the forepeak, in which Oskar Lange secretly wallowed, cursing them all, there was no line the eye could follow that was free from it. *Straker* herself was dying and the men who were forcing her to live now stood silently, their own mortality stitched in sailcloth and wrapped in the Union Flag.

Jack Muir had finished his brief oration, and bowed his head as Beattie Dandridge's body was gently lowered over the side, the ropes supporting his shoulders and feet being paid out by Tilley and Hackett as the boy began his journey in search of peace.

His speech had been inadequate, Muir knew, but he had found it difficult to find eloquence enough.

The men had taken the boy's death badly, almost seeming to resent it, as if, after the carnage they had seen, it had been a matter of spite. The story of his 'accident' in the hold had caused no comment, but the death itself was an evil nudge in the ribs when all of them least needed it. Anger had become a substitute for grief. They stared at Muir.

Barrow suddenly walked to the rail and faced them. His voice was low, but powerful:

> 'I have loved thee, Ocean! And my joy
> Of youthful sports was on thy breast to be
> Borne like thy bubbles onward; from a boy
> I wanton'd with thy breakers – they to me
> Were a delight; and if the freshening sea
> Made them a terror – 'twas a pleasing fear,
> For I was, as it were, a child of thee.
> And trusted to thy billows far and near,
> And laid my hand upon thy mane – as I do here.'

He stepped aside, his face stiff as Tilley and Hackett let go of their ropes. There was a faint splash.

'We will take the memory of Midshipman Dandridge home with us,' said Muir decisively. 'The memory of *all* who have died will not end here.' He had meant to keep his plans from them until the last minute, but now they needed something. He glanced at von Bauer. The German captain was staring over the crew's heads, across his ship. Alongside the man she had once wanted to kill stood Rose.

199

'I have decided that no longer will we wait for what fate, or the men out there, have to offer. Your efforts and the work you have done have committed me. We are going to take *Drummer* back. And if every man does exactly as he is ordered without question, I hope before very much longer to be congratulating you once again. As for *Straker*'s crew – the men who are with us now – I don't think I need to explain that they have no sword hanging over them.' He turned aside. 'I would be obliged if you would tell those who do not understand me exactly what I have said, Captain von Bauer. Accurately, if you please.'

The German captain ignored the inference. He spoke in German and this time there was no doubt that the message was the correct one. Tilley tugged off his cap heedless of the display of scarred scalp. 'Three cheers,' he shouted. 'Three cheers for *Straker!*'

Muir groaned inwardly. Could the boy be forgotten so easily – passed over for a burst of jingoism? But something in Barrow's expression stopped him. *Straker* had found life in death. To lose that strength now would be to throw away Beattie Dandridge's blessing.

Charlie Pickett stood to attention alongside Arnold Prettie, while Bellamy and three men – including the scalded Webster – who had managed to walk from the sick bay to pay their last respects stood swaying behind them. Pickett couldn't swear to it, but half a dozen of the mutineers – German and English – seemed to be staring at *Straker*.

The Committal to the Deep service had been glimpsed behind the rising and falling prow of the windjammer and the faint cheering – odd, that, he couldn't help thinking – had reached them at its end. Tom Garrett had been a good man, a good engineer and a good sailor. He could not remember him ever raising his voice in anger or complaint and he shared a joke with the next. Or had until a few months ago when, for some reason, he had become quiet and unusually withdrawn. Pickett had gently joshed him about the mood he was in but afterwards, alone, Prettie had quietly suggested he dropped it. Tom Garrett was going through ·some form of mental crisis that could only work itself out on its own. Poor Garrett, his last days, for whatever reason, hadn't been happy ones.

'Get these swine to work!' Kapper had come from his cabin and was bleary-eyed with sleep. He stared at the men on deck and at Frank Judd in particular. Judd wasn't at attention, but had watched the Committal to its close. 'Hear me, Judd!'

'Stow it, *mister*,' said Judd.

Karl Recke touched Kapper's arm. 'Leave them, Kapper, it's a private thing and all over now anyway . . .' Kapper pushed him away.

'Where's Coker?' Kapper looked wildly around. But Coker was on the bridge, where he intended to stay after Kapper's last navigational fiasco. 'What you say, Judd? What did I hear?'

Judd ambled towards him: 'I said "stow it", Kapper. This business was private, see? I knew Tom Garrett for a few years, and a couple of minutes saying cheerio isn't going to break your heart now, is it? So let's all quieten down and get back to the job in hand.'

Kapper angled his jaw. 'I've had as much from you, mister . . .'

Bellamy had been staring at a spot between his feet, apparently lost in thought. Now he raised his head to look at the fuming German. 'That man has died,' he said. 'Now will you believe I am not joking? He had the same illness that you have, only in your case I can keep you alive. Unless more food is given to the injured I have decided to refuse to do this. You have no respect for the dead — and perhaps I do not either, for very different reasons. But I respect the sick who cannot help themselves.' Bellamy hoped he had kept the doubt out of his voice. The patchwork of lies, deception, histrionics and more lies had got to the stage where even he — at the centre of it all — had begun to lose the thread. Garrett's death was inexplicable. But Barrow had been unequivocal in his message: the chief engineer had died of ruptured lungs through excessive, unrestrained coughing. Yet the examination he had made before unsuccessfully trying to lance the poisoned gum had disclosed no lung infection, no heart problems, nothing.

Kapper's face was purple. Pickett moved slowly out of his vision and slid a hand under his shirt, feeling for the scalpel stuck into his belt. If Kapper was going to give another performance then this time it would be slightly less one-sided.

But Bellamy seemed completely bored by the German's imminent explosion. 'I will sew stitches in your nose, as someone had to do with Garrett,' he said, 'and that is the only "treatment" I will give unless you are reasonable.'

Kapper pushed through the gathering and walked away, throwing back a string of German oaths.

'He backed down,' breathed Pickett. 'He really did. What's he got, sir, that you could do that to him?'

'I find myself in the position of being the safest man on this ship, Pickett,' said Bellamy. 'Kapper kills me, he kills himself. Quite a delicate arrangement, while it lasts.'

'I think you'll get your food, Bellamy,' said Judd. Despite the surgeon's modesty, it hadn't been that simple or that sure and he must have known it. Kapper wasn't the kind to think ahead and his violence was inspired by itself, with unreliable safety catches.

'*Their* food,' corrected the surgeon. 'Not mine.'

'Poor old Tom Garrett,' said Pickett to no one in particular.

'Garrett's got no problems now,' said Judd. 'We have. So get back to your business, all of you. Including you, Bellamy. Remember you're not treating me for anything and when I say move, you move.' His voice held no threat; it was almost apologetic. Karl Recke looked at him strangely.

Bellamy nodded and walked away, pausing for a moment outside the sick bay and looking back at *Straker*.

'Something wrong, sir?' asked Pickett.

'No.' Bellamy was thinking about Garrett's 'death'. And wondering whether Muir was becoming entangled in his own intrigue.

Judd had turned out to be as much use as a lead lifeboat, Recke was wandering around in a daze, and only Coker seemed to have any guts left at all, but Coker wouldn't lift a finger until he felt himself in danger. Recke, greasy little rat that he was, had been listening when he, Baines, had talked to Judd and there was no telling that he might not go running to Kapper in order to keep his nose clean. And if that happened it would be all over. Baines felt the huge German's feet tread across his grave and shuddered. None of the bastards would help him! Yes, Recke had gone in to talk to Judd. All they had to do now was tell Kapper and they would be able to claim his share – that was it, no bloody question, they were after his gold! He had to move fast. Get rid of Kapper and tell Coker that the German, along with Judd and Recke, had been plotting to do all of them in. Coker could handle it from there.

Stagg Baines smothered a giggle. That would make, how many – *three* extra shares. And he'd be buggered if it would be spread across the board! Two extra for him and one for Coker. Or one and a half each if Coker pushed it – but then Coker would be so grateful when he heard what he heard, he'd most likely give him the lot! All the loose ends would be taken care of. So the swines wouldn't help him now! They'd regret it! Christ, how they were going to regret it!

Walking across the cabin, he took the pistol that Kapper had thrown across Muir's desk and for the third time checked its chamber. The jacketted bullets cancelled out anything Judd or Recke might come up with. How did it go: 'Be not afraid of any man, no matter what his size – when I am with you, dum de something, I will equalise.' He laughed and, reaching for the bottle of surgical spirit he had filched from under Bellamy's nose, filled the tin mug to three-quarters of its level, topping it up with lime juice. The real booze had long gone, but this wasn't too bad. His hand stopped shaking. One bullet, that was all it needed. Kapper's ugly mug would look pretty compared to what one of these little beauties would do to it. The funniest thing was that Kapper himself had given him the gun in the first place. His big hams couldn't cope with it.

Baines wiped his burning lips with the back of his hand and steadied the pistol at arm's length. Turning it around he shared Kapper's last vision. One more shot of liquor. He stuffed the pistol into his pocket and drank.

Night, such as it was, had begun to fall, bathing *Drummer* in starlight. Enough to blunt the sight of the unsuspecting, yet, at the same time, sufficient to illuminate Kapper against the horizon. It couldn't be better!

The surgical spirit had invested Baines with a growing confidence. In less than an hour it would all be over. Judd, Recke, could burble their heads off and it wouldn't do them any good. One thing: Kapper's head wouldn't be burbling any more. Off, yes! Baines giggled again. Good one, that. Bloody hell, why hadn't he done this a long time ago, there was nothing to be scared of, ab-so-lutely fuck all! He had underestimated himself.

The barrel was cold and reassuring against his groin and he hiked at his crotch. First thing he would do was get little Dandridge back, mistake that, letting him go, mistake. *Drummer* rolled and he missed the door handle, staggering backwards across the cabin. Blinking, he tried again and was out on deck. Easy . . . easy.

The night air sucked the alcohol from him like blotting paper until a pungent vinegar smell wafted around him. The bloody ship seemed to be taking the sea badly, it was all over the place! He lurched towards the forrard well deck, swearing, and waited beneath the broken derrick. Kapper would have begun to make his rounds, and he was waiting for him. Every step was drawing the ugly mad bastard towards his last. Coker on the bridge would hear the shot and Baines would give him the thumbs-up, just to let him know he was safe. Important that Coker didn't feel threatened. So many things to remember ... So many ...

'Baines, that you?'

Stagg Baines found himself sprawled across the hatch cover. It was over -- must be! His eyelids were sticking together and his head pounding. He poked at his eyes. Kapper. It was Kapper! How? Christ, he'd fallen asleep! He dug into his pocket for the pistol butt and dragged himself to a sitting position. The German was standing by the rail, thirty feet away.

'Me,' mumbled Baines. ' 'S'all right, Kapper. Just me.' He disentangled the pistol from the pocket lining and stood up unsteadily. His body was shaking and his mouth bloated, a blue-tinged circle forming around his lips.

'What you up to, mister?' Kapper was carrying a four-foot section of wood shaped like a club.

Baines wobbled towards him. There was nothing to worry about. I will eeglise ... ewklise ... The rail caught his hip and he winced, clutching at it to keep his balance. All of them bastards! It took one ... just one ... he didn't need any of them ... ' 'Sme, Kapper, like said, me ...' The German was hiding among the stars, but it wouldn't do him any good. Baines drew the pistol and fired.

'Mister?' A growl.

It had gone. The pistol had disappeared! Baines stared at the space where it had been and couldn't see his hand. Mentally clenching his fist he fired again but this time there was no sound, except for a strange splashing. Kapper was walking towards him. He tried to wake up.

Stagg Baines would be for ever unaware that he was the first man to fire that particular Webley and Scott 0.455. Even less aware that the jacketting on its cartridges was one millimetre thicker than the pistol's bore, an error that had been discovered and hastily rectified in most models a year before, after a number of them had prematurely exploded. Jack Muir's pistol had lain uncorrected and unused for years. The first time it had been fired, the fast-burning seven-grain charge had built up sufficient pressure to blow out the revolver's cylinder, taking with it Baines's hand and a portion of his forearm; all, as it happened, anaesthetised by the surgical spirit swilling around inside him.

Kapper was grinning. He strolled up to Baines and stood aside from the spurting radial arteries.

'Kapp ... 'sme ... Baines ... Stagg ... it went off ... mistake ...' He nodded at his still outstretched arm, hopelessly. 'Look what it's done ...'

The blow hit him casually across the side of the head, the wood ringing with the impact, and he went over the rail without another sound. He was alive, but only just, when the first shark found him.

17 December

Finding sleep more elusive than ever, von Bauer finally abandoned the futile search for it, swung from his bunk and quickly dressed. He had lain listening during the ship's silent hours to the muted piping and the soft signals for the relieving watches to muster – what the British called 'little-one-bell'. It was the middle of the morning watch. Six a.m.

Early that evening he had made his own unofficial inspection of *Straker*, assessing her seaworthiness and the mood of the men. The latter had made him realise that his self-imposed exile was unnecessary and self-defeating. German and English crewmen alike treated him with a respect that was no less than that which they accorded Muir. Forcibly breaking down his own innate reserve, he had talked with many of them at length, finding it a strangely refreshing experience. What were their chances? Would *Straker* hold up? What had been planned? He had tried to assure them as best he could without disclosing that he was not totally privy to what Muir might be planning.

'This should have been done sooner,' Mueller had whispered candidly at one point. Even Detweiler had lost some of the distance he had put between himself and his captain. It had been, on the whole, a satisfying exercise on many counts, and the sleepless hours had consolidated it – spent in thought of the added leverage it would give him. The only imponderable was Muir himself. If the British captain failed, then he too would fail. It needed Muir to build the bridge for him to walk across and open up the struggle that must inevitably follow. The man who smashed a citadel did not necessarily get to rule it. For the moment, however, he would think of it as a partnership.

The lack of sleep had sharpened rather than dulled him and he stepped on deck feeling almost lighthearted.

Straker had changed.

He sensed it as surely as a horseman senses some fickleness in his mount. At first it was nothing tangible, like walking into a familiar room and knowing *something*, some small, omnipresent article had been moved. But which? *Straker*'s trim had altered and she was no longer down at the head, but it was more than that – he had sailed her in all conditions and he had never felt her like this. She was heavy on the decks, as if her scuppers were awash due to blocked waterways. Looking forrard he saw that he had not been the only one to go without sleep that night. New chafing gear had been fixed to the standing rigging; braces and lifts had been made new, the missing foresheets controlling the clews of the foresail replaced; and, most significantly, the two spare lower yardarms hoisted to their trusses. On every serviceable yard the suit of storm sails was furled and secured in its gaskets. All of it had been done in the dead of night and with a stealth that had obviously been designed to escape *Drummer*'s attention. Muir, it seemed, was about to make his move.

'Captain?' Mueller's face was flushed as he strode along the gangway. 'What does it mean?'

Von Bauer shrugged.

'Ask him, Captain – you have a right to know! We all have.'

'Why? There is no possibility of our sailing away, Mueller, none at all. And if the men aboard *Drummer* are the seamen they have so far shown themselves to be, they will have seen none of this. Was Detweiler involved in that furling? It has his trademark. From a distance it would be difficult to detect at all.'

'Hasso knows nothing about it,' said Mueller impatiently. 'Muir has just told him that when the time is right he will be called for, but not until then. We have been below decks, ordered to keep everyone else down there while – *this* was going on.'

'Then I think it best to leave Captain Muir to his own devices for the moment,' said von Bauer. The strange trim was still bothering him. He caught a glimpse of Muir standing on the topgallant fo'c'sle, men moving around him with a pre-determined efficiency. 'That should concern us more.'

Muir craned his head.

The English captain was slowly being obscured by the crates of gold that were being winched up on deck.

The crates were lifted on large all-purpose luff tackle hooked to one another. Two single and two double blocks raised them on an improvised hogshead sling – a basic purchase that allowed a quick change-over from one crate to the next. Even so, Muir was apprehensive. It needed only one crate to slip and split and everything he had planned would smash with it, and the chances of that happening increased with every minute. The men were exhausted, moving in a dream, muscles locked rigid with a cramp that felled them indiscriminately, leaving them pounding the sluggish blood back into circulation. None of them complained. Those who knew what was going on (or part of it) were aware that they were members of a select brotherhood setting in motion the final act, the last chance, and that alone was enough to drive them. The Germans now allowed on deck knew only the physical demands of their bodies, tending the guys, oiling the donkey engine, pressed in the rigging. Muir felt even more admiration for them than for the rest – none had questioned his orders and it was a trust greater than he had dared hope for.

'Pile them high,' said Barrow, checking the rope tension. The crates hovered and bumped one on top of the other, resting on the wooden blocks that allowed the ropes to be unslung beneath them.

'A pyramid,' added Muir. 'Get them into the pyramid.' That way, when needed, two tackles could be used side by side. And they would be seen more readily from *Drummer*. The thought had crossed his mind that maybe they wouldn't be seen at all, and would simply stay there until a bad sea came and washed them overboard. In which case, Jack Muir knew, he was going to look very silly indeed.

'Keep at it, Number One, I'll be back in a jiffy.'

Now came the awkward part.

'Captain?'

Von Bauer gave a nod of greeting, Mueller hovering uneasily alongside him.

Muir felt sorry for Mueller. In a way he wasn't unlike Barrow – and in fact they seemed to have discovered that themselves, striking up what could almost be described as a friendship. Von Bauer had good reason to be grateful. But then von Bauer was von Bauer and Mueller couldn't have had an easy time of it.

'You will have seen our preparations,' said Muir. 'Secrecy was essential. There was little point in bothering you with mere possibilities until practicalities had been resolved. Now I think *together* we can discuss the next move.' For the moment he was prepared to be conciliatory.

'Captain!' burst out Mueller, 'with respect, you cannot be unaware that many of this crew are Germans first and foremost, no matter how they have followed your *diktat*! They have many reasons to listen to Captain von Bauer at a time when their lives are in the balance. And there is no reason why you should not explain . . .' he faltered as von Bauer's hand tapped his sleeve.

'I think not at this moment.'

'The time *has* come to talk, Mueller,' said Muir. He ignored the implication that they should be working on a fifty-fifty basis. That had been settled once and he wasn't going to re-plough it. Mueller, in some respects, was seeing things more clearly than von Bauer.

'The gold is going to be thrown over the side,' he said, aware that the information would drive anything else out of their minds. 'Thrown crate by crate. It will turn a liability into an asset. The guns are working, or so I believe, and so, we hope, is the auxiliary, though I have no way of being certain of either. We will draw Kapper and Coker on to our ground – as, I might remind you, Captain, you once tried to do to us. Unfortunately you lost the element of surprise. As long as there is a little gold remaining they will not sink us or they lose everything. We, apparently, have no guns, and will remain silent until the time is right.'

'You are prepared to lose the gold?' said von Bauer.

'Yes. Rather than our lives,' answered Muir. 'It will bring them. They must try and board us, and I don't believe Kapper will let that be done by anyone but himself.'

'And *when* Kapper comes aboard?' Mueller still had some of the fuel left over from his interrupted confrontation, and his tone suggested he was determined not to waste it.

'Herr Mueller, if I were your captain I would be pleased to have you as my first lieutenant, but I am *asking* you and Detweiler and all the other members of *Straker*'s crew to trust in me – for all our sakes. Disharmony now will drive nails through us and the only man who will benefit is Kapper. If he comes, Kapper will be taken care of. Now, can we go into detail? I suggest we talk in my cabin.'

The 'my' was only faintly accentuated.

The word was spread through *Straker*, and synchronised to the second by the bell sounding the ending of the morning and the beginning of the forenoon watch. Eight a.m. A cloudless sky and the touch of a breeze. Barrow, Offord, Mueller and Detweiler had split the men among them to avoid any suspiciously large gathering on deck, but the substance of their communiqués was identical: within minutes a number of the crew – and this time Muir asked for volunteers – would be required to start dumping the crates of gold overboard from the topgallant fo'c'sle.

The rest were to be assigned stations that they would man only on the piping of the Special Call, followed by a trumpet blast. Their immediate orders were to keep out of sight: disappear into any cranny they could find. There was no shortage of those aboard *Straker*.

Volunteers were to be given select hiding places that they would find quickly accessible.

It had been left to Detweiler to organise one other select group – those who could handle the rigging – and it was inevitable that this would consist of Germans. Muir was pleased when Barrow reported that the volunteers accepted for the fo'c'sle were three-quarters *Drummer*'s old crew. It gave the right balance.

'And they took it well?'

'Well,' said Barrow. 'I told them exactly what was going to happen.'

'The women?'

'The same, sir.'

They were standing at the midships wheel watching the pulleys swing into place.

'I want you to give Garrett some moral support, Number One. His nerves are shot to pieces, and the tension isn't going to help him any. Just jolly him along, gently.'

'Will do. Hackett has done a good job with the guns, by the way. Only von Bauer seems to be a bit of a problem, I'm afraid.'

'Oh God,' groaned Muir. 'What now?'

'I doubt if you will get him to go below, sir. He baulks at, as he puts it, crawling among the ballast of his own ship. He's even more adamant than usual. No doubt you'll be getting it in the neck any moment. He's looking for you.'

'He chooses the damnedest moments to kick up!'

'Sometimes I get the feeling he's not just kicking up but still hasn't accepted that he is not running the show, despite what he says. Or at least that he's still dreaming of some kind of "truce with honour" and if we get out of this you'll give him back his ship and we will sail our separate ways.'

'He can *think* about it,' said Muir. 'That's as close as it comes to possibility.' He looked at his watch. Mueller and Offord were waiting forrard. 'Well, here we go. Say a little prayer for Garrett's handiwork.' He hesitated. Von Bauer was heading towards him.

'Captain Muir!'

'A misunderstanding,' said Muir. 'There will be no need for

you to go below. In fact I would like you to be with me. You cannot disagree with *that*!'

The carpet pulled from under him, the German captain managed to mumble: 'And where will that be?'

'Simply follow me and all will be explained. Now, please, no more discussion.' He raised a hand above his head and swung it down as if clenching an axe. Blocks began to rattle and the pulleys fell. 'England expects *every* man to do his duty, Captain von Bauer,' he said and led the German captain away with the merest hint of a wink to Barrow.

Erlich's discovery in 1910 of arsphenamine turned all previous drug treatment on its tail. The first drug to be manufactured as a specific remedy for a specific disease. Its arsenic base had been rendered harmless to man but poisonous to the germs of syphilis. But in the space of the following four years it was found not to be as harmless as was first imagined. Erlich was forced to reconsider his discovery and in 1914 replaced it with neoarsphenamine, which became the standard treatment. An esoteric piece of medical fact, but one Bellamy had had good cause to remember when he had found the ancient bottle of yellow powder in his medical cabinet. It had never been used, and should have been thrown away. Arsphenamine. He had tripled the dosage.

Friedrich Kapper's fingertips tingled as if they had been brushed with nettles and he rubbed them raw against his chest. For two days, to think of food had been to imagine lumps of glass sliding down a throat that found it painful to swallow water. That morning he had pissed blood and fainted. But the cramps had gone in his knee-joints and the attacks of fatigue with them. Bellamy was holding back the treatment, watering down the dosage, he knew it. When he had recovered consciousness the panic had expressed itself in an overwhelming urge to beat his own body, or if necessary someone else's, into submission. The bloody bitch of a woman would suffer eventually, that he promised: no, he would satisfy himself by whipping the rest into line – including Coker.

He jerked the sailor oiling the hawser to his feet and threw him aside. 'The swining thing is too tight,' he spat, kicking the man away. The effort sank a stone into his stomach. Eyes bloodshot, he followed the wire back to *Straker* and saw the faint splash. For a brief moment the lacuna in his mind robbed him of speech or movement.

Another crate was dangling over the windjammer's side. As

it hit the water a bubbling, foaming gurgle of white sound exploded in Kapper's head.

Roaring, he pounded towards the bridge.

Ship's engines were automated mules. Once they could be cajoled into moving they paced their blindfold circles without thought of night or day. Stop them, and they began to wonder why they had been so unquestioning in the first place.

Tom Garrett, for what seemed the past ten years, had been locked in mental combat with *Straker's* intractable mule – her 1000 horsepower engine. Persuasion had produced no results, and it had taken him a long time to come to the conclusion that, basically, he was dealing with a German who didn't understand his language and had no intention of trying. From then on it had become a quiet battle of wits.

He wiped his hands on his forearm, adding the fifth epiderm of oil, and knew it had paid off. The engine had made its peace. How it had ever worked in the first place was something he would never grasp. Gobbets of jellified oil he had plucked from its throat were spattered around his feet in a black phlegm. Now it *wanted* to move, but there could be no rehearsal, and it might have doubts. He heard a mockery of its beat throbbing in his skull and clutched his jaw. The broken tooth seemed to be growing back into his gum, squeezing the nerves behind his eyes.

'I think I've done it,' he said. He wished she could see him now, the dragon at his feet. Here lay his real strength, one that she had never seen or even begun to understand, despite his meticulous descriptions. None of them seemed to have any effect other than reducing him to a sweating, grimy, awkward oil-grubber who, when the evening was done, spent so long obsessively cleaning his hands that she was asleep by the time he dared touch her.

'Maggie,' he said.

The mute engine glistened. If it worked it would help to take him closer to the real pain. If it rejected him no other decisions would ever be needed. Soon, one way or the other, it would be out of his hands. He swallowed one of the pills Bellamy had given him and tried to think of something else.

Tilley, crouched on the fore deck, had the dubious privilege of seeing the first burst of machine-gun fire scatter across the sea in front of *Straker*. Tiny Winslow and Hollis were guiding the pulley hook down on to another crate and were too engrossed to notice. The rest of the volunteers jockeyed the crate into position as Winslow suddenly hoisted himself up on to the mountain of crates and, with all his sixteen stone, began to tug at the hook which had twisted and jammed in its block. Suspended like a porcelain buddha salvaged from some sunken treasure ship, he patiently waited for his weight to defeat the rope's internal dynamics and then snapped the hook on to the sling, sliding down to the deck as dainty as a suet pudding.

Barrow was supervising the operation. 'Well done,' Tilley heard him call.

It was surreal. Tilley, who had volunteered for deck duty, had been kept minding the hawser, which, considering the circumstances, was a dangerous enough occupation. But the thought of feeding syrup to a wire was becoming unbearable as he watched the men sweat. Pushing aside the bucket he went down to lend a hand. Barrow didn't seem to mind.

'They're turning!' shouted Detweiler from up in the rigging.

Straker began to lose way as the hawser slackened and *Drummer* swung hard to starboard. Barrow looked at the ship. They were doubling back trying to get their Maxims in range. 'Wait for it.'

There was not long to wait. Another shower of gunfire hit the sea fifty yards from *Straker*'s bow.

'Fast as you can, lads,' Barrow regarded the straining men anxiously. All the crates had to be offloaded within the next five minutes. *Drummer* wouldn't use her 4.7s for fear of sinking them, but Maxim fire alone, when they found range, could clear the decks in no uncertain way.

There were five crates left when the co-ordinates of chance met on the figure of Yeoman Hollis and the Maxim found its mark. 'Oh!' exclaimed Hollis with no more stress in his voice than if he had been slapped a little over-boisterously on the back. Barrow leapt for him as he fell towards the whirring cogs of the winch, and tore open his shirt.

'Sir?' said Hollis, waiting for an explanation.

'It's all right, old chap. Easy does it.' Barrow's hand encountered a damp sponginess.

'Oh, I see.' Hollis smiled his last signal and died, the puzzle solved.

Four crates. The machine-gun fire was murderous, sweeping *Straker* like bird-shot. Barrow laid Hollis's head on the deck and roared: 'Almost finished! Keep at it!'

'Is he dead, Mr Barrow?' It was Rose.

'Below, below!' Barrow pushed her to a crouch. 'Get out of this!'

Tiny Winslow clutched his shoulder and gave a bellow of outrage. A splinter of wood stuck out of it like an arrow. Bent double, Rose padded across to him, slapped two fingers around the point of entry pressing the skin taut, and pulled out the splinter with her teeth. Winslow sank to his knees, his eyes rolling.

'You're too big a fellow for a bit of wood to bother you,' said Rose, spitting out the five-inch sliver behind her so he couldn't see it. Winslow scrabbled to his feet.

'Have you bandages?' she called back to Barrow.

'Rose! Get below!' Barrow flung up his hands in despair. 'Yes, over there in the canvas roll.'

She strapped Winslow's shoulder expertly and moved back to Hollis.

'He's gone, Rose, nothing more you can do. Leave us to it! That's an order!'

'Don't tell me what to do with my life, young man – I've kept it longer than you have yours, so I'd be . . .'

The edge of a crate showered sawdust over her as *Drummer*'s guns concentrated their fire over the fore deck.

'Two more!' shouted Barrow. He jammed the hook under the rope. 'Up! Up! Get rid of the damnblasted thing – God!'

Rose shrilled as three men fell to the deck, one crawling in the yellow slime that was oozing from his stomach.

'See to him,' said Barrow. It was worse than anyone could have imagined. The gunfire came at them without pause and *Straker* was hardly moving, providing the easiest of targets. Tilley helped him hook the last crate as Muir came racing from the saloon, appalled at the carnage. 'Get out of here, Barrow, this is too much!'

'Got the bitch!' Winslow engaged the hook, the bandage fluttering from his shoulder as he slammed the support rope up to meet it. 'Take her away!'

'We can't leave it, sir,' shouted Barrow. 'Not now!' The winch hummed.

Muir and Rose were carrying away one of the injured.

'Let her go!' The crate fell into the sea. 'Now all of you, get out of here, at the double!' Barrow lifted bodily the German who was holding his stomach in place and began to stagger to shelter. 'All of you. Here me!'

Crouching low, the men began to scuttle from the deck. Tilley was staring at his arm. Blood was pouring down it and yet he felt nothing. He wiped it away and there was no wound beneath. Again it blossomed scarlet and he looked up. Detweiler hung like a trapped fly in a web, caught high in the rigging, his leg shattered.

'Detweiler!' Tilley raced for the ratlines. But it was too late. Detweiler fell, turning once in his flight.

'Noooo!' Tilley turned away from the dreadful sight, clutching his mouth.

Kapper couldn't keep still. He trod the length of the boat, threatening to capsize them all, spittle lacing each curse as he waved his rifle and swore at them to pull harder. They bent their backs like galley slaves, veins near bursting point, arms straining in their sockets, none daring to catch his eye.

Kapper had left Coker watching in amazement as he had piled guns and ammunition into two of *Drummer*'s boats and herded the nearest men towards them with kicks and curses. A stubbed finger against his chest had been all Coker had known about what going on; an implicit threat.

'You, mister, like all of them!' Kapper had gasped. 'You and all of them! I come back for you!'

The German was in a pitch of rage that left him incoherent.

Only when the boats were pulling away from *Drummer* had Coker seen what was happening on *Straker* and spun the wheel.

It seemed a waste of time. Every crate had gone before Kapper was anywhere near her.

The Maxim fire that had been passing over their heads from *Drummer* had stopped. Kapper fired a wild round from his rifle. A sample. Once aboard not one of them would live! She would sail on with a dead crew. He squeezed the rifle butt, comfortingly, and his face creased. It couldn't be gone ... couldn't be! A thought struck him. 'They will dive for it!' he shouted. 'Dive for it! I'll lash them by the legs like cormorants and drop them down with lead around their waist! If they don't bring it up, they drown.' He was wildly excited by the solution, and began to laugh, a staccato bark that shook his body. 'Von Bauer, do you hear me? I'll feed you to the sea! All of you! And you'll feed me back my gold! You don't know Friedrich Kapper, mister!' He shot another round at the sea. 'Wait for your friends, Baines,' he told it. Baines's bullet had gone right through him without causing a mark – he had healed immediately. A sign. He was indestructible! He tore the shirt away from his chest. 'Look at that, you swine! What chance have you got?'

Bellamy had lost the race. His drugs, momentarily checking the more dramatic symptoms of Kapper's disease, had been unable to kill him in time. The German had reached the final stage of his degeneration – *dementia paralytica*, the surgeon would have called it, and he would have been no more accurate than the men in the boat, who simply knew their leader had gone totally insane.

'Close in!' Both boats were within yards of *Straker* and the ropes that had been put down for Garrett were still trailing her length, left there by Muir to provide for any injured who might fall overboard. The exhausted oarsmen looked at them balefully.

'Tie the rifles round your necks,' said Kapper, his voice carrying to the following boat. 'Up the side, and anyone who drops can swim back!' He grabbed one of the ropes as they hit *Straker*'s side and held them alongside, locking his knees under a thwart.

'Up!'

They began to climb, spurred to achieve what their bodies told them was impossible by the positive results of failure. Kapper waited until the second boat joined them and only then hauled himself up. He looked over the rail. 'What are you playing at?' The boat was hammering itself to pieces, wood splintering from her gunwales, as a man hung from the rope unable to move any further. Kapper shot him through the chest. 'Now, the rest of you – up!'

They were on the midships deck. No sound, no movement. The wheel was unattended. Kapper slid a dividing arm across ten men. 'Go through the ship. Shoot anyone who resists, the rest bring here. Leave the women. *I* want them.' He waved the rest behind him and they followed him like bedraggled ducklings as he marched towards the poop. A sudden shot rang out. 'The saloon,' said Kapper. He began to run.

Without testing the doorhandle, Kapper mangled it with four rounds from his rifle and kicked it open. Muir and von Bauer stood against the far wall, unarmed. The gun that had fired the shot was on the table.

'Shoot now, Kapper, and you'll never know what happened to your gold!' Muir jabbed his pipe stem. 'Do you think we were so foolish as to throw it away? Do you? I wanted you here on board *Straker* to make a deal with you – to get food. My men are dying of starvation.'

'You are going to die, mister. Both of you!' Kapper blinked away a rainbow of light that had begun to flash in the corner of an eye. He stepped into the middle of the saloon, herding the rest around him.

'It was a trick, Kapper – a trick to get you here, and it worked. Now we can talk, face to face!'

Kapper raised his rifle and pointed it at von Bauer. His breathing was heavy.

'You are an ignorant, stupid fool,' said the German captain. 'You believe you can frighten me with that? I have seen you – and the men around you – frightened by a storm! Storms do not frighten me, Kapper, not yours, or any other kind. The British captain is telling you something you should hear. If you do not have the sense to see what he is offering you – against my wishes – for some paltry supplies, then go ahead, compound your stupidity.'

'I do not think you will fire, Kapper,' said Muir. 'You have too much to lose.'

'If the gold is on this ship, mister, then we will find it.' Kapper was unsure which way to jump.

'Not so simple,' said Muir. 'If we had put it overboard and marked its position the crates could be hauled back – assuming, of course, we had left ropes attached to floats.' It wasn't a bad idea, thought Muir, considering it was spontaneous.

Four more of Kapper's men appeared in the saloon doorway and walked directly across to the German, looking troubled. 'The gold has ... gone. All of it. Every crate!' The man half winced from the expected blow. 'And there are no men. They have hidden or gone too.'

'I'll get an answer,' snarled Kapper. 'Tie these two up and we'll see how strong they really ...'

Von Bauer collapsed, falling back against the saloon wall. He held out a hand to support himself and it knocked the barometer to the floor. Muir – as they had rehearsed – hit the switch with an open palm.

The hydraulic lifts that had been designed to smooth any unwelcome guests into embarrassing imprisonment, had been removed. The centre of the saloon did not drift quietly down but fell like new snow over a hidden crevasse. Kapper's rifle, flung into the air by the momentum, seemed to hang there for ever, pointing to the ceiling long after he had gone.

Muir was the first to step to the rim and look down into the snakepit. Kapper was sitting upright clutching his legs as if awakened from sleep by violent cramp. Knee bones shone through punctured trousers and caps of skin. Around him twitched the rest in various awful contortions. Some lay still beneath the heavy table.

Muir looked at von Bauer. 'God help us,' he said.

The German raised an eyebrow and picked up the rifle that had landed on the parapet of the saloon, pointing it at the back of Kapper's neck.

'No,' said Muir. 'They are no danger now. And we are still human. Call the men to their stations and get someone to see to these poor devils.'

Von Bauer smoothed his collar delicately and turned the rifle away. 'If we make concessions at this stage, Captain . . .'

'Otherwise, *Captain*, I will lock you in this saloon to listen to them until I am ready!'

'I am perfectly aware . . .'

'Of nothing!' burst out Muir. 'Just do as I say and spare me your damned reflections. I have mine too!'

Von Bauer swallowed the reprimand and even managed to lace it with a little satisfaction. One more step. And already the Englishman was wavering.

The legacy of Kapper's rage had, in his absence, been more than claimed by Coker. The German's arrogance had taken time to burn him, but now, walking from the bridge, he was gathering a storm. A madman needed an anchor of sanity, that was how he had seen it, but all that had gone to blazes and back in an accumulation of error, idiocy and lousy seamanship. One – they were off course. Two – the future, apart from a plan to casually slaughter *Straker*'s crew, hadn't been considered. Three – Kapper had been reduced to a jelly by Bellamy's rubbish. And four – the whole reason for it all had just been dumped in a few hundred feet of ocean. If that was true and the gold had been ditched, Kapper could come back to *Drummer* with no worry about who was going to hang him. Coker would take that responsibility – if needs be at arm's length over the side.

Prettie was standing at the 4.7 inch gun on the poop deck staring at the silent *Straker*. 'They're signalling,' he said casually as Coker came to stand alongside him. 'See it?' A lamp blinked. 'Reckon you ought to be finding out about that.' There was a curious note of confidence in his voice. Prettie knew Muir of old and the apparent dumping of the gold had suggested a number of possibilities, none of which could be accounted for by sheer cussedness. He was beginning to hope that he might yet discover what it was all about. 'Can you read it? Suppose it's in German.'

Coker grabbed the first German crewman in sight and propelled him to the rail. 'Read it!'

'I ... do not ...' protested the German in fractured English.

'Read the bloody fucking thing!'

A reprieving voice dropped across the man's wretchedness. Withoft, one of Recke's cohorts, climbed on to the poop. 'The gold has gone,' he said. 'All of it. You understand?'

Coker walked in front of the gun, still looking at the windjammer. There was no doubt what Kapper would be doing now. The result of his running amok on *Straker* would haunt them for ever. And you couldn't kill the dead. The ship would have to be dispensed with.

Prettie's shoulder sagged as Coker's fingers tried to meet through the muscle. 'Now, mister, you wake up,' said Coker. 'You aim this gun and you sink that fucking wind-catcher as quick as I could wring your neck.'

Prettie's teeth came together and he clamped his hand across Coker's. 'Press any harder and no matter how quick you can wring my neck, it won't matter.' He flexed his wrist. 'If you want me to fire the gun I need an arm that works.'

The grip relaxed. 'Fire it.'

'And sink a helpless ship?' Prettie made a play of massaging his arm.

One by one Coker drew his fingers across his lips and rubbed the spittle into his palm, examining it with exaggerated patience. 'Do as I say, Prettie.'

'And join you?' Prettie laughed. 'They'd try *me* first, Coker, you know that. It's not signing my death warrant so much as writing it out and oiling the trap to boot! Sorry, no go. And that's only one of the reasons.'

Coker said: 'There is no one left alive on *Straker*, or won't be when Kapper has finished. I'm not killing anyone, Prettie, nor are you. Apart from Kapper and his mob.'

'He wouldn't dare kill them,' said Prettie. '*Kill* them?'

'He'll come back here and the blood won't be just on *his* hands.' He drew a bayonet and held it towards Prettie. 'No more chat, eh.'

Prettie looked around and called for his gun team. If he could stall, just for a little while, something would happen; what, he didn't know, but *something*. The first round splashed harmlessly fifty yards from *Straker*'s bow and he swore at the sight-setter.

'No,' said Coker, '*you're* laying this gun, mister. And if it misses ...' He held the bayonet at Prettie's temple. 'I won't.'

'Pickett, where are you?' Frank Judd stepped over the sick and dying on their makeshift beds and was marooned amongst a sea of moon-pale faces. Recognising him as his father, a young sailor held out his arms and tried to lift himself. 'Da,' he said. Shock and injury had taken him back to childhood. He smiled dementedly beneath a tube of bandages.

'Pickett? Are you in here?' Judd shouted again, uneasily.

'Sir, some food, sir . . .' came a shrill voice, as if in answer. A stump butted against his ankle. 'Water?' And the clamour rose.

'Take me home . . .'

'My back . . . only my back . . . just something for my back . . .'

'Help me . . .'

'Da. Da. Da. Da . . .'

Pickett trod expertly between them from the recesses of the sick bay.

'Pickett, can you handle . . .' began Judd.

'We'll talk outside,' said the midshipman. 'The men are being disturbed.' Judd allowed himself to be spun round and followed Pickett. Someone grabbed at his foot and he shook it loose. 'Don't tread on anyone,' warned Pickett, 'the rest will see it as a provocation and some of them are delirious.' Charlie Pickett would never be a Frederick Bellamy, with the emotionless, detached efficiency that marked his style, but he was learning fast and, in the process, grasping something of the forces that had moulded the surgeon's singular character. Repugnance, disgust, unease and, eventually, pity, had been Pickett's stepping stones to understanding. The torn and mutilated, unless you were a missionary and they gave your life purpose, were initially offensive no matter what you chose to believe about human nature, like being confronted by the gibbering village idiot while contemplating some idyllic rustic scene. At least that was the way it was with Pickett. The sudden deaths of Lorimer and Muswell in the boat had, momentarily, shocked him, but that had been war and, in the end, that was what they were all there to face, at some time or other. This – Bellamy's sick bay – was something entirely different. The ripe smell of sodden bandages mingling with iodine; the twisted shapes of men lying motionless on the few unburned areas of their bodies like victims of an eruption, calcified in lava; the resentful silence of those who knew they were going to die; the screaming of those who were going to live but couldn't accept a future limited by the width of a bed or wheelchair; the babbling of those who had found their own escape.

Bellamy had gone beyond understanding, which Charlie

Pickett knew *he* could never do. For Bellamy, understanding was non-productive, self-indulgent and patronising. Having watched him at work, Pickett had become aware of watching a mechanic repairing ruptured hoses, fractured drive shafts and dislocated bearings. There was no other way it could be done. To sit down and think was to beckon demons – to collapse into an exhausted, dreamless sleep at the end of the day was the most one could hope for. Not a little of Bellamy's abrasiveness had begun to rub off on Charlie Pickett.

'If you'd spent a few days among those men you wouldn't have walked in like that,' he said.

Judd glanced at the yellow bruise across the midshipman's face and seemed about to comment on it.

'It was a good one,' said Pickett, fingering it gently. 'Only I don't know why.'

'Forget that,' said Judd. 'Listen to me, lad. None of this will make much sense to you either, and I haven't got time to explain it all. We're hard up in a clinch and you can take that from me. What I want to know is, can you handle one of the 4.7s?'

'What's been going on, Judd?' Pickett looked around the deck. 'I could hear the guns and ...'

'Guns, for Chrissake!'

'Guns? Yes, a bit. Prettie taught me.'

'Right.' Judd grabbed him by the arm. 'Take the gun I'm going to put you in charge of and act as gunlayer. To hell with the men around you, I'll see to them. Coker is out to sink *Straker.*'

'What?' gasped Pickett.

'Kapper is on board her and ... fire to miss and make it look good. Now come on.' His legs took one pace to the midshipman's two until they reached the forrard gun. 'This man is in charge,' he snapped at the crew. 'Anyone who argues with him argues with me. He's been trained to fire this and we want him here.'

'Kapper gives us our orders,' said one of the Germans in English. He folded his arms and stepped back from the breech.

Judd sighed. 'No he doesn't. Kapper isn't here and ...' his voice trailed away.

The German shrugged and looked around the rest, building strength in numbers. 'These men ...'

Judd's hand shot out and gripped the man's nose, twisting it savagely as he dragged him close enough to ram a knee into his kidneys. He rolled the palpitating figure beneath a foot like pastry. 'Any more questions?'

The sailors moved to the gun.

'There are no more questions, Pickett. Should any arise, call for me. You ...' he said to the man on the deck, 'Go and learn how to use a shovel below. Savvy?'

The man stumbled away, groaning.

'Fire exactly as I said – just sufficient,' said Judd.

Pickett squinted along the sight: 'Sufficient,' he said.

Recke was out on the bridge, Coker still on the poop with Prettie. For once things were going right, thought Judd. He tapped the helmsman lightly on the shoulder and beckoned him out of the wheelhouse and on to the boat deck. 'I'll take over here, get some scran down you and come back in half an hour.'

When the helmsman had gone he walked silently through the wheelhouse and on to the open bridge. 'This is Judd, Recke,' he said, holding his pistol at arm's length and pressing the barrel into the small of the German's back. 'Don't move, don't turn, or you'll be blinking your life away.'

'A coup within a mutiny within a revolution,' said Recke easily. 'I gather your captain has jettisoned the gold. Does it make any difference who holds the guns now?'

'I don't care a stuff what it means to you, Recke, but I'm not taking any chances. No speeches either. For my money half of this can of worms came from your yapping in the first place.'

'In that case ...' Recke bent his body forward, grasped the rail of the bridge and, pivoting on one heel, brought a hand slicing upwards from his crouch to connect squarely with Judd's forearm. The pistol spun from Judd's hand and clattered against the wheelhouse. Easing the safety catch from the pistol he had taken from beneath his shirt Recke waved the astonished Judd back. 'One shot from this and even if it only hits you in the arm it'll knock you out,' he said, holding the 9 mm parabellum Luger two-fisted.

Judd shook his arm and rubbed the already rising bruise disbelievingly.

'An oriental thing,' said Recke. 'I never really believed it would work. It's designed for those of us who haven't got the strength or the inclination to get hurt a great deal. Ingenious but, of course, if the first move goes wrong one tends to pay a high penalty.' He held out the Luger, its grip towards Judd. 'Now we are both a little calmer, you can take it. It would probably break my wrist if I fired it.'

'What's your game, Recke?'

'Just take it. *That* is my "game", as you call it.'

Judd held the pistol and Recke dropped his arms to his sides. 'If you feel I am any danger – which I assure you I am not – then I *reassure* you. I have used up my quota of courage.'

Judd looked doubtfully at the pistol.

'I think you now understand what I was trying to say after your meeting with the unfortunate Baines,' went on Recke. 'This farce had to end some time, it was obvious how futile and desperate it had become. Maybe I was wrong about you and that pistol is about to blow what little is left of my judgement to pieces?'

Judd juggled with the black butt. Then: 'I don't know, Recke. I don't know why the hell I'm here – why I stayed in the first place. I had no illusions about the gold, or about Kapper. But it needed someone on board who might be able to do something when the whole bloody house of cards blew down. Not that I'm expecting anyone to believe it. It happens to be true.'

'*I* believe it,' said Recke. 'Why shouldn't I?'

'Because it was ridiculous, that's why. But here I am and I reckon we might be seeing the last bit of madness before the ... end? What end? Coker is going wild and I don't have to spell out what Kapper is up to. I think we may have left it too late. I've had enough of it, that's all. Are you with me?'

Recke nodded at the pistol. Judd was no longer pointing it at him. 'Would I do that if I wasn't?'

'Prettie and Pickett are at the guns, and that'll be useful. There's maybe half a dozen of us altogether, that's all. You still want to come along?'

'I was along before you were, Mr Judd. And remember not *all* the mutineers on *Drummer* went along gladly with Kapper, they were misled. I think they'll come in with us. But what about Coker ...'

'Coker I can handle.' Judd stuffed the pistol into his belt. 'You're a funny bastard, Recke.'

'One day,' said Recke, 'we must compare notes on that.'

'Last chance, Prettie.' Penn Coker pricked the point of his bayonet behind the chief gunner's ear. 'The next shell hits *Straker* or this blade goes through your neck. No in-between, just one thing or the other.' He glanced briefly over his shoulder. The forrard gun was firing slowly and erratically. 'This isn't a fucking salute!' he yelled. But they couldn't hear him.

Prettie had laid the first round as a sighting shot, deliberately falling short, and had ordered 'Up four hundred' to the sightseer. The second round had passed over *Straker* and was followed by the order 'Down two hundred.' The target was straddled; it meant that the third shot should hit her midships. Which there was no doubt it would, if Prettie hadn't made a few random range adjustments of his own.

A shell was slammed into the breech, and he looked along the rangefinder. There was no doubt that Coker meant what he said. It wasn't an easy shot, but Prettie, with his experience, could have hit her blindfold and his show of blatant incompetence was fooling nobody. So what now, Arnold, what now? Thirty seconds and Much Wenlock would cease to exist, along with his wife, the 'smallholding', a battery of relations, the Red Lion, bowls on Sunday and Maurice the pig. He'd once been offered twenty pounds for Maurice by Larkins the local butcher, but family outrage had interceded and the porker had carried on snuffling into his dotage. Larkins used to kill them by slitting their throats, the blood being made into a renowned black pudding. Feeling the bayonet at his neck Prettie began to envy Maurice his reprieve.

The barrel was two points beyond *Straker*'s stern; any other time a convincing try, but not now. He held it steady, wondering whether h∘ would live long enough to see the harmless ripples spread.

'Fire!' he said, and closed his eyes.

'Coker!'

The blade eased.

Frank Judd stood on the well deck looking up at the poop. 'What's going on there?'

Turning to him, Coker missed seeing the shell fall beyond *Straker*. 'Go away, mister! See to the forrard gun if you want to throw your weight around.' He turned back to Prettie. 'You bastard,' he hissed, looking at the unscathed *Straker*.

'Co-ker!' The sound of the pistol shot splintered his name. Coker whirled. Judd was aiming the Luger up at his chest. 'Next one, Coker, next one! I could kill you now! Come down here, and throw the blade away. Prettie, get out of it!'

Prettie didn't need urging. He threw himself away from the bayonet and straddled the rail, ready to dive into the sea if Coker should come for him.

'You're not so big that a bullet would notice,' said Judd.

Coker flipped the bayonet and stuck it in the top of his boot. Hands on hips he looked down at Judd. 'Without the pistol, Judd? What kind of a man are you *without* the pistol?'

'Take the bayonet out, Coker.'

Coker threw it across the deck.

'Now come.' Judd dropped the pistol and skidded it away with his heel.

The men who had made up Prettie's gun crew had slid from their positions and disappeared. Coker was bad enough, but Coker and Judd together equalled one and a half Kappers: a combination that promised a wide expanse of damage. Prettie rubbed the puncture behind his ear and tried to massage some sense into what was going on. Judd had stepped back as Coker came down to him, and they faced each other, Coker shaking his head, Judd pale. And then they were on each other, like bull terriers, so suddenly that Prettie never knew who moved first. All he remembered afterwards was Coker's flailing fists and Judd on his knees as one them crashed across his shoulder with a force to forge steel. Rolling like ecstatic lovers across the well deck, they used up the repertoire of bar-room brawlers in minutes and began to improvise. Coker's hand, held by the wrist inches from Judd's testicles; Judd's fist desperately trying to connect with the soft flesh of Coker's temple. Coker's nose seemed to be broken, and Judd was coughing from a blow across the throat.

Prettie swung from the rail and ran across to the 4.7. 'Hear me! Both of you!' He spun the wheel. 'Hear me!'

But they were beyond reason.

'Judd!' Prettie aimed the big gun at the rail beneath which they were gouging and kicking. It had to be the most careful shot of his life. An almost impossible one. The thought of Coker standing up triumphant sent a chill down his spine. He fired.

The blast hurled them apart. There was an eerie silence. Judd wiped the dirt from his eyes and blinked, working his jaw and spitting muck from his throat. Coker was on his hands and knees, his clothes in tatters. He had been on top of Judd and had taken most of the force of the explosion. He stared open-mouthed at the deck and with a sudden cry fell on his side, clutching tightly at his ears. Judd managed to stand. 'No more, Prettie,' he said, weakly. Jelly-legged he stepped across to Coker. Panting like a tightrope-walker he tried twice to take his weight on one leg. The third time he managed it. Drawing back his boot he kicked Coker in the face and stood swaying.

'Judd?' Prettie had reloaded the gun.

'I'm all right.' He tore away the remains of his shirt. 'Stay there and use it again if need be. I need Pickett.' He tottered away to the fo'c'sle.

Charlie Pickett didn't need to pretend he was a lousy gunner. The shells had been falling everywhere, like a badly planned firework display, and most of them owed nothing to his intentions. The only fear he had was that he might accidentally sink *Straker*. Prettie made it look too easy. The men around him were beginning to murmur when Judd arrived.

'You lot! Down here.' He had remembered to pick up the Luger. For the moment physical combat was something he would avoid – any one of them could have pushed him over with a finger. None of them seemed to understand, staring at the wild figure waving the pistol as if chancing on a drunken footpad. The pistol wavered in Judd's hand.

'Stand aside!' Recke's voice came faintly from the bridge, followed by the rattle of a machine-gun. The bullets passed over the gun crew's heads.

'*Now* get down here,' said Judd. He shooed them in front of him, looking up at the bridge and keeping a healthy distance from them. 'Below! At the double!' He called back to Pickett: 'Turn the gun. Wipe the deck clear of trouble – but for Chrissake don't sink us!'

Another gun had opened fire. A Maxim ripped across the fo'c'sle. Pickett swung the 4.7 and fired, blowing men and Maxim into the sea and sending with them a slice of *Drummer*'s superstructure.

'More of that, more of that!' shouted Judd as he shoved the men in front of him down the mess-deck hatch and closed it. Other guns had joined in the mêlée and Recke was leaning from the bridge with his machine-gun, picking off various groups. A tremendous explosion from the poop shook them all into silence. Small groups of men, at a loss as to who was firing at whom, stood around the ship, some with their hands in the air.

'Leave them,' shouted Recke. 'They asked for none of this!'

Judd was herding them together as Bellamy came out on deck. 'Get a gun, Bellamy! Arm yourself!'

But Bellamy was already armed and was pointing the pistol directly at Judd.

Pickett leapt across the deck like an injured kangaroo, arms wrapped around his ribs, grunting with each movement. 'No, it's all over!'

Bellamy gave a twitch of annoyance. He had kept the gun hidden for a considerable time and had thought long and hard about whether he could bring himself to use it. Pickett took it from him. 'Right idea, sir, wrong enemy. Judd's with us. I think.'

'Everyone on this ship is in need of treatment,' huffed Bellamy and disappeared back into his sick bay.

'Look there, will you!' Recke was pointing from the bridge. *Straker* was moving. From her stern churned a thick foam and the sails were falling to be braced.

'Jesus Christ on a crutch,' whispered Judd. Not Kapper. He was in no shape for Kapper. No shape for anyone.

It worked. Garrett limply took Barrow's congratulatory hand as the deep-throated rumble of the powerful diesel filled the tiny engine room. 'To run it like this will do it no good at all,' he said. The engine was at full power. 'There's less than two hundred gallons of fuel left and we'll be needing it all.'

'Not for long,' said Barrow. 'One short burst of speed should do it. Can you stay here with it?'

'I can't leave her now.'

'Good man. When you hear the bugle ease it off.' He dashed from the engine room.

Straker was a hive of ferocious activity. Men crawled into the rigging to join others already balanced there on the foot ropes, while yet others hauled on the yards. The gun crews checked and re-checked, as if awaiting a visiting admiral. Muir and von Bauer seemed to be the only ones who were still.

'We should simply release it,' the German captain was saying to Muir, as Barrow joined them. The firing had stopped and the hawser grown taut as *Straker* moved away, pulling her 2000 tons and more against it.

'I cannot risk getting any closer,' said Muir. 'They could be simply holding their fire.' The fake signal they had sent purporting to come from Kapper had given them breathing space, but now Coker must have guessed what had happened. The sudden cessation in the firing was worrying him. A few shells had fallen pathetically off-target, apart from one near miss, and then there had been an explosion at *Drummer*'s stern. Whatever had happened it could be ominous. The masquerade in the saloon had worked to the letter, the auxiliary had responded to the second. So why hadn't *Drummer* responded accordingly? Coker and Judd were desperate men, but they were resourceful too, and it would be an act of misplaced optimism to imagine them standing on board *Drummer* scratching their backsides in confusion.

'Four points starboard,' he said to the helmsman.

'You realise this could go one of two ways, Captain?' said von Bauer.

'Yes.'

'And you still have men on deck.'

'We take our chances,' said Muir. Three of the crew were trying to push Detweiler's body into a sack and Mueller stood watching them, his face expressionless.

'Move her,' said Muir to the helmsman.

The hawser fought against *Straker*, tearing her from her course. Then the sails began to fill.

'It'll break,' said Muir.

'She cannot hold,' muttered von Bauer. 'She is in no condition.' The helmsman was bearing down on the tortured wheel. Barrow added his weight.

'*Give!*' said Muir. '*Give!*'

In answer, *Straker* threw up her head and fell back into the sea as the hawser parted. Chopping off the wave-tops in a shower of spume, it headed :or *Drummer* like a writing water snake, curled in a loop, and sank harmlessly.

Part Four

'Put him down here,' said Rose to the two sailors carrying a body slung between them like a sack of coal. 'Is he alive?'

One of them shrugged. 'If he's dead, then that's one less. He's a German and the question don't bother me either way.'

Rose slapped him hard across the cheek. 'Mercy! Learn a little mercy, my boy. One day you may be begging for it!'

The sailor coloured angrily.

'Put the poor sod down and shut it,' said the other. 'She's right. I might be carrying you next.'

The old woman bent over the body and said: 'Can you speak? Can you hear? We are going to take care of you.'

The men brought from *Straker*'s saloon were laid around her on palliasses. What had happened to them was beyond her imagination. She walked among them with a jug of water. The face was unmistakable: 'I ... hurt,' said Friedrich Kapper. Only his mouth seemed capable of movement. 'The doctor ... get ... him.'

'He will come,' said Rose. 'Rest.'

'Where ... are ... my ... legs. I cannot feel ...' He was turning grey. 'No ... no fault. I didn't ... kill her. Dead inside ... all dead. No!' He tried to twist away from the pain.

'You are safe.' Rose clenched her teeth and smoothed a hand over his brow.

'Doctor! My legs!' He choked on his own saliva and she turned his head on its side, holding the water to his lips. He spat it out.

'You are dying,' said Rose. 'If you have belief call on it now. Confess to me. I am the instrument of Our Father in Heaven, who is looking down on you now.'

Kapper's eyes rolled in their sockets. 'Away. Get away, bitch,' he said, suddenly fully conscious. 'No women.'

Once more she laid her hands on his forehead. 'Feel the pain begin to go,' she said. 'Feel it begin to ...' she snatched her hand away. It was cold, extracting life, not giving it.

Kapper stared at her, a mucous film drifting across his pupils; tail clouds of a hurricane that had blown itself out.

'Fire when I say,' said Muir. *Straker* was closing on *Drummer*, freed of her chains, and the gun crews were on a hair-trigger, waiting for the signal.

'If *they* fire, Captain, then what?' Von Bauer, for all the windjammer's problems, was handling her like a racing yacht, dictating the movements of the wheel by a single finger laid across the helmsman's wrist.

'The answer to that is that they haven't,' answered Muir. 'What do you reckon, Number One?'

Barrow was conning *Drummer* through binoculars. 'Can't make it out. The crew are there all right, but nothing is happening. Wait a minute! The guns aren't pointed at us!' He handed Muir the glasses.

'Nor are they.' They were closing fast and a decision had to be made. If it was left a moment too late and *Drummer* fired first, *Straker* would be blown out of the water. Hackett was looking back from the 'pig-pen' gun as if Muir had forgotten them.

'One over the bow,' said Muir. Hackett's gun barked.

'Well at least the wretched thing works. Where are the other glasses, Number One?'

'That's the only pair intact, sir.'

'You've got better eyes than me. Take a squint and tell me whether I'm seeing things. On the poop, alongside the rail.'

'I see him. It's Pickett. Judd's alongside him. They're *waving*! This is damned strange, sir. I can't say I like it.'

'Nor I,' agreed Muir.

'It would be madness for Coker to surrender now,' said von Bauer. 'It's a trick. Either pull away, Captain, or sink her!'

'Pickett,' said Muir. 'Along with Judd?'

Barrow raised the glasses. 'Judd's gone, but Pickett's still waving. It could be some fancy footwork by Coker, but I can't imagine Pickett going about it so enthusiastically. And those guns are still no threat.'

'Well, we can't wait until they are. Signal them to heave to. Something weird is going on over there.'

'I hate to say this, sir, but look ... a white flag.'

Muir saw it. 'Déja-bloody-vu. Get some boats ready, I can't fire on her like this.'

Barrow displayed a slight hesitation, as if about to make a point, then, changing his mind, nodded abruptly and strode away. Muir guessed that, after his previous experiences, the Number One would have very little faith left in a pulling boat. But ten to one he'd volunteer to be in it.

'You *cannot* fire on her, Captain?' said the German. 'Why? Because she is your ship? Do such things take precedence at a time like this?' He was on the verge of a very real anger.

'They're cutting the hawser free,' said Barrow.

'You must accept my decision, Captain. I don't recall you sacrificing your ship. Men, yes. This time I am not going to sacrifice men if I can do otherwise. Pickett and Bellamy and a hell of a lot of wounded are on board *Drummer*.'

'Being used as bait, Captain.'

Von Bauer began to walk away, but suddenly turned to Muir. 'That ship is out of control, Captain,' he said, flatly. 'They may have the steering, but not the power. It is running away from them! Give me a reason for that and I take off my cap to you.'

'Some kind of hiatus,' said Barrow to Muir. 'It sounds crazy but I reckon Coker has been deposed.'

'Give me *everything* this ship has got, Captain – sail and diesel – and I'll try and give you your reason.'

Von Bauer looked at him through pitch-black eyes. 'Muir, there are times when I almost begin to wish we were on the same side.'

'We are,' said Muir. 'Whether we like it or not.'

Judd flipped the butterfly clips on the hatch coaming. It had taken only the briefest of discussions with Pickett to prove that neither of them had the expertise to close down the engines below and, even if they had, there was no way they could go about it. Engines that Coker had ordered at full power. Contrary messages had been relayed via the telegraph to the sealed-off engine room but there had been no response. The most ridiculous thing of all, the signalling equipment was missing and all the lamps on the bridge out of action, one ripped from its cradle by shrapnel from Pickett's 4.7.

The white flag had cried wolf once before, but it was all they could do.

'How many of them are down there?' asked Judd.

'Fifteen at the most,' guessed Pickett. The hatches had been sealed on the unwitting engineers, as they had on all below, as soon as Coker and the hard core of the mutineers had been taken care of.

'Armed?'

'I doubt it. I don't know.'

They could hear the sound of boots on the ladder and a rapping of knuckles on the underside of the hatch. Voices, shouting. Judd thumped back with a fist. 'They're in a bloody panic,' he said. He touched the two remaining clips. 'Open these and out they come like a jack-in-the-box, no stopping them. They think the ship's about to go down.'

'Even if the stokers have stopped, the boilers aren't going to die down yet awhile,' said Pickett. 'Ease the clips off enough to speak through the gap. Sit on it just to make sure.' He lay flat as the cover lifted an inch and a half above the coaming, the clips hanging on to the last fraction of thread. Two fingers wormed through it and tore at the rubber sealing strip.

'We are not sinking!' shouted Pickett. 'Stop the engines now. If not this hatch will be closed for ever. Understand?'

There was a raised babble of German voices and the sound of someone falling. A different voice: 'Ja. Yes. I understan'. Ja. Schtop. Vill. Open pliss.'

'Stop them!' said Pickett.

'Ja. Open?'

'They don't have a fucking clue what you're saying,' said Judd.

Pickett pressed his mouth to the gap in the hatch. 'Stop the engines and we will let you out,' he said in French.

'What if I stick a pistol through here? They'll get the message,' said Judd.

'And then what? One of us goes down feet first? You fancy that?'

Judd sat silent on the hatch digesting Pickett's warning. A hiss of steam.

'That's it,' said Pickett. 'Must be. Wait!' *Drummer* began to lose way. He smiled at Judd. 'We made it.'

Judd began to tighten the clips. 'Let's get out of here.'

Pickett shook his head. 'Do that and they'll screw us into the ground. If we lie to them, what else can they do?'

Judd shrugged and twirled a clip. 'Have it your way, you're the French scholar. Still, get over there and use your gun if I say. I mean *use* it, this still isn't an old boy's reunion.' Kicking off the hatch he stepped back, his pistol aimed at the pair of staring eyes that rose above it.

'Nein!' The German sailor was torn between holding his hands above his head and using at least one to prevent himself falling.

'They're Recke's men,' said Pickett, 'go easy on them, Judd.'

'Up, slowly,' said Judd. He smiled at Pickett. 'Charlie boy, it seems my role in life is to get people out of the shit and put myself in it.'

The pulling boat was alongside *Drummer*, resting easy; a cygnet against a sooty swan. The sea was calm and Muir took the rope ladder with ease. Pickett held out a hand as he reached the rail and suddenly remembering himself, saluted.

'Welcome aboard sir. Sorry about the delay.'

'Where's Judd?'

'Judd is an asset, sir. He's below, sorting out a few strays.'

Von Bauer heaved himself up the ladder and Pickett grasped him beneath the arm as he clambered over the rail. The two captains stood in front of him.

'Most things are under control,' said Pickett. 'More or less. Recke, Bellamy, Prettie are O.K. What we need to do is secure what we have. But it's your ship.' His right hand began to point towards the bridge and his speech became slurred. 'Srorry, sir . . .' His forehead slid down von Bauer's shoulder and the German captain eased him to the deck. He bent over the boy, unable to rise. 'He is asleep,' he said weakly. 'Help me to rise, Captain.'

Muir took the elbow and levered him upright, feeling the trembling in his arms.

22 *December*

Full circle.

The ocean had moved beneath them and brought them back to the beginning, having taken them nowhere. A long journey in time, but the sea was timeless, and men moved across it like ants on a sundial, casting insignificant shadows.

Jack Muir sat at his desk and turned the broken photograph of the old man in his fingers. The same photograph, but now somehow different. A jigsaw, like everything else.

Full circle.

Leaving what wheels within wheels?

Charlie Pickett had collapsed, asleep on his feet, before he had been able to talk to him. Everyone was still tired and confused and, he suspected, sick of the sea. Muir had begun to welcome the fact that his naval days were numbered, and it would take a long time before he regained the respect he had once had for it all. The question was, what now?

A job somewhere in the City, a home in the suburbs. Now it was a reward, not a mark of failure. Only it wouldn't happen like that. Couldn't. If they made it back home he would have everything he had wanted − *they* had wanted. The focal point of a cocktail party, with avuncular acknowledgement from those who had known he 'could do it' if he tasted a bit cf salt. 'Daddy'. Her 'Daddy's Daddy'. 'Good show, old man'. And Garrett and Prettie, and Hackett and Tilley would move on − an incident in their lives that would simply lead to another, with hardly time to jot it down on a calendar. What was it Barrow had once said in the wardroom: he could never understand why, at the end of a horse race, everyone congratulated the jockey and all the horse got was a pat on the rump. Somewhere in that lay a basic truth. Assuming there were any basic truths left. Muir smothered a yawn. And then there was Frank Judd. Prettie had spoken about the fight in the well deck and there could be no doubt that Judd had turned against the mutineers. But Karl Recke had spoken too. And the story was a strange one. Judd had gone along with Coker and Kapper with an aim to *confounding* them. Recke himself didn't claim the same motivation. So was Judd trying to earn leniency, or was it a way of using what had happened to some future advantage? Or was it true?

Recke and Judd had been quartered in a cabin with a guard at their door while Muir thought about it all. Prettie had objected strenuously, but finally agreed they needed time to take stock.

Hackett had come to him with the air of a man expecting to be clapped in irons, but his 'confession' was so poignant that all Muir could do was listen in amazement. Hackett had buried Oskar Lange at sea as he had been ordered − but had been unable to dump the carcase over the side like garbage. Instead, given charge of sewing Dandridge into a canvas shroud, he had contrived to put with him the remains of Oskar. It was all vaguely bizarre, even distasteful, but Hackett had done what he thought was right: both had had a decent burial. But, coupled with it, was a fear of having somehow transgressed. Muir tried to reassure him, not knowing what to think. There weren't enough beads on Hackett's rosary to cope with it.

He looked at the chart on his desk. He had decided against pushing on to St Paul's Rocks − there were no medical facilities available there − and instead they had sailed due north. The two ships were sailing independently and they were making good way. In five days they had covered more than a thousand miles at an average of nine knots. Now the Cape Verde Islands were falling behind them and the Azores were thirteen hundred miles away. It had to be the Azores. Cape Verde was full of interned German merchant ships and the arrival of *Drummer* and *Straker* would soon have been known in Germany. The Azores would have English ships in the vicinity. In the end even Bellamy had agreed. A few more days.

Barrow was back on *Straker*, this time with a crew he could trust – personally selected by Muir. Coker, in the sick bay, was stone deaf and possibly had a broken back. Baines had never been found. He ran down the list he had drawn up. Bellamy coping. Garrett, despite his personal worries, fairly confident that *Drummer* could hold her own. Von Bauer reasonably acquiescent. Mueller, still stunned by the death of Detweiler, was working as Barrow's other arm. Armgard was dead of a heart attack. Kapper dead. Mason, Spinks, Ludermann, Berkwell, Paisley, Gabzic, Kirkpatrick, Lerner . . .

The unanswered roll-call went on.

Muir felt his head lolling across the desk and shook himself awake. The Azores would change everything. A few more days. He lay down on his bunk. It would be good to be home. Holding her. 'I love you,' he said. What a damn silly life! His hand slipped from under his cheek. *Drummer* was talking. His unease finding an identity, he walked out on to the bridge.

The wind kissed him across a pewter sea that was busy and disorganised. Clouds bumped across the bow. He was soaked within seconds.

Within minutes the storm broke.

23 December

Hand over hand, Charlie Pickett forced himself along the forrard deck, pausing at every other step as a wall of water broke over *Drummer*'s side and took his legs from under him, leaving him dangling helplessly, the lifeline cutting into his armpits. The body was ninety-eight per cent water, Bellamy had told him, and it seemed to the young midshipman that at this precise moment the other two per cent was trying to squeeze its way in for a full house. He shook his head, spitting out salt, and glanced down the line. Half a dozen were draped over it like a troupe of tightrope walkers whose act had ended in near disaster. The deck was a foot deep in curdled foam, gurgling as it drained from the scuppers.

The storm had given them no time to think, each man acting instinctively as the wooden locking bars on the hatch cover were hammered askew by the pounding waves. In the few seconds of protection as the ship rolled to lee, they had lunged for the hatch, grabbing anything that would support them. The next big wave would spring the bars adrift and swamp the hold. The one after that would sink them without compunction.

He found himself alongside Prettie. The lieutenant was thumping his heel against one of the bars. Pickett added his boot and they ducked as another wave came in. The bar held.

'What happened, Mr Prettie? I can't find . . .' shouted Pickett.

Prettie began to slither across the hatch as a surge of water broke his grip, and Pickett grabbed at his leg and pulled him back. Prettie still wasn't satisfied with the hatch and together they worked to hammer the bar further in.

'Beattie Dandridge!' shouted Pickett above the roar.

'Dead,' yelled back Prettie. 'An accident.'

Pickett looked dazed. '*Dead?*'

'Like we'll all be if we don't get back to that lifeline.' Prettie pushed him towards it. 'Now!'

Drummer hit a trough and a wave reared up to hang over them. And fell. They were pressed flat by a ton of water, and the line broke.

'Two points starboard.'

'Two points starboard, sir.'

'Now keep her there.'

'Sir. Holding her, sir.' The helmsman's shoulders were shaking with the effort.

Take each wave as it comes and hit it hard. Jack Muir, his face caked with spray, pipe burning upside down to keep the sea from extinguishing it, squinted upwards as a tremendous wall of water swept across the deck below the bridge. *Drummer* wasn't putting up a good performance. Her bows were more under water than above. Three bodies floated over the side and back again and were gone.

'Hold her!'

'Holding her, sir,' said the desperate helmsman. Offord, Garrett and Mueller were in the wheelhouse.

'Give that man a hand, one of you,' shouted Muir from the bridge. Mueller came out. '*Straker*, Captain! She's having a bad time of it.'

Muir flicked an empty glance back at the windjammer. The

sea was beating around her like a shaken blanket. 'She'll survive.'
She had to.

The world in its turning had a purpose. Even the world
turned upside down. Rose rolled on her seat, holding herself
steady with a hand against the bulkhead. Hannah was gripping
the edge of her bunk, and with each lurch of the ship flopped
like a rag doll. The main table was bolted to the cabin floor
and Elizabeth had jammed her chair against it, making a vice
of her knees beneath and elbows above. Everything movable
was moving – tin mugs clattered among the shards of the water
jug and bowl; a round-backed hairbrush spun like a roulette
wheel; knives, forks, mirrors, hairpins, all shot from one end
of the cabin to the other in a wild cacophony of sound, each
journey grinding the china and glass closer to sand.

'You look worried, Mr Tilley,' said Rose.

Tilley was hanging on to the door handle, legs bent, moving
with the sea. He grinned. 'I'm here for *moral* support, Rose. But
I think it's the other kind we're all needing right now.'

'Have you . . . has it been this bad before?' The girl was pale.
'It feels as if we are going to turn over.'

'We won't turn over, miss. It's a squall. A little storm. Be gone
as soon as it's had its blow.'

Hannah tried to stand and he held out an arm. 'No, ma'am,
don't try to move, that's how accidents happen. If you could just
hold on and ride it out a little bit longer . . .'

'I hate this ship!' burst out Hannah. 'I hate the sea! Every
second I hate it more! We've had enough, can't any of you see
that? Why don't you put us ashore?' Her voice burned accus-
ingly.

'Well, ma'am, there *is* no shore hereabouts. That would mean
going back the way we came. I realise, well, conditions aren't
what ladies might be used to . . . but then, *Drummer* wasn't
built for ladies.'

'You don't have to apologise on behalf of the sea, Mr Tilley,'
said Rose, glaring sharply at Hannah. 'It was our decision to
stay at sea in the first place and if we hadn't made that choice
we wouldn't be here now.' The point went home. It was
the only way to deal with Hannah, Rose had discovered. Since
the Dandridge affair her attitude had changed from one of
morbid despair to a tight-lipped resentment, most of which was
centred on her daughter. Rose guessed something had been said
between them. Something Hannah didn't want to believe.

For her part, Elizabeth had recovered quickly – perhaps too

238

quickly – from the horror of Dandridge's death. It appeared to have left no scars on her mind, apart from a curious reluctance to leave *Straker* for the relative comfort of *Drummer*. In the end she had to be virtually dragged on to her and, ever since, had seemed preoccupied with what might be happening on the windjammer: the only outward sign that all was not well. That and the detached coolness with which she regarded her mother. Some strange emotional fuel was keeping her going. No doubt it would resolve itself.

'I'm quite safe, Mr Tilley,' said Elizabeth, suddenly standing and holding on to the table. 'I'm getting used to ...' The ship rolled and she let herself be carried across the cabin, half sliding, but somehow managing to keep her feet. Gripping the butterfly bolts around the scuttle shield she looked through the dripping glass, craning her head from left to right.

Tilley had made to stop her, but had found himself folded as neat as an envelope flap by the edge of the table. 'I'd rather you didn't do that, miss,' he wheezed. 'If any harm comes to you I'm afraid it's my head on the block.'

'Behave yourself, Elizabeth!' snapped Rose.

'I can see the sailing ship!' the girl said excitedly. Her face grew serious. 'Would it be worse on her, Mr Tilley? Worse than here?'

'No worse. Better maybe. Sailing ships are built for bad seas.'

'Good. But there must be men aboard her who are sick. Perhaps if I talked with the captain ...'

'You are staying with us, Elizabeth,' said Rose. 'No more silliness, now!'

'Not silliness, Rose.' She swung gently against the bulkhead. 'There are some things even you can't understand.'

'You will stay!' Hannah snapped the last word on the subject.

Elizabeth made a small sound in her throat that might have been either a sob or a laugh and looked out again towards the battered sailing ship.

26 December

The storm had long gone, but it had left an indelible mark. Four men dead, both ships damaged and weary: *Straker* minus half a dozen sails and low in the water, *Drummer* having serious trouble with her engines. Minor disasters that paled alongside the news Judd had brought: provisions in the main storeroom had broken loose. Flour, molasses, corn, dried peas and fat had formed a foul, glutinous pudding a foot deep. It had taken the weight of two men even to open the door. Judd had held out a fistful of the inedible mess for Muir to inspect. It had been two days to the feast of Christmas. And, staring at what Judd held, Muir was forced to acknowledge privately for the first time that their chances of survival had virtually vanished. But what one admitted privately was one thing: to admit it publicly would have been to pre-date the inevitable. No one could take much more, that was certain, but to dwell on the thought of a slow death by starvation would have extinguished the faint spark of hope that was keeping them all going.

Over the following two days, Muir had spent his time pacing the decks like a gung-ho cavalry captain, chivvying and joking, oozing confidence from every pore. On Christmas Day he had doubled rations and led the sing-song on deck, challenging his 'choir' to raise their voices loud enough to be heard on *Straker*.

> Fight the good fight with all thy might,
> Christ is thy strength and Christ thy right;
> Lay hold of life and it shall be,
> Thy joy and crown eternally.

A distant cheer, and *Straker* had answered with *Silent Night* sung in German. A celebration of faith, or of tenacity, it didn't matter what label it was given. *Lay hold of life*. And still Muir conducted his rounds. It was the only way. The men's blood was already sluggish as the inadequate diet picked like a vulture at their faculties, and Muir was determined to keep it pumping by whatever means he could.

Keep moving.

'Keep moving,' he said aloud. 'There's nothing else that matters.'

Barrow nodded. Muir's face, no longer public, had momentarily collapsed into a haggard landscape of grey ridges and dark crevasses. They were alone in his cabin, Hardcastle temporarily in command of *Straker*.

Muir waved a hand to the chart on his desk. 'We're eight hundred miles from the Canaries, just over a thousand from the Azores, but I think the latter is the best bet. There's a lot of shipping activity around there and we'll have more chance of meeting something on the way, although I'm beginning to wonder where all the damn ships have gone! Whichever we headed for the food wouldn't last at the speed we're going. Tell me about *Straker*.'

Barrow scratched his jaw. 'Physically the ship is in a bad way, still taking water. The crew are in reasonable spirits.'

'Has there been ... any talk?'

'Tight-lipped as the proverbial duck's fundament, sir. It says a lot for your faith in them.'

'It says a lot for them, Number One. I wonder if it can last? Anything else?'

'As I signalled – the Germans are participating in the running of the ship. Frankly we need them. Some, of course, are still confined. The hardliners who went along with Kapper and Coker of their own free will. The ones I call "Recke's Men" go about ordinary duties. I have given Recke his head – or rather used his influence. It's benign, if unusual. And, apart from that, well ...'

'Yes?'

'Something I can't put my finger on, sir.'

'Try a stab. By the way, what are you eating, or rather not eating? You look bloody thin.'

'With respect, sir, you hardly look flourishing yourself.'

'Touché. And the mystery?'

'Not a mystery so much as a *feeling*, sir. You remember what Rose said about the ship having a presence? Well it's no more and no less than that. Some of the men claim to have seen something.'

Muir clapped a hand to his brow. 'All we need is a bloody ghost to feed!'

Barrow smiled. 'I think they're all a bit this way and that, sir. But it *is* strong. The first sign of problems we're going to have.'

'Don't tell anyone aboard *Drummer*, or they'll want one.' Muir patted the pocket where his tobacco used to be. 'I'll leave you to sort that one out. As far as food is concerned we'll give it a few days and then talk again. Soon we'll be on starvation diet. In the meantime ...' he shrugged.

'Keep moving?'

'Keep moving.'

28 December

The days passed with unrelenting monotony, something *Drummer*'s crew had once been acclimatised to. Now it was different. Each hour, each day they went on living was, paradoxically, one day less, bringing them closer to the inevitable. Watches had been pared back, giving everyone greater time to sleep. When you were sleeping you weren't eating and whatever energy could be conserved was vital.

One by one the men had stopped shaving, and Muir was forced to issue an order drawing attention to the need for cleanliness after five men reported to the sick bay with festering cuts and boils. Dysentry had struck *Straker*. Now all they were waiting for was the first sign of scurvy.

Muir, collarless and crumpled with fatigue, held the report by Bellamy and Offord giving a breakdown of supplies, physical needs, sickness and distances covered daily.

Assuming the weather was favourable, they needed at the very least six days to travel the seven hundred miles to the Azores – assuming they weren't spotted before. They were now making no more than five knots. Bellamy's minimum diet assessment, placed alongside the victualling officer's total food stocks, stretched to four days. To cut back further on rations would, Bellamy noted, mean a host of food deficiency illnesses and an impairment of working ability which would, in turn, reduce the ship's efficiency, such as it was. A case, he concluded, of having a shoelace too short to knot, no matter how one economised in the threading.

Offord, in what was probably intended as a well-meaning addendum, had proffered a short list of historical precedents. Muir read aloud: 'H.M.S. *Sterling*, 1902. Four survivors discovered when boarded by crew of American schooner *Lacona*. *Sterling* had been drifting in the Pacific for seventy-six days after being struck by a typhoon and dismasted. As food ran out the full horror of what fate awaited them drove a section of the crew to insanity. The question of cannibalism, though raised by an Admiralty investigating committee, was hotly denied by the survivors, but certain evidence aboard *Sterling* suggested that . . .' Muir flung the report onto his desk. At times Offord's enthusiasm was too much to stomach.

He was half way through shaving when Prettie arrived. 'Sit down, Guns.' He nodded at the Bellamy/Offord report. 'Cast your eyes over that.'

Prettie read it quickly.

'Damn!' Muir dabbed at a cut.

'Fresh fruit,' said Prettie. 'Lack of it makes the skin sensitive.' He touched two small pieces of paper over cuts on his own jaw.

'Which is what Bellamy is talking about,' added Muir. 'And what I want to talk to you about. It seems to me that, between them, Bellamy and Offord have given us a choice of either starving to death or . . .' he winced as the razor negotiated his Adam's apple '. . . eating each other. Not thrilling alternatives.' He swilled his face, drying it on a towel, carefully avoiding the tiny peaks of blood. Tearing off a corner of the report he stuck the wet paper over them. 'There's been some desultory fishing done over the last week, but nothing that meant much. I want it organised systematically. Our lives could depend on it. Every man that can be spared is to be put at it. I want nets made, lines baited. Three men to each net, marked as a team and given a number. Individual catches recorded. The top catches will be noted and announced daily. The more rivalry the better. I'm deadly serious, Guns. I want it made a big business.' He rubbed a hand across his jaw and the paper came away. 'Signal what we're up to to *Straker*. The same applies to them.' He caught the doubt in Prettie's eyes. 'A reason for living. A purpose. An aim. That's what it's all about.'

'Oh, I realise that, sir. I was just wondering about bait. I used to do a bit of fishing and that stuff in the storeroom – the stuff that broke loose – might be the best ground bait you could devise.'

Muir clipped on his collar. 'I once caught a gudgeon three and a half inches long in the Severn. I was twelve at the time and it took me the best part of a day. Never caught anything since.'

'Now that's one thing I've never eaten, sir. Gudgeon,' said Prettie with a grin.

Muir looked at him. 'My feeling is we'll be eating stranger things than that before this voyage is over.'

29 December

The lights twinkled like St Elmo's fire along the distant yard-arms of *Straker*. *Drummer*'s boat davits had been rigged with lamps and the watch were having a good time of it : flying fish were offering themselves by the dozen to the fishermen. Von Bauer looked down from the bridge (allowed no executive role, he was given virtual freedom of the ship) and watched the excited commotion on the fo'c'sle. A school of dolphins was gambolling less than thirty yards away, their polished snouts gleaming as they broke water, eyes shining green as a cat's. The rail was lined with men calling them like children at a zoo. Muir's madness had its method. Not only had the inter-team rivalry soon grown to a high pitch, but *Drummer* and *Straker* were locked in combat as fierce as they had ever been, if emotions were anything to judge by. Bantering messages were sent backwards and forwards detailing who had caught what.

Be your own saviours, was the message Muir had given them all. Each day's objective was an end in itself and the real end had been forgotten, or at least wasn't for the moment dominating them. In two days they had caught enough to feed both crews three meals. Mathematically it couldn't save them. But von Bauer knew that wasn't the real object of the exercise. The lassitude that had gripped the crews had vanished in a burst of competitiveness. Muir was pulling everything out of the bag to keep them going. The German captain looked ahead into the darkness beyond the lights. The question now was one of stamina. He wondered whether he had much left in reserve. He massaged his neck, feeling the ridge of knotted muscle, the nodules of pain.

A machine-gun raked the dolphins and one flipped its tail high and slapped helplessly against the sea as it lost co-ordination. Its companions dived in shock as grappling hooks bit into the dying creature and it was dragged towards the ship.

A splash of silver. Von Bauer looked away. A light had been rigged on the prow, but the men fishing there had abandoned it in the excitement. In the faint glow he fancied he saw something dancing in the water. The beam caught it again and then it was gone. Von Bauer clutched the rail. *Drummer*'s engines were barely turning as the dolphin was plucked from the sea.

Again! It *was* there – only he had seen it. A brief glimpse but it was enough. He turned to look at the helmsman, who was standing on tiptoe behind the wheel trying to see what all the racket was about. If he or anyone else looked ahead, there was still a chance of their seeing what von Bauer had seen ...

The German captain bent forward in pain, sinking to his knees. Offord came out from the wheelhouse at the double: 'What's the matter? Can you hear me?'

'A pain,' said von Bauer. It only needed a few moments' distraction.

Offord was tutting. 'Do you need a doctor?'

'No, I ...' The helmsman's interest now centred on Offord and von Bauer. Offord undid the German's collar. *Drummer*'s engines picked up as he walked back into the wheelhouse and blew down the speaking tube.

It was the chance von Bauer *knew* would come. He had always known *something* would happen. Hadn't it always? All one had to do was be prepared for luck when others weren't. *Seize* it.

The drifting mine lay dead ahead of *Drummer* and in the next few seconds they must strike it. He was prepared.

He would sink *Drummer*. One way was as good as another.

Rose had never learned the layout of the ship. It was a fairground booth of alleys and companionways. Steps leading to more steps. Even on deck there seemed to be so much that was unnecessary, as if the person who designed it had forgotten to include certain bits and pieces that had to be tacked on afterwards.

She ran towards the bridge. 'Mr Tilley!' But no one seemed to hear. 'Mr Muir! Captain!'

Muir moved back as the writhing dolphin was speared with marline spikes, and turned to see her.

'Captain Muir! There's something,' gasped Rose, 'something ...'

'The girl?' He looked alarmed.

'No, no ...' she didn't have enough breath to shape the words and Muir tried to calm her. 'A dream? A nightmare, Rose?'

'No!'

The dolphin was still and its tail was being hacked off. Muir coaxed her away as the blood swilled towards them.

Rose looked strangely at Muir. Then: 'We are in danger, Captain Muir. Something I can't explain, but terrible danger.'

A sailor who had returned to the lamp at the forepeak suddenly began to call. There was panic in his voice as he stumbled and fell, calling out to them.

'It's that,' said Rose helplessly. 'I'm too late.'

'What is it, man?' Muir turned to say something to Rose, but never began the sentence. *Drummer's* bows lifted, a towering wall of steel rising as if on a hinge. The noise was deafening. The lamp, still shining, traced a trail of light in the sky followed by huge spinning sheets of metal. The explosion threw them flat across the deck, the remains of the dismembered dolphin showering yellow fat as it cushioned them against the foot of the bridge. *Drummer* sucked a fatal lungful of sea into her shattered bow and her stern began to rise.

'Let's have some *calm*! Get those bloody searchlights pointed down here! Judd, Hackett and you men there – get the sick out on deck. Move! That you, sir?'

245

Muir was bent over the unmoving body of Rose. 'She's hurt. What in God's name has happened, Prettie?'

'Torpedo, shell, whatever it is it's taken the sharp end off and I reckon we only have minutes, sir.'

Muir struggled to his feet wiping the foul globules of fat from his uniform and hands. 'Get someone to carry her to a boat.' He trod across the canting deck cupping his hands to his mouth: 'This is your captain. Every boat over the side. You up there on the bridge – get down. She's going under. Leave as quickly as you can! No panic! The yeoman? Where's the bloody yeoman?' He fought his way through the figures rushing about the deck, suddenly remembering Yeoman Hollis was dead.

Offord shouted from the wing of the bridge and began to work the signal lamp.

'Tell *Straker* to get as close as she can without putting herself in danger. We want lights on the water. Then get down here smartish!'

'All boats, sir?'

'Don't be so bloody stupid, Offord.'

'Sorry, sir.'

'Tell her to pick up the men who are swimming and leave those in the boats till last. Get on with it, and don't make it an essay!'

'Sir!'

'Captain!' Bellamy's shirt was flapping outside his trousers and he was visibly shaking from the shock of being plucked from sleep. 'We can't move some of the men in the sick bay. It will kill them! Impossible.'

'Possible!' barked Muir above the sound of escaping steam, rending metal and shouting men. 'Two minutes, Bellamy. Drag them, carry them, anything. If it's a submarine out there we probably only have seconds before the coup de grâce!'

Tilley was leading the Langes along the rail and Prettie and Hackett were carrying Rose to a boat. The starboard rail was less than twenty feet above the sea. A grinding roar. Someone was screaming. The port boats had failed along the side, two of them turning turtle and trapping men beneath them against the hull.

'Let it go! Leave it! These boats are useless!' Muir flung an arm. 'Get to starboard!' Liferafts were already dotting the water. He waited until the last man slithered away from the temptation of the dangling boats and began to descend the face of the deck.

Pickett, a whistle in his mouth, was regimenting the loading of the sick. The boats began to move away. Muir ushered Bellamy in front of him. 'Get into one, man! If you go under they won't have any chance!'

'There are still ...' began Bellamy.

'Get him in!' Bellamy was pushed into a boat.

Something ruptured deep within *Drummer* and she settled deeper. Garrett limped past supporting one of his engineers who was clutching a rag to his bleeding shoulder. All the chief engineer could do was shake his head in mute despair. The scene below was indescribable.

'No more boats!' shouted Muir. 'Over the side.' The ship was threatening to roll, her rail dipping beneath the water. 'No bloody heroics, Offord!' Offord tore off his jacket and pushed himself away from the ship. 'Pickett! Get in there!' He punched the boy gently across the shoulder.

Frank Judd was perched at an impossible angle, still sliding lifeboats across the deck and down into the water. 'Judd! That's enough, in you go!'

'Bugger off,' said Judd absently.

Muir tried to climb towards him. 'An order!' He fell and slid hard into the scuppers, striking his head and swallowing a stomach full of water. He came up driven by anger.

'More of these the better, lad!' cried Judd. 'There's a minute or two yet.'

'I'm telling you, Judd ...' Muir's mouth was smeared with oil. 'My ship!' He looked dazed. Fell again, and a blinding pain stitched itself between his eyes.

'Sod you! You silly bugger!' Judd sat on the last liferaft and tobogganed down towards him.

Drummer was turning like a dying fish. The bridge had begun to kiss the water and great gouts of steam were streaming from her bowels. Bubbles of air broke as if from some subterranean explosion, blistering the surface of the sea. A single semaphore of light still shone from her stern, swinging across the struggling figures fighting to escape the inevitable surge that could whirlpool them down with her. And then, guttering like a snuffed candle, it left only the night and silence. A full minute later the sea gave a single belch of satisfaction and closed finally, a sheet over a corpse.

In the oil-strewn water, those who had not been able to scramble aboard a boat clung like black-faced minstrels to anything that would support them.

'More room here!' shouted a voice. 'This way, this way!'

Charlie Pickett dog-paddled among the foul scum trying to find the source of the cry. Oil was in his mouth and ears and he held his head high to keep it from his eyes. He could hear someone coughing in the water nearby and saw Offord.

'Over there ... behind you ...' he croaked. Pickett turned to see the dim outline of a boat. More voices. 'Here! Here!'

'For God's sake!'

'This way!'

'Where are you?'

'Wait ... wait ...'

They seemed like whispers in the silence.

'Come on, lad.' A hand grasped his arm, but didn't have the strength to pull him aboard. Pickett held on to the side. 'Offord!' he shouted. There was no reply. He tried to lever himself up but the pain was too much. 'Get in.' It was Tilley.

'I can't.' More hands reached for him and he felt his chest explode as he was dragged over the gunwale. 'Shit! Oh Jesus bleeding ...'

Elizabeth Lange put her arms around him and eased him onto the thwart. He looked at her lamely. 'Sorry, miss.' Tilley handed him an oar. 'Try and row, sir, we need to move away quickly now.' His voice was echoed by that of Prettie from a boat ahead of them. 'Get away! The boilers will go. Can anyone hear me? Get away!'

'Have you got Offord?' yelled Pickett. 'He was here, feet away!'

'We have him! Now move!'

Pickett tried to pull on the oar. Hannah Lange appeared behind him and took over. They began to move through a ghastly litter of bodies and debris.

'I can hear someone calling,' said the girl. 'Look!'

A hand was raised towards them as the sailor struggled in the water. A bandaged head bobbed and disappeared. 'McGowan!' yelled Pickett. But it was too late.

The boat began to rise. 'Here it comes!' Pickett bent the girl hard against his shoulder.

A hundred-foot geyser of steam shot from *Drummer*'s tomb, showering the sea with scalding water. The screams burned through the oil blocking Pickett's ears and he felt the girl tremble.

'How many?' Barrow looked over *Straker*'s side. There were problems lifting some of the sick and hammocks had been lowered on ropes.

'Eight boats, sir,' said Hardcastle. 'Quite a few others on life-rafts, some still swimming.'

The crew of *Drummer* had been decimated. A blind parade of oil-covered men was being led across the deck.

'How much more of this?' Hardcastle avoided the eyes of a sailor whose tongue lolled dog-like from his mouth as he fought to breathe.

'Who have we got?' said Barrow abruptly.

'Surgeon Bellamy is aboard, sir.'

'Captain Muir?'

'Not to my knowledge. The women are here. Pickett, Offord, von Bauer, Prettie. Quite a few others.'

'And the boats that have been cleared of survivors . . .'

'Are searching the area as soon as they are unloaded.'

'Good.'

There was a shout from the fore deck, and they ran forward to a group at the rail. 'Down there, sir.' One of the men pointed. 'Judd is with him.'

'Judd, how is it?' called out Barrow.

Judd caught the line thrown down to him, standing over the body of Muir. 'Never felt better. Do it more often if I had the chance.'

'The captain?'

'Out cold. Chuck another line down and you can hoist him up.'

Muir was hitched and drawn up. His face was relatively free from oil but waxen, and his breathing was shallow.

'Take him to my cabin and get Bellamy there fast.' Hardcastle loped off. 'Can you climb a rope, Judd?'

'I could climb a stream of piss at the bloody moment, sir,' came the reply. He began to haul himself up hand over hand, feet walking the side.

'You'd better get cleaned up, Judd,' said Barrow.

Judd looked around the deck, 'Christ, what a mess!'

'Any idea what happened?'

'U boat? A mine? Guessing, I'd say it was a mine. A submarine would have come back for another slice.'

'And nobody aboard *Drummer* saw anything?'

Judd spat on the deck. 'If they did they knew how to keep a sodding secret.'

'Can you hear me, sir?'

'Don't be daft, Number One, of course he can't. He's concussed. Just leave him alone and he'll come out of it in his own good time.' Bellamy scratched slivers of oil from his forearm with a fingernail. 'How in the name of all that's sane are you supposed to get rid of this stuff? Men out there are covered with it like tar babies.'

'The galley is boiling up hot water,' said Barrow. He looked down at Muir. 'Are you sure he's all right? He seems very still.'

'He's in one piece, that's the main thing. Probably thankful for the rest.'

'And you?'

'Me?' Bellamy's mouth twitched. 'I go on. We all go on. It puzzles me how we do. We must be very frightened of death, Number One, to take some of the alternatives life has to offer. To live in agony is better than dying in peace. A strange equation, but proven over and over again. Men who were drawn on the rack screamed for *life*, never for death. Life at any price, eh?' He shook himself. 'I'll keep an eye on the captain.'

Bellamy closed the door as Barrow left. Straightened the sheet over Muir. 'You'll recover. There'll always be enough problems to stop you brooding.' He slammed a palm against the bulkhead. The disintegration began from within. At some point the sap stopped rising and the tree began to turn into a shell. Outwardly still a tree, but one storm and it might snap. Maybe he could shake off the feeling with the help of other people's pain, like Muir had done using the placebo of routine and concern.

It would be refreshing to cry but he had even forgotten how that mechanism worked.

Tilley was in the grip of a major thought that nothing was going to deflect. 'Number One, I know there are problems, and it might seem ...'

'Get on with it, Tilley.'

'Permission to take a boat out, sir?'

'What the hell for? We've picked up every man we can.'

'Fish, sir. I was thinking of fish. The explosion must have flattened a lot of them. They'll just be floating out there. If we could scoop them up before the sharks start beating us to it, I thought ...'

'Good idea, Tilley. Off you go. Good hunting.' He watched Tilley tout for a crew and there was a sudden voice at his shoulder. It was Recke. 'You made it! I didn't see you come aboard!'

'Lieutenant Mueller is alive, sir. He is with Captain von Bauer. Which is what I wish to talk about.'

'Yes?'

'Captain von Bauer has assumed control of the ship, sir. Your captain is ill and under the circumstances von Bauer has seniority. It is also a German ship.'

'Are you serious, Recke?' Barrow shook his head in disbelief.

'No, I am not joking. There are many German sailors on this ship. And maybe we have seen the war is not over. It might have been a German submarine that sank *Drummer*. In which case you have lost *your* ship, Lieutenant.'

'And it might have been a mine and it might have been God knows what! You are putting your weight behind von Bauer on the strength of that? What has he promised you?'

'Nothing. He has nothing to promise. I doubt if he will live to honour any promises anyway.'

'What?'

'He is a sick man. Opium eases the pain of an old injury, but opium in turn causes its own pain. His pride is all he has left.'

'And you think von Bauer's pride is important at this stage? God!' Barrow exploded in disgust. 'When it comes down to a matter of force, Recke, what then?'

'No force, Lieutenant. I would beg – no more violence. The crew of *Straker* have been given arms.'

'*Given*...'

Recke closed his eyes with a sigh. '*Taken*, Lieutenant, *taken*.'

'You mean that von Bauer has taken advantage of the pain and the misery to press on with his own petty ambitions! Damn him!'

'Nothing will be done unless I say so,' said Recke. 'He knows that. But there has to be order.'

'Oh dear, oh dear.' Barrow grimaced. 'Recke, does nothing matter to you Germans, other than who is giving the orders?'

'I am a German,' said Recke stiffly.

'A revolutionary German? Or von Bauer's German?'

'I have made mistakes and out of them has grown a strength I do not want. But, having it, I have to decide.'

'So, because the men will listen to you, you hand them over to von Bauer's keeping.'

'There are, sadly, fewer men. But that in itself could give us a little more time. With good command. It is no disrespect to anyone, Lieutenant, but Captain von Bauer in the past has made this ship perform miracles. He can use every inch of her to get us home. That is the most important thing.' He stared directly into Barrow's eyes. 'I am using him, understand that. For what he can offer, not what he represents.'

'I see,' said Barrow sharply. 'When you have "finished with him", Mr Recke, we will be here.'

Nothing was real, nothing what it seemed. A hinged steel panel cut into a false bulkhead was identified by a code pattern of rivets around its perimeter, only vaguely differing from all the rest but, to the initiated, as meaningful as the notes piped on a boatswain's whistle. Von Bauer pushed against it and squeezed into the narrow alleyway, springs sealing it behind him. Water had seeped in even here, but it was barely enough to reach ankle-high to his boots. He flashed the torch and a rat stared back, stunned, bent its back and plunged away in a series of leaps and splashes.

Von Bauer steadied himself. There were no secrets kept from the rats. They moved in impossible ways through impossible places, indefatigable as Hong Kong thieves. Only the rats knew more about *Straker* than he did.

The alleyway ended in another bulkhead and he had to kick the panel before it moved. Stooping, he stepped through into a small room, no bigger than a water closet. A ladder led upwards, ending blindly against more steel. There was a great deal of rust and he had difficulty in making out the panel. When he did it was more difficult to move than all the rest. The weight of the torch, even clutched waist high, was sending vibrations up his arm and through his neck, but the opium was lying to him sufficiently and he thrust upwards with his free hand, balancing on the ladder. Another room, larger this time, with a table and a bunk seat big enough to sleep on. There were four such cabins hidden below *Straker*'s waterline, sufficient, if the occasion arose, to hide away those of the crew whose knowledge of French was too skimpy to defy close scrutiny by a boarding party. None of them had ever been used. The boarders they had met had been particularly naïve. All but the last one.

He shone the torch. He had spent over an hour working his way through every inch of *Straker*, looking for the answer to a question that itself wasn't clear. But again the opium talked to him and his mind was no longer dulled. It told him that Muir could not have done what he seemed to do. The gold – the whole reason for their existence – could not have been jettisoned. It was unthinkable! Somehow, some way, it *must* be here, at least part of it! What kind of a man could do such a thing? At the end of the hour he was beginning to realise. An Englishman. A stupid, pig-headed Englishman!

The exit from the hidden cabin meant descending through a

hatch in the floor to a genuine alleyway. His torch passed over the room. Hovered.

The thin cord was half wrapped around the leg of the table like a coiled water snake. He pulled it free.

A bootlace.

'You understand, this can only end in more conflict, more trouble?'

Mueller nodded. 'I know what you must be thinking. But I think we are past trouble now. It is survival that should concern us.'

'Exactly!' Barrow smacked his palm. 'Survival! Not this kind of nonsense!'

'Does it truly matter?'

'Yes, it matters. And I'll tell you why. *My* captain is conscious. I haven't told him about von Bauer yet, but when I do, he's going to come out of his corner breathing hell and fury, concussion or no concussion. Recke is not going to be used to prop up the mad dreams of your captain any longer. I have delayed doing anything because I hoped I could rely on your support.'

Barrow and Mueller were standing on the poop deck. The events of the past few hours had shaken both of them, but Mueller had aged visibly. The death of Detweiler in particular had robbed him of vitality.

'Your captain is sick, Viktor. An opium addict who is not rational. Cannot be.'

Mueller frowned.

'His injuries are insupportable without the drug,' went on Barrow, 'and it is beginning to affect his reason. Ask Recke. He told me about the opium.'

Mueller was on the defensive. 'Why should Recke make up such a story?'

'He hasn't made anything up, Viktor, it is true! Doesn't it begin to make sense, now? Right back to the first insane resistance against *Drummer*? Talk to him. Try and reason with him. For his own sake.'

The German lieutenant was silent. Then, quietly: 'Captain von Bauer went below some time ago. He had a torch and seemed ... he was excitable, and, at the same time, distant.'

'I'm sorry. You are close to him,' said Barrow.

'Not close. I have admiration. A certain trust. In a way I like him. Even that. I would like to go below and see that he is safe.'

'Of course.'

'Are you telling me the truth, Guy, or are these more games?'

'The truth. You will discover it. And do you trust me?'

Mueller walked forward to the German helmsman. 'This officer is in command until I return.'

The helmsman didn't seem to care, either way.

30 December

Von Bauer moved slowly along the tween deck, weaving between the iron stanchions and through the cubicles for prisoner accommodation – now empty – probing into every corner. Below lay the main cargo hold where the gold had once been stored. He lowered himself down a ladder. Here, even more than above, the warren of hidden alleyways ran the length of the ship. Undetectable rooms were shielded from tell-tale echoes by cork lined walls. The passageways were lower and narrower and he was forced to crouch, rust flaking as he brushed the sides, making small 'plopping' sounds in the water. *Straker* was becoming flooded, despite all the pumping. The alleyways had begun to smell like sewers. In the confined space the torchlight began to play tricks with his eyes. Walls were closing in on him and the water, bathed in the harsh light, moved like a sheet of glass, slopping in the opposite direction to the ship's roll, totally disorientating. He tried to concentrate. There was something else. Something much more definite even than the overpowering smell of corruption and neglect. It did not belong here. He ran his fingers along a panel and pushed. It would not give. Beyond was the largest of the hidden compartments, a place so secret its existence was known only to Von Bauer himself. It had been designed for the possibility of *Straker*'s being taken into an examining port and held there overnight. Documents and other incriminating material were to have been stored there, along with some crew. It could also serve as a base for a sharp retaliatory attack against a boarding party that, after a few days, had been lulled into a false sense of security. The room held rifles, dried foodstuffs and casks of drinking water. It also held candles. The smell was identifiable now.

Von Bauer braced his back against one bulkhead and kicked out at the other. The reaction in his spine caused a bubble of spittle to burst at his mouth. He was drenched in sweat. It didn't matter. Muir had been here. And he could have come for one reason only – using *Straker*'s secrets to bury his own. The gold was there, beyond the panel. He kicked again and it moved fractionally. With a last desperate effort he smashed it open.

The man was clothed in pantomime rags, his hair beyond his shoulders, a beard roughly hacked into a six-inch mandarin wisp. He was crouching in the middle of the room, holding out a protective arm against the light, eyes rolling. The rifle was crooked under his arm wavering at von Bauer as he backed away. Around him the floor was littered like a gipsy camp; shreds of material, bones, excrement. Apart from that it was empty.

Von Bauer recoiled and the torch fell into the water. For a moment he managed to keep his balance, but then was trampled down as the wild man rushed past him. His shoulder struck a projecting rib of iron and his feet slithered in the slime as he went down, splinters of rust burying themselves in his cheek.

'Captain!' Mueller heard the shot and began to run down the steep stairway. 'Captain!' He took the torch that was swinging from his lanyard and picked out a figure scurrying along the deck.

'Halt!'

A moan.

'Stay where you are!'

The man was crouched behind the opening to one of the prisoner cubicles. Mueller eased himself towards it and, abruptly turning, grabbed the man's shoulder. There was no resistance. The rifle fell at his feet.

'My God! What are you?'

The man smiled, cowering like a dog.

'Over there!' Mueller waved him back and drew the torch over him. It seemed to have the effect of a naked flame. No man could be so thin. His eyes were pebbles stuck into a melting snowman. 'I am ...' he blinked painfully and then seemed to forget what he was about to say.

'You fired that rifle?' Mueller shone the light at it and spoke loudly and slowly, as if addressing a half-wit.

A nod.

'At whom?'

A finger jabbed away. Mueller pushed him in the direction of the stairwell. 'Take me.',

'Yes.' It came as something of a shock to realise the man could talk, was to that extent human.

The scarecrow seemed eager to help. Even where there was

headroom he walked – scurried – in a perpetual crouch. Mueller was forced to break into a trot. 'Where now?'

The man pushed against the panel with surprising strength and looked questioningly at Mueller.

'Go on!' And they were slopping along the foul alleyway. 'Keep in sight of me,' shouted Mueller. He suddenly realised he had stupidly left the rifle where it had fallen.

Von Bauer was lying with the back of his head propped against the bulkhead, his face only inches above the water that covered the rest of his body. Two rats were swimming quizzically around him. Mueller kicked water at them and they stared back contemptuously. One nibbled at von Bauer's shirt. The wild man waved Mueller back agitatedly and bending even lower stalked forward. The rats took no notice, even of the light. He threw himself headlong at them, slithering over von Bauer and momentarily disappearing under the water. When he surfaced he was smiling the smile of the successful hunter, a wriggling rat in each hand. He smashed them against the steel walls in one well-practised movement and they were as limp as a dowager's stole.

'Captain?' Von Bauer's eyes were open, but blood ran from a cut in his cheek. He seemed not to recognise Mueller as he tried to raise him. 'Can you stand, sir?'

The scarecrow helped him drag the captain to his feet and hold him against the bulkhead. Von Bauer tried to move but his legs wouldn't hold him. 'Like that, Captain. Very good. One foot, then another. Slowly.' They staggered like circus clowns, von Bauer with his arms draped over Mueller in front, and held from behind by the soaking skeleton.

It took them fifteen minutes to move the thirty feet of the alleyway. The heat was unbearable and the smell stomach-wrenching. Mueller was light-headed and shaking as he drew open the panel and they sat the captain down. Von Bauer was clutching at his stomach, which was visibly contracting in spasms and he seemed incapable of speech.

'Can anyone hear me?' shouted Mueller. 'Down here!' The meagre diet of the past week had taken its toll. He needed all his strength to keep on his feet and there was no question of carrying von Bauer any farther. He looked at the man crouched by the captain. 'Who are you?'

The man frowned at von Bauer like a child with an injured dog: puzzled why it had suddenly stopped moving. A furtive glance at Mueller and then he leapt. The rifle was back in his hands and he fumbled in the tatters of a pocket for a bullet, slid it into the chamber and pointed it. Along the tween deck. The bullet seemed unaffected by the water. A deafening explosion echoed around them and he ran, still at a crouch, towards the stairwell, head cocked. The rifle boomed again.

Mueller was trying to fight off a terrible weariness that was drowning him in unconcern.

'They will hear.' The last shots were fired into the darkness, guiding them down.

'What in blazes is going on, Number One?'

'You shouldn't be here, sir.'

'I've had the same discussion with Bellamy, so spare me that.' Muir blinked. His head was pulsing. 'The shooting?'

'Von Bauer has gone below, sir. Mueller went after him. While you were ill he tried to take command. I've sent a party of men down to find out what it's all about.'

'Tried to take command?'

'Recke was persuaded somehow to follow von Bauer, and *says* – I don't believe it – that von Bauer has armed some of his men. Men loyal to Recke, for one reason and another.'

'And is that what the shooting is all about?'

'I don't think so. There's something else you ought to know, sir.' He went over Recke's story of von Bauer's illness and opium addiction. 'I think it's more to do with that.'

'The poor devil,' said Muir. 'You don't think he's gone mad or something. Would it affect him that way?'

'I don't know, sir.'

'Nor do I. Whatever, I want von Bauer put under arrest. Recke too, if necessary. Mueller has his head screwed on and should be able to explain things to the Germans. None of it may be necessary if ...'

'Good God, sir,' said Barrow. 'Look over there.'

Von Bauer was being carried by two crewmen, his head lolling loosely to one side, water dripping from him in a trail as they moved across the deck. Mueller seemed to be sleepwalking. But the main object of attention on *Straker* was the outlandish figure that walked behind them, dressed in holes around which a few patches of material had been gathered, small bright eyes darting from a head that was, otherwise, all hair.

'Mueller?' Muir stopped the procession.

'The captain has been injured,' said Mueller. His mouth was slack with fatigue.

'Who is *that*?'

'A ghost.' Mueller attempted a shrug.

'Get Bellamy at the ready,' Muir shouted to Hackett. 'Mueller, this has to be the time and the place, I'm afraid, but Barrow has told me what is going on.' He nodded at von Bauer as he was carried away, 'This may have changed things painlessly. At least for everyone else. I'm asking you to assume control of your German crew. Not Recke, *you*! Tell them to stop being used. Otherwise not one of my men will lift a hand on this ship and it will founder before the day is out. And your captain gets no medical attention.'

Mueller seemed too weary to care about what Muir was saying. Muir followed his eyes to the figure of Recke, who was looking intently at the ragged stowaway. 'Recke?'

'Captain?'

'You have some say with these men, it seems. Now use it, and use it well. Because if you don't this is the beginning of the end. After this, no more. Choose. Are the men around you listening to stories of what may happen to them when they get home, or are they more interested in *whether* they get home? I'll get them home. But if they defy me once more, in any way, then they'll die. We'll all die. Slowly and uncomfortably. And what you believe won't add up to a bag of nails. It will be nothing, Recke. Kaput! Your captain is ill. Mueller is ill. We are all, all of us, ill, in one way or another. Weak — and throwing away what little strength we have fighting among ourselves. The enemy is a common one — the sea. It doesn't care a damn what you believe or what I believe. We're arguing over the bait while the hunter waits. One more storm, Recke, and *Straker* goes down if there is only half a crew.'

Recke spoke in German and the men around him began to move. Bellamy had come out on deck and was remonstrating with the sailors who were carrying von Bauer.

'I have told them to listen to you,' said Recke.

'To obey me, Recke. *Obey* me!'

'That too.'

'Then it is done.'

Recke held out a hand. 'I know this man.' Brushing the matted hair of the scarecrow aside.

Suddenly Muir knew him too.

'Sit down, Rose.' Muir drew forward a seat for the old woman and leaned against the desk. 'How are you faring? The three of you?'

'It could be a lot worse. One learns to put up with most things.'

'The knock you received ...?'

'A bang, it's gone.'

'The young girl is ...'

'Young, Captain Muir. Young and more resilient than we gave her credit for. She has drawn a blind down over what happened and knows that there can be no other way. Hannah has seen her daughter at last grow up — something I wasn't thinking she would ever accept, but now she has to. A little bit of niggling between them, but that will pass. Out of darkness cometh light, Captain.' She had been packing fish in barrels of salt and her hands were chapped as if with frost. 'What has happened?'

'You know *something* has happened?'

'Perhaps something has been laid to rest. What manner of thing I couldn't be saying.'

'You knew what was going to happen to *Drummer*?'

She laughed. 'Hundred years ago I'd have been burned as a witch. 'Twas a long, long time before I came to know not everybody *felt* things in the air around them. Moods, I'm talking about, Captain. Sensing moods.'

'And a little more, Rose? The healing?'

'God alone heals.' She looked him squarely in the eyes. 'You've found Oskar's body.'

'Not exactly, Rose. But we've found Oskar — alive.'

It was the first time he had seen surprise register on her face. Then her expression turned wooden.

'He was deep in the holds and must have been hiding — living — in the alleyways and compartments in the ship. How he managed to stay alive I don't know. How he managed to escape detection is as much of a mystery. *Why* he did it, yet another question. The fact remains it *is* Oskar Lange. The isolation, and whatever experiences he must have gone through down there for weeks have left him, how shall I say, dizzy.'

'Is he sane?' The old woman's shoulders drooped.

'Quite sane. But scatterbrained. It is temporary. Otherwise incredibly fit. Fitter than some of us.'

Rose nodded. 'He would be.'

Muir frowned. 'What do you mean?'

'Tell me, Captain, was there food down there? Where he was?'

'A little, I believe, but it was a storeroom affair, I wouldn't think a great deal.'

'Elizabeth. She knew. For weeks she took all the food she could get; even when Hannah couldn't eat she saved what she had left. And you have seen her, Captain. Thin as a lath. Once I caught her popping biscuits into a bag. She said she sometimes woke hungry in the night. That morning the bag was gone.'

'You mean she was feeding Oskar? She knew he was down there?'

'Elizabeth wanted to come back to *Straker*. She was going to ask you but we both told her no. She was worried about her father.' Her voice trembled. 'Perhaps the young man, the young midshipman, was bringing her extra food. I think he was and . . . that was why . . .'

'But why didn't Oskar contact his wife? Or why didn't Elizabeth tell Hannah he was alive?'

'Oskar would never have let Hannah see him living like that. Better for her to think of him as dead until the time came when he could face her without shame. Elizabeth in many ways is stronger than her mother. But why, why did he hide away from her? What reason could he have had?' She shook her head. 'I don't understand. All I understand is that Oskar was riven with doubts and fears and the only person he could turn to was his daughter. She justified his faith in her.' Rose stood up with a sigh. 'Poor Oskar had made a mess of so many things, one more . . .'

'I want you to prepare her to meet her husband, Rose,' said Muir. 'It won't be easy.'

Rose nodded. 'She needs to break, Captain, before she can truly mend.'

He held open the cabin door.

Speculation, but God, what if the girl *had* been leading Dandridge on simply to get more food for her wild, haunted father in the holds?

'She is a good girl, Captain,' said the old woman, as if reading his thoughts. 'And he was a good boy. It will do none of us any harm to think the best.'

Charlie Pickett's introduction to sick bay routine on *Drummer* had not gone unnoticed by Bellamy. The surgeon had asked the captain if the young midshipman could work alongside him, and though Pickett didn't relish the idea no one could deny Bellamy needed all the help he could get. His problems on *Drummer* were as nothing compared to those on *Straker*.

Pickett had called the surgeon over to look at the sailor who had been at *Drummer*'s wheel when she went down. For the first time since being taken from the water he seemed on the verge of consciousness and was even trying to talk.

Bellamy said: 'He's about to die. His lungs are clotted with oil.'

'But he seems to be . . .' began Pickett.

'He's looking along a dark tunnel and trying to turn away. Talk to him, say anything. All we can give him now is a little comfort. We have precious little of anything else.'

Bellamy walked down the line of cots and a voice called to him. Von Bauer was plainly uncomfortable in the sick bay and Bellamy didn't want him cluttering up a cot, but Muir had insisted he say there for at least a few hours.

'I wish to leave,' said von Bauer.

'You are here for observation,' said Bellamy laconically. He didn't add that 'observation' when the German was unconscious had revealed tell-tale puncture marks in his forearm. 'But perhaps it is in order for you to leave now.' What was the point of making the poor bastard suffer any more? There was enough real suffering around without fabricating it. He helped slip the jacket around von Bauer's shoulder.

'Captain?'

'Yes?' It was the voice of an old man.

'I am available if you feel the need to see me.'

'Thank you.' He was gone.

Charlie Pickett was talking urgently to the dying sailor. 'Again! Can you hear me?' The man opened his eyes. Pickett's mouth was pressed to his ear: 'Again! Say it again!'

Bellamy touched the midshipman's shoulder. 'He's dead.' Stooping he closed the man's eyes with a thumb.

Pickett let out a long breath. 'I heard his every word, sir.'

'He asked for his mother?'

'No, he didn't. He swore that von Bauer must have seen a mine and deliberately distracted us so that we hit it. For a moment it seemed to come to him lucidly.'

'It sometimes does in the last minutes.' Bellamy shrugged and drew a sheet over the dead man. 'Our job diminishes every day, Pickett.'

31 December

'Well, Oskar, my old friend, I reckon you'll do.' Judd, who, with Recke, had been released as soon as Muir had learned the true course of events aboard *Drummer*, put down the scissors and scuffed the hair from beneath his feet. 'Could stuff a blanket with that.'

Oskar Lange stood up from the chair and ran a hand over his cropped head. 'You think, Mr Judd, the captain will let me see them now?'

'I reckon,' said Judd. He knew. Since his appearance Oskar had been quartered with Judd and Tilley and their brief had been simple: to find out what the hell he was all about. For the first few hours the bedraggled German had spoken not a word, vaguely flinching at their approach. Tilley had tried the father-figure ploy and run into a brick wall. Lange was tighter than a clam. It was left to Frank Judd to prise him open, displaying the sensitivity of a stevedore and the subtlety of a water buffalo.

'Now listen here, Fritz. Food is short on this tub and tempers not much longer. Finding you has found one more mouth to feed. [Tilley had tried to point out the illogicality. Oskar had been feeding himself. Judd shut him up.] 'To put it bluntly, if you disappeared now, nobody would care and most wouldn't even notice. Now then, you have a wife and kid and you want to see them, is my guess. If you don't answer my questions, you won't see them. Me and Tilley here had been told to find out what the whole business is about and we'll have our rations cut if we can't. Our captain is a hard bugger and wouldn't think twice about bunging us off in a boat.' [A distinct 'tut' from Tilley. Ignored.] 'I'm going for a stroll. Five minutes, I'll be back. I want you to think about what I've got to lose as far as you are concerned. What you got to lose too.' [Looking at Tilley.] 'Five minutes. If you soft-soap him I'll stick you in a bloody fish-barrel.'

Five minutes later Oskar Lange began to talk. Of the taunts and suggestions that had been made by some of the crew. Of one man who had goaded him with lewd references to his daughter. Late one night, failed flower seller, failed sailor, failed breadwinner, Oskar Lange had asserted his manhood and struck out in explosive rage. And, to his horror, the man had died from the blow. He had dragged the body to the forepeak in the darkness and hidden it above the coiled anchor-chain, already covered with water, and had disappeared, knowing his crime would have been dealt with summarily. In a moment of clarity he had put papers belonging to him into the sailor's pocket. And then, retching with nausea, slit the man's throat, placing the knife in his lifeless hand. The pounding of the water would soon obliterate any recognisable features. From that moment

it was Oskar who was dead. Living the life of the damned.
Tilley had watched Judd's expression. The parallel was strong.
'I've had some experience of "self-defence", son,' said Judd
eventually. 'I think we can sort this out. I'll have a talk with the
Old Man, tell him the story.' And went off to see Muir with his
own, much better, version.

'Now then, she knows you're going down to see her, so listen to
me, Oskar. No bloody nonsense. Hold your head up and sod
everything, right?'

'I am grateful, Mr Judd, Mr Tilley.'

'You were two points off going batty, my friend.' Judd whirled
a finger at his temple. 'No more of it. Your eyes?' Oskar had
been having trouble adjusting to normal light.

'They are better, thank you.' Oskar's nervousness was still
there, but tightly battened down by a desire to please Judd.

Tilley nodded. 'He looks fine. The hair's a bit tufty, but apart
from that . . .'

'You've got a thing about hair, Tilley. So, are we set fair?'
Judd walked around Oskar. There had been no shortage of
clothes. Too many men had died for that. 'Not bad. Right,
Tilley here will take you down, I'm not much good at reunions.'

'Head oop, chess tout,' said Oskar, following his lesson.

'Bloody peacock,' said Judd. Turning to Tilley: 'Sooner you
than me, old son.' He was feeling in his pocket. 'Right, off you
go!' He waited until they reached the door. 'Oskar! Here!
Missed Christmas, but you can't go just like that.' He held out a
small silver chain with a heart-shaped locket at it centre. Tilley
had caught him slipping the tiny photograph he had taken
from it into his waistband.

'Frank?'

Judd pushed it roughly into Oskar's hand and closed the
German's palm over it. 'She might like it. Now sod off! Scram!'

The door, though patched, was still loose on its hinges and
afforded a little space to peep through. Von Bauer pushed it
open a degree. There was no sound. 'Captain?' The cabin was
empty. Crossing quickly to the bunk he felt beneath it, running
his hand along the wooden ledge. His fingers met nothing. He
tried again.

Nothing.

He had gummed them there, the sachets of opium, every one
of them! His hands raked at the wood. They had gone! He
scrabbled on the floor under the bunk, his hands shaking.

'Captain?' Muir stood in the doorway.

Von Bauer struggled to his feet.

'Take a seat, Captain.' Muir helped him to a chair, and the German sat with his hands clasped tightly together to hide the tremors. 'A dying man told us that you steered *Drummer* on to a mine. I believe a dying man's words. I tend not to believe yours. Surgeon Bellamy has confirmed what Recke had already told Lieutenant Barrow about your condition.' He held out a sachet. 'You were looking for these, I believe. I have them all. Any further attempt to disrupt this ship and I will destroy them, one by one. And I will destroy you, Captain, as you destroyed my ship.' He threw one of the sachets to the German. 'Get out, and do what you have to do. But remember who gave you that, and who has all the others, before you try any more nonsense.'

The old man stumbled away.

Muir felt hungry, cold and tired.

Sickened.

Tilley said: 'They know you're coming. It's up to you now.'

Oskar nodded as Tilley rapped on the cabin door and stood back, pushing Oskar towards it. The young girl opened it and, without a word, grasped her father's wrist, drawing him in.

'Oskar.'

'Hannah!'

With a sudden movement Elizabeth raised her father's hand and pressed it to her cheek. The tears brimmed. Rose took Oskar's other hand as he stared, transfixed, at his wife. Then, to Elizabeth: 'I think we should be having a little walk.'

The girl looked as though she would argue, but there was something in Rose's expression that made her think better of it. Oskar scarcely seemed to notice as they slipped out, leaving him alone with his wife.

'You are thin, Oskar. Very thin,' said Hannah eventually. 'Why did you leave us?'

'There was a man ... I killed a man ...' began Oskar. He knew she had been told. 'They would have ...'

She nodded. They were standing six foot apart, as if briefly introduced and then abandoned by a matchmaker.

'Hannah, it has been hard for you. I am to blame.' He bit his lip. She was the same dark, quiet Hannah, but now elusive behind the cold screen of reserve. The beating of his heart slowed, as if plunged into ice-cold water. 'Is there nothing left, Hannah? Why?'

'I had begun to learn to live without you, Oskar,' she said. 'Without anyone. Now ...'

'We are together. Things may not be the same ...'

'The same?'

'As they were.'

'I don't want things as they were,' she said.

He walked closer. 'I love you, Hannah. As I always have. I want *that* to be the same.' He held out his hands, the thin stalk-like wrists pushing the screen away, trying to find her.

'I need time, Oskar. Time!' She shook her head.

'Hannah.' He fumbled in his pocket and brought out the locket. 'For you.'

'Please.' She stepped back. 'You don't understand.'

'Hannah, what is it?'

She bent her head with a sudden weariness. 'I am no use to anyone any more, Oskar.'

'No!' He broke through and held her. 'You are everything! Everything!' And then she was crying with him, deep racking sobs that robbed her of breath. Her arms gripped him tightly around his bony shoulders with a desperate fierceness.

'I won't let you go away from me, Hannah.'

She buried her head in the curve of his neck and he could feel her breasts heaving. She had come back from whatever terrible place had tried to claim her.

Hackett bounced like a castaway on the lashed timbers of the raft, looking up at the rail. 'Loosen left!' he called out. 'Left! *Your* left, you silly buggers, not mine!' He waved his still-bandaged hand at the timber being lowered over *Straker*'s side. 'Now! Let it go!' He stood back as the two men with him grabbed the ropes and the wood spilled around them. Together they piled it up until the makeshift platform found its centre of gravity, and Hackett stuffed a bundle of oily black rags into its heart and nodded. The men began to climb the ladder to *Straker*'s deck. Hackett sliced one of the two tethering ropes holding the raft to the windjammer and stood with one foot on the ladder the other on the rolling platform, holding himself steady with a crooked arm. He bent to the cartridge powder and tried to fire it. At the fourth attempt it began to hiss and he cut the remaining rope and pushed the raft away with his boot. Still hanging from the ladder he waited.

'Give it time,' called Pickett from the rail above.

'The bugger's gone out!' Hackett stared at it malevolently. Most of the crew were watching from the rails as the reluctant pyre dipped and rose, a good forty yards away now and showing no signs of igniting.

'What you do, Paddy, lay the powder across the sea?' Frank Judd gave a bellow of laughter.

'No, see, what did I tell you!' Pickett gave a nod. A thin plume of smoke threaded itself from the raft. A first hint of flame. Then it caught and the wind began to fan it. Five minutes later it was belching black smoke. Judd helped Hackett over the rail. 'Well done, lad!'

'You think it'll work?'

'It's a sight better than throwing out bottles with messages inside them.' Judd looked across at Barrow. 'One of his better ideas.'

Barrow watched the smoke rise in an angry spiral, flattening at the top like a thunder cloud. It could be seen, he estimated, from forty miles away. If there was anyone to look. The men were already preparing another raft. A last desperate signal for help.

Bellamy had been checking on the health of the crew as often as possible and, with a few exceptions, their deterioration was marked. Oddly enough a number of thinner men, like Hackett, Tilley and even Oskar Lange, were faring better. Judd, Winslow and the like had been plagued with boils. But the most tragic blow of all had come in the form of a stroke that had left Rose paralysed down one side of her body. Her spirits were high, but her strength had gone.

'Smoke signals,' said Mueller, joining Barrow at the rail.

'Somebody might be looking our way,' said Barrow.

'If they aren't, how long can we go on?' Mueller was making an attempt to appear alert, but Barrow knew he was racked with constant stomach cramp.

'How long can a body go without fuel?' said Barrow by way of an answer.

2 January 1919

For two days the rafts were piled with wood and silently prayed over as they wrote their forlorn messages in the sky. Only the occasional gull showed any interest, shaking his black-capped head as he waited for food scraps to be jettisoned, not knowing he had come begging at a pauper's home. Those foolish enough to alight were caught and cooked. All over the ship fragments of fish lay invitingly in crude wire snares devised by Prettie. Only

266

one had fallen victim. 'Like goat,' Tilley had adjudged the taste. 'Very *old* goat.'

On the third day, *Straker*'s auxiliary, which had been limping along at quarter power, stopped. Simultaneously the wind dropped.

They rose and fell, but moved forward at a painful pace.

Garrett held the monkey wrench and looked at it as if having suddenly recognised the potential of some primitive weapon. He hated the auxiliary. It was challenging him to get it started and he knew this time he couldn't. There came a certain point when cogs, sleeves, shafts, pumps, fused together in a solid, obstinate mass. One could *feel* the pact they had made with each not to function. It had simply said: no more. Let it!

'I don't *want* you to work, you pig! Can't you understand that? I've nowhere to go, in no rush! A few days and the sea will get you! Rust! I'd like to be here to see that!' He laughed, Garrett's broken teeth and inflamed gums hadn't got any worse, but the act of chewing was torture of the most refined kind and the tough fish and biscuit diet had become impossible to cope with. He had been living off whatever soup could be made, with the occasional entrée of indigestible bread. He had lost more weight than could be coped with by the notches in his belt and it was now tied around his waist. Even despair was no longer any comfort. Day followed day and hope had been eroded like soil on a windswept mountain. Up on deck men could be seen talking to themselves; others climbed masts and forgot what they were there to do. Accidents were commonplace, major and minor, as hunger left them lightheaded. Food didn't bother Garrett. Why eat? Why *do* anything?

Nowhere to go.

He swung the wrench and smashed it against the engine. The second blow split the sleeving. Faster it rose and fell and he was red-faced and panting with the effort.

'Tom!'

The wrench hit grease as he turned, and spun out of his grip. Arnold Prettie gripped him by the shoulders. 'What is it? What's happening Tom?'

'What use is it now?'

'You want to go home, don't you?' Prettie shook him gently. 'Tom?'

'No,' said Garrett. 'Nobody there.'

'What? Don't be stupid! You have a wife – a lovely wife. A child. A new life!' Prettie's face was twisted in concern. He had wondered how long it would be before Tom Garrett would crack, and now it had come and maybe done for them all.

'She's gone,' said Garrett weakly.

'Who? Who's gone?'

'You know who! My wife!'

'When?'

'Months ago,' said Garrett, as if stating an obvious truth.

Prettie shook his head. 'That's bloody daft, Tom. We haven't *heard* from anyone for the best part of a year. Now come on!'

'I *know*.'

'You know bugger all, lad! Think of your boy. You want him to grow up never having known you? It's a hard road for a kiddie without a dad. A bloody sight harder than for a man without a wife. You've lost nothing, Tom. Except a little bit of your mind that's addled with doubt. She'll be there when we get home. What you're thinking is a terrible thing – you think she's gone off. How many men on this ship haven't had the same kind of thought? Women have needs and we all know that, just as men have them. But we've managed without them, Tom, and we know the women we married. You are taking away trust in her because you think *perhaps* she's taken away fidelity to you? If she knew what you were thinking she'd be right to turn her back on you. You'd deserve it. If it's trust you're worried about, how much have you shown, dammit?' Prettie let his hands fall from Garrett's shoulders. 'If you want to let it get the better of you, carry on,' he said softly. 'I can't stop you. Whatever problems might face us when we dock I just know I'd like to be around to face them.' He picked up the wrench and propped it against the engine. 'When I see your wife and son I'll tell them all the lies I can invent. Write them a letter, I'll give them that too. It's not what they're waiting for, but it'll be better than nothing.'

'Arnold.' Garrett stopped him as he bent to leave the tiny engine compartment. 'I think I was going ... my mind ...' he looked at the damaged diesel. 'I've never done anything like this before in my life.'

'We're all doing strange things, Tom. I just hope you haven't done too good a job,' said Prettie. 'Because if you have you've got a hell of a lot of work ahead of you to put it right.' He gave a wry smile. 'Probably what the damn thing needed, a kick in the pants.'

'Don't tell anyone, Arnold. Please. If I can't fix it, I'll tell the captain myself what I've done.'

'Oh, you'll fix it,' said Prettie. 'Now you've fixed yourself.'

January ... 1919.

Whomsoever finds this document is instructed to ensure its safe delivery to British authorities able to make its contents known to His Majesty's Admiralty. A sum of money will be paid for so doing.

Your Lordships —

It is my sad duty to write this and consign it to a watertight cache in the hope that it may be discovered and explain the fate that has overtaken His Majesty's ship Drummer *and the officers and men who served aboard her ...*

Jack Muir wrote for half an hour, his pen moving easily across the paper.

My postscript to the above is simply a wish that all you have read, of necessity a narrative of fact, should not obscure the heroism and valour to which these events gave birth. From the quiet courage of those injured who could only wait, to that of the men who tended them. The men in the rigging who fought not only the elements, but their own failing bodies. Cooks, carpenters, engineers, stokers. I respectfully attach a list of names that, in your Lordships' wisdom, might be considered for posthumous awards.

The former commanding officer of Straker, *Captain von Bauer, salutes the bravery of his officers and men. They were valiant.*

It has been a long battle, but now we are simply sailors against the sea and, in that respect, brothers-in-arms facing the Final Judgement. Let no one think harshly of us.

Our position when this was consigned to the sea was ...

Muir left it blank, like the date. That would have to wait. The wind had risen, blowing black smoke from the rafts across the windjammer, acrid and sour.

Rose smiled. A lopsided grin. One side of her face was paralysed by the clot of blood that had lodged in her brain. But still a smile, her eyes left no doubt of that.

Elizabeth was smoothing the hair from the old woman's forehead. 'He'll be here soon, Rose, Hannah has gone for the doctor.'

'Lisbeth, let nothing worry you. Nothing.'

'I promise.'

'Love your mother.'

'Yes.'

'Like you love Oskar.'

'Yes.'

'Both, Lisbeth, both.' Rose closed her eyes.

The girl turned to see Hannah and Bellamy enter the cabin. The surgeon eased her aside and, crouching by the bunk, felt the old woman's pulse, his other hand on her brow. 'Pain, Rose?'

'Not now.' She smiled again.

Bellamy saw the sweat on his palm. 'Elizabeth, ask Captain Muir if he could visit us.'

'Rose?' Hannah held her hand. 'You will be all right. Can you open your eyes?'

Rose looked at her. 'I'm tired, Hannah.'

'Sleep now.'

'No. Soon. Hannah? Take my strength. Take it all.'

Hannah touched Rose's cheek. 'You have been my strength. And I have been selfish. Worse than that.'

The hand clenched hers. 'Look after them, Hannah. God loves you for your suffering. Don't reject Him. I am going to leave you with something you will not understand for a while.' The hand gripped tighter. The old woman gave a sigh. 'Now you have it.'

'Bellamy?' Muir lowered his voice. 'I'm sorry.'

'Rose isn't too well, sir. I thought a word or two . . .'

'Of course.' Muir knelt by the bunk.

'A little "turn", sir,' said Rose, recognising him.

'We can't have you ill, Rose. We're almost home now. A few hours sleep and we'll be there.'

'You *will* go home, Captain. I know that.'

'Of course we will. You too.'

'I am dying. Old women die, even at sea.'

'No.' Muir looked up at Bellamy. Hannah Lange had walked to the far end of the cabin, a hand covering her eyes. 'Sleep now,' said Muir. 'Tomorrow I will be down here and I want to see that smile again.'

On deck. 'Bellamy?'

'She is very ill. A blood clot. Another will come.'

'And then?'

'She'll die.'

'Christ, Bellamy, can't you stop ringing the plague bell?' He regretted his misplaced anger immediately. 'I'm sorry.'

'So am I,' said Bellamy, deliberately obtuse. 'She's a nice old stick.'

'She wanted to be buried ashore. I remember that. "In the green." I suppose she meant Ireland. We can't even give her that.'

270

'She'll have her "green", sir. "Fiddler's Green." The sea.'
'Have you told Hannah Lange how bad it is?'
'Yes.'
'She understands?'
'She does.'
'Hannah seems a lot more stable since Oskar surfaced. I thought it might send her the other way. If only she had the chance she would be a charming woman.'
'I have a number of things, sir ... If you'll excuse me.'
'Carry on.' Muir watched the surgeon walk away. Bellamy was upset. He had been seeing a lot of Hannah Lange over the past weeks, in an effort to shake her out of her depression. And she was a very attractive woman. 'God,' Muir said aloud. 'You poor bugger!'
He heard the auxiliary burst into life.

'Well?'
'Well what?' Paddy Hackett shifted uncomfortably and looked at Tilley. Tilley looked at Judd.
'Well?' repeated Frank Judd.
'Er, perhaps we should be sharing it,' said Hackett quickly. 'With the rest.'
'To the hunter the spoils,' said Judd, shaking his head. 'Bugger the rest.'
'Funnily enough I feel quite ...' began Hackett.
Tilley frowned. 'It's your birthday, Paddy. Frank has gone to a great deal of trouble.'
'I appreciate that. Yes.' Hackett looked doubtfully at the dish set before him. 'It's very good of you, Frank.' He prodded the oddly shaped offering with his knife. It had been cooked in a sort of thin batter that smothered its identity.
'You, er, *caught* it, Frank?'
'Put up one hell of a struggle.'
'Yes. You caught it fishing?'
Judd sniffed. 'It smells good.'
'It'll be cold, Paddy, if you don't dig in.' Tilley tried to avoid Judd's eye. The big man was deadpan.
Hackett made a tentative incision.
'I once ate a bit of dog,' said Judd casually. 'In Shanghai. A delicacy there.'
'They eat horses in France,' said Tilley. 'Snails, horses and frogs. I once heard that the Chinese eat bats. Arabs eat goat's eyes. Samoans, long pig.'
'Long pig?' said Hackett weakly.

'Humans. Mostly missionaries. Roasted on a spit. They leave the dog-collar on and when it disintegrates he's done to a turn.'

Hackett had no wish to be ungrateful and it was obvious that Tilley and Judd were proud of the birthday feast they had brought him, but what was particularly bothering him at this precise moment was the fact that Judd's 'catch' appeared to have four vestigial stumps that might once have been legs. And, try as he might, he could think of no fish with such an anatomy. On the other hand there *were* still a few cats rambling half-wild below decks. And rats. Plenty of rats.

Judd put his hand over Hackett's knife and sliced a generous portion. A leg? Hackett clamped his teeth over it as gently as a pointer picking up a grouse. Chewed. Swallowed. His eyes moved from Tilley to Judd, Judd to Tilley.

'Happy birthday,' said Tilley. And, to his relief, Judd couldn't stand it any longer. Hackett was into his second forced mouthful when the big man turned away with a roar of laughter.

Laughing with him, Tilley put an arm around Hackett's shoulder. 'He's a sod, he really is.'

Hackett chewed.

'It's a turtle, Paddy! Frank caught you a lovely bloody little turtle!'

Hackett handled the moment admirably. 'Of course. Far too fishy for cat.'

4 January

Oskar Lange was taking his duties seriously. He had the determination of a man on bail. For three days his eyes had burned between the smoking rafts and the horizon, swamped with involuntary tears as they readjusted to natural light. A permanent look-out, he had begun to *will* someone to see them. But will, it seemed, wasn't enough. The swaying crow's nest made a game of holding the binoculars steady and, until he had learned the trick of wedging his knees against the mast and letting the rest of his body ride, he had seen as much sky as sea. He rubbed his eyelids and blinked into the distance. The weeks in *Straker*'s corridors had shortened his vision. Trying to readjust it he focussed on a point in the sea no more than forty yards distant and then began to 'stretch' his sight back to the horizon. It never reached it. Sixty yards away there was a strange movement in the water, as purposeful as a shark's fin. A faint wake. He lost it. The binoculars helped. Where was it? His mouth had gone dry.

'There,' he whispered, scarcely daring to move his neck muscles, forcing his watering eyes to stay open. A blink and it could go away. He shouted at the top of his voice, holding one arm out as a marker. 'See there! See there!'

An answering call, but he daren't look down to see what they were doing. 'See there, see there!'

Every fibre in his body was concentrating on the foot of metal that protruded from the water, marking the trail of the watching submarine.

Pandemonium.

Straker resembled an up-ended ants' nest. Muir and Barrow stood at the rail and the whoops of the men rang out along the deck as they dashed to find the best possible vantage point from which to follow the course of the single eye running alongside them. Karl Recke joined them in a state of intense excitement. 'Thank God,' he said through cracked lips.

'I don't like it,' said Muir suddenly.

'Nor do I, sir.' Barrow shook his head. 'There's no reason why she shouldn't surface. They've been watching us for quarter of an hour, probably more ...'

'If only we had a damn flag,' said Muir, 'apart from a German one. At least it would identify us, and I think that's exactly what all this is about. They must be in radio contact with someone.'

'And if we are identified as *Straker* ...'

'... and the submarine is English, they will probably have heard by now that we are a German raider and they are to sink us. They couldn't afford to wait for any tricks, not with *Straker*'s reputation.'

'And if it's a German submarine then the war is still on,' murmured Barrow.

'Exactly.'

Recke's initial enthusiasm had turned to puzzlement. 'Why do they not greet us?' It suddenly dawned on him. 'You think she is a German?'

'No idea,' said Muir.

Recke's hands gripped the rail. If it *was* German and it took the windjammer, what would von Bauer's attitude be? 'You said the war was over.'

Muir ignored him. 'We're getting nowhere standing here, Number One. Whatever the outcome I want it over and done with.'

'We could run up a flag of ...' his voice trailed away.

'No. No more white flags. Get the yeoman to stand ready to

signal again. And muster every man in drill order along the rails. I don't want a bloody sound. We've lost most things, but not our self-respect.'

They stood to attention as best they could, shoulder to shoulder, and from a distance looked less the vagabonds they were. A collection of badly bundled sores and scars and aches and blisters. Young men who had grown to middle-age; middle-aged men who had become old; old men who had almost reached the end. All in a matter of a year. Slowly, very slowly, the grim realisation that had come to Muir and Barrow had muted them, and the order for silence was unnecessary. There was now nothing more to be said. To be blown from the water, or to know that the war was still going to demand of them, was an alternative that encompassed them all, whether British or German. The only thought left was that somehow there might be something in between. A little bit of luck long owing.

Muir looked down from the poop at his bedraggled sailors swaying with tiredness, and the poignancy of it made him clench his teeth. Christ, they needed that luck! But one half of him knew a torpedo was just as likely.

'Wish I had some tobacco, Number One,' said Muir, à propos of nothing. 'Strange how one misses things.'

'We pose no threat, that's obvious. So why don't they damn well surface and have done with it?' Barrow was tense.

'*Straker* posed no "threat",' said Muir. 'But it nearly did for you, Number One. They're just being cagey.'

Hollis's substitute was steadily signalling, spelling out *Straker*'s identity and situation. Not the simplest of messages.

'In the war that *Straker* fought, a truth was a lie,' went on Muir. 'And that's her problem now. *Our* problem. *Straker* lived by deceit – I don't condemn her for it – but once the deceit is laid bare it leaves nothing to fall back on. Von Bauer lived with that every day of his life, and it took courage, because there was always the chance that the time would come when crying wolf would rebound on him. Another ruse. That's all a *real* cry would mean. In a way *Straker* lost her soul because of it.' He coughed artificially. 'All of which isn't worth a fart in a colander if the bugger in that submarine is feeling tetchy.'

Five minutes passed. Some of the men were wavering. A few had begun to whisper to those alongside them. Others glanced back to Muir on the poop. He was looking at his watch.

'She's coming up, sir!' Barrow stubbed a finger. 'She's

moving.' The submarine's periscope contracted abruptly. 'She has to be rising.'

The sea heaved and opened like a broken wound. A conning tower, then the hull. Before it had drained water, men could be seen leaping from the tower and manning the gun.

'It's British!' someone yelled. A roar went up.

'This is it, Number One,' breathed Muir. 'The next few seconds.'

The gun didn't fire.

'I think they believe us, sir.'

'I think they do, Number One. They're being careful, but I think we've passed the acid test.' He bit at a fingernail in lieu of a pipe.

Von Bauer closed the cabin door, dragged the small table across and pushed it on its side. Whatever else he could find he wedged alongside it against the door. When he was satisfied he sat on the bunk, took three sachets of opium from his pocket and lay them at his feet. Muir's 'rationing' had been conserved for this moment and the strain had been excruciating. Sleep a nightmare he couldn't face – a nightmare equalled only by day. His lips were cracked and bleeding and there were strange bruises on his cheek he couldn't account for. He could hear cheering from the deck. That didn't matter. Now he must get it right. A failure now would be unforgivable. No more failures. He mixed the sachets in water and filled the syringe. Injected. The second injection caused him pain. He waited. Soon no more pain. Filled the syringe with the rest of the liquid.

The cabin door shook and he was gripped with panic. Before he could move, the table toppled and the chairs crashed across the floor. Karl Recke forced himself into the cabin.

'Go away, Recke!'

Recke stared at the hypodermic and tried to grasp it, but von Bauer held it away. 'Everything is all right, Recke.' He stood up stiffly, fumbling with the syringe. Recke managed to grab his hand. 'What are you doing?'

Von Bauer tried to shake him off. 'Have you no respect?'

Recke didn't relax his grip. 'This is not the way to end it, Captain! You will be taken care of.'

'I wish to be left alone,' said von Bauer as if dismissing a meeting. The opium was beginning to take effect.

'Captain, you must listen to me!' Recke tried to squeeze the hypodermic from his hand, but von Bauer resisted. With a sudden surge of strength he jabbed. The needle entered the corner of Recke's eye and sank into his brain. He stepped back as Recke fell to his knees and then pitched across the floor. That was sad, very sad. But it saved a trial. It was inevitable that Recke should discover who was the stronger. Why hadn't he seen it? Strange. He could have been a good sailor.

The needle was unbroken, merely a little blood flecking its tip. Von Bauer found a place to puncture his arm and sank into his final sleep.

11 January

Now, at the end of it all, he should have felt elated. Instead Muir felt only a strange numbness.

The submarine captain had shipped supplies aboard *Straker* and they had set sail for the Azores. The captain's name was Winstanley, and to Muir he looked scarcely old enough to ride a bicycle. He had watched the smoking rafts for a day and had followed *Straker*, assuming they were intended as a lure. The sailing ship's description fitted that of a German raider and London had wirelessed him to proceed with extreme caution. For his part Muir had told the young captain the bare bones of their odyssey.

At the Azores the badly injured were taken off, along with the bodies of von Bauer and Karl Recke — *Straker* had claimed her victims right to the end.

They shared a burial with full military honours. *Straker* had taken on more stores and refitted her sails. It had been a new ship that sailed for England, high in spirits and fresh as only reprieved men can be.

But in the five days it had taken them to come within sight of Pompey, after the two-day stopover in the Azores, Muir had had his share of idiocies. Some lunatic at the Admiralty, thoroughly discomfitted by the sudden reappearance of a written-off ship with all its attendant problems vis à vis his filing system, was asking information on crew complement and days at sea, with the attitude of someone not altogether sure it wasn't all a hoax. Muir sent his own messages via the accompanying submarine. They were brief. *Straker* would stand off Portsmouth for half a day after mail that had accumulated there over the past year had been brought aboard. The hard core of mutineers would be taken off quickly and the rest of the Germans treated civilly. The message had been directed to Vice-Admiral Orrage-Potter, his wife's uncle. A boor and a dunderhead, it was possibly the only time in his life he had proved useful to anyone. Muir's requests were granted.

He went on deck. Pompey was enveloped in a thin winter mist. The auxiliary thumped *Straker* along, sails furled. The news they had heard as rumour a lifetime ago had been true. On 21 November, two hundred German ships had approached Rosyth, sandwiched between the guns of the British Fleet. They flew the flag of the Imperial German Navy, not the flag of the revolutionaries. The second biggest naval power the world had ever seen had surrendered without any resistance. Perhaps it was as well von Bauer never had to face the final truth.

Judd was at the wheel, Barrow alongside him.

'Going back a bit in time, eh, Judd?' said Muir.

'It is that, sir.'

'He could once do this with his eyes closed,' explained Muir to Barrow. 'Just the wind on the backs of his ears telling him how the ship was moving.'

'A trick,' said Judd. 'Showing off.'

Muir coughed. 'I think I ought to tell you now, Judd, that the business of the coxswain will not be raised further. It was a case of six of one and half a dozen of the other in my opinion, and to pursue it would only add to a complicated situation. The surgeon has testified that the coxswain had a thin skull case. His "fall" was unfortunate. Anyway, the poor devil's dead. That's not to say you aren't very lucky, Judd. *Very* lucky. Never again, eh?'

'I think my old friend the sea and me part company soon, sir. Thank you, sir.'

'You have someone waiting for you?'

'My son and his wife should be, sir.' He nodded at the port. That's if they know we are coming in.'

'That was the first thing I did, Judd. People will have heard well in advance.'

'In that case they *will* be there. Permission to make a comment, sir?'

'Go ahead.'

'Bloody good performance, sir,' Judd rumbled uncomfortably.

Muir looked at him and then winked at Barrow. 'I had some good teachers.' He fingered an ear-lobe in memory of Judd's long-ago chastisement, and grinned.

He and Barrow strolled to the rail. 'We put in in a couple of hours,' said Muir. 'Any problems?'

'No. Standing off has meant that quite a few of the men's relatives can be here and it's made for good feeling.' He gave a click of the tongue. 'I'm afraid Prettie's wife is dead. Terrible business. He got the telegram this morning. Three weeks old.'

Muir closed his eyes. 'What happened?'

'Influenza. There seems to be a lot of it about. Many of the letters tell of an extraordinary epidemic.'

'Yes, I heard something about it,' said Muir. 'How has he taken it?'

'Garrett says he will look after him when they get ashore. They're friends. He's bearing up.'

'He deserved better.'

'Didn't they all,' said Barrow. 'Recke.'

'Yes, Recke. And von Bauer.' He shook his head. 'I don't suppose we'll ever know what went on in that cabin.'

'My personal feeling is that von Bauer had gone beyond rational thought. He was living in a strange world.'

'I think we all were.' Muir tugged at the lapels of his uniform. 'I think Mueller ought to know, Number One. I would have told von Bauer and now it only seems right that his number two should . . .' He shrugged. 'He's a good man, Mueller, and I don't want to leave him with a lie. Does that sound strange?'

'No, sir. I think Viktor Mueller has had enough of lies. In his way he liked von Bauer, but I think he hated the life they led. He's a straightforward kind of chap and he never got used to keeping a dagger under his cloak.'

'I want you to tell him, Number One. If I do it will be formal, and I don't want to give the impression of crowing. Not now. There is nothing to crow about.'

Mueller had spoken very little about his background; no mention of a wife and no indication of close ties with anyone. It was as if his personal history began and ended with life at sea and his service in the Imperial German Navy — both of which were facing, for a time at least, suspension. Barrow could only guess at the mixed thoughts that were now racing through the German lieutenant's mind as he stood at the rail on the foredeck, his greatcoat collar turned up to his ears, watching the hazy coastline draw nearer, as clouded and uncertain as the future.

'Viktor?' Barrow had tried not to startle him but Mueller jerked his head sharply, almost angrily. Seeing it was Barrow he softened. Nodded in the direction of the land. 'I wonder what will happen? Of course we will be prisoners. But what does that mean? A prison? A camp? It's a strange thought, *to be a prisoner*, I haven't felt it until now. It makes me feel somehow unclean. Stupid, *Straker* took enough in her time, and I never thought of them being anything other than sailors who for the moment had lost their ships. On land it's different, of course.'

'Captain Muir reckons your stay will be a brief one,' said Barrow. 'As soon as the formal surrender is negotiated you will be free to go home.'

'I hope that is the case,' said Mueller. 'I have an ageing mother and father who need my support. Things cannot be easy for them now.'

'If there is anything at all I can do . . .' said Barrow.

'If somehow it is possible . . . I speak for myself, but it applies to all the men . . . if it is possible somehow to tell our people that we are alive. That would be enough. It would give them a lot.'

'I will talk with the captain.' Barrow was finding it difficult to broach the subject that had brought him here. 'Viktor, I want you to come with me. There is something you should know.'

Mueller seemed reluctant to move, and Barrow couldn't blame him: he'd had enough.

'It will only take a moment.'

Mueller shrugged. Barrow led him below decks in silence, hating every second of it. He stopped in front of a bulkhead, cut into which was a small door, more an inspection panel, requiring a man to bend himself double to enter. He loosened the wing nuts on it and drew it open. Mueller frowned, at a loss.

'It is impossible to enter,' said Barrow, 'but I had to show you rather than simply tell it.'

'We are, where?' Mueller suddenly took stock of his position. 'Beneath the saloon?'

'Yes. Beneath the saloon. This, as you know, is the well down which the floor was designed to fall. A lift shaft. If your captain hadn't told us of it then possibly we wouldn't be here now.' He drew a breath. 'When it fell with Kapper and the rest in it, the saloon floor didn't hit its normal base. The gold had been laid ingot by ingot to a depth of some five feet beneath it. The collapse of the saloon sealed it away, apart from this hatch. It was the only hiding place on the ship that your captain couldn't know about for the simple reason that if the saloon had fallen it would normally have left no space beneath it. It was impossible to know it hadn't travelled its full journey.'

Mueller said: 'How much of it is here?'

'All of it. The crates we dropped over the side were full of gravel ballast. Which is why men died to get rid of them before we were boarded and it was discovered.'

'Your men moved it?'

'Yes. It was a monstrous effort in the small space of time we had.'

'And afterwards none of them spoke about it?'

'No. They were sworn to silence.'

'Loyalty indeed,' said Mueller. 'The curfew, the fact that Captain von Bauer *knew* something had altered the trim of his ship ...' He looked desperately tired. 'So simple. What more can I say? Lumps of metal dug from the earth to make trinkets. If only we could all have thought of it like that.' He tried a smile. 'Of course we never can.' He held out a hand. 'You are to be congratulated. My captain would have congratulated you, maybe even laughed a little.'

Barrow shook his head. 'I don't want to take your hand, Viktor, not for something like this. That was not the point.'

'I know. There was no reason why you had to tell me. As parting friends, then?'

'Gladly.'

'Good.'

The crowds began to gather along the quay as the two tugs eased *Straker* towards her mooring.

'If it suddenly vanishes I don't think I'll be surprised,' said Bellamy, nodding towards the port. He had come out on deck with the two women.

'If it does, prepare another berth in the sick bay,' said Muir.

Hannah Lange had her arm around Elizabeth's waist. With her other hand she was fiddling with a small silver locket at her throat.

'It really is going to be all right this time, Hannah,' said Muir.

'We know,' smiled the girl.

Her mother nodded slowly. 'Captain Muir, I ...' she swallowed. 'There are things I need to say and yet ... there is too much to say ...'

'There are things to look forward to, Hannah. Nothing to be said.' Before she could go on: 'Warm baths, good food – and a place that isn't trying to deposit you on your *derrière* every minute! One of the good things about going to sea in ships is getting back home. Take my word for it. Now do you have everything?'

'Mr Barrow gave us the money,' said Elizabeth. 'We will repay it, of course, but it is very good of you.'

'You won't repay anything. Tilley has offered to arrange accommodation ashore and show you the sights. It won't be necessary for Oskar to go through the normal channels for a while, but a policeman will eventually come to your hotel and he will be required to give some undertakings. A formality. Don't let it worry you.' He didn't tell her that swinging *that* with the Admiralty had been as easy as arranging a state visit for the Kaiser. He had leaned heavily on Hannah's American parentage.

'You will be there?' asked Hannah.

'I have to go to London. But I will be back.'

'Please visit us, Captain.'

'I will,' promised Muir. They could hear the shouting of the crowds. Muir excused himself. The rail was already open fore and aft and the gangplanks ready. Ropes were flung to the quay.

Straker touched land and was still.

The German crew were taken off first, to be driven to barracks outside the town. A detachment of Marines marched off the hard core of men who had instigated the mutiny on *Drummer* and had been locked below. The rest of the crew had been given a few hours' grace before they reported to a shore base and were re-kitted. Five days' leave would follow immediately. Muir had tried to make it more, but the Admiralty had insisted they be available for questioning. It was obvious that *Straker*'s travels were going to be turned over in every detail. A rear-admiral and a commodore were already in his cabin, drinking gin and reading the log. He hadn't yet told them about the gold. He was saving that. But now he wanted to be alone.

He watched.

He watched the young man and girl embrace Frank Judd as he reached the bottom of the gangway, Judd lifting her in his huge bear-hug and spinning her like a top. The young man was limping, but shook off Judd's obvious concern with a grin and a fist feinted at the big man's solar plexus. Judd roared his joy, as uninhibited as a Cossack as they pushed through the crowds, ruffling heads as he went.

He watched Charlie Pickett and an old lady, whose regal presence kept the jostling crowds at a respectful distance, looking the lad up and down as he presented himself, tugging a wayward collar tidy until she was satisfied. A tiny woman with the face of a Japanese doll. Pickett bent to kiss her. And her hands were suddenly buried in his hair as she clutched his head down to her shoulder.

He watched Bellamy shake hands with a ramrod-backed old man who might have been his father, and then watched them move on together towards the ambulances and the sick.

He watched Hackett and Tiny Winslow, along with four or

five others, shaking hands with members of the crowd, determined to have their carnival as they headed for the nearest pub, waving back at *Straker*. Or maybe 'waving' wasn't exactly the gesture they were making.

Tilley took the women ashore, talking to Oskar Lange as he went. They seemed to have a lot in common. His hair had grown and peeped from underneath his cap.

Tom Garrett stood at the top of the gangway, looking away from the crowd, Prettie beside him. 'Guns' pointed down and turned Garrett by the shoulder. The young woman and child were having trouble making their way towards the ship.

'Clear a path there!' shouted Muir to the Marines on the quay.

Garrett stumbled blindly down.

Muir saw the little boy explore his face with his fingers, tug at his jacket.

The few minutes were over.

13 January

'Damned incredible!' The Admiral's name was Fitzroy, an old sea dog who had listened to Muir's two-hour account of what had happened on board the two ships with the hunger of a man re-living past glories. 'I can only repeat: "damned incredible".' Fitzroy raised himself from behind his foredeck of a desk, took a cigar from an onyx box and pushed it across to Muir. 'Green Havanas.' He puffed. 'All this, of course, will go higher, I'm just the old buffer who reports it all back. There'll be the usual damn inquiries, fleets of brass and enough paper to fell a forest.' He glanced out of his window over the Mall. 'Snowing.' The cigar glowed as he turned to Muir. 'There'll be promotion, of course. Automatic. Should have congratulated you on that straight away. Seems a bit lame after what you've just told me. But heartfelt, just the same.'

'Thank you, sir.'

'Don't thank me. Facts speak for themselves. There'll be a medal or two flying around, I shouldn't wonder. Good thing to have, keeps people off your back.'

'There are a number of people I would like to put forward for promotion, sir. And decoration.'

'Course, course. That goes through me, as it happens. I'll tell you the procedure later, plenty of time for that.' He looked again at the falling snow. 'Lunch?'

'My wife is waiting for me, sir.'

'Silly of me. Yes.' He turned from the window. 'Just before Armistice, Muir, our Fleet was locked up waiting for the Germans to come out. They didn't, as it happened, so we couldn't move either. Now there were lots of things we wanted to do with the Fleet rather than see it kick its heels. Damn silly stalemate for two countries supposed to be blowing each other off the map. Bit of a disgrace, in my opinion. We knew and they knew that in a toe to toe battle, numerically at least, they wouldn't stand a chance. It was eyeball to eyeball, except they were tucked away in one port, we were tucked away in another. Nobody moved. For months.' He examined the end of his cigar and seemed satisfied. 'There was the need for a trial of strength. They have a damn big navy, Muir, and it had to be knocked out. The only way we realised it could be done was by tickling the trout. Have one of these cigars; they're not half bad.'

Muir lit one, feeling uneasy.

'So it was decided that we'd give them a prize so big they couldn't ignore it. As it happens there are more German spies in Capetown than there are taxi drivers in London, and it was a good place to start. A ship was loaded with gold there and two escorts were sent over to bring her — "secretly" — to England. It worked. The Germans knew exactly what had been loaded and what it was worth within a few hours of it being loaded. They knew its destination too. The story was spread well. The German economy had been rattled ever since the blockade and that ship's cargo was a carrot they couldn't afford to miss. The idea was that the German Fleet would come out to take it, and we would then come out to take *them*. We needed to meet them on the open sea. As it happened, your Captain von Bauer intercepted the goldship before anyone else could. And then came the Armistice, which none of us had reckoned for. What I'm trying to get round to — and it doesn't change anything that happened — is that the gold aboard the ship bound from South Africa, wasn't.' He looked at Muir. 'It was lead. Covered in a thin film of real gold.'

Muir's cigar had gone out.

'I hope you understand.'

'I think I'm trying to, sir.'

'Difficult. Yes.' A long pause. Fitzroy looked at his watch. 'Your wife will be waiting. Please give her my apologies.'

'We're all so very proud of you.' His wife clasped his hand in hers as they walked from the Admiralty to the waiting car, and he felt her shiver.

'Who's that?'

'The McIlvanney's chauffeur. They lent him for the day. You know I *hate* driving in the City.' She shuffled the cold away, burying herself deep in her fox fur. 'I've arranged a table at the Savoy. A few friends. Do you mind terribly, darling? *Darling?*'

'I'm sorry, I was thinking. Yes. Yes, of course.'

'Your promotion, darling?'

'I think that will be coming through.'

She breathed: '*Commander* Muir.'

'Yes.' The shop windows slid past like blind eyes. 1919.

It had to be a good year.

Postscript

Morris Wylie – 'Tilley' – died on 15 November, 1934, at the age of seventy-four, and was buried in a now overgrown grave in a Portsmouth churchyard. For the last six years of his life he had worked as nightwatchman at the factory of Josiah Parkes, glue-makers. There were no mourners.

Arnold Prettie lived to the age of eighty-one, at sixty-nine marrying his housekeeper. He was better known as the founder of the 'Prettie Homes' for the children of impecunious families. He died peacefully in his sleep in 1967.

Frank Judd was mine host for six years at the *Doggett's Arms* in Bermondsey (latterly called *The Dog and Drummer*). In 1925 he collapsed while celebrating the birth of his grandson and was confined to a wheelchair. His stories were still the main attraction of the *Drummer* until his death at the age of seventy-six.

Tom Garrett, as founder of 'Garrett Engineering' was a wealthy man within ten years of leaving the Navy. His wife bore him one more child, who married Arnold Prettie's daughter, Jessie. Garrett outlived his wife by less than a month.

Viktor Mueller, after a long spell in hospital with a virus infection contracted aboard *Straker*, went on to become managing director of a German shipping line. He died in a traffic accident in Hamburg in 1930.

Oskar Lange and his wife and daughter lived somewhere in America, no doubt finding the anonymous security they had searched for for so long.

Bellamy, one of the pioneers of study into psychosomatic illness, was knighted in 1929.

Guy Barrow never went back to sea. His stud of racehorses occupied him fully for the rest of his life.

Jack Muir became something of a celebrity and social lion until his divorce five years after the war's end. Then he disappeared into obscurity.

Charlie Pickett is now eighty-one, and very much alive.

If he wasn't, no one would ever have known the true story of the Goldship.